Praise for

Romeo, Romeo

by Robin Kaye

D1115178

Kaye's writing is just about perfect for this kind of story, as she balances... romance, sex, and family, all of which come together with ease. The result is the totally irresistible *Romeo, Romeo*.
—A Book Blogger's Diary

The author has crafted this story line so well it's easy to relate to the players and fun to read. I adore her writing style and found this a great book from first page to last.
—The Romance Studio

Debut author Robin Kaye strikes gold in *Romeo, Romeo*—and deserves to have her name added to your favourite new author list.
—Book Loons

The author does a wonderful job of drawing large Italian families and two passionate people who fall in love... I found *Romeo, Romeo* to be a quick, entertaining, and easy read.
—RomanceNovel.tv

Robin Kaye's *Romeo, Romeo* is sensational! I loved everything about this novel. The story, characters, and writing are all five-star material.
—Crave More Romance

Delightfully funny and wonderfully romantic, I stayed up all night to read this book!
—Night Owl Romance

Praise for

Too Hot to Handle

by Robin Kaye

I didn't miss a single breathtaking word of
this fine novel. Readers will be hooked on
Too Hot to Handle. I know I was!
—Romance Junkies

If you like Janet Evanovich, you will enjoy Robin
Kaye. This book is an easy victory for Robin Kaye and
I look forward to more of her accomplishments.
—The Burton Review

Robin Kaye is a master at romance, and her
second novel is even better than the first.
—Armchair Interviews

A romantic story that will have you laughing
and crying… From page one, Robin Kaye
captures your attention.
—My Two Blessings

Ms. Kaye has style—it's easy, it hits the spot and it
has everything that you need to get caught up
in a wonderful romance.
—Erotic Horizon

This story sizzles with sex appeal, as does Dr. Mike
Flynn. This book had me laughing so hard,
I could not put the book down.
—Deb's Desk

I very, very highly recommend this book to all
contemporary romance readers and anyone who
wants to fall into a beautiful, sensual love story.
—Book Reviews by Bobbie

Breakfast in Bed

ROBIN KAYE

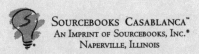

SOURCEBOOKS CASABLANCA™
AN IMPRINT OF SOURCEBOOKS, INC.®
NAPERVILLE, ILLINOIS

Published by Sourcebooks Casablanca, an imprint of Sourcebooks, Inc.
P.O. Box 4410, Naperville, Illinois 60567-4410
(630) 961-3900
FAX: (630) 961-2168
www.sourcebooks.com

Printed and bound in the United States of America
QW 10 9 8 7 6 5 4 3 2 1

Chapter 1

REBECCA LARSEN SHOULDERED OPEN THE DOOR OF HER new Park Slope apartment and surveyed the wreckage. A pizza box lay open on the coffee table, containing the remnants of a sausage and mushroom pizza of indeterminate age. By this point, Becca was on her last nerve. Her cat had shrieked for the entire trip from Philadelphia to Brooklyn, and as Becca gazed about the room, she began to feel a sensation akin to entering the Twilight Zone.

Annabelle, Becca's best friend, sister-in-law, and resident of the apartment until two weeks ago, wasn't a neatnik by any stretch of the imagination, but Becca had never seen her leave this much of a mess. Empty beer bottles littered the remaining space on the coffee table, and a pair of very large shoes lay underneath. Men's shoes. Becca's sense of unease escalated. It definitely looked as if there was a man living there. Yep, the XXL fleece hoodie thrown on the couch was her first clue; the second was the singing that came from the direction of the bathroom seconds after the hiss of the shower started.

Becca grabbed the baseball bat she found leaning against the wall by the closet and skulked to the bedroom. The bed was unmade, which wasn't startling, but the collection of men's jeans hanging off every surface as well as a mess of jockey shorts and socks on the floor certainly was. Not as much, though, as the voice coming from the shower. It was a rich bass baritone, and if she wasn't mistaken, he was singing an old '40s tune. God, who sings songs from the '40s? Whoever it was had a smooth, smoky, sexy-as-hell voice that was hot enough to make a woman melt like chocolate in a two thousand-degree kiln. The guy in the shower had one hell of a voice. Too bad he was also going to have one hell of a bruise.

She spent some time thinking about whether she should hit him while he was in the shower or wait until he got out. He'd gotten through the first stanza of his song and the whole chorus before she decided to wait until he emerged. The shower curtain might severely curtail the speed at which the bat would hit, and then there was the problem of proper aim.

Pushing the door open with the end of the bat, she watched the steam roll toward her and bring with it the scent of yummy-man. A man who smelled like that at any other time would have her following him just to get a whiff. His scent was clean, with citrus and spice overtones that made her mouth water. The body that stepped out of the shower bare-ass-naked stole the breath from her lungs, the attack plan from her memory, and made her thankful she was a woman who could appreciate the human form because she'd never seen one finer. Her eyes wandered back to his face just in time to see the corner of his full lips lift to form a grin. If looked at separately, each part of his face—the Roman nose, sapphire blue eyes, curled spiky black eye lashes—was almost pretty, but something about the way they fit together and the addition of his five-o'clock-shadow-before-noon, stole the prettiness from his face and made it arrestingly gorgeous. He was the Sicilian version of a Greek god. He had to be the most beautiful man she'd ever seen in person, and as a sculptor, she'd seen more than her fair share of beautiful people. Too bad she disliked him.

Rich Ronaldi looked over his shoulder to find his sister's best friend staring wide-eyed at his bare ass. Well, maybe it wasn't only his ass she stared at because when he turned, she got a load of the full monty.

Becca rested the end of the bat she carried on the floor. "Excuse me, but what the hell are you doing here?"

Rich had never been the shy type, but the women who got a load of him in the buff were usually invited to do so. Becca, Miss prim-and-proper-ice-princess, wasn't. He wished he knew where the damn towels were. He'd just moved in, well, in a figurative sense of the word. He'd stayed there for a few days, and he had a towel somewhere, but knowing himself, it was on the floor along with his dirty socks and underwear.

If he'd known she'd be coming by, he'd have kicked them into the closet or at least under the bed. But then, Becca was the last woman he'd expected to darken his doorstep. He had no clue why, but since their first meeting, he got the distinct impression she wasn't overly fond of him. "How did you get in here?"

Becca didn't seem to grasp the fact that standing naked in front of a woman who wouldn't normally give him the time of day is not the most comfortable thing to do. She didn't turn away or hand him a towel, not that there was one at hand. He brushed past her into the bedroom, saw a towel hanging off the footboard of his bed, and quickly tied it around his waist. The only reaction he saw from Becca was a blink.

"I used my key. What are you doing in my bedroom, taking a shower in my bathroom, which is conveniently located in my apartment?"

Rich let out a laugh. "Hold on. I'm the one asking the questions here. This is my apartment. I'm leasing it from Rosalie and Nick."

She crossed her arms, the action pulling her baggy sweatshirt taut across her chest. A chest he forgot she even had. When he realized he was staring, he returned his gaze to her face and found her rolling her eyes.

"You're impossible. So is your story since I'm subletting the apartment from Annabelle. It was her apartment, and now it's mine. You need to leave."

She looked like one of those sexy Anime cartoon characters. She was tall, just a few inches shorter than his own 6'3", and thin with long, long legs and short, choppy, platinum blonde, perpetually tussled hair that gave her a sexy as hell, just-been-fucked look. Rich mimicked her stance, careful not to spread his legs wide enough to dislodge the towel, though it would serve her right if he did. "You're wrong. Rosalie and Nick own the apartment. They rented it to Annabelle, who has since moved out. I moved in. If anyone is leaving, it's you."

"Well then, we have a problem. Because as of right now, I'm living here."

"Not with me, you're not."

"Exactly."

He waved his arm to encompass the whole apartment, and the whole mess he had scattered across it. "Possession is nine-tenths of the law."

"The only possession I see here is your mess. Everything I own that's not in storage is now in the living room, so, in that respect, as in others too numerous to count, you come up…" She looked him up and down with a critical eye. "…decidedly short."

Rich had half a mind to whip off his towel just to show her how very short he wasn't. He was a man comfortable with his body and his um… size. Shit, he'd never had any complaints in that department, and from the look in Becca's eyes when she ogled him—and it was an ogle—she didn't have any complaints either. He was sure she was just trying to get a rise out of him, which she wouldn't. She wasn't his type.

No, Rich's type was a woman like his girlfriend, Gina: a little bombshell. She was all black-haired, copper-eyed, and built like a woman. She was a barely five-foot package of pure TNT. Gina dressed like a woman. You'd never find her wearing an old sweatshirt five sizes too big and a pair of low-slung baggy jeans. "Shit." He looked at the clock. He was going to be late. He was meeting his dean at the Harvard Club and then heading uptown for a date with Gina. "I don't have time to talk about this. I have somewhere to be. Why don't you go out to the living room and let me get dressed. I'll call Nick and Rosalie on my way and find out what to do about this mess. You can spend the night tonight because I have other plans, but I have to tell you, babe, you're gonna be looking for another place to rent."

Becca pulled her cell off her jeans and flipped it open. "I'm not leaving until after I've spoken to Mike and Annabelle. We'll see who'll be combing Craigslist for a place to hang his mess. And let me tell you, *babe*, it's not going to be me."

Rich didn't bother to wait for Becca to leave before reaching for his towel. Thankfully, she stormed out and slammed the bedroom door behind her. Rich found a clean pair of jockeys and pulled them on wondering what else could happen. He went to the closet, ripped the plastic off his dry cleaning, and slid on his lucky shirt—the blue one everyone said matched his eyes. He looked around for his favorite pair of 501s, stepped into them, and while he buttoned the fly he scrounged around for clean socks. He had to go for the emergency pair of red socks he'd gotten for Valentine's Day last year. He hated them but kept them in his gym bag for emergencies. It looked as if he had to wear his boots to hide the damn socks, and sometime in the next day he either had to do figure out how to do laundry, find a laundry service close by, or go to his mother's. He tried to remember if he picked up the last of his laundry he left there. After stuffing his wallet in his back pocket, he slid on his watch and ran his hand through his hair. Perfect. Well, perfect except for the temporary lodger banging around in the next room.

Becca paced the apartment waiting for Rich to dress. The man was completely exasperating. Moving to Brooklyn meant she'd be the only single female in a gaggle of couples. The payoff for overlooking all that togetherness was that she'd be close to her newfound brother, her best friend turned sister-in-law, and her little niece- or nephew-to-be. She could always sneak out of whatever stifling function she was talked into and escape to her own apartment if it got to be too uncomfortable. She just didn't expect to be stuck moving in with the only other unmarried person she knew in Brooklyn. The fact that Rich Ronaldi had played a starring role in all her fantasies since the day she met him only added to the numerous reasons that he was the last man she wanted to be alone with. He was a regular menace.

When he stepped out, he'd gone from Mr. Wet-and-Wicked to Mr. Urban Chic. He wore great boots, perfectly faded jeans that lovingly hugged his thighs, ass, and well, everything else a pair of well-designed jeans is supposed to hug. She turned her back on him and stepped into the kitchen. "Do you want some coffee before you leave?"

Rich shook his head. "I'm late as it is, and as much as you try to be the lady of the house, you're not. Making coffee isn't going to change that, Becca."

The way her name rolled off his tongue, dripping with sarcasm and something else she thought it best not to consider, made her want to call the cops and have him thrown out. But if she did that, she'd have to prove residence, which she couldn't. She'd also have to explain to Annabelle why she'd had Rich thrown in the clink. Becca tossed a filter in and counted the scoops of coffee hoping it would help in the same way counting to ten did.

Nope, no luck there. She measured the water, filled the machine, and was still as angry as ever.

Rich followed her to the kitchen and was now leaning on the breakfast bar staring at her. "I need to go. I'll be back late, if at all. Feel free to help yourself to anything in the kitchen. Stay the hell out of my things. We'll get this mess sorted out, and you can be on your way first thing in the morning. I don't think Gina would look too kindly on you staying with me."

Becca didn't bother holding back her laugh. "Oh yeah, she's got a lot to worry about there. Get over yourself Richie. The only thing I'm interested in is my apartment."

Rich plucked a leather jacket off the back of the kitchen chair, went to the door, and picked up his keys. "Sorry to tell you this, babe. But that old saying, blood is thicker than water, is just as true today as it was when the Germans penned it. Of course, the Italians have taken it to a new level." Rich winked. "Don't wait up."

Rich walked up the steps of the Harvard Club and headed toward the bar. He didn't belong to the prestigious club, but Craig Stewart, his old friend and new boss, the dean of psychology at Columbia University, did. Rich stood in the doorway of the bar and looked for Craig.

The two had a long-standing lunch meeting there once a month. It began when Rich had been one of Craig Stewart's doctoral candidates. Even while Rich taught at Dartmouth, he'd fly down to the city every couple months and always met with his mentor and friend.

When Rich had woman or job troubles, Craig was the first one he'd call for advice. Thankfully, Craig was quick to help him out of the last mess he found himself in. Now Craig was not only a friend and a mentor, he was a boss.

"Rich, over here."

Rich nodded and worked his way past several tables to the bar. Craig stood a few inches shorter, quite a few years older, and about fifty pounds heavier than Rich. Rich accepted the beer Craig pushed toward him as he tossed his jacket on the back of his stool. "Thanks. I'm sorry I'm a little late. It was a family thing. It couldn't be avoided." He held up his glass, and then took a long drink from it. "How are you?"

"Good. I saw your research on schools was cited, and you were quoted in the science section of the *Times* this morning. You didn't mention the *Times* had picked up on your work. Congratulations."

With everything going on that morning, Rich had completely forgotten about it. "I'm sorry. I should have said something, but I can't take all the credit. There were two other co-authors."

"Yes, but the article said the researchers were led by you. It's good for you and good for the department." He slapped Rich on the back. "I'm proud of you. But I have to say I've been a little disappointed that Emily and I haven't seen you at the house. We saw you more when you were up at Dartmouth."

Rich always got along well with Craig's wife, Emily. But now that Craig was his boss, Rich wasn't sure exactly how to treat the relationship. "I've just been busy trying to get things set up the way I like them, moving into my new place, getting my office settled, ordering new books for next semester. You know how it is."

"That I do. I invited Jeff Parker to join us in about a half hour. I know you met at the faculty mixer, but I thought since you're both new to the faculty, you might want to get better acquainted. He's got a great jump shot, and I know you're big on basketball."

Jeff was the professor in office next to Rich's. "Sure."

Craig took a sip of his drink and set his glass down. "I heard from your old dean yesterday."

Rich had just taken another swig off his beer and tried not to choke on it. "Oh?"

"He wasn't too happy with the way you left things with his daughter."

As if he hadn't made that crystal clear during the last six months of Rich's tenure at Dartmouth. "Shit, Craig. She's a grown woman. How the hell was I supposed to know she was my dean's divorced daughter? Darcy has a different last name, and thank God, she looks nothing like her daddy. If she did, I wouldn't have got in bed with her in the first place."

"I understand, Rich. I do. But don't you think you're getting a little old for this? Even you have to admit that your serial dating has brought nothing but trouble to you your entire life. First, there was that problem with the law."

"Hold on, I was seventeen. And that had more to do with stripping cars than with my dating life."

"Still, it was your girlfriend who turned you in."

"Yeah, but I turned my life around. I did my six months of hell in military school. I paid my time, and my record was expunged. You would never have known about it if I hadn't told you."

Craig rested against the back of his stool. "I still can't believe you live the way you do after going through military school for even six months. Your place always looks like a frat house after a weekend party."

"Which is why I spent most of my time in military school in the brig. I could never get a quarter to bounce on the bed after I made it. Then I got nailed for paying someone else to shine my shoes, buckles, and iron my uniforms."

Craig laughed. "That explains how you remained a slob. Still, you're a thirty-four-year-old man. Aren't you getting to the point where you want to settle down?" When Rich looked at him with what he was sure was a blank, confused expression, Craig continued. "Have a committed relationship, maybe get married, and have a few kids? Isn't that what you want?"

"Where are you going with this?"

"I just thought that since you're back home now that you might want to reevaluate your life. You have a great opportunity at Columbia if you play your cards right. You're on the right track, but you can't afford another problem like the one you had at Dartmouth. You're exactly where you want to be. Now you can look forward to having more of a personal life. You know, settle down, have a committed relationship, get married."

Rich looked into his beer. He wasn't sure if this was his friend, the happily married man, or if it was his boss, the dean of Columbia's psych department, speaking. Still, since Rich was working his way toward a full professorship and tenure, he didn't want to do anything to screw up his future. He could get away with leaving one Ivy League University on less-than-good terms, but not two. "As a matter of fact, I've been seeing someone here for some time. She's the reason I stopped seeing Darcy in the first place. Now that we're both in the city, I was thinking of taking the relationship to the next level." It made sense. Gina was great. She was a lot of fun, easy on the eyes, good in bed. What more can a guy want?

"I'm glad to hear it. You can bring her to the benefit dinner Emily has been nagging me to drag you to. She hasn't seen you since you moved back."

"Sure, we'd love to go. I've yet to meet a woman who doesn't love to dress up and do the town."

"Great. The benefit is in two weeks. I'll get the tickets and let you know all the details later."

Just then, Jeff Parker joined them.

Craig stood up and Rich followed suit. The three shook hands and went to the club room for lunch and psych department talk. Still, it was better than the conversation Jeff's arrival put an end to. Now, if only Rich knew which Craig Stewart he had that conversation with: his friend and mentor, or his boss.

Rich knew something was wrong when he entered the apartment Gina shared with her sister and brother-in-law. The way Gina's brother-in-law, Sam, a big cop with a bad attitude, stared at Rich made him want to run in the opposite direction. What was it with people not liking him on sight?

Rich smiled, doing his best not to fidget. His experience with cops made him uncomfortable to say the least, and Sam didn't seem thrilled to have his sister-in-law mixed up with an ex-juvenile delinquent. Although his record was expunged, the fact that it was expunged didn't look good on the background check Rich was sure that Sam ran on him. "Beautiful day, huh?"

Sam just stared.

"The leaves are changing, I'll bet the Park is gonna be crazy today with everyone taking in the fall colors."

Rich found himself taking a step back when Sam shifted his weight. "Is Gina ready to go?"

Sam crossed his arms and Rich wondered where the man found shirts to fit over his huge biceps. He looked like the incredible hulk without the whole green skin thing happening.

Tina, a slightly younger version of her sister, Gina, entered the room, took one look at the situation, and stood between him and Sam. Rich fought the urge to cross himself.

She poked Sam's chest. "Sam, stop this." She turned to Rich. "Sam and I are going out for a little while."

Sam held Tina's coat for her. "We'll be close by and could stop back any moment. Understand?"

Rich nodded. "Okay, but we're not staying—"

"Yes, we are." Gina teetered in on her four-inch heels and all but pushed Sam and Tina out the door. "Give me an hour before you send the SWAT team in, okay? Tina, maybe you should put a leash on him or something." She shut the door behind them and locked it. "Sit down, Rich. We need to talk."

Nothing good ever came after the words, "we need to talk." Rich examined his actions over the last week and wondered if it was something he'd done that caused the I'm-so-not-happy-to-see-you look on Gina's face, and the way she kept her back up as if she was trying to steel herself against God only knew what.

Rich sat on the couch and watched Gina pace the room while he tried to figure out the problem. Before he'd moved down a few months ago, Gina would visit him in New Hampshire once or twice a month. She never wanted to go out because she had an aversion to any place that wasn't New York, so they stayed at his place, usually in bed, which worked for him. Come to think of it, since he'd moved back to New York, he and Gina didn't do much together that wasn't horizontal either. Maybe that was the problem.

She continued pacing, and he had half a mind to grab her and haul her onto his lap. Whatever she had to say couldn't be as bad as all that. After all, they'd never really had any problems. He closed his eyes and cursed silently. They must have had some problems since she was obviously working up the courage to do something. Rich had a strong feeling it wasn't going to be something he'd enjoy. He'd lived with his two sisters long enough to know that women had all sorts of problems with the men in their lives that the poor slobs were never privy to. Maybe if Gina had said something, he could have avoided whatever this was. Gina turned and crossed her arms under her breasts, which always had the same effect on Rich.

"Richie."

He pulled his gaze away from her abundant cleavage and brought it to her face.

Gina rolled her eyes. "I'm not cut out for this."

"This?"

Gina nodded. "Yeah, this..." She motioned from herself to him and back again. "I didn't sign up for a relationship. It was different when you lived in Maine—"

"New Hampshire."

"Whatever. We saw each other once or twice a month for a day or two, and it was fine." She blew her inky bangs off her forehead. "This full-time girlfriend thing. It's just not working for me. It's too much pressure. You're everywhere. And well, since you live here now, it's really killing my social life."

Rich stood. "Social life? You have a social life?"

"Because of you, no. I don't."

"Good."

"Good? You think that's good?" Gina said something in Spanish that even after four years of taking it as a foreign language, Rich couldn't make out.

He figured it had something to do with God and possibly death. Maybe it was better he didn't know the exact translation. "Look, Gina. Why don't we just talk about this? What's the problem?"

"You."

"What about me?"

"Pretty much everything. It's nothing personal, Richie. You're a nice guy. I liked it when you were just someone I slept with whenever we got together. You're great in bed, and well, that's always been fun. You know?"

Rich nodded. Yeah, he knew.

"Now you're talking about relationships, and well, I like you, but let's face it, you're just not relationship material."

"I'm not?"

Gina shook her head. "You're like a little boy. You expect every woman you know to clean up after you, cook for you, and do your laundry. I'm surprised you've learned to cut your own meat. Face it. You're a mama's boy. You don't need a girlfriend. You need to move back in with your parents so your mother can take care of you. I'm not interested in being a maid with benefits. I want more, and you're not it."

Rich stood. "Hold on, Gina. Give me a chance. I can change."

She laughed. "Come on, Richie. You're hopeless. You've been treated like a prince since birth. Your mother thinks you're the Second Coming. I'll bet she still does your laundry."

"I can change. I'm a grown man. I'm intelligent. I have three post-secondary degrees. I'm sure I could figure out how to do laundry."

"Sure you can. If that's what you want to do, go for it. But don't do it for me. I'm sorry, Richie."

When Rich left the apartment, he saw Sam leaning against the wall in the hallway with his arm around his wife. Tina shrugged as if to say that's the way things go sometimes, gave him a sad smile and a wave. Rich nodded and turned toward the elevator. He just wanted to go home and do an imitation of Brian Wilson holed up in bed for a week or two, eat bags of Sara Lee biscotti, and watch cartoons and hockey on TV. He couldn't believe he'd been dumped. He'd never been dumped before. Well, except for that time when he was seventeen and his girlfriend slept with his best friend, Nick Romeo, and then snitched to the cops, which led to his and Nick's arrest for grand theft auto. But the only reason she did that was because she found out he was about to dump her first. Women.

What was he going to do now? He was supposed to show up at some charity thing two weeks from today with a woman on his arm to prove to his dean he's respectable, stable, and in a committed relationship. Fuck, he had to get Gina back because there was no way he could find another girlfriend and establish a committed relationship in the next two weeks. He was good, but not that good. Besides, how hard could it be to turn into relationship material?

He stuffed his hands in the pockets of his leather jacket, pulled up his collar, and headed into the cold fall wind toward the subway and home. That's when he remembered that Becca was at his place. Great. Just what he needed. Another woman who thought he was worthless. Shit. He couldn't even go home so he went to the next best place, his home away from home—DiNicola's.

Becca moved her cat, still in his carrier, from the living room into the spare room. While he slept, finally, she cleaned her new apartment and made a strategy for getting rid of the unwanted man in her life. She had a feeling it would be difficult. But then, over the years, she'd learned that nothing worthwhile was easy.

She jumped at the sound of the intercom buzzing. Shit, she wasn't sure what she should do. For all she knew it was Richie's girlfriend, Gina, at the door. Richie said she wouldn't be happy to find out that Becca was staying there. On the other hand, it might be a fast way to get rid of Rich Ronaldi. She smiled as she pressed the button for the intercom. "Yes?"

"It's Rose Albertini, Richie's aunt."

Becca leaned her forehead against the cool plaster and buzzed Aunt Rose in. She looked in the mirror and pushed the hair off her forehead wishing she'd had a minute to clean herself up a little. Taking a deep breath, she opened the door. Becca had met Aunt Rose twice before—once at Annabelle and Mike's engagement party, and then, of course, at their wedding. Annabelle always said Rose was scary, but the little old lady who walked in carrying a lasagna didn't look the least bit scary. "Oh, it's'a you. I thought I recognized the voice. Not too many got your accent."

"Accent?"

"Yeah, you know, you sound like you talk with your teeth clenched. That's'a no good for your jaw. It'll give you pain as you age. Mark my words."

Rose walked past Becca into the kitchen, popped the lasagna into the oven, and turned it on. "You take'a this out in forty-five minutes when it'sa nice and bubbly. Leave the foil off for the last few minutes to brown the top a little if'a you like. I put'a the gravy and the cheese in the Frigidaire. You heat the gravy and make sure you save the leftovers. I made enough for you and Richie. He'll be hungry after tonight. You take care of him, eh?"

"I hardly think that I'm—"

"Ah, you don't like my Richie, do you? My Richie—he's'a good'a boy, you'll see. Spoiled, but good." She rubbed her hands together as if she were wiping away any argument and looked Becca over from bottom to top. "You too skinny. *Mangia, mangia.* My Richie, he don't like skinny girls."

"Mrs. Albertini—"

Rose waved her hand. "No, you call me Aunt Rose. You're practically family." She moved toward Becca, reached for her face, and kissed both cheeks. "You'll like my lasagna. Later, when you want, I teach you to cook. Put some meat on those skinny bones." She looked away and shook her head. "Aye, yi yi, you and Richie, you got a lot to work out. But don't worry, you're good for him, and when he grows up, he'll be good for you too."

"I'm sorry Mrs... I mean, Aunt Rose. Rich and I aren't... we don't even like each other. Honestly, you've got it all wrong."

"Like? Who said anyting about like? You think me and my Vito liked each other?" She laughed. "You don't need to like each other. Well, not at first." She waved her hand. "It'sa the fire you like. The rest, you learn to live with, and then to love. You listen to your Aunt Rose." She tapped her temple. "I know what I know."

The only thing that Becca knew as she followed the old lady out of the apartment was that Aunt Rose needed some serious therapy. Still, the look she gave Becca when she tapped her temple gave Becca the willies. Becca could see what Annabelle meant.

The old lady turned and raised her hand. "No need to thank me. Just take care of my Richie. You're a good'a girl. Skinny, but that won't last."

"It won't?"

"No." She kissed Becca again. "A little meat on your bones and you'll be a beauty. You Catholic?"

Becca shook her head. "Presbyterian."

"Ah well, I guess you can convert. Eh?"

"Convert what?"

Aunt Rose just patted her cheek. "You're going to be fine. You wanna watch your cat though. Somethings a'no right with him."

Becca grinned. "No kidding. Thanks for the lasagna, Aunt Rose."

"*Prego, ciao.*"

Becca watched Aunt Rose through the window. Tripod's yowl had her rolling her eyes. Aunt Rose was right about one thing. There was something definitely wrong with Becca's cat. She wasn't sure if it was that he lost one of his hind legs or it was his personality problem. Probably both. After checking to make sure the dog door that Rosalie's dog, Dave, used was locked and dead-bolting the door to the garden, she let Tripod explore his new home while Becca changed the sheets on the bed. She'd be damned if she was going to spend the night on the couch, or God forbid, on that torture rack of a futon in the den. No, if possession was nine-tenths of the law, Becca was going to possess the memory foam mattress. That was for damn sure. Rich could just take his pick of either the couch or the futon; she'd even be nice and leave him a pillow and a blanket.

Chapter 2

"AW SHIT. WHAT HAPPENED TO YOU? YOU GET DUMPED again?"

Rich looked up from searching for answers at the bottom of his Scotch glass to find a fuzzy Vinny DiNicola staring at him. Vinny was a bear of a man with dark hair and a unibrow that reminded Richie of a prickly black caterpillar, only bigger. He wore a white cook's coat over black and white checkered pants, both splattered with the special of the day. The only thing about Vinny that had changed since Rich was a kid in trouble was his hairline. It was receding, badly.

Rich tossed back the rest of his drink and slid the glass toward Vinny. "This is the second time in my whole life I've been dumped. It's not like it happens every day."

"And every time you do get dumped, you end up at my bar. At least this time you're not underage." Vinny filled Rich's glass and slid it down the bar to him. He poured himself four fingers of Jack Daniels, raised his glass in silent toast, and drank most of it before slamming it down on the bar, punctuating the act with a satisfied "Ahhh…"

Rich just gulped down more Scotch and thought about calling it quits. The drinking, not his life or anything. He was depressed, sure, but more than being depressed about losing Gina, he was depressed about what she'd said. Rich waited until he had Vinny's attention. "Do you think I'm relationship material?"

"Not for me, you ain't."

Rich tried to focus on Vinny. Yes, he was definitely getting drunk. He could tell because he actually had to concentrate to get the glass to his mouth. When you have to aim for your own mouth, chances are, you're well on your way to oblivion. "Shit, Vin. You know what I mean. Gina said I wasn't relationship material."

"Yeah, well, she's got a point."

Rich was looking at Vinny, but if that was Vinny talking, he wasn't moving his lips, and he was throwing his voice. Rich turned his head in the direction of the voice and saw his brother-in-law Nick sitting beside him.

Nick grabbed Rich by the back of his neck and gave it a shake before giving him a shoulder bump. "Mona called, said you needed some male bonding time, whatever the fuck that means. She said I had to get my ass over here. This had better be good. I was home, curled up with my wife and my dog, watching the Islanders trounce the Cunucks." He shot Rich a look that was somewhere between a smirk and a grimace and reached across the bar, grabbed the remote control, turned on the Islanders game, and muted the volume.

Vinny poured Nick a drink. "Gina dumped Richie and said he wasn't relationship material."

Nick nodded. "Smart girl."

Rich went to smack Nick but forgot he had his elbows on the bar and was resting his head on his hands. He remembered just before his face hit the bar.

Nick grabbed Rich's left arm, and Mike, his other brother-in-law, grabbed the right.

"Hey, Mike. When did you get here?"

"Just now. Nick called me. Said you were in deep shit and needed some medical advice." Mike nodded to Vinny with the same expression Nick wore.

Nick gave Rich a tug. "Yeah, like how to get your head out of your ass."

Rich slid off the barstool. "My ass isn't in my head."

Mike laughed. "Sure, whatever you say."

His brother-in-laws helped turn him around. "Where are we going?"

Nick pushed Rich forward. "Vinny's office. Drunks are bad for business."

"It's a fuckin' bar. Bars encourage drinking."

"Drinking yes, drunks no." Mike opened the door for them.

The next thing Rich knew he was sitting in a hard chair with a cup of coffee in his hand. He aimed for his mouth again and forgot the content of his cup wasn't Scotch. It was hotter than hell. Shit!

Vinny looked over his boys and laughed. It wasn't long ago that Nick and Mike were both in the same place Rich was. Of course, they did it at different times and over different women, but still, they both came to DiNicola's to get plowed.

Vinny took another sip of his Jack and tried to remember that saying about the course of true love never running smooth or some such crap. But come to think of it, Nick and Mike had both been a whole lot more upset about losing the women they loved than about why they'd been dumped. Maybe Rich didn't really love Gina after all.

Rich moved to stand, but Mike put a hand on his shoulder and pushed him back down into his chair. "I gotta get Gina back. I'm supposed to have a date with my dean to show that I'm a responsible guy and involved in a committed relationship."

Vinny put his feet up on his desk and pulled his office bottle of Jack out of his bottom drawer to refill his glass. "Why do you want Gina back if you're datin' your dean?" He took a sip. "You think that's smart? Ever hear that saying, don't shit where you eat?"

Mike laughed. "I thought your dean was a man."

Nick almost spit out his Jack Daniels. "Oh yeah? This is almost worth missing the game."

"I don't have a date with my dean. I have to bring a date to this charity thing my dean invited me to. I gotta get Gina back in the next two weeks, or I'm screwed. But she says I'm not relationship material. What's a guy got to do to be relationship material?"

Vinny was right. Rich didn't love Gina. He just needed her to look settled so he could keep his job. Hell, Vinny should do this shit for a living. Was he good or what?

Mike sat down. "Well, you have to think of the woman you love before you think of yourself."

Nick leaned against the desk and took a sip of his Jack. "If she's anything like Lee, you have to do her laundry, clean up after her, cook, make sure she eats." He paused. "Oh, and bring her coffee and chocolate in the morning. Believe me, your life will be much more enjoyable if she starts her day with caffeine and chocolate. Sex works too."

Rich looked appalled and squeamish, like the first time a guy has to go to the store to buy tampons.

"Yeah, that's good." Vinny nodded. "Mona likes it when I rub her feet. You know? She's always wearing those spiked heels of hers, and though they make her legs look great, they're hell on her feet."

Rich groaned. "You gotta be kidding."

"Vinny's right." Mike nodded. "Plus, feet are erogenous zones."

Nick smiled. "Everywhere is an erogenous zone if you're talking about Lee."

Rich was incredulous and looking a little sick as he eyed one brother-in-law and then the other. "Hold on, those are my sisters you're talking about. I don't want to hear this shit." He slumped in his seat. "I don't know how to do laundry. Or cooking. Why can't I just feed them Mama's leftovers? I guess I could have her come over and clean the apartment."

Nick shook his head. "You can't have your girlfriend clean your apartment and expect her to think you care about her. That doesn't scream 'marriage material.'"

Rich tried to stand only to fall back into his chair. "Shit, I know that. I was talking about Mama. I'll call her to clean the apartment."

Mike laughed. "Your mother cleans your apartment?"

Nick joined him. "Yeah, she probably does his laundry too."

Rich looked from one to the other. "Yeah, so?"

Vinny tried not to laugh, but really, Rich was a total putz. "Oh shit, he's serious. Boys, he's got a lot of work to do. He has to figure out how to take care of himself before he can take care of somebody else."

Nick nodded. "Yeah, he's got to learn how to cook, clean, and take care of a woman."

Rich sat up a little straighter. "I'll just hit the bookstore on the way home. They're open late. I'll find a book on cooking and cleaning. Like a Martha Stewart training manual for men. How hard can it be?"

Vinny took a deep breath and tried to break it to the schmuck real gentle-like. "Richie, this stuff you ain't gonna learn out of a book or fancy classroom. This is the kind of thing you can only learn by doin'. You see what I'm sayin'?"

Richie's mind wasn't moving at the usual light speed, but it wasn't moving slowly either. "You can help me then, right Vinny?"

Vinny backed up a little and held up his hands. "Sorry Richie. Between the restaurant and my family, I ain't got time to help you out."

Nick crossed his arms. "Don't look at me. I have my hands full taking care of business, Rosalie, and Dave. I don't have time to whip you into a Domestic God."

Mike took a step back. "Me either. Between setting up the practice, Annabelle's pregnancy, and remodeling the brownstone, the last thing I need is an apprentice. Sorry bud, you're on your own. You'll just have to learn to become a Domestic God the same way we did. Trial and error."

Richie shook his head. "I don't have time to learn by trial and error. I need a coach. Where can I find a Domestic God coach?"

Becca ignored the light shining through her closed eyes and tried to block out the morning. Her nose peeked out over the covers and was cold, but the rest of her felt as if she was sleeping up against a furnace. There was nothing she loved more in life than warmth, and for the first time in ages, she was blissfully warm. Life was good. She smiled as she turned her face into the pillow hoping to block the light so she could sleep longer, but what she found instead was hair. "Oh, God, no."

"Oh, yeah."

Becca was sleeping on someone, a very big someone, a very big, naked someone with… "Oh, God." She was draped over Rich Ronaldi, who had one hand on her ass, and the other on her leg, which was, at the moment, thrown over his… "Oh. God."

Rich rolled over on top of her, his morning erection pressed hard against her thigh. Of course it was the first time in over two years she'd slept with a man and come in close contact with anything that didn't require four AA batteries. Her body knew the difference and was doing its own version of a happy dance. Her heart beat a mile a minute, her breathing was ragged, and her every nerve ending was on red alert.

"Oh baby, you feel so good."

Becca's brain went straight into panic mode. This was a disaster. The man talking in his sleep on top of her had a girlfriend and was the last person in the world she'd sleep with under any circumstances. What she didn't understand was how he got into bed with her in the first place. She knew she'd been exhausted, but she should have felt the bed move or something, right?

She pushed against his shoulder, and he didn't budge. His eyes were closed, and under the five o'clock shadow, or in this case, the six o'clock shadow, his lips formed a satisfied smile, like a little boy who had just found his favorite Hot Wheels car. She tried to pry herself out from under him, but he was two hundred pounds of dead weight.

He nuzzled his nose in her neck, and her traitorous body responded. It didn't seem to matter that her body had no right feeling the way it felt or reacting the way it did. Every time she moved, it made things worse, and harder. Not to mention more difficult.

She was either going to have to wake him, which, under the circumstances, would be unbelievably embarrassing, or wait for him to roll off her.

Rich smiled and thanked the dream gods for giving him such a gift. He took a deep breath and wondered what they called the scent she wore. It was earthy and rich, with a touch of musk and maybe patchouli mixed with hot, wet woman. He kissed her neck, his lips tasting her skin. It all felt so real—the heat of her body surrounding him, the noises she made, the way she whispered, and the bite of her nails on his shoulders…

He shifted his hips and pulled her long legs around him.

"Rich! Wake up."

"Oh baby, I am up."

"Good, then get the hell off me."

"What?" Rich opened his eyes and saw Becca's eyes green with anger and dark with arousal. He may be more than half asleep, but he was awake enough to know he wasn't the only one turned on. Of course, all it took was the thought that he'd almost had sex with someone who hated his guts to deflate him. "What the hell are you doing in my bed?"

That's when she hit him. Hard. "It's my bed, and I locked you out."

Rich didn't remember coming home last night, much less being locked out of his own bedroom. "I told you to stay out of my stuff. My bedroom is my stuff." God, all this yelling was doing nothing for his blaring headache. He'd forgotten she was even in the apartment. Rich rolled off her, taking the covers with him. He didn't do it on purpose, but he wasn't sorry he did. Wow. Who knew that was hiding under the butt-ugly sweatshirt and baggy pants? Damn, with a body like that—

"Do you mind?"

"Not at all." Rich remembered how she gave him a long once-over yesterday when he was bare-ass-naked. He took his time doing the same. So he wasn't much of a gentleman. Shoot him.

Becca scrambled off the bed and grabbed the first piece of clothing she could put her hands on, his blue shirt. What was it about a woman in a man's shirt and nothing else? Hell, she might as well have been wearing a French maid costume for all the good it did. Seeing her standing there naked was less of a turn-on than seeing her naked under his shirt. He groaned and bunched the covers over his lap as he sat trying to cover any evidence of his raging hard-on. Christ, he was going to hell. He wasn't sure what he did wrong, but it looked like she was about to tell him. Loudly.

He held up his hand. "Before you go off and yell at me, let me just say that I had no idea you were in my bed when I passed out in it last night. I didn't even remember you were here in my apartment, and I'm sorry—" The look she shot him said she wasn't buying it. Neither was he. "Okay, maybe not sorry, but I sure as hell didn't know that what I was dreaming wasn't a dream. I mean what were the chances that you, someone who wouldn't give me the time of day, would spend the night cuddled up to me? That wasn't a dream, was it?"

Becca shook her head but didn't say anything. He couldn't believe it. She was left speechless and blushing—everywhere. The longer he looked, the redder that porcelain skin of hers turned. He couldn't help but smile. There were definitely worse ways to wake up. He was just glad she wasn't the violent sort. He rubbed his shoulder that was sore from her punch. Okay, he was glad she wasn't armed.

Becca held his shirt down around her thighs; the movement gave him a great cleavage shot. Christ, was she trying to kill him?

"This was obviously a big mistake, and well, you didn't mean it, and I certainly didn't mean it. So why don't we both forget it ever happened."

Rich let out a bark of laughter that made his head feel as if it were splitting in two. He took his head in his hands to hold it together just in case it wasn't his imagination. "You can do whatever you want, but I have a feeling I'm going to remember this one until the day I die. Sorry, sweet-cheeks."

"You're insufferable." Becca turned an even darker shade of red. The look on her face was priceless.

"And you're quite the morning person, aren't you?" Who knew a pissed off princess could be so hot. And to think he thought she was an ice princess. Maybe that was what she wanted everyone to think. But standing there wearing nothing but his shirt, Rich saw there was nothing cold about her. Damn. She gave Rich a whole new appreciation for his lucky shirt.

Becca stormed into the bathroom and slammed the door. He'd never be able to wear that shirt again without picturing her in it. Maybe he should have it bronzed. He stood, grabbed a pair of jeans off the floor, pulled them on, and decided to go shirtless to remind her she was wearing his shirt and to piss her off. He remembered how she'd checked him out the first time they met at Annabelle and Mike's engagement party, claiming she was an artist and checked everyone out the same way. He didn't buy it, just like he didn't buy the size comment yesterday. He'd been around the block enough to know when a woman liked what she saw. It was clear Becca Larsen just didn't like that she liked it, and the thought of making her a little more uncomfortable was too good to pass up. Just for shits, he left the top button of his jeans undone. Rich scoped out the room. Lying on the dresser was a matching panty and bra set. Bingo.

Damn, Becca wasn't a plain white cotton kinda woman either. Rich smiled when he pictured her wearing the little scrap of satin and lace and thanked God for his great imagination because chances were, he'd never get to see her out of her big, baggy, ugly-as-shit clothes again. That was a real shame.

Rich leaned against the dresser holding her underthings. He knew he was pressing his luck, but hell, he really enjoyed pissing Becca off. It just became his new favorite hobby.

Becca spent the last ten minutes brushing her teeth, finger combing her hair, and doing her best to calm down. She washed her face and tried to wash the feeling of his body on top of hers from her memory bank. God, why did he have to feel so damn good? Probably because the only male she'd had on top of her in the last two years was Rosalie's dog, Dave. And as sweet as Dave was, and as much he seemed to enjoy sucking on her toes, Rich had it all over him. Hell, a man like Rich had it all over ninety-five percent of the male population. That is, if personality wasn't a requirement. Unfortunately for her, it was.

She couldn't believe she slept all wrapped up with him like that. How did that happen? And why couldn't she seem to get her hormones under control?

Maybe she should start dating again. Whatever loser Mike, Annabelle, and Rosalie saw fit to fix her up with couldn't possibly be a worse choice than Rich Ronaldi.

"You had better be dressed because I'm coming out." She opened the bathroom door to find him standing there in a pair of Levis, and nothing else as far as she could see, and she looked, though she really didn't want to think about the reason behind her interest in his apparel. She couldn't help but notice that he'd left the top button of his jeans hanging open, and there was no telltale elastic waistband showing to disprove her initial conclusion that he was going commando. All she saw was a treasure trail of dark hair running over a full six-pack of hard abs straight down to the button fly, and from the fit of his pants, it looked as if he was happy about something. She just wasn't sure if it was because he stood there holding her underwear or because she still wore nothing but his shirt.

She stomped up to him and ripped her lingerie out of his hands. "Do you mind?"

"You wearing my shirt?" He crossed his arms. "Not at all."

"You're really pushing your luck, Ronaldi. If you don't get out of here right now, the next time you sing in the shower, you'll be singing soprano. Get my drift?"

"I'm just trying to be of service." He scratched his chest, gave her a nod, and sauntered out of the bedroom as if she hadn't just threatened to unman him.

"Sure you are."

Becca took a long, hot shower and wondered if cold showers only worked for men. Thankfully, there were simpler and more enjoyable ways to solve that problem. God knew she needed to do something to get her mind off Rich Ronaldi and the fact that she was essentially an embarrassingly horny, born-again virgin. Not that the born-again virgin thing was planned. It wasn't. She didn't swear off sex until marriage or anything. She just swore off sex until she found a guy she thought would be an improvement over her Battery Operated Boyfriend. A battery operated boyfriend was reliable, well, as long as you had batteries. Although the reliability was a definite plus, it didn't hold you all night long, and it certainly didn't keep you warm. She got the holding and the warming part of the deal, just not the sex part. Not that she wanted to have sex with Rich. Okay, she was attracted to his body, but the attraction ended there. Unfortunately, her hormones didn't seem to give a flip that he was as far from a dream date as a guy could get when it came to personality. God, how depressing.

Tripod sat on the edge of the tub waiting for Becca to turn off the water, and if she wasn't fast enough for his taste, he'd yowl. Tripod could make a Siamese in heat seem quiet.

"Okay, okay, I'll get out." She turned the water off, and Tripod jumped into the tub with her, chasing the last of the water to the drain before rolling around the wet tub.

Becca closed the shower curtain and peeked out into the bedroom finding it empty. At least Rich hadn't snuck back in. She locked the door before dropping her towel and dressing. She threw on her favorite lie-around-the-house clothes. They may have looked like sweats, but they were cashmere. The tank, the drawstring pants, and the sweater wrap felt like a heavenly, decadent secret. She was finishing up her makeup by the time Rich rapped on the door.

"Are you about done in there? I'd like to take my shower sometime today."

Becca opened the door giving a silent thank you to Tripod for hurrying her along. "You didn't mention a time limit."

She strolled past him and headed for the coffee only to find it cold. It was the same coffee she'd made yesterday. "You couldn't make coffee?"

Rich stuck his head out the door. "The only coffee I make is instant. It's safer that way."

"Safer?" Her question never reached its destination. He'd already left. He was taking a shower—oh no. Tripod. She ran for the bedroom and just turned toward the bathroom door when she heard Tripod yowl.

"What the... Ow! You little son of a—"

Becca was through the door before she even realized it. A very naked Rich was wielding the toilet bowl brush like a sword. It was like that movie *Groundhog Day*, only today, he was the one armed. And a very unhappy, wet Tripod was under the back of the toilet bowl, hissing.

"Don't hurt him."

"Hurt him?" Rich dropped the toilet bowl brush back into its holder and turned on her. "He bit me!"

Becca tried to move toward her cat, but Rich seemed to take up the entire bathroom. He was large. "You sprayed him."

"How was I supposed to know there was an attack cat in the bathtub?"

Well, she had to give him points for that. She really should have told him that Tripod was out and about. But after this morning she had a hard, no, make that a difficult time thinking of anything but waking up draped over Rich. Hell, the way things were going, she spent more time with him naked than dressed. Not that she was complaining. His abs were nicer than that Cuban figure model's back in freshman year. She wondered if she was in over her head here. Just about the same time she noticed that she'd allowed her eyes to linger, she saw Tripod was staring too. Since the cat was known to jump really high, even after the loss of his leg, it would probably be a good idea to cover certain things up. She rolled her eyes. Yeah, from the looks of things, it was already up, so it definitely needed cover.

Becca pulled a towel off the rack and handed it to Rich. "You might want to put something on until I get Tripod out of here. You wouldn't want him to bite more than just your calf."

Rich wrapped the towel around his waist. That did nothing to change the fact that her mouth had become as dry as the Sahara during a hundred-year drought and that a few other places on her body seemed to have the opposite problem.

Rich cleared his throat. "Why don't you get your animal out of the bathroom so that I can shower?"

"I would, but the thing is, Tripod doesn't like to be picked up when he's in attack mode."

"Attack mode, huh? He sounds like he's as much trouble as you are."

So, okay, Rich was up by four in this unfortunate exchange. "He didn't mean to hurt you. You startled him. He likes to play in the water, but not while it's running, unless it's the toilet or the faucet where he can stay relatively dry."

"You might have mentioned that, or that you let some wild cat out in my apartment."

"Tripod isn't wild. He's a Bengal."

"A what?"

"A Bengal. It's a breed of cat that's a second or third generation cross between an Ocelot and a domestic shorthair.

"Like I said, wild."

Rich looked at the back of his calf, and Becca saw where Tripod had broken the skin. "He's up to date on all his shots."

Rich didn't say anything.

"Tripod's not your everyday house cat. Bengals are usually larger and I think more beautiful than your average cat. They have a pelt instead of an ordinary cat's coat. They love water—"

"No shit."

Becca nodded. "They're great hunters…" Probably not something she should really talk about now. "And they're smart. And since they're sometimes bred with Siamese, they tend to be a little loud, and well, Tripod's more temperamental than your average kitty."

"Is the attack cat persona part of the breed, or is it just him?"

Tripod's crouch got more pronounced; he was all set to pounce. Becca hissed, and Tripod put his butt back down on the tiles. "I don't know. I think it has more to do with him missing a leg than his breed. I found him on the side of the road with a broken ankle—he'd been hit by a car. I took him to a vet, and they couldn't save his leg. I don't know what he was like before the accident."

"And you kept him?"

Becca shrugged. "He grows on you—"

"Like mold."

"Look, I'm sorry. Let me get his toy, and maybe if you step out of the bathroom, I can get him to come out."

Becca went to get the birdie—which was nothing but a bunch of brightly colored feathers tied to a string on the end of a bamboo pole. She always thought of it as fishing for kitties. It worked like a charm. Tripod followed the birdie, his butt bouncing like it was on top of a pogo stick. Once they got out into the bedroom, Becca let Tripod catch and kill the "bird" while Rich kept a wide berth and snuck into the bathroom, locking the door behind him.

"Good going, Tripod. If he kicks us out, I don't know what we're going to do. Do you think furnished apartments are rented month-to-month to people with

disabled kitties?" Tripod answered her with his meow
that sounded more like the word "noooo" than anything
else. He used it every time he wanted her to stop something or if he was answering a yes or no question in the
negative. Most people would think Becca was crazy, but
after spending a few months living with Tripod, she was
sure he knew exactly what he was saying.

Chapter 3

RICH STROLLED OUT OF THE BEDROOM IN RECORD TIME probably just to piss Becca off some more. He was really good at that. He wore another pair of perfectly faded Levis, which he filled out way too well for her taste, and a long-sleeved, cobalt blue T-shirt that brought out the blue in his eyes and showed off that incredible chest she'd spent the night using as a pillow. Damn, she'd almost talked herself into forgetting about that.

Rich followed her to the kitchen and leaned against the breakfast bar, staring at her as if he could see beneath her clothes. It was unnerving, and she reminded herself of all the reasons she didn't like him.

"I know you don't like me much."

Becca took a cup from the cabinet. Ah, and he was a mind reader too.

"I don't know why, but it doesn't matter."

"It doesn't?" Wow, he was good. Not in that way, she reminded herself. And no, she wasn't even that curious. She poured the coffee.

He shook his head. "It might be a good thing."

She looked up from the cup she was filling. "How can my not liking you be a good thing?"

"I need help, and I know it might come as a shock, but most women find me attractive. That would just complicate matters."

"Color me surprised. Since you know I don't like you, I suppose I can give up pretending that I do."

He nodded and smiled a sinfully sexy smile that made her hormones do the cha-cha. She stepped out of the kitchen, picked up the sheets, blanket, and pillow she'd left for him in the living room, and returned them to the closet. Anything to get away from him. The man was a threat to her equilibrium. Unfortunately, he followed. "Okay, so since I don't have to be nice, and you're weirdly happy about that, why don't you just leave?"

"I have a proposition for you."

"No."

"No?"

"That's my answer to your proposition."

"Don't you even want to know what it is?"

"Not especially, but I will listen if you promise it will get you out my door sooner."

He smiled again, and she rolled her eyes. She just wanted to be alone already. When it came down to it, she wasn't much of a social person. She spent most of her time alone in her studio, and she was happy to do it. She didn't need a man or company to keep her happy.

"Gina dumped me. She said I wasn't relationship material because I don't cook, clean, and do my own laundry. How hard can it be? I just need a trainer."

"A trainer?"

"Yeah, like a domestic coach. Someone to show me the ropes. So I learn whatever I have to learn to make Gina think I'm not such a bad bet." He might as well have asked her to streak through Times Square during rush hour. His chances would have been better. He stood and walked toward her, forcing her to look up to him, which ticked her off all the more.

"Why?"

"My dean suggested that I should settle down."

"And why is that my problem?"

"It's not. See, the thing is, I thought we could, you know, help each other. You need me. I need you. This is my place, and there aren't many furnished apartments that take man-eating, three-legged attack cats."

"I'm not that desperate, and the jury is still out on whose place this is. But setting that aside for the moment, why should it matter who you're with or not with? Isn't the whole idea of a man having to settle down to be good at his job archaic? And I'm sorry to have to tell you Rich, but you have as much a chance of becoming Mr. Perfect as Tripod has of growing his leg back."

Rich really didn't want to get into his inauspicious departure from Dartmouth. He'd left there with his professional integrity barely intact. When he was offered a position at Columbia, Rich thought things were looking up until yesterday's meeting with Craig and then Gina.

There were times when Gina reminded him of plastic explosives, easy to mold but dangerous as hell if you lit her fuse. Unfortunately for Rich, all it took to light her fuse was to surprise her by moving nearby, thereby removing the long distance portion of their relationship, and, without knowing why, the ecstatically happy part of it too. He looked over at Becca, and she didn't look like she'd cave any time soon.

"Things happen. Relationships break up. It's not unheard of. What's the big deal?"

"Becca, please. You don't understand."

Becca sprawled on the couch, getting good and comfortable, and her damn cat jumped up on her lap turning around a few times before curling up and covering his eyes with his front paw as if to shield them from the light. Becca was going to make him beg. He could feel it. Shit. The woman was impossible. If she'd asked him to help her out of a bind, he'd have done it for free, but no. Not Becca. This was going to cost him big time.

"I've got all day. Enlighten me."

"No." He didn't want to enlighten her. All he wanted to do was strangle her. No other woman he'd ever met could take him from calm to homicidal with one look, nor had he met a woman who could get him hot by doing exactly that. He wondered what the hell he'd done to deserve this kind of torture. Okay, there were plenty of things, but had he known what the payback would be, he never would have done them, that was for damn sure.

He took a deep breath and let it out slowly. One of his exes, a yoga instructor who had incredible flexibility (which led to equally incredible sex) once told him that breathing deeply relieved stress. Unfortunately, it wasn't helping now. All it did was make him wonder what kind of perfume Becca wore and why he found himself standing close enough to get a whiff. She was a damn witch.

The woman wore a Mona Lisa smile, that one that says *I know a hell of a lot more than you ever will, and I can't wait to use it to torture you.* "Fine. Leave. It's no skin off my nose."

Rich sat and leaned over her so that they were nose-to-nose. "You help me out with the whole domestic issue, and I'll let you stay."

She sputtered. "You'll let me stay? You'll let me stay?"

Rich tried not to smile; she was really cute when she was steamed. Her pale skin turned pink, okay, red, and the white blonde hair just made it seem redder, then her eyes darkened to a scary shade of green, almost like the color of the sky before a tornado. Maybe Little Miss Larsen wasn't such a cool customer after all. Maybe she was just waiting for someone to light her fuse. Lucky for him that was one of his strong suits. "I told you, blood is thicker than water."

Becca became one with the couch in order to get her face as far from his face as possible without running away. God she was fun to fuck with, figuratively, although he wouldn't mind finding out if she'd be fun literally since he was newly single. Damn, he really needed to stop thinking that way, for his own sanity if for nothing else.

"If you remember correctly, I'm Mike's sister. So I trump your whole blood is thicker than water theory. Mike's not going to be too happy to see me thrown out on the street."

Rich smiled and licked his lips just to get a rise out of her. She was easy. Okay, maybe not easy in the way he suddenly wished she was. What he meant was it was easy to piss in her paddling pool. "I'm sure Mike and Annabelle would love it if you and Killer moved in with them. Just imagine the two of you living in the love nest with Mr. & Mrs. Incessantly Happy. I give you an hour tops before you're fighting Annabelle and her morning-noon-and-night sickness to pray to the porcelain god."

Ah, he was finally getting to her. And that was a good thing because he really needed a coach. He just wished he could look at her the way he looked at Coach Como in high school. Even the way he looked at the girls' coach, Mrs. Southern, with the harelip and the speech impediment. Unfortunately, since he felt Becca beneath him, imagined her naked, and worse, knew what she looked like wearing nothing but his lucky shirt, it would be impossible to see her as anything but a goddamn sexual fantasy.

"I get the bedroom."

Rich's mind was still stuck on the sexual fantasy thing, and the mention of any word with bed in it spelled trouble. Big trouble. He backed away and sat, pulling a pillow over his lap to hide any embarrassing evidence from her and the cat.

His silence must have unnerved her. "Well?"

He shook his head. "I thought I'd let you use the guest room unless you'd rather share the bed."

"Over my dead body."

"Well, that's a shame, but not unexpected. I'm sure you'll be comfortable in the guest room."

"Ha!"

"The way I see it, you have three choices. You can stay on the futon in the guest room, you can stay with Mike and Annabelle, or if you ask nicely, we can share the bed. We will have to discuss your borrowing my clothes though."

It was time to face facts. Becca had no choice but to cave to Rich. All her belongings were in storage for three months until her new apartment in the brownstone she bought with her brother and sister-in-law was remodeled. She didn't have the time or energy to find another place that would accept her and her disabled cat while she was supposed to be supervising the construction on her apartment and studio and trying to get her work into galleries.

Rich might be cocky and arrogant, but she wasn't sure how much of that was bravado. He was a guy, and guys hated getting dumped. Plus, he wanted to win this Gina woman back badly enough to try to change, so he couldn't be as arrogant as he seemed. Could he?

She cautioned herself not to think too highly of him. After all, he wasn't much of a gentleman. If he were the least bit gentlemanly, he'd give her the bed, not just offer her half. What a jerk.

She kicked herself for putting a stop to Tripod's planned attack on Rich's dick. It would have served him right if she'd let Tripod have his way with Rich. It would have almost made up for the anger and frustration he'd caused her. The man really had a way of getting under her skin, and he knew it.

Rich had his head buried in the refrigerator and his really nice ass facing her. "You made lasagna?"

"No, your Aunt Rose brought it by for us yesterday."

"Us? As in you and me?" He pulled out the tray and set it on the counter beside the gravy and cheese. "My favorite breakfast. Leftover lasagna."

"Yes. Your Aunt Rose has this weird idea that there's something more between the two of us than animosity."

Rich groaned. "What exactly did she say?"

"I don't remember."

"What do you mean, you 'don't remember?'" His hands flew up and down in front of him, as if he was tossing an invisible pizza. "Think! What exactly did she say?"

"Geez, overreact much? What does it matter?"

"It matters a whole hell of a lot. Aunt Rose knows things. She says shit, and the next thing you know, it comes true."

"Are you telling me she's clairvoyant?"

"Hell, yeah! She's been getting me in trouble with my parents since I was in diapers."

Becca crossed her arms and rolled her eyes for good measure. "It doesn't take a psychic to figure out a guy like you. Anyone with an IQ over fifty would have no problem doing that."

"Yeah, well explain how Aunt Rose knew Annabelle was pregnant at her engagement party."

The hair on Becca's neck stood up. "A good guess?"

"Okay, how about this. The one time I got picked up by the cops, she called my parents and told them to meet me at the police station before I was even arrested. They were there waiting for me."

Becca suddenly didn't feel so good. She pulled a chair out and sat down hard.

"Oh God." Rich crossed himself, picked up the cross he wore around his neck and kissed it, and then ran his hands through his hair before kneeling in front of her. "You have to tell me."

"No. There is no way. I'm not going to put any ideas into that fertile mind of yours. Besides, it's not as if you can ask her to take it back." Though if she could, Becca definitely would.

"Maybe we could do something."

"Like what?"

"I don't know. Maybe we could go to a priest and get some kind of protection."

"You actually believe a priest could ward off a curse?"

"It was a curse?"

"To me it would be. To you, it would be the best thing that ever happened to you."

Rich took her hand, and Becca felt all the blood that left her head a few seconds before rushing through her ears. Her heart beat so loudly it sounded like a stampede of elephants was running though her, and she tingled all over. The last thing she ever wanted to do was tingle with Rich Ronaldi.

"What did she say?"

"She said you are spoiled and that you need to grow up."

"And?"

"And she said there was something wrong with my cat."

"What else?"

"Nothing."

"Don't lie. Nothing you just said would give you reason to almost pass out."

"She said that I'm good for you and that you don't like skinny women."

Rich smiled as if he didn't have a care in the world, which she guessed he didn't. She, on the other hand, wanted to die.

"I don't usually like skinny women, but you're growing on me. You looked pretty good wearing my shirt."

Becca tried to pull her hand out of his to hit him. Unfortunately, he might have been a little psychic himself, because he knew not to let her go.

"Well, if that's all she said, it wasn't as bad as I imagined."

"What did you imagine?"

"I don't know. If she didn't even ask if you were Catholic, I guess I don't have to worry." He gave her hand a squeeze and went to heat up his food. Becca thought she'd never eat again.

Rich kept one eye on Becca as he microwaved his lasagna. The color had yet to return to her face. He had a feeling she wasn't telling him the whole story when it came to Aunt Rose. Since there was little he could do to change the fact that Aunt Rose told Becca whatever it was she saw and scared the life out of his new roommate, he might as well enjoy the results. Anything that left Becca speechless, thereby silencing her sharp tongue, could only be good news for him.

He took the plate out of the microwave and sat opposite Becca at the table. He cut a piece of lasagna and, blowing on it lightly, took his first bite.

One thing he could say about his aunt was the woman could cook. She made lasagna that rivaled his mother's. He groaned in appreciation. It was unusual to have a meal this good without first having to be tortured by his family. Rich didn't feel the least bit guilty that Becca took the heat for the food he was consuming. The fact that she still hadn't regained her composure was a little worrying. She seemed to be the type to bounce back fast. Not today. Maybe the double whammy she received with Aunt Rose last night and waking with him this morning was more than even Becca could handle.

With his stomach full and his hangover almost gone, Rich felt pretty good. Having a blonde beauty sitting across from him didn't hurt either, especially since all it took was a blink of his eye to picture her naked. Yeah, compared to yesterday, things were looking up. He had his coach, he had a plan, and he even had an intriguing woman living with him. Okay, it was platonic, but just because he couldn't touch didn't mean he couldn't look. Did it? He was a guy, after all. If he had anything to say about it, when they lowered him into the ground, he'd be checking to see if he could see up any woman's skirt. He slid the last noodle around his plate soaking up the rest of the gravy, brought it to his mouth, and sucked it up with a slurp. "Hungry?"

Becca stared as he licked the last of the gravy off his lips. Her darkened eyes widened. She shook her head as her color rose.

Rich wiped his mouth with a napkin and hid a smile. She might not be hungry for food, but she was hungry for something. Hmm. "So where do you want to start?"

Becca blinked. "Start what?"

"My training."

"You weren't serious about that, were you?"

"As serious as Pearl Harbor."

He waited for Becca to come to the realization that he wasn't pulling her leg.

"You're really going to learn how to be, what would you call it, a domesticated man?"

Rich shook his head. "My brother-in-laws call themselves Domestic Gods. 'Domesticated man' sounds wimpy. We're not wimpy. We're Domestic Gods."

Becca laughed, not a polite little giggle. She let out a bark of laughter that turned into a sexy belly laugh and ended in almost a snort. Not as sexy, but really cute, especially since she seemed embarrassed by it.

"I'm a fast learner."

Becca threw the tail of the sweater-thing over her shoulder covering the hint of cleavage she'd displayed earlier. "Did it ever occur to you that most people pick this stuff up by osmosis? You observe people cooking, cleaning, doing laundry, and imitate them? If you were such a fast learner, you wouldn't be begging for training from me."

"I never beg."

Rich was disappointed when her retort was interrupted by a knock on the door. Becca raised an eyebrow, stood giving him one of her annoying half-smiles, and went to answer the door. "Wayne. Henry. How are you two?"

Ah, the upstairs neighbors.

Wayne balanced a tray of cookies in one hand and pulled Becca into a hug. "We just stopped by to bring something sweet to the sweet and to welcome you."

"Thanks, guys."

Wayne looked over her shoulder at Rich. "Are we interrupting something?"

Becca returned his hug. "No, not at all."

Liar.

Wayne tsked. "Such a shame."

"Believe me, it's not." Becca pushed Wayne away, rolled her eyes, and reached for Henry. "I was wondering when I'd see you." She motioned toward Rich. "Do you know Rosalie and Annabelle's brother, Rich?"

Henry, the taller of the two, gave Rich a nod. Wayne walked across the living room toward Rich, giving him a very thorough once-over while he set the cookies on the breakfast bar. "Just in passing a few times at the girls' weddings. Hi."

Rich stood and shook Wayne's hand. "Hello. It's nice to see you both again. I've been meaning to go up and reintroduce myself. I like to know my neighbors." Rich picked up a chocolate chip cookie and took a bite. "Mmm, good. Thanks for these."

Wayne looked perplexed.

Henry's gaze traveled from Rich to Becca and back again. "Your neighbors? I thought Becca moved in."

Becca groaned. "There's been a mix-up. Rich rented the place from Rosalie, and I rented it from Annabelle, so unfortunately, for the next three months, Rich and I are going to be roommates."

Tripod jumped up on the couch and meowed—if you can call it that. It sounded more like a siren or maybe like a baby's wail.

Wayne turned to Rich. "You have a cat?"

Rich took a step back. "Don't look at me. Killer is Becca's."

Wayne turned back to Becca. "Killer?"

Becca reached over and scratched Tripod's neck. "His name is Tripod, and he doesn't like Rich. Who could blame him?"

Wayne and Henry looked from Becca to him like spectators at a tennis match. Rich couldn't help but laugh. "Other than me?" He took a tentative step toward the couch and turned to Wayne and Henry. "That thing attacked me. It's possessed." Of course, the spawn of

Satan rubbed up against Becca and then jumped to the floor doing his three-legged hop over to Wayne and wove his way between his and Henry's legs. Tripod even let them pet him. "I turn the shower on him one time, and I have an enemy for life."

Becca picked the beast up and rubbed her cheek against his head. He was purring like a motorboat. "Rich, really. Pouting is so unattractive." The damn cat even meowed to agree.

"I don't pout." Everyone stared at him.

Wayne backed away and nudged Henry. "Well, we can see you two are busy sparring. We won't keep you. Enjoy the cookies. You can return the plate anytime." He shot a pointed look at Becca.

Henry nodded. "Rich, nice to see you again." He gave Becca a kiss on the cheek. "We'll see you soon. Have fun settling in."

Becca grabbed Henry's arm. "You don't have to leave."

Wayne and Henry exchanged looks, the two smiled to each other, and Wayne answered for Henry. "Yes, we do. Sorry doll, you're on your own. Have fun."

Rich put his arm around Becca, earning a hiss from the possessed one who leapt from Becca's arms, and a smile from Wayne. "See ya. Thanks for stopping by." He waited for them to close the door and pulled her a little tighter to his side. He really liked the way she felt. He found out that what he thought were plain old ordinary sweats—which he had to admit looked better on her than on any other woman he'd ever seen—were made of fabric so soft it made him want to touch her, as if just looking at her didn't do the trick. "Where were we?"

"I'm not sure."

She turned her head so they were nose-to-nose. Her breath fanned his face, her eyes sparkled, and her face flushed.

Becca stepped back and missed Rich's warmth. She'd never felt delicate until just now. Rich was big, hot, hard, and she seemed to fit right in the crook of his arm. Actually, she seemed to fit pretty well on top of him and underneath him too. What the hell was she thinking? Okay, she knew what she was thinking, but she had absolutely no right to think it. He was semi-attached, and she was horny.

She touched her forehead. "Oh, I remember. You were asking about where we should start to turn you into Gina's Mr. Perfect." She smiled as he shook himself out of his stupor. Okay, so she was physically attracted to him. She was attracted to plenty of other men. It just seemed like more with Rich because she'd woken up naked with him. So she hadn't been able to quite get past that, but she would. Just as soon as she could get a little privacy and fresh batteries.

"Right. Where do you want to start?"

Becca pulled her sweater-shawl around her to make up for the loss of body heat and to cover any evidence of her arousal. No need to give him any reason to stare at her almost nonexistent chest. "How about with some ground rules. After all, we'll be living here. Together. Platonically."

Rich cleared his throat. "Right."

"Since you're so interested in becoming a Domestic God, you are responsible for all the cooking and cleaning."

"All of it? You have to be kidding."

"Come on now. I have to supervise and teach. You have to practice, practice, practice."

Rich sat on the couch and groaned. "Fine."

"And just because we're sharing the apartment temporarily doesn't mean we're sharing anything else. This is a purely platonic partnership."

"Right. So, you're going to be my coach? You're going to help me get Gina back?" He stood, turned to her, and grinned so wide she needed shades.

"Yes."

"Great!" He grabbed her, swung her around as if she weighed no more than a feather, and set her back down. "We better get started. We only have two weeks."

"What?" Oh God, what had she gotten herself into?

Chapter 4

TRIPOD WAS RINGING. OKAY, MAYBE NOT TRIPOD. BECCA'S phone rang, startling Tripod who had been sleeping on it, which explained why Becca spent the better part of an hour searching high and low for the damn thing and was unable to find it.

"Hello?"

"What is going on there?"

"My, Annabelle. Aren't you in a fabulous mood today?"

"I'm pregnant. What the hell do you expect?"

"Still not glowing, huh?"

"Not unless I glow when I turn green. What I want to know is how it's possible to throw up more than I consume."

Becca tossed herself on the futon. The damn thing was a torture rack. She really needed to get herself a bed. "One of life's great mysteries. Just think, in February you'll have a little baby or two."

"Two?"

"Yeah, twins runs in the family, remember?"

"Oh, no way. There's only one bun in this oven."

"You're sure of that?" Becca rolled over and tried to get comfortable. Impossible.

"Nice try, Larsen. You thought if you got me worked up about the idea of twins, I'd conveniently forget that for some unknown reason you're living with my brother."

"Platonically."

"How in the world did you end up living with Richie?"

"Why are you asking me? It's all your fault. You're the one who sublet the apartment to me without checking with the owner who had already rented it to Rich."

"Oh, God. I'm so sorry. I never thought to ask. What are you going to tell Mike?"

Becca sat and wrapped her long arm around her even longer legs. She shook her head wishing she could be the least bit normal. "What do you mean?"

"Mike's not going to like the idea of his little sister living with anyone, especially not Richie. You know that Gina just dumped him. Maybe you can use Ben's guest room over the gallery, but then Mike would probably like that even less than you living with Rich."

"Yes, I'm aware that Gina dumped Rich and that Mike still hasn't forgiven Ben for proposing to you—"

"He's my boss and my friend. He only proposed to me because he needs to get married. It was nothing personal."

"Right, like Mike's ever going to buy that one. But where and with whom I live is none of Mike's business. I'm a grown woman, and I can live with whoever I want. And just in case he didn't notice, I'm almost as big as he is. If he wants to see his little sister, he'd better find the few pictures of me when I was a kid. I'm anything but little now."

"Mike's still not gonna like it."

Becca couldn't take the singsong tone Annabelle used. It wasn't as if Becca was happy with the arrangement. That didn't mean she was going to let Mike, or anyone else, have any say in the way she lived. "Mike has no say in the matter. Besides, aren't I a little old for him to be pulling the whole protective brother routine? I've lived my whole life on my own. The last thing I need is for my newfound brother to start telling me I'm not living up to his standards either."

"Whoa, sensitive much?"

Becca lay back down. "Maybe. But the fact stands that I want to stay in Brooklyn to be close to the brownstone, and I have nowhere else to go. I don't have time to find a temporary residence since I'm supposed to be supervising the remodeling. I lost my loft in Philly so even if I could commute, I can't go back. Not to mention that I have Tripod here with me. As harmless as a three-legged cat should be, Tripod's not. He already bit your brother. Besides, it's only going to be for a few months. I can live with anyone for a few months, even Rich." She hoped.

"You sure? You know, you can come stay with Mike and me. It'll be like old times."

"And break up your perpetual honeymoon? I don't think so, but thanks for offering." Becca heard rattling in the background.

"Oh God, Mike. Shut the refrigerator. I can smell it. Becca, I have to go. I'm going to be sick. Bye."

All she heard was dead air. Well, that's one way to get out of an uncomfortable conversation with Annabelle. Becca only felt a little bad that Annabelle was probably tossing her cookies, but not bad enough to call back to see how she was. The last thing she wanted to do was explain this mess to Mike, her newfound, possibly overprotective half-brother. Sheesh, you'd think he was smart enough to know that she was capable of taking care of herself. Hell, she was the most independent person she knew.

There was a knock on the door.

"What?"

Rich stuck his head through the opening. "I washed the dishes and started the dishwasher."

"Good for you."

"It wasn't so bad."

Becca stood and smiled. "You stuck our dishes in the dishwasher. I don't want to be a downer, but it's hardly rocket science."

Rich turned, and she followed him into the living room. "Bec?"

Becca had her eyes locked on Rich's back. He had one of those backs she loved. Broad shoulders tapering to a thin waist and a really nice tight ass. "Hmm?"

Rich increased his speed. "Should there be bubbles coming out of the machine?"

Becca raced after him. "You're kidding, right?" She drew in a deep breath when she looked over the bar and saw the kitchen floor covered in soapsuds. Nope, definitely not kidding. "What the hell did you do?"

Rich looked genuinely upset, as he should, since he was going to be the one bailing bubbles. "I did just what you told me. I filled that little cup with the yellow dish soap."

"Rich. I said the dishwasher soap, not dish soap." She kicked off her shoes and slid barefoot into the fray. So much for her favorite cashmere sweats. She should be getting combat pay.

Rich checked his watch. He was going to be late for Sunday dinner at his parents' house, but there was no way he could get out of cleaning up the mess he made. Becca looked as if she wanted to kill him, and he did feel awful. Her pants were all wet and clinging to her mile-long legs. She was shivering, too.

"Why don't you go change out of those wet clothes? I'll finish up here." It wasn't that bad. He was able to see the black and white tiles through the bubbles now. Another ten minutes, and he could be on his way. "I'll get this cleaned up before I leave."

"Hot date?"

"Gina dumped me, remember? I have dinner at my parents' every Sunday. I can't get out of it. As it is, I'll be late."

"Oh, right. I've heard all about your weekly family dinners. Annabelle compared them to shock therapy."

He didn't try to hold back the laugh. "Yeah, that's not a bad description. Though I doubt shock therapy patients get tiramisu for desert."

"Is it worth it?"

"The tiramisu? Definitely. Mama's tiramisu is amazing. You wanna come?"

She backed up a step. "No, thanks. I have enough torture from my family. I don't need yours too."

Rich went on soaking up the bubbles. "Oh, it's not that bad. And what's wrong with your family? Mike is great, and your dad seems nice."

"Yeah, they're great."

Something in her tone of voice made Rich stop mopping. All of a sudden the in-your-face, not-afraid-of-anyone, come-at-you-with-a-baseball-bat, fiercely independent woman he spent the night and morning with seemed to disappear, turn into a five-year-old whose mother forgot to pick her up from kindergarten, and reappear in the blink of an eye. If he hadn't been watching closely, he'd have missed it.

Becca held out her hand. "Give me the mop. Go ahead. You're going to be late. I'll finish cleaning up."

Rich shook his head. "No, it's fine. I'll take care of this. You're cold and wet. Go change. It's not like I don't have a good excuse for being late. Maybe I'll be lucky and miss round one."

"Or you'll be thrown in the ring when you get there."

"I can hold my own."

"Yeah, as long as it doesn't involve soap or a mop. Good luck." Becca shrugged, wrapped her sweater more tightly around herself, and tiptoed across the small kitchen, careful not to slip. Rich watched her duck into her room, shook his head, and finished mopping.

By the time Rich had the kitchen floor suds-free, he was a half hour late. He rushed to his room, dried his feet, and put his socks and boots back on. Passing Becca's closed door, he wasn't sure if he should say good-bye or just leave. He hadn't heard a peep out of her or her damn cat. He stood outside her door and remembered the last time he went to her room. She'd been lying down. Maybe she was taking a nap, or maybe she was avoiding him. The thought of her locking herself in her room so she didn't have to deal with him rubbed him the wrong way. Rich knocked on her door.

"Yes?"

He pushed the door open and stuck his head in to find she'd rearranged every piece of furniture. "You moved the furniture yourself?"

Becca pushed a small dresser closer to the wall and wiped her hands on her jeans—she was back to wearing the butt-ugly baggy jeans. "Yeah, Tripod wasn't much help."

"If you'd have asked, I'd have moved everything for you."

"Thanks, but I don't need help. I'm a big girl."

He looked her up and down, not that he needed to. He'd seen her naked, and he knew a few things about her body. She was tall, she had the most incredible legs he'd ever seen on any woman, and he'd seen his share. She was a natural blonde, and she was anything but big. "You might not have needed help, but you could have had it. There's a difference."

"Thanks for the offer, but I'm fine." She moved a lamp from the dresser onto the desk. "See ya."

Rich really hated being dismissed. Especially by Becca. But she was right, he had to leave, or he'd never hear the end of it. He left her door open, grabbed his jacket, shrugged it on, and headed for his parents'.

He parked his Highlander behind Nick's Viper. Annabelle had the front door open and waiting for him before he even hit the kill button. Damn, she had radar as good as Aunt Rose's.

"Where's Becca?"

Rich climbed up the steps. "Home with her cat. Why?"

"She's not coming?"

Rich held up his hands to protect him from Annabelle's future assault. He didn't need any psychic powers to see that coming. "I invited her. Maybe if you hadn't told her the family dinner was like shock therapy with food, she'd have come."

Annabelle rested her clasped hands on her bump. "Compared to her family, ours is normal."

Rich let out a bark of laughter and shrugged out of his jacket. "Normal?" He put his arm around his little sister and gave her a sideways hug, kissing the top of her head. "We put the fun in dysfunctional. We aren't the least bit normal. Believe me, I've seen normal, and we're about as far away from that as we can get." There was no place in the foyer to throw his jacket. He turned to the closet because he knew he'd get a smack upside the head if he didn't hang it up.

"You go ahead and believe that. You want to know real torture, go eat at the country club with Becca's mother. The woman is obsessed with her social status. Her bible is *The Social Register*. And she thinks women should be petite. Poor Becca hasn't been petite since birth. Bitsy calls her an Amazon and has been pushing cosmetic surgery on her since she was fifteen. Every year she gives her a Christmas card with a check for a boob job and a card for a plastic surgeon."

Rich couldn't believe his ears. He tossed his jacket on a hanger and pushed aside the others to squeeze it in. "You're kidding. Becca's beautiful, and she has a great body. There's nothing wrong with her tits."

He turned just in time to see Mike, his brother-in-law and Becca's big brother, scowl. Fuck.

Annabelle stood in between her brother and her husband. What is it with men and their little sisters? "Don't even think about it, Mike. Rich doesn't need intimate knowledge to know Becca's beautiful. He's not blind."

Rich was looking awful guilty for a guy who didn't have intimate knowledge. Hell, as far as Annabelle knew, no man had had intimate knowledge of Becca's body for a very long time, and Annabelle knew everything there was to know about Becca, up to and including her latest vibrator purchase. Annabelle might be repressed, but Becca sure wasn't, so she routinely conversed about her toy collection, and much to Annabelle's mortification, had even given Annabelle a vibrator as a Christmas gift last year.

Mike wrapped his arms around her from behind, his hand resting on her belly. "I didn't say anything."

No, but the amount of tension running through his body told her how much he hated the fact that Rich saw Becca as the beautiful woman she was. Annabelle tilted her head back to rest on his chest as she looked at his face. "Becca's a grown woman. She's not a little girl who needs a big brother to fight off bullies. Besides, my brother's not such a bad catch."

"What?" Both Mike and Rich said in stereo.

Rich backed up a step and shook his head. "Hold on. There's nothing going on between Becca and me. She doesn't even like me. Besides, she's helping me get Gina back. Believe me, we're just sharing the apartment temporarily. We're platonic roommates. She's sleeping in the guest room."

Rosalie had sauntered over with her husband Nick. "What are you talking about?"

Rich nodded hello. "I asked Becca to teach me to be more domestic so I can get back together with Gina. Becca's gonna teach me how to cook, clean, and do laundry."

Annabelle laughed. "And she agreed?"

Rich nodded. "She needed a place to stay, and I needed a coach."

Rosalie groaned. "Richie, are you sure Gina broke up with you because you're a slob and not because she's not interested in being tied down? The last I heard, she wasn't looking for anything long term. That's why when you were in New Hampshire I thought you and Gina were good together. I mean, it's not as if long-distance relationships ever work out. Since when are you interested in committed relationships, anyway?"

Rich didn't look too happy with Rosalie or her line of questioning. "A guy's gotta grow up sometime. Don'tcha think? I'm ready to settle down."

Nick put his arm around his wife. "I know there's pressure on you from your dean to look respectable and settled, and hey, maybe you are ready. Gina might be a different story. You know, just because you're ready doesn't mean Gina is. "

Rich crossed his arms. "Gina broke up with me because she thinks I'm not relationship material. Those were her exact words. That's why I asked Becca to teach me to be more domestic. I need to get Gina back, and all I have to do is show her I've changed."

Annabelle could tell Mike was trying not to bust out laughing. She swatted his thigh for finding this whole mess funny.

Mike hugged her a little tighter before he spoke up. "You make it all sound so easy. So, you're going to learn how to cook and clean and then what? Are you going to call her and say 'Hey baby, I've changed. Come and get me?'"

Rich obviously hadn't planned that far in advance. "Rosalie, maybe you could help me. You know, tell Gina how much I've changed. I did the dishes this morning.

You can ask Becca. She taught me how. I don't think I've ever seen the kitchen cleaner."

Rosalie shrugged. "I guess I can mention it. I'm not sure it's going to help though. Maybe the best thing for you to do is move on. I don't think Gina is waiting for you."

"Dinner's ready," Mama yelled. "Rosalie, come help me in the kitchen."

Everyone moved toward the dining room except Annabelle and Mike. She thanked God Mama didn't ask for her to help. Annabelle spent the morning hiding in the back of the apartment because Mike had made toast. For some reason the smell of toast made her sick, well, the smell of toast and just about everything else, too. Annabelle took a deep breath through her mouth so she wouldn't smell anything that would have her running to throw up and turned in Mike's arms.

He was still scowling. "I don't like the idea of Becca living with Rich."

"That's too bad, but Becca didn't ask for your opinion or permission. Besides, it's only temporary. She'll be spending most of her time at the brownstone anyway."

Mike didn't say anything, but Annabelle knew he wasn't happy.

"Do us all a favor and try to keep your feelings to yourself. If not, you're going to offend your sister, my brother, or both of them." She wrapped her arms around his neck and kissed him until she felt all the tension leave his body and another kind of tension take its place.

Someone behind them made a production of clearing her throat. Annabelle cringed. Only one person clears her throat like that. Aunt Rose.

"Come to supper. You two already made'a the baby. Give it a rest. Eh?"

Rich lingered after supper. He felt weird going back to the apartment. He'd never been the sensitive type, but he had to admit it was uncomfortable living with someone who openly stated that she didn't like him. He wasn't sure why either. He was a likable enough guy. But there was something about him that bugged the crap out of Becca.

"Annabelle?" Damn, she looked as if she was half asleep.

"Hmm?"

"Why do you think Becca doesn't like me?"

"She doesn't like you?"

"No. She admitted it the other day."

Annabelle shoved a pillow behind her back. "I don't know. What did you say to her?"

Rich thought back. He had been adamant that the apartment was his; he probably could have been nicer about it. But it's hard to remember to be polite when you're stark naked. "We just had a disagreement over whose apartment it was. She was impossible."

"Yeah. When she thinks she's right, there's no talking to her. I'm surprised she didn't throw you out."

"She tried. But we came to an agreement." After he'd slept with her.

"It'll take a while, but she'll come around. You'll see."

"I don't know. She seems really standoffish."

It didn't help that he'd made a total fool of himself when he flooded the kitchen with bubbles. Not that it was really his fault. She didn't mention that there were two different dish soaps. Still, she obviously didn't think he was the sharpest pencil in the box. Normally he wouldn't care, but he didn't want to spend the next three months with someone who thought he had the IQ of an amoeba.

"She doesn't trust people easily. It comes with the territory."

Rich took a sip of his beer and looked at Annabelle over the top of his mug. "Huh?"

Annabelle opened her eyes. "She's been burned a lot. You know, Becca's got money. The Larsens are an influential family. A woman in her position has to wonder if a guy is into her, her bank account, or her social standing. Let's just say, she hasn't had the best luck with men. I'm hoping that improves now that she's out of Philadelphia. Her family was really well known there. She couldn't get away from it."

"If she's got so much money, why doesn't she look like it? Heck, yesterday she looked like she'd gotten her clothes at the Salvation Army. Why is she fighting over the apartment? Why doesn't she go and stay at the Plaza or something?"

Annabelle rolled her eyes. "Hey, just because she's got money doesn't make her a spoiled debutante. If anything, she's a reluctant debutante. It's a real bone of contention between her and her mom. Which is probably one of the reasons she doesn't just go to the Plaza. She knows what's important in life, and money isn't in the top ten."

After a while, Mike joined them in the family room. They spent the next hour talking while Mike gave Annabelle a foot rub. Those two were so good together, it was enough to make Rich almost jealous. He tried to see him and Gina together like that, and he couldn't.

Monday morning dawned cold and gloomy. Becca had slept like shit. God, she needed to get a real bed. She'd never be able to survive three months of this. If it wasn't the lumpy futon keeping her awake, it was the thought that Rich was in the next room naked, or Tripod's snoring or wanting to be fed. The little stinker sat on her chest and yowled, and when that didn't work, he bit her nose.

"Fine. I'll feed you." She pushed him off her chest, rolled out of the bed that was four inches off the floor, and stubbed her toe on the damn frame. She pulled on a sweat jacket and hopped out of the world's smallest room and ran right into Rich and his coffee. The coffee wasn't hot, thank God, but it was still wet, and all over the front of her T-shirt.

"Shit, Becca. I'm sorry."

"No, it's my fault." She pulled her wet T-shirt off her chest as Rich dabbed at it with… what the hell? He held a handkerchief. Like her dad used. She'd never known a guy who still used handkerchiefs. Well, not straight ones anyway. She pushed his hand away. "It's an old T-shirt. Don't worry about it."

She dragged her hair off her eyes and really saw Rich. He'd pulled a Dr. Jekyll and Mr. Hyde. Gone was the Richie she'd spent the weekend with. He'd been transformed into Dr. Ronaldi, Mr. Monochromatic. He wore great shoes, gray slacks, a gray sweater she itched to touch, and a wicked-cool, gray car coat. Very hip and very yummy, in a cool, Hugo Boss kind of way. Damn, if she'd had professors who looked like him in college, she'd never have skipped classes. "Did I get you?"

"Did you get me, what?"

"The coffee. Did I get coffee on you, too?" She couldn't help it. She ran her hand over his chest and abs, checking for wetness—well, that was her excuse anyway. What could she say? She was a sculptor and very tactile. The sweater felt heavenly, so did the way his stomach muscles rippled at her touch.

Rich laughed. "No, I think you took the brunt of the spillage. I really am sorry. I'd help you clean up, but I have to get going, or I'll be late. I have office hours early this morning and then classes. I'm cooking dinner tonight."

"You are?"

"Sure. I've never tried, but how hard can it be?"

"What are you going to make?"

He leaned against the wall. "I don't know."

"Rich, you don't just 'cook dinner.' You need to plan the meal, make a list of ingredients, and from there make a shopping list. You want to make sure it's well balanced, you know, a protein, a starch, a couple of vegetables."

"Okay, well, we can figure all that out later. Do you want to meet me at the market after work to pick something up?"

Becca blew out a breath. She wasn't sure if she wanted to strangle him or hug him. He was so clueless. "We're going to shop together?"

Rich tilted his head and looked at her quizzically. "That's usually what happens when two people meet at the market to buy stuff for dinner. How 'bout I call you before I leave the office and figure out when to meet. Are you going to be around?"

"Yes. I have to go check out the demolition in the brownstone, but I'll be back this afternoon."

"Good. I'll call you later."

Rich grinned and raised an eyebrow before bending to grab the briefcase he'd set down when he mopped her off. As he straightened, she had the weirdest urge to kiss him good-bye. Becca took a step back. "Yeah. Have a good day." Damn, she needed to get dry, get dressed, and buy a damn bed; maybe then she could get a decent night's sleep.

Tripod yowled and nipped her calf.

"Okay, okay, I'll feed you first. Did anyone ever tell you you're a pain in the ass?"

Tripod answered in the affirmative and hopped beside her to the kitchen.

After the cat was fed, the coffee made, and the mess Rich left in the bathroom and everywhere else he went was cleaned up, Becca curled up on the couch with her now lukewarm coffee and her unfinished to-do list. On the top of the list was buying a bed. Lord knew, she didn't want to sleep on that futon ever again. She also needed to stop by the brownstone to check the progress of the company she contracted to demo the third and fourth floors where her new apartment and studio would be built. She could pick up her work table while she was there. She already missed having a place where she could pound clay and sketch the vision she'd had in a dream the night before during the two minutes she'd actually slept. And the third task was to go through her slides to show the gallery owner in the neighborhood her work. The last time she was in town, she dropped in to introduce herself and was invited back to show the owner her work. The final, and probably most difficult, task on the list was to call her father.

He'd emailed her that he'd be in town and would like to meet for lunch. Up until a few months ago, they hadn't talked for almost two years, since the day of her brother Chip's funeral. He and Becca's mother made Annabelle, Chip's fiancé and Becca's best friend, even more miserable than she already was. There was no excuse for that. Since her parents' divorce and her father rediscovered his old love and found the son he never knew existed, he seemed to become human again. He also said he wanted back into her life.

Becca was thrilled her father found happiness after all these years, but that didn't mean she was comfortable with the new and improved Christopher Larsen, MD. They'd never been close, and since her brother's death, even the obligatory birthday and holiday phone calls had tapered off. Now it was as if he thought something was wrong if they didn't speak once a week. She spent most of the uncomfortable conversation they had explaining that she was fine, she wasn't avoiding him or angry, and she was sorry she didn't think to call. It was as if he thought because he was now available to her, she'd automatically need him. Well, she didn't need him. He'd made sure of that. There had been a time she had prayed for her father's attention, but that ship had sailed.

Becca dressed in a pair of wide-legged pants—not dressy, but not jeans either—a French cuff shirt, an oversized "boyfriend" sweater. Not that Becca had a "boyfriend" sweater that was actually a boyfriend's. She added another check on the pro side of her "live boyfriend vs. Battery Operated Boyfriend" list. BOBs didn't have wardrobes one could pilfer.

She scrolled through the contact list on her cell for her father's number. She might as well get it over with.

"Hello?"

Becca checked her watch. It was almost nine. "Hi, Dad. Did I wake you?"

"No," he whispered. "Hold on."

A door snicked closed. "There, that's better. How are you, Rebecca?"

Other than curious? "Fine. I'm getting ready to leave. I'm just returning your call."

"Yes. What are your plans for today?"

"I'm off to buy a bed, then I need to check out how the demo is going at the brownstone."

"Good. Colleen and I are meeting Mike and Annabelle at the brownstone for lunch. You can join us. It'll be," the words like one big happy family were left unsaid, but that's what he wanted, "nice to see you. You can show us the plans for your new apartment and the studio you and Annabelle will share."

"I don't know…"

"You said yourself you were planning to be there, and you have to eat."

He had set her up. She made a mental note to avoid that kind of trap in the future. "Okay. I'll be there around 12:30."

"12:30 it is. And Rebecca…"

"Yes?"

"Thanks."

Becca slipped into her leather jacket, tossed her purse over her shoulder, and slid her sunglasses on. "It's okay. I'll see you this afternoon. Bye." She disconnected the call and dropped her cell into the outside pocket of her purse before leaving and locking the door behind her.

Chapter 5

BECCA LET HERSELF INTO THE BACK GARDEN OF THE brownstone to check out the workers' progress before they knew she'd arrived. The forty-yard dumpster that was delivered the other day was almost filled to the brim. Shading her eyes from the sun, she examined the structure. It had good bones, or so the architect said.

Becca had meticulously salvaged everything worth saving, including all the trim, fireplace mantels, and light fixtures, which were already in the process of being stripped and cleaned. With any luck, most of it would be reused. If the amount of noise was anything to go by, the demo of the third and fourth floors was well underway. She stepped back as a shovelful of debris flew out of the large tube that ran from a third-floor window into the dumpster.

She did a quick walk-through with the supervisor and talked him into helping her load the pieces of her small sculptor's table into the car. She had dropped it off on her last visit and was amazed at how much she'd missed having it around, even though she'd spent most of her last week at home packing. She used that little table for everything. It had a tilting top perfect for sketching, but when the top was down it was strong enough to pound clay on too. It wasn't very pretty, but it was amazingly functional, and she was all about function. The best part was when it was disassembled. It was small enough to fit into the trunk of her little BMW Z4 Roadster.

She thanked the supervisor, closed the trunk lid, and locked the car. Now all she had to do was get through what would certainly be an uncomfortable lunch before having the rest of the afternoon to work. She had already rearranged the furniture in her room so all she'd have to do was put the table back together and slide it into the corner.

It was almost time to meet up with her father. Becca put a hand on her stomach and willed it to calm down. These family get-togethers always made her nervous. Using her key, she went into the brownstone and took the elevator up to Annabelle and Mike's second-floor apartment. She knocked before letting herself in.

"Your sister's here. Everybody decent?" Becca set her purse down on the hall table and met Mike and Annabelle as they were entering the living room. "The two of you look green."

Mike wrapped his arm around Annabelle. "She's not feeling well."

Becca looked from one to the other. "Is morning sickness contagious?"

Annabelle rested her head on Mike's shoulder. "It looks that way. I've heard of sympathy pain, but not sympathy nausea."

Becca rubbed her hands together. "So, are we all finished puking?"

Mike scowled, and from the look of it, Annabelle was having a hard time hiding her smile. She patted Mike on the back. "So it seems."

"That's a good thing." Becca tossed her jacket on the back of the sofa. "Just in time for lunch. You look fabulous, by the way. I love how the green tinge to your complexion contrasts with the fuchsia blouse. Very Lilly Pulitzer."

Annabelle laughed. "You should know. What are you doing here?"

"Meeting you for lunch. Dad said he and Colleen would be here, too." She looked from Mike to Annabelle. "Are you two still planning to eat?"

Mike gave Annabelle a nudge toward the sofa and headed to the kitchen. "Belle only eats baked potatoes and Five Guys Hamburgers and fries."

"Those are the only things I can keep down, so don't break my chops."

He returned, tossed Becca a bottle of water, set another bottle on the coffee table, sat beside Annabelle, and handed to her what looked like a glass of ginger ale. "Here, drink this. It's room temperature—just how you like it."

Annabelle took a sip as Becca cringed. "Gag. Room-temperature soda?"

Mike shrugged. "Whatever works."

Becca couldn't help goading her brother. "If it works so well, maybe you ought to try some. You look as if you could use it."

He wrapped his arm around Annabelle. "Very funny."

This part of the whole family thing was really working for her. She and Mike fell right into a typical brother-sister relationship—even if they started it twenty-six years too late—and Annabelle was her best-friend-turned-sister, which was great. If only the whole parental front was so easy.

Annabelle looked as if she felt a little better. She

set her soda on the table, turned so her back rested against Mike, and her face radiated mischief. Becca braced herself.

"How are the Domestic God lessons going?" When Mike grumbled, Annabelle quieted him with a look. "Rich said he did the dishes. I lived with him for years and never once saw him do anything in the kitchen but eat, drink straight from the milk and OJ containers, and make a mess. How did you manage to get him to actually clean something?"

Becca sipped her water and shrugged. "He asked me to show him how. Far be it from me to discourage someone who wants to do all the cooking, cleaning, and laundry. I just hope his first adventure in dishwashing isn't the start of a trend, although, he did manage to get the kitchen floor cleaner than I've ever seen it."

"The floor?"

A knock at the door heralded the entrance of Christopher and Colleen. Mike's parents and Becca's father and from the looks of it, her soon to be stepmother, not that Becca had a problem with Colleen, well, except for the fact that the woman hugged her every time she saw her. Of course, that was just Colleen. She hugged everyone, and today was no different.

Mike answered the door and took everyone's coats. As soon as she got out of hers, Colleen went straight to Annabelle, gave her a hug and a kiss, and handed her a greasy bag of something that smelled heavenly. She gave Annabelle's belly a pat. "Five Guys hamburger and fries for mum and the babe."

When Mike grumbled about nutrition, she shushed him as she hugged him, kissed his cheek, and wiped the lipstick off. "When I was pregnant with you, I couldn't keep much down either. All I wanted was steak and kidney pie. I was surprised when you didn't come out with your very own crust."

Becca was next in line so she accepted Colleen's hug and then Christopher's. "Hi, Dad."

"Becca, it's good to see you." He gave her an awkward pat on the shoulder.

Man, Colleen sure had her work cut out for her if she was trying to turn him into a cuddler.

"It's good to see you too."

The five of them stood there looking at each other for an awkward moment until Annabelle took a French fry out of the bag and chomped on it. "I don't know about you, but I'm starved. Why don't we eat before it gets cold?"

Mike laughed. "I only made salads and sandwiches. They're already cold."

Dad looked relieved and with his hand on Colleen's lower back, followed Annabelle to the dining room. Mike didn't look happy. Becca wasn't sure if it was due to Annabelle's diet or Dad's hand on Mike's mother's back. Either way, Mike was going to have to get over it.

Becca helped Mike put the food on the table while Annabelle and Colleen got drinks, and her Dad looked uncomfortable. She took pity on him. "Dad, I was surprised to hear you were in town. Taking a few vacation days?" She sat down, took a spoonful of the potato salad, and passed the bowl to him.

"Yes, I came to spend some time with Colleen and catch up with a few friends, but I also wanted to see how you were settling in."

"You did?"

Colleen walked behind her and trailed her hand over Becca's shoulders before sitting next to Christopher. "Of course he did. You're his daughter, and he loves you."

Becca nodded like a good girl and put together her sandwich. She didn't know what to say to that. Of course he loved her in his own way. She smiled at her father. "I'm sharing Annabelle's old apartment with her brother Rich."

"The psych professor?"

"Yes. It's only temporary until my place upstairs is finished, and it's close enough so I can keep an eye on the construction."

Her father put some mayonnaise on his sandwich. "Where will you work?"

"I finished the last piece I was working on in the loft, and I don't want to start anything big until I get into the new studio. I'm doing some preliminary work, you know, getting ideas about what I want to work on next, making sketches, models, going through my slides, stuff like that."

"You could use this time to market the work you're sitting on."

"I'm always doing that. I actually have a meeting with a gallery owner here in Park Slope later this week, but I also have my hands full with the construction."

"You're going to have to show your work to more than one gallery owner, Becca, if you want to get anywhere in your career. That's why I talked to an old friend. He's interested in showing your work."

Becca shook her head. "You talked a friend into showing my work sight unseen?" She was on a slow boil. Her dad didn't look up from fixing his sandwich so he didn't notice.

"He owes me a favor. I helped his son get into medical school. He said if I ever needed anything…" He looked up and finally realized there was something wrong with this picture.

Becca wiped her mouth and tried to calm down. Saying what she was thinking probably wasn't the best idea, but then neither was her father pawning off her work to a respected member of the art community for payback. Not that she knew who the man was, but in her experience, highly successful men ran in packs. Dad would never stoop to an association with someone who wasn't at the top of his game or business. "No thank you."

Great, now her dad was pissed. "What do you mean, 'no thank you'? I had to pull a lot of strings to get you this opportunity."

"I never asked for your help. Just because you're willing to offer it doesn't mean that I'm willing to accept it. I've already explained to you ad nauseam that one of the reasons I moved here was to make it in the New York art world on my own merit. I don't need you pushing my work on someone because he owes you. It's one thing for you to set up an introduction, which would have been helpful. What you did was insulting."

She stared at her father who gave her the same look he'd given her since she was a child when she did something he wasn't pleased with.

"What's wrong, Dad? Do you think I'm so talentless that I can't make it on my own?" She held up her hand. "You know, don't bother answering. It's obvious that you do. I guess it's a good thing I'm wealthy, huh? That way you'll never have to worry about your daughter being a starving, talentless artist." Becca stood and placed her napkin beside her uneaten lunch. Both Mike and her dad stood. Such gentlemen. "I'm sorry, Annabelle. I need to go. I'll call you later."

Annabelle nodded. Of course, she understood perfectly.

Becca's dad threw his napkin on the table and pushed his chair back. Colleen stood then too. "Christopher, let her go. You can apologize later after she's had a chance to calm down."

"What?" His growl followed Becca out of the room. Unfortunately, Mike did too.

"You know he hates it that you don't need his money or his help, don't you?"

Becca couldn't talk. She was too close to tears, and the last thing she wanted to do was start bawling. She nodded.

Mike pulled her into a hug. "I'm proud of you. But remember, sometimes men can't help doing stupid things for the women they love, even if that woman is a daughter. Are you going to be okay?"

She nodded against his shoulder. "I'm fine."

Mike gave her a crooked smile that looked just like her father's.

"What's so funny?"

"I was just thinking that I hope I have sons." He kissed her cheek. "I'll call you later."

Becca left with a smile on her face that stayed until the elevator door closed then she went home and set up her work table. She needed to work. She needed to pound some clay.

Rich tossed his briefcase on the desk in the classroom, took out his notes for the lecture and the tests he'd finally graded. He handed them back to his students as they shuffled into class. From the look on their faces, his students knew with amazing accuracy how they did before they even checked their grade.

"Okay class, when everyone takes their seats I can get started." He rested back against his desk, crossed his feet in front, and waited until he had everyone's attention.

"Today I'm going to talk about cognitive development. Humans' cognitive ability lags far behind physical ability because the association areas of our brains are the last to develop. Remember, one of the main causes of brain growth after birth is making new connections between existing neurons."

Rich turned toward the white board and wrote "Jean Piaget." "Jean Piaget is the main theorist on cognitive development. He suggests that people create schemas, which are mental models of how the world works. Would anyone like to tell the processes that govern schema change?" Rich saw Brad Stanhope searching his notes. His hand tentatively went up. "Brad."

"Assimilation and accommodation."

"Good." Rich wrote "assimilation" on the board.

A knock at the door interrupted his train of thought. Dean Stewart poked his head in. "Excuse me, Professor Ronaldi. If I can have a moment?"

"Certainly." The door closed. "This might be a good time to review Piaget's four stages of cognitive development, why he suggested that the stages occur in an invariant developmental sequence, and whether or not you think most of the guys at the frat party the other night actually reached the formal operations stage."

Rich opened the door and stepped out.

"Ah, teaching Jean Piaget. Your specialty. With an interesting bent, I hear."

"Yes, well, it's one way to keep their butts in the seats."

"You could take attendance."

"Yeah, but what would be the fun in that? This is much more challenging. Keep it interesting, and they will learn. I wish half my professors realized that."

Dean Stewart raised an eyebrow. Oops, "Present company excluded, of course."

"Of course."

Dean Stewart reached into the breast pocket of his jacket. "I wasn't sure if I'd see you later, so I thought I'd better give you these tickets to the benefit dinner before I forgot. Emily has been harping on me."

Rich took the envelope. "Thank you."

"Emily and I are looking forward to meeting your girlfriend."

"She's looking forward to meeting you both as well. Thanks for dropping the tickets off, sir."

The Dean slapped Rich on the back. "Go on now. You've got a lecture to give."

"Right." He folded the envelope, put it in his back pants pocket, and went back into class. "Where were we?"

Brad Stanhope raised his hand. "You were talking about assimilation, accommodation, invariant developmental sequence."

Rich laughed. "I see I got your attention there. Good." Rich picked up his marker again. "So maybe you'd like to share with us the difference between assimilation and accommodation," he said as he wrote on the board. Rich looked over his shoulder to find Brad searching through his notes. "Would anyone care to define these?"

The rest of the class flew by, and in the back of his mind, all Rich could think about was how screwed he was going to be if he couldn't talk Gina into giving him another chance. The dinner was just over a week away.

By the time he finished his lecture, the class was already packing up. "Your assignment, due a week from today, is a one thousand-word essay on Piaget's four stages of human cognitive development." He opened his file and took out the stack of assignment sheets he passed around to the accompaniment of his students' groans as they left. "If you have questions, see me. My office hours are posted on the department's website. Have a good day."

Rich followed the class out and saw Brad waiting for him outside. The kid was having trouble keeping up, which was amazing considering the guy's overall intelligence. "Do you want to come to my office and talk about the paper?"

Brad nodded but kept looking at his feet.

"Come on then." Rich led the way to his office, unlocked the door, and held it open for Brad. "Have a seat, and let's look over your notes. We'll figure out why you're confused. It'll be fine." After helping Brad outline the paper for the better part of an hour, Rich made lecture notes for the next week's classes, put together an exam for his three thousand level class, ordered review materials for next semester's courses, and ran to teach his last class. In between all that, he wracked his brain trying to come up with something to make for dinner. When he met Becca later at the market, he didn't want to look as if he had no ideas. He didn't know what Becca would like to eat. All he knew was Italian. Rich poked his head out his office door. "Hey Jeff, what are you going to have for dinner?"

"I was thinking of going to the pub for a burger. Do you want to join me?"

Damn, that's not what Rich was after. "Thanks, but no. I'm supposed to cook dinner, and I was trying to think up something to fix that was pretty much idiot proof."

Jeff walked in. "You have a date?"

Rich nodded toward the chair across from his desk and sat in his. "You might say that. I'm supposed to cook, and I never cook."

"A steak is easy if you know how to broil."

"Broil?"

"Yeah, there's a funny flat pan with cuts in it. You just put a steak on it, sprinkle salt, pepper, and garlic powder on top, put it as close to the top of the oven as you can, and turn the broiler on. Then all you have to do is turn it over once halfway through."

"How long do you cook it?"

Jeff shrugged, "It depends on how thick the steak is and how well done you like your meat."

"Sounds like too many variables."

"The only thing easier than that is spaghetti. A jar of Prego and a salad, and you're good to go."

"Shit, I'm Italian. I don't eat sauce out of a jar. My mother would kill me right after she brought her sauce over, cooked me dinner, and watched me eat."

"Well, there you go, then. Problem solved."

Not quite, but Rich wasn't going to say anything. "Yeah, thanks for your help."

Jeff stood. "You want to get a beer or something after work sometime?"

Rich stood too. "Sure, that would be great. I hear you play hoops."

"Whenever I can."

Rich tossed him the basketball he kept on his shelf. "One on one?"

Jeff shot the ball back. "Anytime. Good luck tonight."

"Yeah. Thanks, man." He had a feeling he was going to need it.

Jeff went back to his office, and Rich still had no idea what the hell to do for dinner. He called Becca as he packed his briefcase.

"Hello?"

"Becca, it's Rich."

"Oh, hi."

"Are you all right?"

She sniffled. "Yeah, I'm fine. Why?"

"You sound like you caught a cold."

"No. I'm good. What's up?"

"I'm leaving my office now. Why don't I call you when I get off the train so you can meet me at the market, and we can grocery shop together."

"Yeah, okay."

"Becca, are you sure you're all right? You sound a little weird."

"I'm fine. I'll see you later. Bye."

Rich pushed his way out the door of his office and locked it behind him. He headed out of Shermerhorn Hall and wished he'd brought his umbrella. It looked like rain, but with the way the wind was whipping, it probably wouldn't do much good. He took off for the subway at a brisk pace hoping to beat the rain.

After setting up her workspace and pounding on some clay, the only thing Becca wanted to do on this dreary, cold, rainy day, which sadly matched her mood, was to curl up in her new bed. She had paid an extra hundred and fifty dollars for same-day delivery, but it was worth it. She wanted to make a cocoon with her thick down duvet, drink hot chocolate, and lose herself in a good book. Instead, she ran through the wind-whipped rain down 7th Avenue so she could do the last thing she wanted to do—grocery shop with Rich. She found him standing under the market's awning looking just as wonderful as he had that morning. Running her fingers through her short hair, she confirmed what she already knew—it was sticking up in all directions. "Hi"

He studied her until she wanted to squirm. "You are sick. I thought you sounded bad. You shouldn't have come out in this weather."

"I'm not sick. I'm fine. Come on, are you going to make me stand out in this cold, or are we going shopping?"

She must look worse than she thought since seeing her father had put her in the mood for a good cry. After she set up her workspace and took out her frustration on some poor defenseless clay, she popped her copy of *PS I Love You* into the DVD player and cried her way through the whole thing while eating popcorn and a dark chocolate candy bar with raspberry filling. The candy bar was better than sex. What she remembered of it, which probably wasn't much. Now, not only were her eyes red and her skin blotchy from crying, she had after-a-popcorn-binge bloat and after inhaling the decadent chocolate bar, with her luck, tomorrow she'd have a zit the size of Tahiti on her nose. Rich opened the door, and Becca strode in.

Becca jerked on a mini-shopping cart that was pushed into the back of a line of them and met enough resistance to grab it with two hands and give it a double jerk. It didn't move. "What do you want to make?"

"I don't know. What do you feel like?"

Rich nudged her aside, wrenched the little cart out from inside the others with absolutely no problem, and gave her a superior look.

Becca forced herself not to roll her eyes. "I loosened it for you."

Rich sat his briefcase in the kiddy seat and smiled. "Sure you did."

She chose to ignore that. "Rich, it's not going to help you to learn to make what I like. For all you know I might live on a diet of ToFurky hot dogs on spelt rolls."

"To-what? You're kidding, right?"

"Of course I'm kidding. But the point here is that you're supposed to learn to cook what you want."

"Who says I don't want Foturkey or whatever the hell that stuff is? The only food I ever ate at home was Italian. In my house, a hamburger was a flat meatball. I asked my mom to make fried chicken, and I got chicken parmesan. When I wanted a casserole like the other kids, I got lasagna. Not that I'm complaining."

Becca raised an eyebrow to that, but kept her mouth shut.

"I learned how lucky I was the first time I went to a

friend's house for dinner. His mom heated spaghetti out of a can."

She made a face, because let's face it—no one should eat spaghetti out of a can. That's just too gross for words.

He must have thought she didn't believe him. He stopped her and started talking with his hands. "No shit, the stuff was orange, and she plopped some Miracle Whip on some lettuce and called it salad. I feigned illness and ran all the way home.

"Okay, no canned spaghetti. How about meatloaf? That's American." Becca pushed the cart toward the produce section.

"Meatloaf is just a big meatball."

"Not the way I make it. And it's an easy recipe. I think even you might be able to manage it."

"Okay, American meatloaf it is."

"Actually, it's German. Our cook used to make it."

"You had a cook?"

She took a plastic bag and filled it with a few hearts of romaine. "Yeah, a cook, a housekeeper, a nanny, two groundskeepers, then there was the stable hand, a handyman, and a pool boy." She tossed the lettuce in the cart and began examining the cucumbers. "The pool boy didn't last long. Dad caught him fooling around with Mom in the pool house." She handed two cucumbers to Rich who stood there looking confused. She wasn't sure if it was the cucumber that confused him or the thought of her mother with the pool boy. "It's for the salad. Put them in a bag."

He nodded, stuck one under his arm, and then tried to rip a bag off the roll. Becca watched and finally took pity on him and pulled one off and opened it.

"Your mom was making it with the pool boy?" He dropped the cucumbers in the bag Becca held.

"Yes, it was embarrassingly cliché. We had the Main Line's version of *The Graduate*. Nat was living in the pool house while on summer break from Penn. I still don't know if my mom knew that Nat was seeing both of us, but it wouldn't surprise me. Personally, I think he was hedging his bets. If it worked out with me he'd get my trust fund. If it didn't, he'd get tips from Mommy Dearest."

"Wow, and I thought my family was fucked up."

"Yeah. Lucky me, I get a prize for having the world's most fucked up family."

"But even worse than that, I can't believe you dated a guy named Nat. Is that spelled with the 'G' or without?"

Becca laughed. "Without, but now that I think about it, he was kind of a pest." She caught herself smiling and shut it down. "Okay, we need to buy ground round, ground pork, plain breadcrumbs, onion, and applesauce."

"Applesauce?"

"For the meatloaf."

"You put applesauce in meatloaf?"

"Yes. Do you want to learn how to cook it, or should we move on?"

"No, I mean yes. I want to learn, but I never heard of applesauce in meatloaf."

"You probably never heard of a lot of things, which is why you need a coach, right?"

"Right."

"I know we have brown sugar, Dijon mustard, ketchup, and eggs at home."

"We do?"

"Yes, those are called staples. It's the food most kitchens have on hand. What kind of vegetable do you want to make?"

"We need to make vegetables, too?"

"When was the last time you ate just meatloaf and nothing else for dinner?"

Rich shrugged.

He was such a guy. "Baked potatoes or mashed?"

"Which is easier?"

"Baked."

"Fine." Becca chose a bag of Yukon Gold potatoes and tossed it in the cart.

"What about a vegetable?"

"Isn't a potato a vegetable?"

"No, it's a starch. You need at least one veggie, preferably green."

"Like escarole?"

"What?"

"You know, it's kind of like spinach, but not. It's definitely green though."

"That's a new one on me. Do you have a translation?"

"For what?"

"Escarole."

"It's escarole—what's to translate?"

The grocer behind them cleared his throat. "It's flat leaf endive, and we have some over there." He pointed to something next to the lettuce.

Becca smiled at him and noticed that Rich stepped closer to her. Men. "Thanks for the help." She stepped away. "How is it cooked?"

"Mama makes it with olive oil, lots of garlic, and some onion." He took several handfuls and stuffed it in a bag. From the look of it, they'd be eating endive for a year.

"She sautés it?"

"How the hell do I know? She puts some oil in a pan with onion, then the garlic, and then the escarole, and stirs it until it gets droopy."

"Oh yum. Droopy endive. I can hardly wait."

"Hey, I didn't make fun of your meatloaf with applesauce."

"You're right. I'm sorry." Becca turned so Rich couldn't see her smile and headed toward the butcher in the back for the meat. "Why don't you go get the applesauce and breadcrumbs?"

"Okay." Rich took off with the cart, and Becca watched as he walked away. So did the other three women waiting in line for meat.

The person next to Becca, a beautiful woman in her early thirties wearing a gorgeous suit and four-inch heels that made Becca cringe just looking at them, sighed. "He's so helpful."

The one in front of the line nodded. "Not to mention gorgeous."

The one in the middle checked out Becca. "Did you just move in together?"

Becca nodded.

The middle woman cracked a smile. "Yeah, the only time men shop with you or take you to the airport is in the first three weeks of living together. It's all downhill from there."

Becca shook her head. "Oh no. We're not living together living together. We're just roommates."

"Miss, what can I get you?" The butcher asked the woman in the front of the line.

She ignored him, drew in a quick breath, and stuck her chest out. "He's single?"

Becca crossed her arms. "Technically, I guess he is. But I know he's trying to get back together with his ex."

"Miss?" The butcher asked again. She held up her hand to stop him.

She studied Becca and gave her a look that told her she was definitely lacking. Of course, it's not as if Becca had dressed up to go grocery shopping. She wore her old comfortable sweats, which, after a three-block run through the rain, were soaking wet. What is it with these short, beautiful women? She gave Becca the same look her mother did every time she tsked about her being too tall, too skinny, or too flat-chested.

"Technically single is fine with me. I can change his mind about his old girlfriend."

The woman next to Becca turned to her adversary. "I saw him first."

The one in the middle moved in. "So what?"

Becca turned to the butcher. "May I please have a pound and a half of ground round and a half pound of ground pork?"

The butcher eyed the three women in line before her as they took off down the canned fruit aisle. "Sure, lady."

Becca waited for the meat to be weighed and wrapped wondering what the three women on the Rich hunt were going to do to him and to each other.

She thanked her lucky stars she wasn't with a guy like Rich. She had been before and knew it was way too much trouble. She once dated a man almost as good looking as Rich, and she dealt with women throwing themselves at him continuously. She knew what it was like to have to look perfect at all times. Of course, her mother loved him, but the only thing that Becca felt was trapped. She would never forget the first time he visited her studio. She had looked forward to sharing her work with him, but all he did was comment on the fact that she was covered with the clay she'd been working with and how much better she looked with makeup than without. He wasn't pleased that she wasn't prepared to change her clothes before getting into his new car. By that time, she knew there was no future with Mr. Persnickety and wished he'd have just left her there.

"You better not make that face for too long. It might stay that way."

Becca blinked and saw Rich standing beside her. "That bad?"

He shrugged. "I just hope you weren't thinking about me just then. I'd have to start sleeping with one eye open."

She laughed. "You can rest easy. Believe it or not, my world does not revolve around you. There were a few women who'd be more than willing to take on that job."

He looked confused.

"The women who took off after you when they found out you were single? Didn't at least one of them hit on you?"

"There were three women helping me pick out the applesauce. I got the organic stuff." He held it up to show her. "I couldn't find the breadcrumbs though."

"Oh?" Becca looked over his shoulder to see if the women had followed him. Sure enough, they were on their way back, and Becca did not want to be there when they arrived. "Okay, I think they might have it in the baking aisle." She turned to leave.

"Becca?"

"What?"

Rich slid the meat off the top of the refrigerated case. "Forgetting something?"

"Oh right." She turned and walked away.

Chapter 6

RICH WAITED FOR BECCA TO OPEN THE DOOR TO THE apartment. The handles of the plastic bags cut into his hands.

"How long does this take to cook?"

Becca turned the key in the deadbolt. "It has to bake about forty-five minutes."

"I'm hungry now. I worked through lunch."

"So, make a sandwich. I didn't eat either."

"I thought you had lunch at Annabelle and Mike's with your parents."

Becca kicked the door opened. "Yeah. I didn't stay to actually eat anything."

"How come?"

Becca tossed the bag she held onto the counter. "How do grilled cheese sandwiches sound?"

Her smile was a little too practiced. Something went down she didn't want to talk about. "Good."

She pulled out a cast iron frying pan and set it on the stove. "Great. Have at it. I like mine pretty toasty but not burnt."

"Huh?"

She rummaged through the refrigerator and took out a few things.

"I don't know how to make grilled cheese."

Becca sighed, which put his back up. "Don't you dare treat me as if I'm stupid. I have three post-secondary degrees. I know a thing or two."

"Yeah, just not anything to do with the kitchen."

"Thanks for the news flash. Aren't you getting tired of pointing out my ineptitude?"

Becca smiled a real smile this time. "Not yet." She didn't bother to try stifling her laughter. "All you have to do is put a couple pieces of cheese in between a couple pieces of bread and butter both sides of the sandwich, fry it until it's brown on the bottom, flip it over, and once the bottom is browned and the cheese is melted, it's done. Cut it in half—I like triangles—and eat. It's easy. I'm going to change out of these wet clothes while you cook."

"It doesn't sound too difficult. Go on."

Rich opened a package of cheese like he'd never seen before. It didn't come from a deli. It was wrapped in plastic, and it said that it was made from milk. What the hell else do you make cheese out of?

Rich buttered four slices of bread, stuck a couple pieces of cheese in between, and placed them in the hot pan. They sizzled. There, that wasn't so hard. He opened a few drawers looking for a flipper thing. He found one and stuck it under the corner of the first sandwich, peeked under and it, and it wasn't browned yet. He had it under control.

He stuck his head in the refrigerator and grabbed a beer. He popped the top, took a pull, and waited a few minutes before he grabbed the frying pan. "Fuck!" He burned his hand on the metal handle. "Shit!" He ran cold water over his hand and caught Becca poking her head out of her bedroom door.

"Everything okay?"

"Of course."

"It smells like something is burning."

"Oh fuck." Rich grabbed a towel, folded it a couple times, and held it in his burned hand. He gently held the handle and turned the now burned sandwiches. Shit. He was cursing under his breath when he noticed the smoke. He looked down and found that the towel was smoldering. Shit, shit, shit. He threw the burning towel into the sink and ran the water over the flames that erupted.

He remembered there were potholders somewhere. He began opening drawers looking for them. There was one hanging off the refrigerator. He grabbed it and checked the sandwiches; the one side was golden brown. Rich took two plates out of the cupboard and slid the sandwiches onto the plates, putting the burnt side down. Becca wanted it cut in triangles. Sheesh. Demanding much? Rich went to the silverware drawer, took out a knife, and cut them both in half. He took a bite of his—it was a little crunchy but not bad. Okay, so, it wasn't good, but it was edible. Not that he would have eaten it if he were home alone. But Becca would be stepping out of her bedroom any second, and he'd be damned if he'd let her know he couldn't stand his own cooking, such as it was. It was a little crunchy and chewy, but hey, it was only a little burnt, along with his hand, which throbbed with every beat of his heart.

Becca returned just as he stuffed the last piece of his sandwich in his mouth. Her hair was now dry, and she'd changed into yet another one of her old baggy sweats. He smiled. She was beautiful in a kind of girl-next-door way even though she wore some god-awful clothes.

"Your sandwich is ready. I even cut it in triangles like you asked."

"I'm impressed. It looks great."

"It does?"

"Yes." She picked up a piece and took a bite.

From the look on her face, he knew she changed her mind. Then she kind of gagged and put her hand in front of her lips while she pulled something from her mouth. Oh, man. He screwed up.

Becca held a piece of plastic between her fingers. "Rich, you're supposed to unwrap the cheese before you cook it."

"Right."

"What happened to yours?"

"I ate it."

"Please tell me that you just forgot to take the plastic off mine and not yours."

Rich shook his head and wondered if he should call Poison Control. He then gave Becca a look that dared her to say another word.

She turned away, and he knew she was laughing. "Okay, let's start making dinner because I'm hungry."

Rich wondered if he'd gotten off easy. Although when you consider that he might have just poisoned himself, and he did burn the shit out of his hand, maybe not so much.

Becca handed him a big bowl. "Put the meat in here." She took an onion out of the bowl on the counter. "Have you ever chopped an onion?"

"No."

Becca showed him how you cut the ends off, for some reason, starting with the hairy end. Once she got all the skin off, she told him to cut it in half and mince the onion.

"What does mince mean?"

"Chop in really small pieces."

"Why didn't you say so?"

"I did. You just don't have a big enough vocabulary."

"Fabulous." Rich cut the onion in half.

"That's the wrong way."

"What do you mean it's wrong? You said to cut it in half, and I did."

"The other way is better."

"Will this way work?"

"Yes.

"So what's the big deal?"

She kept her mouth shut, thank God, because his hand was throbbing, and she was getting on his nerves. It seemed to take forever to mince the onion even though he only needed a half a cup. He definitely saw why it would be easier if he'd cut it the other way, but he got it done. "Okay, what's next?"

"Put it in the bowl along with the meat. Then you want to add an egg, a cup of applesauce, a cup of bread-crumbs, and then mix it," She took a bread pan out of the cabinet. "And put it in here. Then we bake it."

"That's all there is to it?"

"That's it. If you don't include putting the glaze on, cooking the potatoes or the endive."

"Escarole."

"Whatever. Just mix it all up."

"With what?"

"Your hands."

"Can't I use a spoon or something?"

"Not unless you don't want it mixed well."

"Fine." He stuck his unburned hand into the cold meat and started mixing.

"Rich, you have to get in there with both hands."

"Why?"

"Because that's how it's done."

Rich had been hiding his hand on the side of the cool bowl, which felt pretty good actually. He pulled it off the side and hesitated just a second before Becca grabbed his wrist.

"What did you do to your hand?" She sucked in air between her teeth. "Ouch. Did you just do this?"

"It's fine." Shit, he really hated that she caught him.

"Did you put anything on it?"

"Yeah, I ran cold water over it."

She smacked his shoulder.

"Thanks, Bec. That makes it feel so much better."

"You need to put burn cream on this and a bandage."

"It's fine."

"It is not. Don't put your hand in there."

"Yes, ma'am."

She pulled him out of the kitchen with all the meat gunk still stuck on his right hand. "What are you doing?"

"Taking you to the bathroom. There's a first aid kit in there. I'm sure there's some burn cream."

He didn't have much choice but to follow her.

She bent over, took the first aid kit out of the cabinet beneath the sink, and rummaged through it. "Here we are. Now…" She tucked his arm between her arm and her breast.

Her breast pressed against the inside of his arm, her back pressed against his front, and since their legs seemed to be the exact same length, her bottom pressed tightly against his fly. He took a deep breath and held it but only breathed in her perfume, which definitely didn't help matters, and tried not to squirm.

"Don't worry, it won't hurt."

At the moment, pain was the last thing on his mind. That was until she sprayed his hand with something that brought any happy thoughts to a screeching halt. "Ow! Shit!" Pain bright and sharp cut through his hand and ran straight up his arm. He tried to jerk it away, but she was strong and held firm.

"Stop being such a baby."

She blew on it, which did make it feel a little better, but not enough to forgive her for the pain she inflicted with that damn spray. He was going to make sure that stuff disappeared. "I'm not a baby."

"Right. You're a big strong man who screams from a little antiseptic spray." She spread some white cream over the burn and then wrapped it in gauze, taping the pieces together so it stayed on. She released his arm, turned to face him, and smiled. "There. All better."

"You didn't kiss it."

"What?"

His hand was still on her waist so he pulled her closer just to see what she'd do. "If you're going to call me a baby, the least you could do is kiss it and make it all better."

Becca sucked in a deep breath and tried to calm her heartbeat. She knew there was a way to do that, biofeedback or something, but right now, it was impossible to think of anything but this strong hard guy pressed against her.

She swallowed. "I'm not going to kiss your hand."

He smiled that knowing smile of his. "Do you want to kiss something else?"

Was he joking? "No?"

"Is that a question?"

Yeah, he was definitely joking, but then he was looking at her mouth too. Maybe because she'd just licked her lips. This was so not good for her equilibrium, especially since the bathroom seemed to shrink in size. "No. It's a no." She just wished she meant it, or at least sounded like she meant it.

He let go of her hand and laughed.

Damn him. She never knew that to expect from Rich. At first, she thought he'd give up on this stupid quest after his first mishap, but he hadn't. He was sweet to work that hard to get Gina back, but Becca couldn't help but wonder if Gina deserved it. And okay, it had crossed her mind what it would be like if he was going through all this trouble for her. That's natural, right?

Rich was a complete disaster in the kitchen, and well, just about everywhere else, but he was really cute about it. She knew he'd probably freak if he knew she thought so. Men weren't supposed to be cute. But every time he made a mistake, the range of emotions that crossed his face were nothing short of adorable. She would love to have seen him as a little boy.

Becca stepped back and made herself busy cleaning up after her Florence Nightingale duties and decided not to look too closely at the reason why Rich played the starring role in all her dreams since she'd met him at Annabelle and Mike's engagement party. Not that it really mattered; fantasies of Rich were nothing more than her visual for sexual stimulation. After all, she was a relatively normal, healthy twenty-six-year-old woman with needs. Why tax her brain to find someone else when she had Rich, the Italian Adonis, living in the same apartment? Between BOB and the incredibly vivid memories of Rich naked, attaining physical satisfaction hadn't been a problem. That didn't mean Becca was content. Far from it. Rich was fine for a fantasy relationship, but that wasn't what she wanted in reality. Not even close. It didn't escape her that when it came to figuring out what she did want, she never seemed to have enough time to concentrate on anything but her artistic ambition.

Becca wanted to make a name for herself in the art world. She wanted her sculptures in galleries and museums. She didn't question her own talent, unlike her parents. She knew she was good enough. Her problem was getting the attention of the right people. She needed to do some serious networking. She was in a new town, making a fresh start without having the family name hanging around her neck like an albatross. When she made it, she wanted to make sure it was her talent that cinched the deal and not her family's name.

Rich hadn't disappeared when she turned away from him as she hoped he would. He stood there watching her.

"You've been a little off today. What's wrong?"

"Other than you trying to poison me with plastic wrap?"

"Yeah, other than that."

She walked past him to the kitchen, and he followed her like a puppy. Tripod hopped beside him looking at Rich with adoring eyes. That was a switch.

"What did you do to Tripod?"

"Nothing. We bonded last night after I got home."

"Over ice cream? I found the evidence on the coffee table."

"Fine, the little guy likes ice cream, so shoot me. Oh, and don't think I fell for you changing the subject."

"I don't need to change the subject. I don't have to answer you at all."

"No, but you want to. I can tell."

Becca stuck her hands into the bowl and took all her frustration out on the meat. She mixed it while deciding whether or not to tell him. Aw, what the hell. It's not as if he could tease her about it. She had so much ammunition on him, he wouldn't dare.

"My father told me he'd pawned some of my work off to a gallery owner in the city who owed him a favor."

Rich rested his elbows on the bar across the counter from her. "That's good, right? You get your work out there. Maybe you'll even sell some of it."

Becca growled and slammed some meat into the waiting loaf pan.

"Or maybe not."

"Why does everyone think I need a favor to get my work shown? I'm good at what I do. I don't need someone pulling strings for me. I can do it by myself. That's why I moved here in the first place. To get away from my family."

"I'm starting to see a pattern here."

Becca raised an eyebrow but didn't ask what he meant by that. She wasn't sure she wanted to know.

He pushed himself from the counter and walked into the kitchen, stopping right next to her. "Why do you feel you have to do everything all by yourself? Are you afraid of owing someone? Or are you trying to prove something to everyone who's doubted you? Are you going for the big 'I told you so?' Oh, I know. You're questioning yourself. You're trying to prove it to yourself."

She did her best to ignore his presence. "I don't need to prove anything. It wouldn't have been insulting if he'd introduced me to the man and let me sell myself. If something came out of the meeting, that would have been wonderful, but I want my work shown because it's good, not because my daddy got somebody's kid into med school." When she looked back up at Rich he was staring. "Stop treating me like one of your lab rats or a troubled student."

She pressed the rest of the meat into the loaf pan, washed her hands, and then tossed it into the oven with a little more force than was necessary. Every time she moved, she had to walk around Rich. He was always in her way; she wished he'd just disappear. On her way back to the sink to scrub the potatoes they danced around each other again until she faked left, moved right, and bee-lined up the middle to the sink. She felt Rich watch her while she scrubbed and dried the potatoes. "To make baked potatoes, you first have to scrub them. The rest is optional." She gathered what she needed and pulled a pan out of the cupboard.

"The rest of what?"

He stood close and looked over her shoulder as she poured olive oil onto her hand and rubbed it into the skins. "I dry them, rub them with olive oil, and then kosher salt. It makes the skins crispy."

"Leave it to you to complicate baked potatoes."

Becca poured kosher salt into her hands and began

rubbing it into the oiled potatoes. "You'll thank me when you taste them."

"I thought I was supposed to do this."

"Yes, but with your burnt hand, you can hardly rub salt into the potatoes. Why don't you get the ketchup, brown sugar, and Dijon mustard out. You can make the glaze. You're right handed, correct?"

"Yeah."

Anything to get him to move the hell away. "Good. Get a measuring cup. Mix a half-cup of ketchup, a quarter of a cup of brown sugar, and a teaspoon of Dijon. When the meatloaf is almost done, I'll drain the grease, glaze the top of the meatloaf, and let it cook another fifteen minutes."

He took the ketchup and mustard from the fridge. "When do we make the escarole?"

"It shouldn't take too long to make. Maybe ten minutes or so. We'll start it after we glaze the meatloaf."

"How do you know this stuff?" He had his back to her as he pulled things out of the pantry.

"I used to hang around the kitchen with Madge, our cook. She was nice. I learned a lot."

"So your mom didn't teach you to cook?"

Becca laughed, breathing easier since he wasn't crowding her. "My mom wouldn't be caught dead in the kitchen. In the divorce, she got a house, the cook, and the housekeeper. Good thing for Dad that Mom was such a witch. They didn't stay with her. No matter how much she offered to pay them, it wasn't enough." Becca looked around the kitchen for something else to do while Rich made a mess measuring the ingredients into a bowl. "I thought I'd show you how to iron tonight."

He looked up and caught her eye. He finished what he was doing and wiped his ketchup-smeared good hand on a clean towel. Men. "Do you think that's a good idea? I haven't had much success with heat today."

The way he said it brought back the weirdly sexual thing in the bathroom. Her pulse rate doubled, and she had half a mind to just tell him to have anything that needed ironing dry-cleaned. That's what she did. After all, who had time to iron?

"Do you want to learn this stuff or not?"

"Yeah. I do. Bring it on."

Becca smiled. Oh yeah. "Let's go get some of your shirts and a couple pair of pants while the meatloaf cooks." She strode right into Rich's bedroom and opened his closet. All his shirts were hanging in dry cleaner's bags. The blue shirt she'd worn the morning after they woke up together hung on the footboard of the bed. She grabbed it.

Rich's eyes widened. "I don't want to iron that."

"Why?"

"Because that's my lucky shirt. What if I screw up?"

"If you do screw it up, it wouldn't be very lucky. Would it?"

"How about we start off with something easy, like my lucky handkerchief?"

"You have a lucky handkerchief?"

Rich stuck his hand in his pocket and shrugged. "It will be lucky if I don't burn the shit out of it."

"I guess we can start with a handkerchief if you're too scared to start with your lucky shirt."

"I'm not feeling lucky tonight." He held up his wounded hand. "Obviously."

Becca didn't want to touch that with a ten-foot pole. "Fine, where do you keep them?" He looked confused. "Your handkerchiefs?"

"Oh." He pointed to a basket of folded and ironed laundry.

She reached into the basket and rooted around and pulled a handkerchief out. "Your mother did your laundry?"

"Yeah, so? She likes doing my wash for me."

Becca laughed. "Rich, no one likes to do laundry. Not even your sainted mother. Go get the ironing board. It's in the closet by the back door."

"Oh, okay."

Rich disappeared and Becca took another look around his room. The place smelled of him, in a good way, like his cologne mixed with something that was all Rich. Whatever it was made her mouth water. She wondered if he tasted as good as he smelled.

"Becca, how do you get this to stand?"

When she turned the corner into the living room, he was pulling the legs away from the table. Okay, he was forcing it. "Stop!"

She pushed him to the side, held the ironing board, and pressed the lever underneath. The legs scissored out. "There you go, big guy. Did you remember to bring the iron?"

"What do I look like? An idiot?"

She didn't need to tell him he looked great with his sleeves rolled up showing off his muscular forearms; he had the arms of a masseur, not a professor. Shouldn't professors be pale and kind of not-built? At least all the professors she had were pale and not-built.

"I'll take that as a yes."

"No. Don't get all sensitive on me now, sheesh. What do you need? An atta boy?"

"An answer to my question would be helpful." He put the iron down on the board and bent to plug it in.

Becca rolled her eyes; he also had the nicest ass she'd seen in well, how long had it been since she worked with a male model? A while. She really needed to start dating. "We need to fill the reservoir with distilled water."

"Why?"

"Because tap water contains metal, which gunks up the works."

"Is that a technical term?"

"Do you need it to be? I think I saw some distilled water under the kitchen sink." Rich went to get it, and she watched even though it was self-torture.

He returned with the water and eyed the iron apprehensively.

"You pour the water in that hole there, and there's a clear tube that shows the water level. Don't overfill it."

"Why?"

"Do you want to iron in a puddle?"

"I don't know. Why do you need water in the first place?"

"To steam it."

"Why steam? Why not just heat?"

"Steam gets the wrinkles out better."

"Then what's wrong with ironing in a puddle?"

"Why do you have to question everything?"

"Probably because I want to know the answers."

"Okay, it's kind of like a wet spot on the bed. You have a great time making it, but no one wants to sleep on it."

"I don't mind."

"You don't mind what?"

"Sleeping on the wet spot. I'm a guy. I take great pride in creating wet spots, and sleeping on them just reminds me of all the fun I had."

"Right, you say that now. Guys will say just about anything to get the opportunity to create the wet spot, but in my experience, they roll over and start snoring, leaving me in the puddle."

"Sorry babe, but you just never slept with the right guys."

"Oh," Becca rolled her eyes. "I forgot. You're such an expert."

Rich chuckled in that sexy, deep-throated way he had. The kind of chuckle she'd be able to feel if she were up against him.

Becca took a step back because if she didn't she'd be tempted to see if she was right. "Okay, have at it. Iron in a puddle if you want. Just be careful of the steam. It can burn, and you only have one good hand left."

"That's it?" That little boy look was back. He stared at the iron as if it were alive and on the prowl. "You're not going to help me?"

"Rich, it's not thermonuclear fusion. It's a hot hunk of metal you push around on a piece of fabric to flatten it. If you press that button on top, it'll shoot out a burst of steam. If you hit the blue button, it'll squirt water out of the top there. I'm going to check on the meatloaf and wash the endive since you're wrapped up literally and figuratively."

"Right. It's just a hunk of hot metal that spits."

Becca turned her back on him and walked the few feet into the kitchen. When she tossed the endive into a salad spinner, she peeked at Rich, and he was still eyeing the iron like it was a poisonous snake. He set the iron down on the handkerchief, pushed the steam button, and a cloud of steam blew out with a swoosh. He didn't move the iron. A few seconds later he pressed the blue button and watched as water squirted out on the table in front of the iron. He still hadn't moved the iron. Sheesh. Becca had a feeling his handkerchief wasn't very lucky. She thought about telling him he had to actually move the iron, but what would be the fun in that?

Chapter 7

RICH LOOKED AT THE LIST IN FRONT OF HIM AND CRINGED. What the hell was it with Becca and lists? Tuesdays were his early days, so he came home instead of playing basketball with the guys in order to do his domestic duties. It had been a week and a half since he and Becca started living together in a depressingly platonic way, and every day she'd leave him a list of things to do with detailed instructions on how to go about doing them. He hated that about her. He didn't know why she didn't just show him how to do it. It was way more fun watching Becca do just about anything than reading her lists and instructions, and Lord knew, the instructions weren't helping to make him into a Domestic God.

Today Rich had to clean the bathroom and do his laundry. He and Tripod seemed to have come to a truce of sorts once Rich discovered Tripod's love for potato chips, popcorn, ice cream, and coffee. The little bugger scarfed all the junk food he could fit in his little body, and then he'd fall asleep on the couch all curled up with his paw over his eyes and snore. Rich never knew cats snored; unfortunately, he also learned cats fart. Tripod nearly gassed him out during a movie marathon while in his ice cream coma. No more spumoni for him.

Rich looked at Tripod, who sat beside him on the couch drinking the last of Rich's coffee out of his and Tripod's favorite mug, the one big enough for his head.

Tripod loved coffee almost as much as ice cream, and Rich loved how much fun Tripod became with a little caffeine, as if he wasn't already the coolest cat on the planet. Tri was Rich's shadow, hell, the little guy even slept with him most of the time. Rich didn't mind as long as Tripod followed the rules and slept on his own side of the bed. "Are you finished with your coffee, big guy?"

Tripod flicked his tail and belted out a short rrup, which meant "yup" in cat-speak. Rich picked up their cup and brought it to the kitchen. Instead of just throwing it in sink, he actually put it in the dishwasher because Becca was on him to clean up after himself. Obviously, he was avoiding the next thing on his list. The laundry— okay, so he'd been avoiding it all. He considered himself lucky that Becca let him take his suits and shirts to the cleaners. Sometimes he wondered if she was having a little too much fun ordering him around. Rich really missed his old cleaning lady; she used to do all this stuff for him.

Laundry first. He went into his room and Tripod jumped into the middle of things while Rich stripped the sheets, burying the cat in bedding. When he picked up the spare pillow to pull off the case, he smelled Becca. "I swear she's everywhere."

Tripod murmured from somewhere beneath the pile of sheets.

Rich tossed it all into a laundry basket and carried the pile to the utility closet, feeling the solid weight of Tripod in the basket along with sheets, towels, and whichever piece of clothing happened to be on the floor under the pile. He set it down. "Come on, Tripod, time to get out of there unless you're into taking a ride through the wash. Seeing how much you enjoyed the shower, I'm thinking that's a no."

Rich picked up each piece of bedding and stuffed it in the front-load washer while Tripod flipped out and did some cool break dancing moves before he started pouncing on an imaginary adversary.

Becca's directions said not to overfill the machine, though she never told him how much to fill it. When it was full, but not packed, he closed the glass door, pulled the detergent drawer open, and checked Becca's directions for the amount to use. The last thing he wanted was to have to shovel bubbles again, although from the look of the black and white tile floor, it could use a wash.

Rich started the machine and waited to make sure the thing actually worked. So did Tripod. Both of them stared at the glass window, and when the laundry started circling Tripod tried to catch the black sock that had somehow managed to find its way into the washer. "That should keep you busy." He left Tripod to it and went to tackle the bathroom.

Cleaning the bathroom wasn't so bad, well, after he learned the very important lesson that if you mix cleaners, you create toxic gas. After he'd washed his timesaving concoction down the drain, spent ten minutes with the window open and the fan on, he started all over again. This time he followed Becca's directions on which cleaner to use and where to use it. On the plus side, Rich was sure he had the cleanest drains east of the Hudson and that his nose hair would grow back eventually. He hoped.

While Rich cleaned the bathroom, he noticed the metal hamper built into the wall. When he opened it just to see how it worked, all of Becca's clothes fell out. Since his to-do list was all but finished, he thought he'd do a good deed and stuff Becca's clothes in the wash for her. He tossed the load into a basket and went to put his wash in the dryer and Becca's clothes in the washer. After that, he thought he and Tripod deserved some DVR time.

After eating a few sandwiches and watching last week's episode of *TopGear*, Rich removed his sheets from the dryer and tossed all of Becca's clothes in. He turned on Animal Planet for Tripod, while he separated stray clothing from sheets and went to put his bed back together, missing the fact he could no longer roll over and get a nose full of Becca on his spare pillow, or Becca's pillow, as he'd begun to think of it.

Rich wished he had paid attention when they taught him how to make a bed in military school. But since military school had been the last place in the world he wanted to be besides jail, and he'd been scared spit-less, he acted tough and dumb. Since Becca moved in, he'd been spending so much time tossing and turning in the middle of the night thinking about her sleeping in the next room, he awoke to find his bed looked as if something had detonated in it. Every morning he'd put his bed back together the same way, and it hadn't held up yet. Well, except that first night. The bed was well intact when he'd woken up naked on top of an equally naked Becca.

Tripod's yowl pulled him from his rather explicit daydream so Rich went out to see what Tripod was so excited about. He wasn't in front of the television watching the monkeys swing around the screen, which is where Rich had left him. Rich put his hands on his hips and waited for the next blast. Sure enough, not a second later, Tripod all but screamed. Rich ran after the sound, and when he turned the corner behind the kitchen into the sunroom/mud room, smoke poured out of the utility closet. Fuck.

Rich ran in, grabbed Tripod, and hightailed it back to the kitchen to get the fire extinguisher from under the sink. Tripod bounced beside him as he ran back to the utility room, opened the door to the dryer, and filled it with extinguisher foam. Becca was going to kill him. At least he'd get out of laundry duty. Rich figured if he burned her clothes once, he'd never be allowed to touch a dryer again.

Gathering Tripod up in a towel, Rich went to answer the door. Wayne and Henry had been banging but busted through after using their own key. "We saw the smoke pouring out of your apartment and called 911."

The fire truck pulled up a minute later, and the firefighters had Wayne, Henry, Rich, and Tripod wait outside until they made sure there was no further danger and gave them permission to return to the premises.

To Rich, the wait seemed like an eternity. It was ten minutes to anyone not holding a three-legged cat wrapped in a towel who knew how to make good use out of his claws. When the all-clear was sounded, Rich walked through the doors, Tripod still thankfully contained in a towel, and sat on the couch. His eyes stung from either the smoke or his little chemistry experiment in the bathroom—possibly both. His arms stung from Tripod's attempts to rip him to shreds, and his ego stung from yet another failure. Of all the billions of people who did laundry, why did he have to be the one to incinerate the contents of the dryer? Especially since that dryer contained what Rich figured was most of the lingerie owned by his roommate—the same roommate who had been known to come after him with a baseball bat.

Becca ran screaming into the apartment and threw herself in his arms. Tripod yowled, but she didn't seem to notice. She was too busy running her hands all over Rich.

"Oh God, are you okay?"

Rich put Tripod in a football hold so he could calm Becca down.

"He's fine."

"Who?"

"Tripod. It really looks worse than it is."

"What does? You're covered with soot. You smell like smoke and chemicals. You're scorched."

"We're fine. I just have Tripod wrapped up until the firefighters let me close the doors. He's already spent time outside, and I think he's more interested in freedom than in coffee and Animal Planet."

"What?"

"Never mind. Look, Becca. There's something I have to tell you."

"You mean there's more?"

"It's about the fire."

"Don't worry about that. The important thing is that you're safe. The damage is minor, or at least that's what the firefighter on the stoop said."

"Yeah, well. I guess so, but still, you might want to sit down."

Becca turned as white as his sheets were before he'd washed them with his socks. Unfortunately, the socks were black and red. Now his sheets were a kind of grayish pink—not that he really cared. He called that a success in light of the way his second try turned out, and if bad luck continued to plague him, no one would ever see the color of his sheets again. As upsetting as that thought was, it was nowhere near as awful as the prospect of telling Becca the news.

Becca sank down into the couch, which seemed to engulf her. She looked almost fragile, and Rich wanted to kick his own ass.

Becca wrapped her arms around herself. "Just spit it out, Rich. You're scaring me."

"The fire was in the dryer."

"You burnt your clothes?"

"Not exactly."

"Okay, what did you burn?"

Rich resisted the urge to cross himself.

"Excuse me?" A male voice interrupted. Rich and Becca looked up to see a firefighter had walked in. "This looks like the culprit." He held up a wire. "It went through one of the holes in the dryer and apparently hit the heating element and threw enough sparks to ignite the contents."

Becca turned to Rich. "Why would you wash a wire?"

The firefighter chuckled. "It's an underwire, ma'am. You really should use a lingerie bag if you're going to machine wash and dry your unmentionables.

Becca's eyes widened. "My unmentionables?"

Rich cringed and nodded. "Yeah, that's what I wanted to talk to you about. I was trying to do you a favor."

"A favor?"

"I was cleaning the bathroom like you told me to, and I found your laundry in the hamper.

"So you had the urge to wash my clothes?"

"I was trying to do something nice for you, and well, the first load of laundry I washed didn't turn out so bad."

"Dude." The firefighter interrupted. "You torched the lady's underwear?"

Rich nodded.

"You need to replace the dryer. That one's toast."

Rich stood and shook the man's hand. "Thanks, I appreciate the help." Rich couldn't miss the pitying look the guy gave him.

"Good luck, man. We're out of here."

Becca didn't say anything as the firefighter left the apartment. Rich watched her carefully, not sure how she'd retaliate. Whatever he expected, it was not for her to walk into her room and quietly close the door.

Rich didn't see her until the next morning when he was getting ready for work. He'd spent the rest of the evening feeling like crap about the fire and was waiting for Becca to come out and ream him. He'd pay to replace the dryer and all the clothes he'd ruined. He didn't care about that. What bothered him was the look on Becca's face when she'd walked away from him the night before.

He cursed under his breath and grabbed his briefcase, ready to leave for work. He looked over his shoulder and saw Becca shuffling out of her bedroom all warm, sleepy, and sexy even though she wore hundred-year-old ratty sweats. Unfortunately for him, he knew what was under them. "Oh good, you're up."

Becca didn't say anything; she just stared at him.

"I didn't want to wake you before I left, but I wanted to tell you that I'm going to see Gina tonight, so if all goes well, I probably won't be home to cook dinner."

Becca smiled, the look of relief clear on her face. "Good luck with that. Do you want me to write a note expounding your Domestic God virtues?"

"Thanks for the offer, but I don't think it'll be necessary." And truth be told, there wasn't much to expound upon. Shit, if this didn't work he wasn't sure what he would do. The dinner with his dean was in two days. If Gina didn't give him another shot… no, he wasn't going there.

He slid into his jacket, turned, and caught Becca watching him with a strange look on her face. "What is it?" He checked his fly, yup, it was zipped, and his tie was straight.

"Nothing, you look fine. I was just, you know, woolgathering."

"Okay, well, have a good one."

She stuffed her hands into the pocket of her sweatshirt. "You too."

Wednesday evening Rich sat at the bar of his and Gina's favorite rendezvous—a quiet little place halfway between his office and hers, waiting for her. He'd practiced his speech most of the day, lucky for him it was an exam day, but from the look on his students' faces as they left, he was one of the few feeling lucky. Unfortunately, he couldn't remember what he'd planned to say. A lot of good all the practicing did him. He would have been better off grading papers. With spending every spare moment cooking and cleaning with Becca, he was way behind on his paperwork. Who knew housework was so time-consuming? Of course, if he weren't such a complete screwup he wouldn't have to do most everything over again after cleaning up whatever it was he destroyed.

The minute Gina walked in, Rich knew he was fighting an uphill battle. She didn't look at all happy to see him. Damn. He stood to pull out a stool for her, and when he bent to kiss her, she turned her head so he barely hit her cheek. She wore a body-skimming, long-sleeved red sweater dress that, even with her coat on, stopped all traffic and most of the conversation in the bar.

"You look great. Thanks for meeting me."

"Thanks." She smiled at him and allowed him to help her off with her coat—the coat he almost dropped when he saw her dress. It was a lipstick red with a very deep V-neck that showed off her rather amazing breasts that he knew for a fact were real. The soft material, what there was of it, clung to her like a second skin. He wondered if she wore a bra because he saw no signs of one. Lord knew she wasn't wearing panties. He took her arm and helped her up on the barstool. He always thought she was tiny, but most women were compared to him. But damn she was short. He never really noticed before, but after spending two weeks with Becca, who was anything but, Gina's shortness was glaring. Even with heels, she stood at least a foot shorter than he.

Gina swiveled the stool to face the bartender and graced him with a genuine smile, much more genuine than the one she'd given Rich. Christ, this did not bode well for his plan. She confirmed his thought when she turned to him after she ordered her drink. "What do you want, Richie?"

Okay, so she wasn't in the mood for small talk. "I've missed you."

She laughed. "Come on, you expect me to believe that? I know you, remember?"

So she was right, he really hadn't missed her. Of course he'd been so busy trying to do everything possible to become a damn Domestic God he hadn't realized it, not that he'd admit it to her. He took a swig of his beer. "If I didn't miss you why would I have gone through all the trouble to learn how to cook and clean?"

Gina had taken a sip of her martini and choked when she heard that. After she stopped coughing, she wiped the mascara from under her eyes and held up her finger to stop him from saying whatever it was he was about to say so she could get her hysterical laughter under control. After taking a few calming breaths, she looked him in the eye. "So, you're learning to cook and clean. Hmm. I can't imagine why unless maybe you suddenly got the hots for Martha Stewart?"

"No."

She patted his chest. "Honey, I'm happy for you. I'm sure your next girlfriend will appreciate it. But I told you before—you shouldn't have bothered for my sake. I'm not interested."

"Hold on, when you broke up with me you said it was because I wasn't relationship material."

"You're not. Well not for me. You're cute and sweet, kinda like Tom Hanks in that old movie *Big*."

"He played a child in a grown man's body."

"Exactly." She looked at her watch and downed the rest of her martini. "I've got to run, but thanks for the drink. It was nice seeing you again."

"That's it?"

"What did you expect, Rich?"

"I thought you'd give me another shot at least. Come on, Gina. I have this dinner thing Friday night. Come with me. It'll be fun."

"A dinner thing?"

"Yeah, it's a charity dinner with my dean and his wife. You know. Dinner, dancing. It'll be a good time."

"So that's what this is all about."

"What's that supposed to mean?"

"You don't want me. You just want a date." She shook her head. "I'm sorry. I really wish I could help you out, but I'm kind of seeing someone."

"You are?"

"Annabelle introduced me to him actually."

"Annabelle?"

"Yeah, I gotta run. I'm late as it is. Good luck with your dinner. I'm sure you'll have no trouble finding someone else to go with you."

Rich stood and helped her with her coat. He just nodded, and she reached for him and gave him a hug. "Bye, Gina."

He sat back down and watched her leave—along with every other guy at the bar. Rich wondered if she'd always dressed like that—loud enough to cause an accident. It had been two weeks since he'd seen her, and he'd spent just about every free minute with Becca who couldn't be more different. When Becca wasn't wearing those God-awful ratty clothes, she dressed with a quiet, sophisticated sexiness that if put up against Gina would make Gina look almost garish. Now that he thought about it, Gina probably wasn't the right girl to take to the benefit dinner. The right girl was right under his nose the whole time. Becca. Now if only he could figure out how to talk her into going with him.

Rich just needed a plan. He'd make dinner to thank Becca for all her help, and after a bottle of wine or two, when she was all happy and relaxed, he'd ask her if she would do him a favor. After all, it was only one dinner. Dean Stewart would like Becca. The only glitch that Rich could see was that Becca really didn't like him. Although after she got over his burning up all her lingerie, she seemed to dislike him less. Either that or she just got tired of talking about it. With any luck and—knowing Becca—a lot of begging, she'd go to the dinner with him.

Rich remembered Becca said she liked salmon so he stopped by the fish market on the way home. He wasn't sure how much to buy, but after getting advice from the guy behind the counter, he had enough for dinner for two along with a foolproof recipe written on a piece of butcher paper.

Thankfully, the cashier had overheard his conversation with the fish man and took pity on Rich reminding him to purchase a few lemons. She even suggested making a side dish, which would never have occurred to him. She took him by the arm down one of the grocery aisles and pointed out a bag of yellow-colored rice that she said was easily prepared in the microwave. Rich could definitely handle a microwave. He thanked her while she rang up his sale and asked her if she had any other advice. She suggested that he stop at the vegetable stand next door and buy the ingredients for a salad, maybe some fresh broccoli, too, which she told him could also be cooked in the microwave. The woman was a Godsend, and if she wasn't old enough to be his grandmother, he would have asked her out to the damn dinner.

Rich juggled the packages and unlocked the door to the apartment. Tripod was waiting for him like he did every night. Tripod jumped off the couch and meowed as he hopped beside Rich to the kitchen. He shook his head. The cat sounded like he was carrying on a conversation and doing all the talking.

Tripod had an entire vocabulary of distinctly different yowls and meows. Short, clipped ones that Rich swore sounded like they had a question mark behind them, snarky, more guttural yowls to show displeasure, and he'd even heard a snort or two, as if the cat were laughing at him—not that he hadn't given him plenty to laugh at.

If Becca went to the dinner with Rich, he could let it slip that they were living together, which wasn't even a lie. There was no need to tell his dean it was only a temporary arrangement. That would prove that he'd settled down. After all, he'd never lived with a woman before. Heck, he'd never even come close. With most of his relationships, he tried to keep women out of his apartment. Not only because he'd have to have his cleaning lady over before his date, which wasn't worth the hassle or expense since he could just go over to his date's place, but because it made things much easier after the relationship ended.

He still had nightmares about the one time he'd made the mistake of giving his key to a woman. A few weeks after they'd stopped seeing each other, Rich had come home to find her waiting naked in his bed. A difficult thing to explain to the almost naked woman he'd been working hard to get into said bed. Actually, since woman number one had fallen asleep waiting for him, Rich technically succeeded in having two women in his bed at one time—every guy's fantasy. Unfortunately, his fantasy quickly proved to be a nightmare.

The memory sent a chill up his spine as he removed the rubber band from the bouquet of flowers he'd bought. He stuffed the stems in a vase he found above the refrigerator, pulled the hose from the sink, and squirted some water into it. The flowers didn't look too good. He probably should have bought one of the arrangements already in a vase. They sure looked better than his, but he had his arms full of packages and wasn't sure he'd make it home without dropping something.

He took out the directions the fish man had given him. It said to use a Pyrex pan. What the hell was a Pyrex pan?

He grabbed his phone. It was good to have a chef on speed dial. "Vin, it's Rich. Man, you gotta help me out."

"What happened? You burn down the apartment again?"

Rich put the wine in the refrigerator to chill and got himself a beer. He wedged the phone between his ear and shoulder while he popped the top off the beer. "Shit, does everyone know about the fire?" He held the phone, tipped the beer up to his lips, and took a swig. Thankfully, he'd finished swallowing before Vinny stopped laughing.

"Of course. What are you, nuts? Remember that wedding reception in the church basement? The maid of honor's dress caught on fire when they served flaming cherries jubilee, and the band started playin' the "William Tell Overture" while she ran around screaming like a banshee?"

"Yeah."

"Yours ain't as good, but it's close. Especially when I tell them that all your girlfriend's bras and undies were in the drier."

"Becca's not my girlfriend."

"Sure, that's why you were washing her lingerie. What man washes a woman's panties if he ain't getting into them?"

"Becca was just teaching me how to do laundry, Vin."

He snorted. "God, that makes the story even better."

"Anything I can do to help."

"So, if the place ain't on fire, what the hell are you callin' me for? I gotta get ready for the dinner rush."

"I need to know what the fuck a Pyrex pan is."

"You're kidding."

"No, I'm making dinner for Becca, and it said to cook the fish in a Pyrex pan."

"You know what a lasagna pan looks like? It's thirteen by nine, usually clear glass, but I got one from Corning that has pretty blue flowers—"

"Stop, for Christ's sake. I know what a lasagna pan is." He had one on the counter he was supposed to give back to Aunt Rose.

"What kind of fish you makin'?"

"Salmon. The fish man told me a foolproof recipe. He said any idiot could make it."

"Yeah? What is it?"

"You just stick the fish skin side down in a greased pan. What kind of grease am I supposed to use?"

"You got that cooking spray?"

"How the fuck do I know?"

"Well, look in the cabinet next to the stove. If it ain't there, try lookin' over the stove."

"Is it yellow with a red top?"

"Bingo. Just spray it on, don't forget the sides."

"Gotcha."

"Then what?"

"He said to slather the top of the fish with mayonnaise like frosting a cake. I'm supposed to make sure I cover all of the fish showing and then sprinkle the top with onion powder, garlic powder, parsley, and dill. Then just bake it at 375 degrees for 15 minutes. He said it'll get so you can flake it with a fork."

"That ain't Italian."

"No, but it's easy. And with any luck, it'll be edible. Right now that's the best I can hope for."

"Why don't you just bring her here? Mona's been dying to get another look at her."

"Vin, I'm trying to impress her."

"You sayin' my cookin' ain't impressive?"

"No, I'm sayin' I'm trying to impress her with mine."

Vinny let out a low chuckle. "Yeah, well, good luck with that. You got anything else you wanna ask before I get back to work?"

"No, not that I can think of."

"See, I told you you should'a come to work for me when you were a kid. If you had, you'd know how to cook good Italian food like me. But no, instead you went and stole a car."

"You're right. I should have gone to work for you."

"Okay, if you get into trouble, just call. I can send Sonny over with some salmon all cooked, maybe you can like, you know, pretend you made it or somethin'."

"Vin, she's not dumb."

"Right, well, call me if you need help."

"Thanks, I appreciate it."

"No problem. What else do I gotta do? It ain't like I got a restaurant to run or anything."

Rich laughed and disconnected the call.

Becca stood in the trendy West Side gallery and watched the woman who worked there examine her business card as if she were checking a fake ID. The snob factor of the gallery was evident by the accent, dress, and degree of angle on the woman's surgically photo-shopped nose. After hitting three West Side galleries on her list, Becca suddenly realized that styles of facial features like the little pert ski-jump nose and the pouty lips were becoming an honest-to-God trend. What would Victoria Hyde-Taylor do if the fat-lipped look ever went out? Do cosmetic surgeons do lipectomies?

Becca kept the smile on her face as she handed Victoria the last of her application CDs in the hand-decorated case she'd created last night. The cases were pieces of modern art. "On here I've included my art exhibition application form, resume, jpegs of my work, PDFs of several articles, and brochures from past shows."

"I see." Victoria looked down her short ski-jump nose at the CD case.

"What is your typical response time?"

Victoria shrugged her shoulders. "You'll hear from us if we're interested."

Becca was tempted to take back that CD case; it was beautiful and would probably end up along with her CD in the circular file as soon as the door closed behind her. "Well, thank you for your time. I look forward to hearing from you. Have a nice day." Becca didn't wait for Victoria's response before leaving. She stopped at the Starbucks on the corner and drowned her sorrows in a Venti Caramel Macchiato on her way home. She needed to change out of her trendy artist clothes into her construction worker outfit and get over to the brownstone.

Between her gallery visits and dealing with the constant problems at the brownstone, Becca was in a shitty mood. It didn't help that Rich told her he had a date with Gina. At least the construction guys were fucking up royally so she had someone to take her bad mood out on. Worse than that, Annabelle seemed to know that Rich had a date with Gina too, and got a real kick out of mentioning it to Becca repeatedly. It was all she could do not to spit, but she wasn't about to let Annabelle know that Richie was growing on her.

She was woman enough to admit, if only to herself, that she didn't hate him anymore. Maybe she'd go as far as to say she liked him. He was a nice guy, and he was cute, especially when he got embarrassed every time he messed up. And what woman wouldn't like a guy whose first thought in a fire was to find and save her cat? Heck, she'd even admit that she turned to mush when she saw him sitting there holding on to her snarling cat and looking so ashamed and embarrassed. She had to pretend to be mad at Rich just so he could save face. Men had such fragile egos. If she told him not to feel bad, it would have driven him nuts.

When she turned the corner and saw the fire engine, she had kind of freaked out. The knowledge that Rich was almost definitely in the apartment turned her blood to ice. Visions of Rich burnt or overcome with smoke filled her head as tears filled her eyes. She'd been in full panic mode when the firefighter stopped her while she was sprinting into the brownstone and assured her no one was hurt. She'd heard what the firefighter said, and she still had to practically sit on Rich to assure herself he was still alive and well.

So, even though it was no surprise to her that he was growing on her, she was still floored by the lightning bolt of sheer jealousy that shot through her when he oh-so-casually said he was going out with Gina. She told herself that it was human nature to feel a little jealous. After all, she and Rich had spent every night together cooking, cleaning, laughing at his foibles, and watching TV. They'd become friends kind of. Now he was off drooling over Gina who hadn't so much as called him in the last two weeks. Becca stopped herself. She didn't know that for a fact, but she was pretty sure Rich would have told her if Gina had called. If not, Annabelle certainly would have.

Annabelle sure had a great time rubbing Becca's nose in the fact that Richie had a date, and Becca hadn't had one in two years. Like she needed reminding.

Maybe she should think about getting another cat. One who'd be more cuddly than Tripod. That shouldn't be so hard to find. Hell, probably most of the big cats would fit that description. She figured she'd turn into one of those eccentric old women like Leona Helmsley who would leave money in her will to her nieces and nephews as long as they took care of her cats. Even one of the construction workers referred to Becca as the Queen of Mean today. Maybe she was channeling old Leona.

Becca grumbled as she unlocked the door because she dropped the DVDs she picked up to watch tonight. She kicked the door open, tossed her purse on the table, and bent to collect the movies when she realized she wasn't alone. Someone was in the kitchen, and she knew it couldn't be Rich since whatever was cooking smelled really good. Maybe his mother or Aunt Rose had the key and wanted to surprise him? Or, oh God, what if Gina was cooking?

Becca didn't remember him saying she should make herself scarce, but then she was half asleep, and she had a hard time hearing what he said with the blood rushing though her ears after he dropped the G-bomb. She grabbed her purse and was halfway out the door when Tripod screamed at her.

"Shhh…"

Rich came out of the kitchen looking like something right off the pages of her Porn for Women Calendar. She just wished it was the XXX one she had stashed where no one could find it.

"You're home."

All he was missing was the "honey." She was speechless. He didn't look upset. He looked happy to see her. What the hell was going on?

"I called Annabelle to see what time you left. I made dinner and didn't want the fish to overcook." He looked at his watch. "It'll be done in about ten minutes if you want to change. You look like you had a hard day." He took her messenger bag off her shoulder. "Can I get you a glass of wine?"

"What?"

Rich tugged her jacket off, and she was too stunned

to stop him. "If you hurry up, you can get a nice hot shower. You have sawdust all over you." He gave her a shove toward the bathroom.

Becca saw the dining room table had been set. There were even flowers. Ugly flowers, but flowers all the same. "Look, Rich. I can see you have plans, and I don't want to intrude. I can just go back to Annabelle's and hang there." She craned her neck to see if Gina was anywhere near; she wasn't in the kitchen. Oh, God, maybe she was already in the bedroom.

"Becca, I cooked dinner for you. I'm making salmon, your favorite. I think it's going to be good. Come on, you could at least try it."

"What? I thought you had a date with Gina."

"Well, yeah. Afterward I stopped at the store to pick up something for dinner. Now hurry up and get into the shower, I don't want you to get sawdust all over the food and then complain about my cooking."

He pushed her into her bedroom. She really did need a shower, so she took off her clothes and threw on her robe. When she stepped out, Rich shoved a glass of wine in her hand and told her he'd started the water. She had seven minutes before the fish was done. He gave her another shove and closed the door behind her.

Becca took a short shower, which left her two minutes to dress. What does a girl wear when her friend who happens to be a guy cooks dinner and even brings her ugly flowers? She always got a kick out of wearing her scruffy clothes around him, just to tick him off. Then she remembered the way he seemed unable to keep himself from touching her when she wore her cashmere sweats—not that she was going to wear them again, that might look as if she wanted him touching her, which she definitely didn't. But she could dress a little nicer.

She threw open her closet and pulled out a lounge set her mom bought her that she didn't hate. She'd never worn it because she had no one to wear it for—not that it was overly sexy or anything, it was just too nice to hang around the house in unless she had company. It was winter white with a gathered Queen Anne neckline, long tight sleeves, and pants you wouldn't know were to sleep in unless you touched them. She debated whether or not to wear a bra with it. Since she currently had a real shortage of bras, and unfortunately wasn't well enough endowed to make a bra necessary, she'd go without. Tossing the shirt over her head, she sighed as the material flowed over her. Damn, if she'd known Tencel—a fabric made from bamboo—was this soft and silky, she'd have worn the PJs before. She pulled on the pants and ran her hands through her hair. It was almost dry, one of the perks of having short hair. She took one last swig of her wine for Dutch courage. After eating more than a few of Rich's creations, she thought she needed it.

Rich did his best to make everything look presentable. The rice looked fine. The cashier was right, it was great in the microwave. So was the broccoli. The salad looked like salad. Rich figured even he would have trouble screwing that up. The oven timer went off, and he grabbed the oven mitt, proud that he remembered, but the fact that his hand still hurt whenever he got near anything hot probably helped his memory. He was beginning to wonder if it was psychological. Being a psychology professor, it wouldn't surprise him. Still, he was getting to be an old hand at this cooking thing. He took the fish out of the oven, set the pan on the stove, and with a fork, stuck the fish, and—wonder of wonders—it flaked. Amazing!

He took the fish out of the pan and put it on a plate with some rice and broccoli. He placed a few pieces of lemon beside it, like they do in the restaurants, and set them on the table just as Becca left her room.

Rich stared. He couldn't get over the transformation. She'd come home in her jeans and sweatshirt, looking angry and tired, not to mention dirty, and ten minutes later, she looked edible. She was all white and flowing and well, gorgeous.

"You cooked this? By yourself?"

Rich did his best to collect himself. "Yeah, I got the recipe from the guy at the fish market, and I called Vinny once. I didn't know what a Pyrex pan was." He pulled out her chair for her and waited for her to sit. When she did, he put his hand on her shoulder; he wanted to see if what she wore was as soft as it looked. It was.

Becca placed her napkin in her lap. "Wow, I'm impressed. Everything looks great. I didn't think I was hungry, but now I'm starved."

Rich filled her wineglass and sat. "A toast."

Becca held up her glass.

"To the future."

Becca touched her glass to his. "To the future." But the look on her face was a mixture of hurt and disgust.

Rich watched her over the rim of his glass while he took a sip. "What's the matter?"

She shook her head. "Nothing. You know, just the normal annoyances. Framers who can't read blueprints who put walls up in the wrong places and tell me I'm wrong. What about you? How'd it go with Gina?"

Rich noticed she still hadn't taken a bite, so he figured he might as well try it. It would also get him out of answering her question. He took a forkful of fish, managed to get a little rice on there, and took a bite. He couldn't believe it. It tasted great. He motioned for her to taste it and watched as she took a tentative bite. She chewed, her eyes widened, and she moaned. Yup, Becca actually moaned. Rich couldn't believe that getting a woman to moan by feeding her was almost as much fun as getting her to moan the old fashioned way.

"Oh my God, this is amazing. Wow." She took a sip of wine, and her little pink tongue darted out to lick a drop off her lips then she shoveled another forkful into her mouth.

"Thanks." He tried the broccoli, and even that tasted pretty good. It wasn't his mother's— she must do something special to it. Knowing her, it probably involved olive oil and garlic. Still, it was nice and crunchy and the most amazing color green, almost as pretty as the color of Becca's eyes.

Becca was quiet while she ate, and eat she did. She cleaned her plate, another first. Rich kept refilling her wine, waiting for her to loosen up so he could ask her if she'd help him out. He'd just wing it. It had always worked in the past.

When they finished, she stood and picked up her plate. He took it from her. "No, I've got it. I remembered what you said and tried to clean as I went, so it'll be an easy job. Why don't you take your wine and see what's on TV? Or better yet, why don't we watch one of the movies you brought home?"

Becca looked guilty. "You said you were going out with Gina. I didn't think you'd be home so I got chick flicks."

"I don't mind, just as long as next time I get to pick." When he looked up from piling the dishes, he knew he hadn't gotten away with it.

"You never told me what happened with Gina."

Rich shrugged. "She's seeing someone else. Annabelle of all people fixed her up with him."

Becca looked a little pissed on his behalf. "So you did all this for nothing?" It was nice of her not to say I told you so, because she had.

Rich topped off her wineglass and his, finishing the bottle. "I wouldn't say that. I fed you, didn't I?"

"Yeah, and it really was great. Still, I'm sorry, Rich."

"I was thinking…"

She followed him into the kitchen carrying her wine and the empty bottle. "That sounds dangerous. Even more dangerous than you doing laundry."

He ignored the cut. "I still have that dinner to go to with Dean Stewart, and since I never mentioned Gina by name, I thought that since you were here and we're technically living together, maybe you'd go with me."

"You want me to lie?"

"No, more like *act* as if we're together. You don't have to come out and actually tell a lie."

"Oh yeah. That makes all the difference." She threw her hands up, and when she realized she was still holding her wineglass, slammed it on the counter shattering it. "Shit."

The sound of shattering glass startled him. "Are you all right?" He grabbed her hand and examined it. She could have really done a job on herself, but he didn't see a scratch, thank God.

"I'm fine." She pulled her hand from his and moved to pick up the pieces.

"Don't touch it. I'll clean it up."

Becca huffed. "I broke it. I'll clean it up."

Christ, she was difficult. "I thought you said I had to do all the cooking and cleaning? So would you let me do it already? I'd really rather not add your blood to the mess."

"Fine. Clean it up if you want. You can cook dinner, ply me with a few glasses of wine, and clean up after me. It's not going to help your cause."

Rich made sure she was well away before bringing the garbage can to the counter. With a few pieces of paper towel, he swept the glass into it. "Come on, Becca. It's one night. It'll be fun. Dinner, dancing, and you'd really be saving my ass. Please, Bec. I'm kinda desperate here."

Becca rolled her eyes as if she didn't believe him. "Don't tell me you don't know anyone else."

"I've been gone a long time, and since I got back, I've been seeing Gina. I really don't know anyone but my students. You're it, Becca. Please?"

She crossed her arms under her breasts, which did amazing things to the look of that top she was wearing. Christ, his professional life might be hanging in the balance, and he was concentrating on her breasts. He was most certainly going to hell. He thought back to the last time he went to confession. Yup, definitely to hell, and he'd get there quickly if his brother-in-law, Mike, knew what was going through his mind. He was so fucked.

Becca walked over to the couch and flopped down. "So that was the reason behind the dinner and the wine. You were just trying to soften me up so I'd go to this dinner with you."

"No."

She tossed a pillow at him. "You are so busted. That's exactly what you did."

He tossed it back. "No. I'll admit to wanting to help you get into the right mood before I asked you. But that's not why I cooked dinner. I cooked dinner because you looked kind of sad this morning, and I wanted to thank you for all the help."

She sat up a little and pulled the pillow to her chest. Rich mentally rolled his eyes. Christ, he had to get his head out of the gutter.

"No kidding?"

She had the same look in her eyes now as she did when she found him sitting in the smoke-filled apartment holding on to Tripod for dear life. He wasn't sure what that look meant. "No kidding."

She put the pillow down, stood, and walked over to him. She smelled really good. He knew it was her shampoo and soap, because he'd sniffed them when he was in the shower, but it smelled a whole lot better on her. "Well, in that case." Becca stood so close; he was too stunned to do anything but put his hands on her waist. "You're welcome. And since you're so desperate, I'll go to the dinner."

"Thanks." The next thing he knew Becca was hugging him. Man, it was so nice to be able to hug a woman and not have to practically kneel to do it. She was the perfect height, and she wasn't wearing a thing under that outfit of hers. He swallowed hard. Damn, he was going to hell.

Chapter 8

BECCA DIDN'T THINK SHE'D NEED ANY EVENING GOWNS when she moved to Brooklyn, so she stored them all right along with her furniture. Now, not only did she have to go to a formal charity benefit with Rich, she had to shop.

"Annabelle, I need help."

"What's wrong?"

"I need to buy an evening gown. I have a thing to go to tomorrow and I just found out about it last night. All my gowns are in storage."

"Ooh." Becca could picture Annabelle settling in for a nice long inquisition. "You met someone?"

Becca groaned. "You could say that."

"Do I know him?"

Oh God, she really didn't want to go there. But she couldn't very well lie. After all, Rich might mention it, but if she did tell Annabelle, she'd have to give her a blow-by-blow of the whole thing. Still, it couldn't be helped.

"I'm going to a charity benefit with Rich because Gina wouldn't, and he needs a date. I'm doing him a favor."

"You're going out with Richie? That's great!"

"Annabelle, stop right there. I'm saving your brother's ass. It's not a date, so you can pull that train of thought right off the tracks." Becca couldn't help but wonder what her late brother Chip would have said about this. Hell, he'd have a field day watching their mother go crazy when she found out Becca was seeing Annabelle's brother. He was probably posthumously laughing his ass off at the irony. Mother couldn't stand Annabelle when she and Chip were together. Now that Annabelle and Mike were married and owned the family estate and the trust due to Mike as firstborn, Becca's mother's extreme dislike of Annabelle had increased exponentially. The thought that Becca was dating another Ronaldi would send Mother over the edge.

"The lady doth protest too much, methinks."

Becca pulled the phone away from her ear and stared at it before remembering she actually had to say something. "Since when do you quote Shakespeare?"

"I've been reading some of Mike's books. You know, that Shakespeare is really great once you get used to all those thees and thous, but don't change the subject. You're going on a date with Richie."

"Technically, yes, but I'm not happy about it. He's in a jam, and I said I'd go with him. It's a pity date."

"You better not let him hear that. Richie never had a hard time getting a date."

"I'm sure. He just has a hard time getting a date that would impress his dean."

"Are you saying his usual girlfriends are bimbos?"

"No. Look, I need a dress. Are you going to help me find one or not?"

"Of course. I never need an excuse to shop. In fact, I have a friend in the garment district who has the most amazing designs. Since you're so tall and skinny, you might just fit into his samples. You can get them for a steal."

"Great. I'm going to need shoes and probably a shawl or cape too. It's getting cold at night."

"No problem. Marcello will fix you up. If he doesn't have what we need, he'll know who does. I'll give him a call and see if we can meet in the morning."

"Okay, thanks."

"Just meet me here at nine, and we'll take the train in together. Oh, and Bec, is Richie okay?"

"Yeah, he's fine. Why?"

"Well, Gina said she told him she was seeing someone else."

Becca couldn't believe Annabelle had gotten into the middle of this. "Did Gina also tell you that she ratted you out?"

"What are you talking about?"

"Gina told him that you introduced her to Mr. Wonderful. Rich hasn't mentioned it, but I don't think you're his favorite person right now. Look, I have to go. He's almost finished with the dishes, and we're supposed to watch a movie."

"What are you watching, *James Bond, Mission Impossible, Die Hard, Iron Man*, or is he going retro with something like *Rambo*?"

"I picked out a few chick flicks. I didn't think he'd be here tonight. Not one of them has a gun in it."

"And he agreed to watch them?"

"Of course he did. I'm not planning to tie him to the TV or anything."

"Right. He'll make fun of the movie while you're watching it. He can be so annoying."

Becca smiled. Rich Ronaldi was all that and a bag of chips.

Becca struggled into the tight, tight black dress. If she'd

known she'd attend a benefit wearing a dress she'd swear was at least a size too small, she would have gone without the candy bars and popcorn she'd eaten in the last few days. She took in her reflection in the mirror over her dresser top, blinked, and looked again. She couldn't believe her eyes. She actually had cleavage. Amazing. She ran her hands under her breasts thinking she should wear more halter tops. The dress dipped so low in the back, she was afraid that if it gaped while she sat, everyone would see the crack of her ass, something she wasn't into sharing. Marcello gave her some double-sided wardrobe tape, just to be safe, even though he and Annabelle checked and swore it wasn't gaping. Becca fingered the stuff, but the thought of pulling tape off her butt later didn't sound all that appealing.

"Becca, are you ready?"

She checked the time. She still had five minutes. Didn't guys understand that there was more to getting ready than just getting a shower and putting on clothes? Becca ran her hands through her hair, messing it up a little more. It looked pretty good with the little natural curl she had along with some mousse and scrunching. She turned and watched as the beaded ribbon that tied the halter dress at her neck swung back and forth across her naked back like a pendulum, drawing the eye down to the dangerously low waist.

"Almost."

He tapped on the door just as she slid into the silver, jeweled heels and checked her matching evening bag.

She swung the door open. "What?"

Rich stood there with his mouth gaping, and his eyes locked on her chest.

"It's a miracle. I actually have cleavage. Who knew?"

Rich still didn't say anything. He just stared.

Becca took a good long look at him in a tuxedo. "Yeah, well. If you'll stop your shock-induced gawking we can leave." She pushed him aside and walked past, heading to the coat closet.

Rich gave his head a shake, swallowed audibly, and took a deep breath. "You have a shawl or something to cover up with, right?"

"My cape is in the coat closet." She opened the door and pulled it off the hanger.

"You're going to wear your coat inside?"

"No. Why would I?"

"You can't go like that. "

Becca looked down. Her breasts were secure inside the top, then she checked to make sure her butt was covered. "What do you mean?"

"You're half naked."

"I am not." Becca took a hold of the slit skirt and shook it. "I'm wearing yards and yards of fabric."

"Yeah, it's just not covering what it should."

Becca knew the back was a little low, but it was not sleazy looking, and although you could see some cleavage, it wasn't as if she was falling out of the dress. "You better not be saying what I think you're saying."

"I don't think you should wear that. Everyone will see you." Rich mumbled something in Italian she didn't understand.

"Excuse me?" Becca couldn't believe her eyes teared. God, how could this be happening again? It had been years since boys and girls stopped calling her a dog, but one word and all the anger and humiliation cold cocked her. She blinked back tears, and let the anger fill her. Her hands fisted, and the damn fake nails she spent a hundred bucks on bit into her palms.

"Don't you have a jacket or something you can wear over it?"

"I left all my evening wear in Philly. I know this is a news flash, but I wasn't planning to go to any balls."

"Yeah, well. I wasn't planning on you either. Come on." He took her hand and pulled her out the door stopping only to lock it.

"What are we doing?"

"We're going to buy something to cover you up on the way to the dinner."

"Rich, you're being ridiculous."

"No, I'm being smart. I don't want guys following you around all night drooling."

Becca let out an unladylike snort. Her mother would die of embarrassment, not that it mattered. He couldn't wait to cover her up. "Right. You don't need to rub it in Rich. I know what I look like."

"I'm sure you do. Jesus, Becca. Couldn't you tone it down a little bit? I know you're beautiful, but when you do that with your hair and your makeup? Shit. Every guy in that room tonight is going to be picturing you naked. It's not going to look good to my dean if I get into a brawl keeping men away from you."

"What?"

"You heard me. You don't think you could go back to your room and well, you know, come out looking less hot?"

"You're picturing me naked?"

Rich rolled his eyes and said something in Italian. "I've been picturing you naked since the first day I met you. You're a beautiful woman, and I'm a guy."

"You're a perv." A perv who thinks she's beautiful. Could he be serious?

"Maybe, but so is every other red-blooded male."

"This is hardly a J-Lo dress. Everything is covered."

"It's sexier that way. It only hints at what you've got going on underneath. Every guy is going to be wondering if you're wearing panties."

Becca rolled her eyes.

"Well, are you?"

"That's none of your business."

"I know you're not wearing a bra cause your nipples were poking out before you crossed your arms."

"Fine."

"Fine what?"

"Let's go and get a shawl. I saw a really pretty silver one at Bloomingdales the other day, and it's right on the way."

Rich rocked back on his heels. "So, are you going to, you know, take off whatever it is that's making you look so hot?"

Becca groaned. "If you're making a joke, you can stop. I'm not falling for it."

"I'm dead serious."

"The only thing I did different was my hair and the dress, and there's no way I'm taking the dress off." She turned and walked out the security door.

Rich mumbled something… if she didn't know better she'd sworn he said, "Not yet, you're not. Maybe later."

Rich helped Becca out of her coat and tossed it on the bar of the coat check as he and every other being with a "Y" chromosome watched as she pulled that silver shawl around her. It was holey material—not to be confused with something worn to church. This thing was like fishnet with holes so big he could almost stick his fist through it.

He cursed under his breath. He'd been sporting a semi-hard-on since she opened her damn bedroom door. That dress hugged her like a second skin, and with her hair all messed and sexy it let every man know exactly what she'd look like on a bed beneath him. Her lips were painted and glossy, which drew his eye to them, and he wondered if she tasted as good as she looked.

Becca was busy looking at anything but him. If she continued down this track, they'd never survive this night or make anyone believe they were a couple.

She stepped away. "I'm just going to run to the ladies room and check my lipstick."

Rich grabbed her wrist. "Hold on. One thing first."

"What's that?"

"This." He pulled her toward him, causing her to fall into him, wrapped his arms around her, and kissed her. She wasn't expecting it. Her gasp gave him the opportunity to deepen the kiss. She was stiff in his arms until he licked the inside of her lower lip. She tasted sweet and felt just as hot and amazing against him as he remembered from that morning he'd woken up on top of her.

In her heels, they were eye-to-eye, chest-to-chest, and thigh-to-thigh. Rich didn't have to crane his neck down to kiss her, and feeling her body against his had him counting backwards from one hundred by threes. His hand traveled beneath that useless shawl to the bare skin of her back as he sucked her lower lip into his mouth and nibbled on it, teasing a moan from her. He slowly slid his mouth off hers to her ear. "There, now that we got past that, you can check your lipstick."

"Why did you do that?" She sounded breathless, more curious than upset, and she certainly wasn't jumping out of his arms.

"Because I wanted to, and since we're supposed to be a couple, I figured we'd better look like one. Couples kiss and touch each other."

She looked a little disappointed. "Oh, right, you did it for show."

Rich threaded his fingers through her hair and tilted her head back to look into her eyes. "I wanted to kiss you, but I wouldn't have if we weren't acting like a couple. Especially since you don't want anything to do with me, right?"

"Right." She stepped away and wrapped her new shawl around her, trying to hide her physical response to him. She didn't succeed. He buttoned the middle button of his tuxedo, needing to do the same as he watched her walk away. He was almost sure she wasn't wearing panties.

Rich turned and saw Dean Stewart and Emily just a few feet away. They waved and made their way over to him. Emily smiled and gave him an air-kiss, something that he'd never gotten used to. Everyone he knew outside academia kissed each other—men, women, it didn't matter—but then Italians were big on kissing. They also kissed both cheeks, and there was no pretending about it. When Italians kissed, it was a real kiss. Rich shook Dean Stewart's hand. "Mrs. Stewart, you look beautiful." Rich was glad he didn't have to lie. She was a very beautiful woman. He figured she was in her late forties but looked more like mid-to-late thirties.

"Always the charmer. I must say, Professor, you're looking quite dashing yourself, even with the lipstick on your mouth. I don't think coral is your color though."

Rich groaned and reached for his handkerchief.

After a few swipes, Mrs. Stewart smiled. "There you go. Not a trace of either the lipstick or the woman who bestowed it."

Rich liked Emily. He grinned and pointed toward the ladies room. "Becca will be out in a second."

She laced her arm through her husband's. "Ah, Becca. Craig couldn't remember her name."

"Rebecca Larsen." Rich looked up and grinned when he spotted Becca walking toward him. She didn't so much walk as glide. Wearing those killer heels, she stood a full head taller than Emily and a few inches taller than the dean. Her eyes widened a little when she noticed Rich had company. She pasted on a smile, lifted her chin in that regal way she had, and stopped beside him. He put his arm around her. "Becca, I'd like you to meet Dean Craig Stewart and his wife, Emily."

Becca took a deep breath and jumped in. She'd attended countless affairs similar to this, which was why she hated them so much. "So nice to meet you." She'd grown up unsuccessfully avoiding her weekly cotillion classes, which taught her important skills like which fork to use, how to make small talk, and get through hours of conversation without ever saying anything. She'd mastered the foxtrot, waltz, mambo, and merengue, and how to avoid social faux pas. If only her mother could see Becca now. She'd be so impressed.

Emily could have passed for any one of Becca's mother's friends except her smile was warm, genuine, and not Botoxed. "I've been dying to meet you, Becca. I've known Rich since he was one of Craig's doctoral candidates. I've always wondered what kind of woman would finally capture his attention. You must be happy to have him living in the same city."

"Yes. It's been wonderful having him so close by."

Rich laughed at something the dean said and turned his attention back to her and Emily. "Can I get you ladies a drink?"

He took their orders. Becca saw the gleam of inquisition in Emily's eyes. She was waiting for the men to leave so she could get all the goods on her relationship with Rich. Becca had no idea what she should say. They really should have discussed it, but Becca couldn't blame Rich. She hadn't been the most available person since the fire. Obviously, Rich thought she was mad about it, and she'd done nothing to correct him. If she had, he would have asked what was wrong, and she was really in no mood to tell him that when she saw the fire engine outside their place, she'd lost it because for some unknown reason, she was beginning to maybe fall for him a teeny, tiny bit, possibly.

Becca smiled at Emily, wishing Rich would hurry up with those drinks. "So, Mrs. Stewart—"

Emily waved her hand. "Becca, no need for such formality. Please, call me Emily."

"Okay, thank you. I was just wondering what you do."

Emily laughed. "That's funny. I was wondering the same about you."

Good, something Becca felt comfortable discussing. "I'm an artist."

"Oh, what's your favorite medium?"

"Sculpture mostly, though I really enjoy oils, too. I do that mostly for myself though. Right now, I'm working on marketing my work to the galleries in New York."

"Really? Have I seen your work?"

"Not here. I have some in several galleries in Philadelphia. That's where I was working until recently."

"I'd love to see your portfolio. I'm in charge of a local arts council and could introduce you around if you'd like."

"Yes, that would be great." Becca couldn't believe it. "The same arts council holding this benefit?"

"Didn't Rich tell you?"

"No. I'll be sure to kill him later when we get home."

"Home? I know it's none of my business, but I wasn't aware you two were living together."

"It's just temporary until I have my new place remodeled."

Rich and Craig chose that moment to appear, and Rich handed Becca her drink before interrupting, "Unless I can talk her out of it. I really love having her around."

Emily gave Rich an approving look. "I see. I wish you all the luck in your quest. I was surprised when Becca told me she's an artist."

Rich shrugged. "Really? I thought I mentioned it. Her work is incredible. That's another thing I'll miss if she leaves. Not nearly as much as much as I'll miss her though." He pulled Becca back against him. "I don't know about you, but I think art adds so much life to a home."

"I agree. I hope you'll invite Craig and me over so I can see some of Becca's work. It's so hard to judge sculpture by photos, don't you think?"

Rich took a sip of his drink and nodded. "Definitely. We'll have to have you over for dinner soon. As soon as Becca gets settled. She just moved in a few weeks ago."

Craig smiled. "Yes, we'd like that. Then maybe you can make your family lasagna you told me about. From the way you spoke about it, I assume you cook. I love real Italian cuisine."

Becca gave Rich a sideways glance. She noticed Rich didn't refute the dean's assumption. "He told you about his family's lasagna, did he?"

Craig shrugged. "Rich just said that since you've been so busy with the remodel of your studio space, he's been taking care of all the cleaning and cooking. It sounds as if you've got yourself quite a helpmate."

Becca took a sip of her drink and tried not to spit it out. She covered her laugh with a cough and cleared her throat. "Yes. He's one of a kind, isn't he?"

Rich pulled her tighter against him. "Come on, Becca. I promised you a dance. What do you say we check out the dance floor before we find our table?" He nodded to the Stewarts, and before she had time to reply, pulled her away.

Becca humphed. "Thanks for giving me a choice."

Rich kept her moving, weaving through people, saying excuse me, and nodding to those he knew. "Thanks for the glowing recommendation. One of a kind? What the hell is that supposed to mean?" He reached the dance floor, pulled her into his arms, and held her close as he swayed to "Enchantment," a slow Corrine Bailey Ray song.

"One of a kind is not necessarily a bad thing. It's not as if I ratted you out. I just didn't lie."

"I didn't lie either. I have been doing all the cooking and cleaning—just not cooking lasagna."

"What's up with you talking about my work?" She had no choice but to wrap her arms around his neck.

"I've seen the few pieces you have in your bedroom."

His hand trailed over her back so gently in contrast to his words, though his voice deepened when he mentioned her bedroom. "You have? What have you been doing? Searching my room when I'm not home?" She drew her head back to look at his eyes, inadvertently pressing her pelvis to his. She tried to give herself a little breathing room, but he wasn't allowing it. Further exasperated, she smiled a hard smile. "I don't know why I'm surprised. You went through my laundry. And if that wasn't bad enough, you torched it."

"Am I ever going to live that down?"

"Apparently not. Nor will you live down the fact that you just invited your boss and his wife for a gourmet dinner and gallery showing. Rich, all my best work is in storage."

Rich's hand lightly trailed from her neck down her spine to her lower back. It was mesmerizing. "Is that all that's bothering you? We'll go down there together and pick up whatever you want to show her. No big deal."

"What about you making lasagna?"

"I'll either get my mother or my aunt to make some, or you can hit up Aunt Rose for the recipe. Didn't you say she wants to show you how to make it?"

"Hold on. You said I'm too busy to do any of the housework or cooking. Now you expect me to clean up after you and your big mouth?"

"I was just trying to show him I'm a settled down, homebody kind of guy. Besides, you're the one who said we were living together. You don't want Emily to think you'd live with someone like me, do you?"

He dipped her, and when she tightened her hold on his neck, he smirked. Damn him. "Don't look at me like that and expect me to melt or anything. I'm immune to you."

"That's a shame because I'm not immune to you." He pressed close against her and proved his point. "Why did you think I wanted to cover you up?"

"I thought… never mind. It doesn't matter." Becca stared at his slightly crooked bow tie, praying he'd change the subject.

Rich tipped her chin up so she couldn't avoid his eyes. "What did you think?"

"Let's just say I went through a few awkward teenage years and was teased mercilessly. When you told me to cover up—"

"Christ, Becca. I'm sorry. But you gotta know that it's hard enough being around you when you're in those baggy clothes you wear. When you look like this, well, it's painful. You take my breath away."

"Great, Rich. You say things like that, and I can't stay mad at you."

"Good. What do you say we spend some time making up?"

Before she could answer, he kissed her. Just a soft sweet kiss that made her toes curl. When he started singing "Fly Me to the Moon" in her ear, she melted. He certainly didn't play fair.

Chapter 9

RICH SPENT MOST OF THE NIGHT DANCING WITH BECCA when she wasn't dancing with Jeff Parker and a few of the other people from his department. The fact that she danced more than one dance with Jeff really set Rich's teeth on edge. Sure, he and Jeff played basketball together a few times, but it wasn't as if they were buds—not that Rich would put up with one of his best friends holding Becca the way Jeff was. Time to cut in.

Rich tapped on Jeff's shoulder and smiled back at Becca who looked happy to see him. When Jeff didn't automatically let go of Becca, Rich consoled himself with getting even on the basketball court next week. "Go find your own date to dance with. Becca's with me." He'd said it as a joke, but if Jeff had waited another second to respond, it would have been no laughing matter.

Jeff met his eyes and seemed to get the picture. "Sure, thanks for the dance, Becca."

Becca took Rich's hand. "You're welcome."

Rich pulled Becca against him where she belonged and smiled. It wasn't as if he liked dancing, well, he never had before. Becca was easy to dance with, and she followed him perfectly—dancing with her was effortless. Besides, it was the only way he could do what he needed to do: stay an appropriate length of time so they didn't look rude and still hold her. Once he had Becca in his arms, he didn't want to let her go.

He nodded to the Stewarts as they danced by. The dean seemed suitably impressed, not that Rich had any doubts that Becca would impress them. He was surprised by how much she impressed him. He'd learned more about her tonight than he'd learned in the three weeks they'd lived together. "You never told me you have a degree in finance and economics."

"Unlike some people I know, I don't go around bragging about how many degrees I have."

"Touché. What else don't I know about you?"

"That's an impossible question to answer."

"Okay, who was your first boyfriend?"

"Robby Parsons in seventh grade. He took me to a movie, his mom drove, and we held hands."

"Your last boyfriend?" She gave him an exasperated look. "What? You know my last girlfriend, and I have no idea whose heart you broke most recently."

"What makes you think I broke his heart?"

"Because no one would be stupid enough to let you go."

"Rich Ronaldi, if I didn't know better, I'd swear you were trying to separate me from my panties, if I were wearing any."

"Would that be such a bad thing?" His voice was so gravely he hardly recognized it.

"Probably."

Rich danced her into a dark corner of the dance floor and kissed her again. This time he kissed her like he'd wanted to since that day he'd woken up on top of her. When she moaned low in her throat, he pulled away.

Becca's eyes were dilated, her lips swollen, and she tightened her hold and kissed him back. When she broke the kiss, she stopped dancing and stared at him, seemingly amazed.

Rich took a much needed deep breath. "What was that for?"

Becca smiled that half smile she used only on him, and his blood pressure shot up another ten points. "I changed my mind. Let's go home."

Rich was proud that he resisted the urge to pick her up, throw her over his shoulder, and run to the car or the nearest hotel. He even took the time to stop by the table, grab her shawl, and say good-bye to Dean Stewart and Emily. The coat check seemed to take an eternity, the valet parking attendant several lifetimes. Once they got in the car, Rich was incapable of keeping his hands off Becca. Fortunately, she seemed to have the same problem. The first red light they hit, he leaned over and kissed her. By the third light, she had his tie off and his shirt opened to the navel, and he was thanking God for the easy access slit in the skirt of her dress. He was having such a good time, he wasn't sure if he should pray for red lights or not. All he knew was that he'd never gotten so worked up in a car, which was amazing, considering he wasn't in the backseat parked under the Brooklyn Bridge. He was driving.

Becca couldn't remember ever making out in a car. Rich was undeniably the best kisser she'd ever locked lips with, and what he could accomplish in the sixty seconds it took for a light to change was worthy of a standing ovation, not that he let a green light stop him.

He made quick work of parking in front of their apartment and hustled her into the building before he wedged her between him and their front door while he simultaneously kissed her, untied her dress, and unlocked the apartment. Talk about ambidextrous.

Becca fell back as the door swung open, only to find herself scooped up into Rich's arms in a move so smooth, it was right out of a sappy romance. Every time she saw some guy pick up a woman and carry her off to bed, she groaned, because really, shit like that never happened in real life. She would have told Rich to put her down if he hadn't used that opportunity to suck her breast into his mouth. Not that he would have heard her since she held both his ears. He kicked the door shut, carried her to his bedroom, and sat her down while he slid her dress the rest of the way off before laying her back on the bed.

"Your sheets are pink."

He lost his jacket, toed off his shoes, and joined her. "Grayish pink. I mixed some of my socks in with the sheets when I washed them."

He was fully clothed, unbuttoned for easy access, but still, she lay there in nothing but a thong and jeweled silver sling-backs. "You have too many clothes on. Do you really own red socks?"

"Apparently." He pulled his shirt over his head, not bothering to finish unbuttoning it, before stripping down to nothing. He looked as good as she remembered. "God you're beautiful."

"Hey, that's my line." His lips quirked as he studied her; she could almost feel the visual caress. "You are too."

Rich slid her shoes off before kissing his way up her leg. Everywhere he touched came alive, leaving her incapable of thought. By the time he tugged her thong off while he nibbled her belly, kissed his way around her tattoo, and tugged on her bellybutton ring with his teeth, she'd lost her patience and her sanity. She couldn't take much more of his kind of torture. His finger slipped inside her, spreading her wetness as he tempted and teased, driving her slowly mad without giving her even the hint of satisfaction.

Becca arched beneath him, and from the shocked look on his face, surprised the hell out of him by rolling them both over. One little move, and he'd be right where she wanted him, inside her. The feel of him long and hard and pressed against her had her on the edge. It was too soon though. She had some torturing of her own to do. She kissed him as his arms came around her, grabbed her hips, and arched to meet her.

"God, you're so wet. Bec, I need a condom, baby. Hold up."

"Not yet."

"What?" When she slid down his body and nipped his shoulder, he groaned. When she wrapped her hand around his erection, he blew out a breath and cursed. By the time she'd finished tracing his stomach muscles with her tongue, he was shaking.

"Enough. Becca, I… Oh God."

Becca nuzzled his erection, licked him from base to tip, as she traced his pulsing vein with her tongue. Tasting him, she swirled her tongue around its head and sucked him deep into her mouth as he groaned. Oh man, she missed this. Rich's hand tangled tightly in her hair, as he throbbed in her mouth. She missed this power. His every gasp spurred her on. She took him deep, and he pulled her off, tossed on her back, and she found herself covered with two hundred pounds of hard, heavy-breathing man. He kissed her long and hard, drinking her in, stealing the air from her lungs. She dragged her mouth away from his. "Oh God, Rich. Please. Now. Hurry."

Rich let out an evil laugh. "What's the rush, Becca? We have all night. And tomorrow."

He kissed her slow and sweet in direct contrast to the treatment he was giving the rest of her body. She was so close to the edge when he sucked her breast into his mouth and slid his fingers deep inside her, she had to fight the urge to come. Becca grabbed the sheets as he slid between her thighs, his mouth joined his hands, and she lost the battle.

Watching Becca come was one of the most amazing things Rich had ever seen. Sure, he'd seen plenty of other women come, but he wasn't sure if he ever really paid that much attention. He was so into it, it was all he could do to keep from joining her. He watched as she rode the wave of orgasm, and he tried to make it last. He loved how she tasted, how she sounded, and the way her body reacted to his every touch. Her skin was all pink. Her eyes were wide as he drank her in just before she screamed his name. She grabbed his hair, pulled him to her, and kissed him, sucking his tongue into her mouth with such force she had him reaching for a condom and praying to God he wouldn't embarrass himself as he rolled it on with shaking hands.

Heaven was all he could think as he slid into her. So hot, wet, and tight that it stole his breath. She bit his shoulder, wrapped her legs around him, and exploded, drawing him in deeper, milking him, driving him to the edge of madness. He clenched his jaw and withdrew, trying to slow it down, make it last, because shit, he wanted to make this last forever. When he slid back into her she met him thrust for thrust, urging him on, her heels digging into his back, her nails biting into his shoulders, and when she came again he joined her, driving into her until his arms refused to hold his weight, and he collapsed, crushing her beneath him.

"God, you are so much better than Bob."

Bob? Who the fuck was Bob?

Becca smiled as she nuzzled Rich's neck, savoring his weight pressing her into the bed and the frantic pace of his heart against hers as they both tried to catch their breath. When he made a move she held onto him more tightly. "Not yet."

He pushed away, rolled off both her and the bed. When she saw his face she couldn't believe her eyes. To say he looked pissed would be an understatement.

"Rich?" With her next breath his face showed disgust mixed with something else. He trudged to the bathroom before slamming the door.

Becca pulled the pink sheet off the bed and wrapped it around her. She didn't bother knocking before she walked in on him. He had his hands on the edge of the counter and his head hanging down so she couldn't see his face.

"Do you mind telling me what the hell just happened?"

Tripod walked in, jumped on the counter, blurted out a meow Becca had never heard, and head butted Rich's arm. Rich turned on the water in the sink to let Tripod play before he grabbed a towel and wrapped it around his waist. He had yet to look at her. When he did, she wished he hadn't. If she didn't know better she'd say he was hurt. "Rich?"

"It's not often I hear the mention of someone else's name right after I make love to a woman. I suppose you think I should be happy I'm better in the sack than some poor schmuck named Bob?"

She had no idea what he was talking about, but whatever it was, it was a big problem. "Huh?"

"I think the exact quote was 'Oh God, you are so much better than Bob.'"

Becca covered her mouth with her hand trying to hold in her laughter, but it spilled out anyway. "God, I'm sorry. You don't understand—"

"What's not to understand, Bec? What do you think this is? A freakin' Olympic sporting event? What was my score?"

She got a grip on her laughter, not that it was a funny, ha ha laughter; it was a nervous laughter. "I'd give you a 9.5 but only because you screwed up the dismount. Rich." She took a step toward him, and he stepped farther away. "Bob isn't a person."

Rich quirked a brow at her, crossed his arms, and gave her a look that dared her to fuck with him.

"B. O. B. My Battery Operated Boyfriend." Her face was on fire, and she couldn't make herself look him in the eye. Becca never blushed before, and she certainly had no trouble talking about sex. Until now. She forced herself to meet his glare.

He didn't look like he was going to break something anymore. He looked more shocked than mad, then he let out a laugh and grinned. "Christ, I'm sure glad I'm better than a fucking vibrator. I can't believe you were so surprised. It's not like that's much competition."

"I beg to differ. It's been two years since I found any man more attractive than Bob with a set of weak batteries."

Rich pulled her into his arms and tilted her head up so she looked him in the eyes. "We're talking a vibrator, right? Not some weird life-like doll or something?"

She nodded.

"Well, either you have met some real duds, or you've got incredibly high standards."

"Probably both."

"Only a 9.5, huh?" He ran a finger from the base of her throat down to where the sheet met her breast.

"You gotta admit the dismount was lacking. But if you make it up to me, I'll consider changing your score."

He crowded her against the counter and nuzzled her ear. "Ah, I do love a challenge."

Rich awoke with his stomach growling. He was starving, but he wasn't sure what exactly he was hungry for. He held Becca in his arms, his hard-on pressed against her. Still, a man needed sustenance, and since he noticed that Becca hadn't eaten much the night before, chances were, she needed to eat too. He slid away from her. The movement encouraged Tripod to belt out his morning request for wet food. All it took was any sign of life, and the little bugger started in. "Shhh." Rich didn't want Tripod to wake Becca so he got up, and without taking the time to dress, ran to the kitchen to feed the cat.

While there, Rich decided that bringing Becca breakfast was a great idea. She'd be suitably impressed.

After all, Rich had never before brought a woman breakfast in bed so it had to mean something, plus, it would take away any excuse to leave said bed until afternoon, which, when you came right down to it, was probably the reason some guy came up with the idea in the first place.

He grabbed a couple of mugs from the cupboard and filled them with water, measured out a heaping teaspoon of instant coffee into each, and stuck them in the microwave. While he waited for them to heat, he took his stash out of the pantry. The last bag of Stella Doro biscotti. The microwave dinged. He stuck the bag under his arm before taking the two hot mugs out of the microwave and carried them into the bedroom.

Rich set Becca's coffee on her bedside table along with the biscotti and sat beside her, pushing her long choppy bangs out of her eyes. "Wake up, sleepyhead."

Becca grumbled something.

"Come on, I brought you breakfast in bed."

She cracked her eyes open, pushed herself onto her elbow, and took the cup he handed her. "Thanks."

He opened the bag of biscotti as she sat. "The breakfast of champions."

When Becca took a sip of coffee and made a face, Rich tried his to make sure it was okay. "Shit. Hold on." He took the coffee away. "I didn't heat it enough."

"You microwaved coffee?"

"Yeah, it's instant. You know, stick a heaping spoonful of instant in a cup, fill it with water, and microwave for a minute. I guess it takes longer if there are two cups. I never did two cups before."

"Lucky me."

Loud banging came from the front door. "I'll get it. You stay right where you are." Rich pulled on a pair of jeans. "Okay, okay, I'm coming. Keep your shirt on." He opened the door to Mike and Nick. Mike stepped in wearing sweats and carrying a basketball. "Hey, did you forget we're playing this morning?"

Rich rubbed his stubbled chin before scratching his chest. "Yeah, I did. Look guys, it's not a good time. I'll catch you next week." He tried herding them out the door when Mike pushed by him.

Tripod ran out of the bedroom followed closely by Becca wearing nothing but a sheet. "He's making a run for it. Close the door!" She stumbled over the sheet and came very close to losing it completely. Rich pulled her behind him as Nick slammed the door before Tripod found freedom. Mike stayed deadly silent, though when a guy looked the way he did, words were superfluous.

Nick grabbed Mike's shoulder. "Come on, bud. Time to go."

Mike shrugged off Nick's hand and stood toe-to-toe with Rich. "You're sleeping with my little sister?"

Rich didn't see much point in denying it. "Yeah, so? You're sleeping with mine."

"I married Annabelle."

"Not until after you knocked her up."

Mike moved forward. Nick grabbed him, and Becca pushed Rich out of the way. "Stop it Mike." She pounded on his chest. "You have some nerve walking into my home and talking about me as if I'm not even here. News flash: I can sleep with whoever I want."

Rich heard that, and before he could stop himself, turned her to face him. "The hell you can."

Rich had seen Becca mad more times than he cared to remember, but he'd never seen her like this. "You—" She pointed to Mike. "Need to leave before I hurt you. And as for you—" She poked Rich in the chest. "Remember what I said about Bob?"

"Yeah."

"I lied."

Rich fucked up. With his luck, Becca was probably calling every man she knew just to show him she was capable of sleeping with anyone she wanted. Like Rich didn't know that. Christ. He wasn't an idiot, and he sure as hell wasn't blind. All he needed to do was somehow get them back to the place they were five minutes before Mike and Nick showed up.

Rich heated the coffee and knocked on her door.

"What do you want?"

Rich opened the door and peeked in. She was lying on her new bed wrapped in his pink sheet looking gorgeous. "To have breakfast in bed. I heated up the coffee, and I'll split the biscotti. Can I come in?" For some reason, a pissed-off Becca was really attractive. Her eyes sparkled, her skin glowed, and knowing she wore nothing under that sheet had Rich reminding himself he had to concentrate on something other than sex if he ever wanted to have it with Becca again.

Becca shrugged and pulled the sheet wrapped around her higher, tucking the end tightly between her breasts.

He sat beside her, set their coffees on the table, wrapped his arm around her, and went in for a kiss. She pulled her mouth away so he kissed her neck instead.

"You think you can come in here, offer me bad coffee and a bag of store-bought biscotti, and I'll forgive you for being an ass?"

Rich took her earlobe into his mouth and nipped it. "No. I figured I'd have to say I'm sorry for what I said to Mike. But I have to tell you Bec, I have a real problem when it comes to you sleeping with other guys. What happened last night was real and had absolutely nothing at all to do with my job or your art."

She scooted away from him. "Right. Tell me that if it was Gina at the benefit with you last night, we'd be together."

Well, shit. "Gina and I broke up weeks ago."

"Yeah, but you were doing your darnedest to get her back. Don't try to deny it. I have the charred underwear to prove it."

"Okay, fine. But when I did meet with her that night, I was thinking about you. I was thinking about how you're the one I want to be with. I like spending time with you, even outside of bed. You fit me better."

Becca crossed her arms. "How much does that have to do with me bailing you out of a mess with your boss?"

"As much as you sleeping with me had to do with Emily wanting to see your work."

She moved forward so they were almost nose-to-nose. "I never slept with you for any reason other than I wanted to."

"Yeah, well me too. I've wanted you since the day I first saw you. You, on the other hand, disliked me on sight."

"I didn't like the way you treated Annabelle. She isn't a child, and she hasn't been for a long time."

"I'm her big brother. I'm supposed to take care of my little sister."

"Right, so you agree with Mike coming in all pissed off because I slept with you?"

"No."

Becca picked up her coffee, took a bite out of a biscotti, and around the cookie in her mouth said, "Then you're a hypocrite."

He was tempted to lick the crumbs off her lip. "I am not. I was just checking out the guy sniffing around my little sister. After I realized he wasn't a putz like Johnny, I left him alone. It's not like I threatened to break Mike's kneecaps or anything. Besides, if a guy isn't willing to deal with a woman's family, he's not into her enough to be sleeping with her."

"Easy for you to say."

Rich took a sip of his coffee and watched her over the rim of his cup. "Meaning?"

"Nothing."

"That nothing means something."

Becca looked at him as if he was crazier than usual.

"It's one of the nine words women use. You know, like fine, whatever, don't worry about it, and nothing." She didn't say anything. She stared at him like a shrink would a psych patient in Bellevue. "In woman-speak 'nothing' means this is something big, and you'd better stay on your toes, or you'll get into a fight. The fight will probably end with the word 'fine,' which means you're totally screwed, and you should shut up."

"What does 'whatever' mean?"

"It means fuck you."

Becca ran her hands through her hair, leaving it
sticking up a little. She looked at him so sternly. The
fact she wore nothing but a pink sheet and had her hair
sticking up changed the picture from scary to adorable.
"Where do you get this stuff?"

Rich shrugged. "I read it in an email once. But
after years of studying psychology, I've found it to be
completely accurate."

Becca let out a long sigh.

"Uh oh. That sigh means you think I'm an idiot, and
you think you're wasting time arguing with me about
nothing. Which brings us back to the fact that 'nothing'
means something, so you might as well just tell me what
it is so we can deal with it. Then, if you don't end up
sighing again, we can get right to the make-up sex."

"Did it say that in the email?"

"No, I'm only taking this forward to a logical, yet
positive, conclusion." Rich waggled his eyebrows and
grinned, but the way Becca looked at him, he might as
well have given her the one finger salute.

"Positive for whom?"

Rich pulled the sheet from between her breasts.
"Both of us. But you'd better hurry up and tell me
what the problem is. We have a lot to do today, after
the make-up sex that is." He unwrapped her like a
present, took the coffee out of her hands, and laid her
back against the pillows. "You really need to start
talking, Becca."

Her phone rang, and before he could stop her, she
grabbed it and checked the caller ID. "It's Annabelle."
She pulled the sheet around her as if Annabelle would
see her as she flipped open her phone.

Becca knew this was coming, and she wasn't looking forward to the conversation, especially having it with Rich lying beside her. He definitely wasn't taking the hint that he should leave.

"I was wondering how long it would take for Mike to tell you."

"Not long. He's in a state."

"That's too bad for him. But Annabelle, I don't need a keeper."

"You surprised him, Bec. Give him some time. He'll be fine. Eventually. You and I are another matter entirely."

"It's not like that. Rich and I are just, you know."

"Having sex? Yeah, I'm familiar with the concept. I'm just shocked. You haven't had a date in like forever, and now you're sleeping with my brother?"

"Can we talk about this some other time?"

"He's there, isn't he?"

Becca just nodded and handed the phone to Rich. "Hi, Princess. Becca can't talk right now. We're in the middle of a quasi-fight. I gotta say though, I'm looking forward to the make-up part."

Becca couldn't hear what Annabelle said, but she could imagine it involved a death threat. Mike wasn't the only one who was idiotically protective.

"Uh huh, sure. She'll call you later." Rich flipped the phone shut. "There, I got rid of her." He turned off her phone and handed it back. "She's not expecting your call until much later."

Rich stood and finished off his coffee. "Come on, we've wasted enough time, and if we're going to leave, we better get a move on. It's a long drive." He took her hand and pulled her to her feet. "We'll talk in the shower and on the way."

"Hold on. Where are we going?"

"To pick up your art. Come on Bec." He tugged the sheet from around her forcing her to pirouette. "You gotta keep up with me, babe. I don't have all day to explain this stuff. You said yourself we have to get your work out of storage, and today is as good as any. I guess since you're not talking, the make-up sex is gonna have to wait."

"I don't need you—"

He kissed her, silencing her. When he sufficiently scrambled her brain, he smiled. "Of course you don't need me, but you'll appreciate my help. I promise."

Becca let out a frustrated breath. She really hated when he took advantage of her lack of ability to think when he kissed her. It was becoming a habit. He led her, naked, to the bathroom, started the shower, and pulled her in alongside him. She'd never showered with anyone before, well, not since she was two years old, and she and her brother used to bathe together. She didn't remember it, but she'd seen pictures—not that it counted. What the heck was she supposed to do with this huge hunk of man in a little tub? He pulled her close and spun her directly under the shower. Before she knew it, he'd switched places with her, had shampoo in her hair, and was well into the lather part of lather, rinse, repeat. Only Rich added a massage to his list. "Oh, God that feels good."

He worked his way down, massaging her neck, shoulders, and back. By the time he turned her around to rinse, she didn't know if she was more relaxed or turned on. The two had seemed diametrically opposed until now.

Becca wiped the water from her eyes and opened them before grabbing his shampoo. "Your turn."

"Nope. I'm not finished with you yet." He picked up the bar of soap and started lathering it in his hands. He pulled her back to his front and began washing her chest.

All the air shot out of her lungs as he teased and pulled on her nipples. His hard sex was cradled in the crack of her buttocks, and his breathing was affected. "Okay, you'd better hurry up, and tell me whatever you need to."

"Huh?" His hands moved lower, dipping in and out of her bellybutton, sliding down her hips and back again. He might as well have been a nervous sailor the way he avoided the Bermuda triangle.

"Talk to me, Becca."

She rested the back of her head against his shoulder and arched her back, pressing her bottom against him. "Okay, sure. Where are the condoms?"

"No, baby. Not before we talk."

"What the hell do you want to talk about?"

"What you meant before when I said a guy who is sleeping with a woman should be willing to deal with her family."

The pleasantly turned on feeling disappeared with the water down the drain. She turned, looked at him, and shook her head. He put her in a no-win position. "Just because we're sleeping together doesn't mean we necessarily need to have a relationship beyond sex."

"Okay, you're right. I've had sex without a relationship before. But you and I do have a relationship beyond sex, we're friends, and we're partners. We're in this thing together."

Becca took as large a step back as she could in the tub and eyed him warily.

"You still want Emily to see your work, right?"

"Yes."

"Then that makes us a team. You and I working together to accomplish a goal." Rich took her hands and pulled her back against him, under the water.

"Our goals are different." Becca couldn't believe how thick Rich was being. He just got shot down, and he still had an erection.

Rich nibbled on her shoulder, moving toward her neck. "Yes, but they are dependent on us working together. Without that, neither of us is going to succeed."

"But our goals have nothing to do with our sleeping together."

Rich stepped away, water suddenly hit her back. "Bullshit. We have a relationship, we have sex, we have conversation, we have a lot of things."

She turned and looked him in the eye. "We're pretending to have a relationship. There's a difference."

"When you agreed to pretend to be my girlfriend, that was true. When you and I made love, all the pretending went right out the window."

"No it didn't."

Rich looked as if his head would explode. "So you'd sleep with anyone?"

She took a deep breath. No need for both of them to lose their tempers. "You know that's not true."

"Oh, okay. You don't sleep with anyone in two years except me, and it doesn't mean anything."

Becca raked her bottom teeth against the side of her thumb before she let go of it and pointed it at him. "It doesn't mean any more than you sleeping with me after just getting dumped by your last girlfriend."

Rich smiled. "Would you feel better about us if I hadn't had another girlfriend in two years?"

"Yes." She looked at him and caught her mistake. "No. I…"

Rich wrapped his arms tightly around her, drawing her close, and kissing her. He made love to her mouth, crowded her against the cold tile, and pressed his erection against her, leaving her squirming.

Rich released her mouth as he picked the condom packet off the shower caddy behind her. "I want you, Becca." He whispered in that deep gravelly voice that made her melt. "But I only make love to women I'm in relationships with. What's it gonna be?"

"Sex?" She tried to kiss him back, but he pulled away.

"Don't split hairs. Either you're with me, or you're not."

She shook her head. "Then no." She pulled the edge of the shower curtain open and got out of the suddenly cold water, grabbed her towel, and ran back to her room.

Chapter 10

"Shit." Rich put down his razor and did his best to blot the blood running down his neck while wondering what the hell he was going to do about Becca. One minute she was hot, wet, and ready, and the next she told him no and climbed out of the shower. "No" was not a word he heard often, and certainly not one he liked.

He tied a towel around his waist as he walked out of the bathroom, and without knocking, opened the closed door into Becca's room. "You can't just say 'no' and walk out."

"You're wrong. I can and I did." Becca wore her old ratty sweats and was torturing a big hunk of what looked like clay. She slammed it on an old wooden table in the corner of her room, picked it up, and slammed it down again.

Rich took a deep breath, crossed his arms, and leaned against the dresser. "So that's it. You're going to ignore everything between us?"

"The only thing between us is a lie."

"No it's not, and no matter how much you pretend it is, it's not going to work. Why don't you tell me what the hell you're so afraid of?"

She pushed the rolled sleeves of her faded green sweatshirt higher and pounded on the clay. "Let me get this straight. Just because I don't fall in line and buy into your little convenient scenario, I'm afraid of something?"

Rich laughed. "Babe, there is nothing convenient about you. Nothing whatsoever. And believe me, if all there was between us was sex, I wouldn't bother."

Well, that stopped her. She looked over her shoulder at him and swallowed.

"I'm going to get dressed. If you want to go like you are, that's fine. But in case you want to change, you better get a move on."

She checked her wardrobe as if she didn't remember what she'd thrown on before she took out her anger on that poor defenseless piece of clay.

"Huh?"

"We're going to pick up whatever art you want to show Emily. Remember?"

"I can do it myself."

"Right, I'm sure you'll fit a whole hell of a lot of your work in that little Roadster you buzz around in. Get real." He turned and walked out, leaving the door open. "You have five minutes."

Rich refrained from slamming the door and left his open just to tempt her. He muttered to himself while he pulled on his clothes. He found himself muttering a lot since he met Becca. She drove him crazy and not always in a good way, though he had no complaints about the way she drove him crazy last night. No. No complaints at all.

Rich knew what it felt like to pretend. Hell, he spent his life pretending to be the perfect son, pretending to be the perfect professor, and even once or twice pretending to be the interested boyfriend. When it came to Becca, Rich wasn't pretending, and from her reaction to him, neither was she. There was no pretending incredible sex.

Meaningful sex. There was no pretending when it came to making love.

If anyone was pretending anything, it was Becca pretending that it was nothing more than a means to a mutually beneficial end. The hell with that. He'd play along for now, but somehow he'd prove her wrong. He had no idea how he'd do it, but he would. Maybe just being cooped up together for a whole day would do the trick. Since that was about the only thing he could think of, he'd go with it. She was smart. She'd figure it out in time. He just hoped she'd figure it out quickly because this pretending shit was getting really old.

Rich took his phone off the charger and speed-dialed his mother. "Hi Mama. Look, I can't make it to dinner tomorrow."

"What do you mean you can't make it? What are you doing that is so important that you will snub your family?"

Rich sat on the bed and pulled on a sock. "Eh—I'm going to miss Sunday supper. That's not a snub to the family so don't break my chops, Ma. I have to help a friend move."

"So you'll come by on Monday and pick up your food?"

"No, Ma. I'm good. I started cooking a little for myself."

"What? You don't know how to cook. You can't cook."

Rich pulled on his boot. "I can too. It's not rocket science, Ma. Thanks for the offer, but I'm cooking for myself, and I even did a couple loads of laundry." He didn't bother telling her that he dyed half of it and incinerated the other.

"You got a girlfriend cooking and cleaning for you. It's that Becca your sister is so fond of. You're living in sin with her. Your Aunt Rose said she was staying there—"

"Mama. Stop. I'm not living in sin." Well, at least not as much as he'd like to be. "But a man's gotta know how to take care of himself. A very intelligent woman once told me that no matter how wonderful a mother you are, you don't like doing my laundry."

Rich expected his mother to deny it and was surprised when she didn't.

"Richie, you feeling okay?"

"I'm fine, Ma, but I'm running late. I gotta go. I'll talk to you later in the week. Bye."

For an SUV, the Highlander was tiny. Rich took up all the space, and even with the sunroof opened, most of the oxygen. Becca opened the book she brought along, pretended to read, and did her best to ignore him. It wasn't working, but she wasn't about to share that little tidbit.

Rich cleared his throat. "Do you want to tell me where we're going? I'm heading in the general direction of Philadelphia, but it would help if I had an exact location." He took the GPS off its stand and tossed it into her lap. "If you're afraid to speak to me, you can just punch in the address."

"I'm not afraid to speak to you. I choose not to."

He turned on the radio, and the song they'd danced to last night filled the car. She switched the station. He raised an eyebrow and switched it back. "My car, my tunes."

Becca punched the address of her father's house into the GPS, handed it back to him, reopened her book, and turned as much as possible to face the window trying to ignore him.

The ride seemed interminable. She concentrated on turning the pages of her book even though she hadn't read a word. By the time they pulled into the driveway, she was ready to scream.

She directed him through the estate, past the stables, the pond, the greenhouses, and several servants' houses to the main house. She was out of the car before he killed the engine.

Rich took his time peering through the windshield at the mansion. She remembered Annabelle's first reaction, sure Rich had no doubt been exposed to more than his sister, but she doubted he'd seen anything quite like it. She always referred to it as the living mausoleum. When he climbed out of the car, he surprised her when he didn't say a word. He just followed her up the steps to the front door.

When Becca stepped inside, Madge, who had been their cook since Becca and Chip were in diapers, came running toward her and enveloped her in a hug.

"Becca, why didn't you call to say you were coming? I would have cooked something special." Without letting go of Becca she eyed Rich. "And who might you be?"

Rich held out his hand, or at least Becca thought he did, since Madge reached around Becca, and it felt as if Madge was shaking hands.

"Rich Ronaldi. I'm Becca's—"

Becca pushed out of Madge's forceful hug. "Roommate."

Rich nodded. "Right."

It didn't sound as if Rich believed it. The way Madge eyed him told Becca she didn't believe it either. Great. There was nothing worse than Madge when she thought Becca kept something from her. Madge could give Rich's Aunt Rose a run for her money when it came to knowing stuff.

"Rich is Annabelle's brother, and through no fault of our own, we got stuck sharing an apartment until the renovations are done with mine, so stop looking at me like that."

Madge smiled. "Oh, I see how it is."

Becca rolled her eyes. "No you don't. Rich and I are here to pick up some of my work. He has a big car, and I don't. We won't be staying for dinner."

Madge smiled at Rich and nodded. "Yes, Ms. Becca. Whatever you say." She turned to Rich. "So, it looks as if you're just a delivery boy."

Rich smiled back. "Yes, ma'am. It looks that way, doesn't it?"

"Madge, we're just going to get a few pieces, and we'll be out of your way."

Madge tsked. "You'd better call your father. I'm sure he'd like to see you."

Becca forced herself to smile. "I will." She reached over and gave Madge another hug and kissed her cheek. "We'll be down in a little while."

Becca was halfway up the main staircase before she looked back to find Rich hadn't followed. He was kibitzing with Madge, which was exactly what Becca wanted to avoid. "Rich, are you coming?"

He winked at Madge and took the steps two at a time. "Ah, right. We're pretending I'm a delivery boy now. You'll have to tell me when we start pretending something else so I can follow along."

Becca ignored him and kept walking.

The only thing keeping Rich from gawking at the crystal chandelier and the hand-carved woodwork and the massiveness of the place was that he was too busy gawking at the way Becca's ass looked in the jeans she'd changed into. He thanked God that she did have a few pieces of clothing that actually fit her rather spectacular body that, for some reason he'd yet to discover, she worked so hard to hide. He followed her up the stairs to the third floor and down a long hallway. He waited for her to open one of the closed doors they passed, but she strode to the end and then up another set of stairs. These stairs weren't as wide and not carpeted. They curved like the steps into an old basement, only they led to the fourth floor.

"These are the servants' stairs. Not that the servants live up here anymore. All of them have their own homes on the estate, but old service quarters make great play-rooms and storage rooms. Chip and I ruled up here."

Rich walked into an attic room that looked as if it was at one time a living room. He smiled. It was black with all the different constellations painted on the walls and ceiling.

Rich stopped to take it in. "Very cool."

Becca shrugged and sat on the old leather couch, rested back, and looked up at the ceiling. "I had fun painting it. It also pissed off my mother, which was an added benefit."

Rich sat beside her and lolled his head back. "How come she didn't make you repaint it?"

Becca shrugged. "I think that was about the time she washed her hands of me."

She didn't say it with even a hint of sadness, just matter of fact, like someone would talk about the weather.

"So that tattoo you have…" He reached over, slid the hem of her shirt up, and pulled the waist of her jeans down enough to reveal the sign of Gemini on her bikini line. The pillars framed a woman who looked like Becca dressed in a toga, reaching for a man facing away from her. Rich ran his finger across it, and Becca sucked in a breath of air in response. When he'd examined it closely the night before, he thought it was a picture of Becca and Mike. But now he wasn't so sure… "I take it you're a Gemini."

"In more ways than just one. Chip and I are twins. We were born May 29th, which made us Gemini twins."

Rich put his arm around her and pulled her a little closer. She didn't make it easy. She needed to be worn down. Wearing people down was something of a gift, so he wasn't too worried. "You don't talk about Chip much. So the tat. Did you get it about the same time you painted the room?"

Becca shook her head. "No, I got it a few years ago. I had it done after my brother died."

Rich took her chin in his hand and turned her face to his. "It's beautiful." When their eyes met, he had the feeling it was the first time she actually saw him since before Mike and Nick showed up.

He couldn't help but smile at the look of wariness he saw. "You're beautiful." He kissed her softly on the lips. Her eyes widened as he released her. "So, where are we going next on the tour?"

Becca stood to get away from him, and he followed as she tugged her top down and her jeans up. "It's not a tour. I have my work stored up here where it won't get into anyone's way."

Rich followed her down a hall and into a room that must have been thirty feet long by a good twenty feet wide. It had paintings hung and leaning against the walls, shelves and tables covered with pottery and sculpture of all sizes. Big dormers let in the light. The room was painted white, which only accentuated all the color on the canvases. "You paint, too?"

She shrugged. "Not well, but I enjoy it."

Rich laughed. "Yeah, right. Has anyone ever told you that you're your own worst critic?"

"No. They usually tell me I'm right. Everyone but you, that is."

Rich tried to take it all in. There were some pretty amateurish paintings, but some of them were nothing short of stunning.

The light from one of the windows seemed to spotlight a small bronze of a mother and child. It was very art-deco looking—the woman had long curling hair, kinda like Annabelle's. Shit, that was Annabelle. Her face anyway, and she was kissing the head of a baby who nuzzled her breast, its face hidden.

"You did this?"

Becca worried the hem of her top between her fingers. "Yeah. I made it as a shower present for Annabelle."

Rich circled the small round table, looking at it from all angles. "God, it's gorgeous. Breathtaking."

Becca shrugged. "Thanks."

"You have to bring this. Emily will love it. Besides it's nice and small."

Becca put her hand on the baby's head and slid it down its back to where it melted into the stand. "I don't know. I'm worried it might be bad luck. The baby's not here yet, and if something happened—"

"Nothing's going to happen. But if you're worried, feel free to stick it in the back of my closet. Annabelle would never venture there. Believe me."

"Her and me both."

Rich ignored the comment and moved on to the next table. It was an old, tile-covered table that held a group of five separate sculptures. There was a woman in a dress sitting with a book in her hands surrounded by children.

Becca stood beside him and crossed her arms. "I plan to have these enlarged at the foundry. The local library is building a small park on the land beside it. Once it gets closer to completion, I'll have them cast in bronze and donate them."

Rich touched the book the sculpted woman held. It was a perfect copy of one of his favorite books. "*Treasure Island*, huh?" He moved behind Becca. She was so rigid that she made a few of her statues look relaxed. He rested his hands on her shoulders and gave them a squeeze. "Will you have it enlarged to life-size?"

She bunched up her shoulders. "I'd like to. That way kids could sit with them and read."

"I think it's going to be amazing."

Becca broke away from his touch and took a bronze off a nearby shelf and set it beside the others. It was a sculpture of a life-like mare grazing while her colt nursed.

Becca turned away from him and pulled out her phone and dialed. Her body language screamed discomfort. "Daddy. Hi. I'm here at the estate to pick up a few pieces of my work."

She wandered the room as she listened. Rich followed her to a modern piece and touched the cold metal. It looked something like a wave. But when he walked around it and saw it from another angle, he wondered if it was some kind of modern rocking chair.

She turned her back to him again. "It was a spur of the moment trip. There's no need to—no, really. Don't feel as if you have to come home. Oh, okay. I'll see you in a few minutes then. Bye." She flipped her phone shut, and she certainly wasn't happy with the outcome.

Rich laughed. "You actually call your father Daddy?"

Becca shrugged. "I guess. I never thought about it."

Rich walked around the cool sculpture trying to read her and having no luck. Sometimes it's best to just ask the question. "Are you unhappy to see him for all the usual reasons, or is it specifically because I'm here?"

"I'm not unhappy to see him. It's just awkward. We'll get past it eventually, and believe me, it has nothing to do with you."

Rich bent low and tested the weight of the metal sculpture. It was lighter than he'd imagined it would be. "Let's take this too." He left it where it was, and when she moved to pick up another, Rich slid past her and beat her to it.

He let out a grunt when he lifted it. It was heavy as all get out. It only stood about two feet high, but was made out of white marble. Cool and smooth, the sculpture was of a nude woman riding astride a horse and holding its mane as it flew over a fence. He set it on a nearby table. The look of ecstasy on the woman's face was stunning. Rich swallowed. "This reminds me of how you looked last night."

Becca felt herself blush. She watched Rich's face as he studied the piece she called "Freedom." To Becca, that particular sculpture was her definition of the word, a chance to escape, to ride. Sometimes it meant riding away from something; sometimes it meant riding to something. The way she looked at it changed with her mood. But every time she rode she felt free, and it seemed as if Rich understood that. She felt like an animal being studied in its natural environment. He saw too much, read her too well, and was getting entirely too close. She felt completely unprotected, like by coming here, he'd stripped her of her shield. Shit, she knew coming here was a bad idea.

"Do you have anything to wrap these in?"

"Yes." She needed some space so she went to the storage room and took her time pulling out several moving blankets. When she returned, he was checking out her earlier work. "Do you think we can fit all the small pieces in the car?"

Rich didn't turn around. "I'm not sure, but we should be able to fit most of them. I'll put the seats down."

She'd never felt so exposed. He had a way of studying everything. He took a small piece off the shelf. "What's this?"

Becca took the less than perfect statue from him. It was the first piece she'd ever done. One of the kitchen help had snapped a picture of her feeding her colt. She turned the picture into a sculpture in clay. She fell in love, both with the colt and with the art of sculpture.

The piece was very rough; her arm was around Russet's neck as she fed him from a bottle. He was almost as big as she was. She remembered the day she'd begun work on it. Becca had learned very early to appreciate the moments of life that were perfect, and sculpture gave her a way to freeze time. An image of Rich's face—the way he looked at her the night before—flashed through her mind. A perfect moment in time.

"That's you." His voice broke through her thoughts.

She reached for the piece and pulled it from his hands. "We're not taking that."

"How come? How old were you when you did this?"

Becca went to put it back where it belonged. Hidden. "I was about twelve, I think. It's not good."

Rich pulled it back out. "You think this isn't good? Bec. It's beautiful. Heck, you were a fuckin' prodigy or something. Look at the way the two of you are leaning against each other. It's my favorite."

She laughed. "Yeah, right."

"It's you without your armor on. It's the you you hide from everyone but me."

"You are so completely arrogant it's amazing."

Rich rocked back on his heels. "It's not arrogance. It's confidence."

Becca rolled her eyes and took the sculpture from him a bit too forcefully before putting it back on the shelf.

He definitely saw too much.

"Becca?"

She turned toward her father's voice. She was almost happy for the interruption. "Up here, Daddy."

He walked in wearing his golfing attire. Heck, he had his glove still hanging from his back pocket. "Dad, you remember Rich Ronaldi, Annabelle's brother." She accepted her father's awkward hug, pulled away as soon as she could, and took a step back. Her dad and Rich shook hands.

"Nice to see you again, Mr. Larsen."

"Rich."

The look her dad gave Rich made Becca want to put an immediate stop to it. "I have to start moving my work to Brooklyn, and since Rich has a nice, big SUV, he's offered to help."

Nope, he didn't buy it either. What, did she have a sign on her forehead that said she made a mistake, let her hormones rule her head, and had sex with Rich Ronaldi, or had Mike called and ratted her out? No, he wouldn't dare.

Rich took one of the moving blankets off the stack she'd brought out earlier and folded it under his arm. "I guess I'll get started while you two visit." He picked up the largest piece and headed down with it.

"You didn't have to cut your game short."

"I didn't. I just chose to play nine holes instead of eighteen." Her father wandered around with his hands clasped behind his back. "You told me you were going to store some of your work up here. I just had no idea you'd done so much."

What did he think she'd been doing all these years? "These are only the small pieces. I have a few of the large ones in the old equipment barn. I needed to bring them in on a truck. I'm hoping to move them into the studio once it's built. Part of it will have a thirty-foot ceiling."

He nodded. "There is one piece that Colleen and I both love. It's the modern granite one you have stored in the barn. I'd like to buy it."

The shock must have shown on her face.

"If it's for sale, that is. Colleen says it belongs in the foyer."

Becca didn't know what to say. He'd never shown any interest in any of her work, much less mentioned that he liked it.

"I know how you feel about having your work displayed here."

"You do?"

He nodded, stuck his hands in his pockets, which he never did, and looked at his feet. "You never wanted it here, but it would mean so much to Colleen and me."

"Daddy, I never said I didn't want it displayed here. I just didn't want to push it on anyone. Mother always called my work dust collectors. I just assumed you felt the same."

He looked pained. "I'm sorry if I ever gave you that impression."

Becca shrugged. "If you like the granite piece, consider it a wedding gift. You are going to ask Colleen to marry you, aren't you?"

When he didn't answer, she laughed. "Maybe that'll be the incentive she needs."

Her father finally smiled a real smile. They were rare. He put his arm around her and gave her a sideways hug. "Thanks for the vote of confidence."

"Anything I can do to help."

Rich returned and raised an eyebrow. Obviously he'd caught the mood change. "I put the seats down, so all we need to do is get these downstairs."

Dad picked up one of the statues they'd gathered to take with them. "We can use the dumbwaiter, and once they get down to the third floor, just put them in the elevator."

Rich looked over the stack of blankets he held. "That old elevator still works?"

"Of course it does. What did you think it was there for? Decoration?"

Rich laughed. "Yeah, actually, I did. You have to admit, it's beautiful."

Her father laughed. "That elevator has a lot in common with my daughter—beautiful, capable, and hardworking."

Becca almost dropped one of her sculptures on her foot when she heard that one. "I'm outta here before he starts comparing me to the dumbwaiter."

With the three of them working, it didn't take long to have the SUV filled with lovingly wrapped sculpture.

Rich had everything in the Highlander; he waited in the foyer for Becca to tell him what she wanted to do next. Her father stepped out and shot Rich an intimidating stare. Rich didn't intimidate easily.

"What are you really doing here with my daughter?"

Rich pushed himself off the wall he leaned against and mimicked Larsen's stance. "Becca has the opportunity to show her work to my dean's wife, who happens to head up a small foundation for the arts—"

"If Rebecca needs money—"

Rich held up his hand to stop Larsen. "No, I don't think money is the driving force here. Becca wants to get her work shown, and Emily Stewart has the connections to make that happen. If she likes Becca's work, she'll give Becca the exposure she needs."

"I told her I could get her into one of the best galleries—"

"Oh yeah. She really loved that idea."

"You have some nerve judging me."

Rich shrugged. "I'm not judging you, but if you haven't noticed, every time someone offers to help your daughter with anything, she shuts him down. She won't let me even help her rearrange her furniture."

"I have no idea where that independent streak came from. Certainly not her mother."

"I've got an idea. It was nice seeing you again, Mr. Larsen." He shook the man's hand. "Tell Becca I'll be waiting in the car."

Rich opened the door and skipped down the steps. No wonder he and Becca understood each other and got along so well. They were alike in so many ways. They both spent their life having people do everything for them, which sounds nice at first, until you see that people either won't allow you to do things for yourself or think you're incapable. Rich rebelled, got into trouble, and was finally sent to military school. It looked as if Becca escaped into her art.

When Becca joined him outside a few minutes later, she looked no happier than she had that morning. She stepped beside him and leaned against the car facing into the cold wind. "Rich, I'm sorry to keep you waiting. I know you want to get home." The temperature dropped, and a wall of clouds moved in. She hugged her jacket to herself.

He pulled her close to him and wrapped his arms around her. "I'm in no rush. Why the long face?"

She cuddled closer; he couldn't help but smile.

"I got a call from a friend. I guess Dad was at the club when I called, and well, word spread. A few of my friends are meeting at The Big Easy. It's a restaurant and bar not far from here."

"You want to go?"

Becca shrugged. "I know you probably have things to do…"

Rich opened the door for her. "We do have to eat." He helped her in, walked around to his side of the car, and got behind the wheel. He started the car and turned around the circular drive. He got to the gatehouse where the driveway stopped. "Which way?"

It's amazing how much a person can learn about another after only a few weeks of living together. Rich knew from the set of Becca's shoulders and the way she rubbed the cuff of her jacket between her thumb and forefinger that she was nervous. He didn't know why, after all, she still held a good bit of mystery. The look on her face screamed she wasn't into sharing.

Rich tried for a supportive smile as he held the restaurant door open. Music spilled out along with the sound of conversation. The place was crowded, which was probably typical for a Saturday night. Becca stopped and scanned the room. He knew the second she'd spotted her friends by the plastic smile she wore and the way she raised her chin in acknowledgement. When he followed her line of sight, he saw a dark-haired woman waving.

"I see them."

So did Rich. He put his hand on the small of her back as he ushered her across the bar to the four or five tables Becca's friends had pushed together and surrounded.

Introductions were made and measurements taken. Several of the guys wore matching rugby shirts as well as the bruises from a recent game. Rich didn't catch many of the names. What he did catch was the shimmer of tension like heat off a desert highway in July at noon. That was pretty hard to miss, and it wasn't only coming from Becca.

The women surrounded Becca and did that air-kissing thing. Becca hugged one of the biggest of the rugby guys the same way she hugged her brother, but it was the way he hugged her back that had Rich wanting to give him a smack upside the head.

"Tristan, this is Rich Ronaldi." She stepped closer to Rich. "Tristan and I grew up next door to each other. He and my brother, Chip, were best friends."

Rich nodded, but didn't like the guy on sight. He didn't know if it was the way rugby boy looked at Becca, like he was undressing her with his eyes, or the way he looked down at Rich as if he'd just stepped in something. Probably it was way he looked at Becca, since Rich couldn't give a shit what this bozo thought of him.

The dark-haired woman, Kendal, pulled Becca away and whispered something in her ear while staring at Rich. It probably would have been a good idea if Becca had told him what he was supposed to be pretending now. Becca was more tight-lipped than usual, which only served to stir everyone's curiosity. It took awhile for everyone to settle down and make room for the newcomers. Rich rubbed the back of his neck and surreptitiously looked around for a server. Unfortunately servers were scarce, and Rich was thirsty.

He leaned over and whispered in Becca's ear. "I'll go get us drinks. Be right back."

She smiled at him and returned to her conversation.

Happy for a reprieve from the weird vibes coming from Becca's friends, he made his way to the bar and signaled the bartender, content to listen to the guitarist play a Beatles tune, while he checked out the beer taps. He turned to see the other set of taps and caught the rugby boy approaching. Rich nodded an acknowledgment and wished the bartender would hurry up. When she noticed what's-his-name, she came right over.

"Hi, Tristan. What can I get you?"

Tristan. Right, that's his name.

Tristan leaned over the bar and smiled at her. "My friend was here first. It's Rich, isn't it? What'll you have?"

"Yeah, thanks. I'll take a Grey Goose dirty martini, a pale ale, and whatever he's having." She nodded and turned away, obviously knowing Tristan's drink.

They watched in silence as she poured and delivered the drinks.

Rich took a sip and then pulled his wallet out of his pocket.

Tristan set his beer back on the bar. "So, Rich. Is Becca all right?"

Rich looked back over at Becca. She seemed fine to him. "Yeah, why wouldn't she be?"

"After what happened, I'm surprised to see her back here. I mean, going through something like that's got to be devastating, not to mention social suicide."

The only thing that Rich knew of that must have been devastating in Becca's life was her brother dying, but it wasn't as if that had happened yesterday. It had been a few years. As for social suicide, Rich knew Becca well enough to know that she had the social aptitude of a diplomat. He'd seen her in action. He crossed his arms and without a word dared Tristan to continue.

"I'm talking about Becca losing the entire estate and half her trust fund to her father's bastard son just a few months ago. It wasn't surprising when she turned tail and ran to New York. The only surprise is her having the guts to show up back here as if nothing happened."

Rich calmly paid the bartender and thanked her. He tucked his wallet back into his pants and motioned for Tristan to move closer. He put his hand on the guy's shoulder and brought his mouth close to his ear, so as not to be overheard.

"A couple things you should know. First is, that bastard you spoke of is my brother-in-law and one of my best friends. The second is that Becca found him and welcomed him into her family. Unlike you, she is not ruled by money or the whims of the social elite who have nothing more pressing to do than sit around pronouncing judgment on their so-called friends." He released the guy's shoulder when he realized how hard he'd been gripping it. "Obviously all your money and your position in *The Social Register* haven't given you what you really need: manners. Now excuse me, I'm going to take Becca her drink."

Rich turned back to the bar to get the drink and found Becca already sipping her martini. She had her mask firmly in place, which made Rich want to rearrange

Tristan's face. A broken nose and jaw would be one way of giving the man a little character. "Hi Tris. I see you and Rich are getting to know one another."

Rich wrapped his arm around Becca and kept his mouth shut.

"Becca. I was just telling Rich—"

"That I turned tail and ran. Oh, and I committed social suicide. My my my. You sure make my boring move to Brooklyn to be closer to my brother and sister-in-law so much more interesting than it really was. I know you see work as a four-letter word, but if you should ever decide to do something useful with your life, you might want to try writing fiction. You seem to have a real gift."

God she was sexy when she completely deflated someone. Maybe it was the regal way she held her head while delivering the final blow. Rich considered the differences in their styles and decided he'd much prefer cleaning the asshole's clock, but then Becca's way did have some advantages. Every time she got that queen-of-all-things look about her, Rich's pants got tight.

Becca finished her drink, slipped an olive between her lips, and slid it off the toothpick. Rich couldn't take his eyes off her mouth. She chewed, swallowed, licked her lips, and set the glass on the bar before taking his hand. "Let's go say good-bye to everyone and then go home."

Oh yeah. He definitely liked the sound of that.

Chapter 11

BECCA SHRUGGED HER JACKET ON AND WALKED OUT OF the restaurant into the stark cold and away from her world. Well, she thought, that was a bit dramatic, but no less true. She never fit into that world, but still, it was what she knew, what she spent most of her life rebelling against, and today, what she'd finally put behind her.

Rich had held the door for her with one arm and wrapped his other around her as she walked through. She tilted her head until it rested against his and took a deep breath, soaking in the comfort he offered.

When they reached his car, instead of opening the door, he pinned her against it and kissed her. She was expecting a pity kiss, but when her eyes met his, she saw no pity there. She saw need, hunger, urgency, and something else she was unable to label. It whipped around them like a live wire, and as his mouth met hers, the shock of it stole her breath. The taste of Rich mixed with the bitterness of the beer he drank and the rage of emotion that bubbled within him was as sharp as his teeth against her lips and tongue as he ate her mouth.

Rich pulled away, and breathing heavily, he stepped back and scrubbed his face with his hands. "Jesus, I'm sorry."

Becca almost melted onto the pavement. If he didn't look as shaky as she felt, she'd have taken offense. Still, since she was unable to speak, all she could do was raise an eyebrow.

"It's that queen thing you do. It turns me on so much I can't control myself." He inched closer to her and pushed her hair out of her eyes. "You were amazing in there. I would have preferred to make it so he spent the next six weeks eating through a straw, but I enjoyed watching you decimate him."

"Happy to entertain."

Rich did a double take. "You didn't let that asshole upset you, did you?"

Becca took a shaky breath. "Assholes, plural. And no, I didn't let them upset me. I don't know why I'm surprised they turned on me. I've seen it a hundred times before."

Rich looked like a cartoon character just before its head blew off. "I got the weird vibes, but I didn't know they—"

He turned as if to stomp back and take them all on. She caught his hand to stop him. "It's okay. They just saw most of the money they thought I had, half my trust and the entire estate, go to Mike. Since they don't have much in their lives except their trusts and their estates, they're suffering from 'there, but for the grace of God go I' syndrome. They're afraid it might be catching. After all, if it could happen to the ultra uptight and respectable Larsens, it could happen to any one of them." She looked into his very confused face.

"So that huge windfall that Mike was given—"

She shook her head. "He wasn't given anything. The trust and the estate are Mike's birthright."

"But still, if you hadn't found him, all of that would be yours."

Becca shrugged.

"And you still told your dad about him?"

When she looked into Rich's eyes, she expected to see the same disbelief and in more than a few of the people she'd once thought her friends, the same disgust. Instead she saw pride and what looked like admiration. She wasn't sure she was comfortable with that either.

"He's my brother. I wanted him in my life and in my father's life. I love him."

"You didn't know him."

"I didn't need to. I already lost one brother. I'd give the world to get Chip back. How could I ignore the one brother I still had?"

Rich pulled her to him. "Bec." He almost sounded hoarse. "You're doing that queen thing again. What's it gonna be? Are we going home, or are we going to the nearest trashy hotel so I can make love to you all night without having to be in pain for two hours beforehand?"

Becca pulled away from him and climbed in the car. "I choose door number three. Let's go to a nice place I know. It's a B&B with room service. That way we can have breakfast in bed, and it might actually be edible."

Rich closed the door and walked around the car, gingerly sat, and turned to face her. "Hey, I'm working on the breakfast in bed thing." He looked longingly out the side window. "But Bec, the trashy hotel is right across the parking lot."

She laid her hand on his fly, pressed against his erection, and squirmed in her seat. The way he sounded made her melt. Okay, it was way more than that. It was the way he looked at her and saw all of her, even the messy parts, and seemed to think they were okay. It was the way he was ready to do damage to anyone he thought would hurt her, but let her handle the situation on her own. And it was the way he wanted her. God help her, she wanted him too. Bad. "I guess you better drive fast then."

"God, you're killin' me here, Bec."

"There's a nice place just a couple miles down the road. I'll make it worth the wait."

Rich pulled up in front of the B&B and left the engine running. "You wait here, and I'll see if they have any rooms available."

Becca shrugged "I don't mind coming in."

He kissed her quick and pulled away. "Yeah, but I'll have a really hard time keeping my hands off you. I'm hoping that little cottage over there is free."

"It's a carriage house."

"That's just a snooty way of saying garage. Frankly, I'd rather stay in a cottage than a garage any day, but I want to be as far away as possible from other people. I love making you scream."

"Okay, but Rich?"

"Yeah?"

She squirmed a little more. "Hurry."

His face split into a grin that shone in the dashboard light just before he got out and jogged up the front steps of the main house.

Becca tried to remember what underwear she had on. She peeked and was glad she wasn't wearing an ugly sports bra because when she got dressed that morning she was so mad, the last thing she thought about was sleeping with Rich Ronaldi. Killing him, sure. Having wild monkey sex, not so much. Making love to him, never.

So much had changed, but she wasn't sure what caused it. Maybe the forced confinement made her open her eyes to what was going on between them. He had a way of holding a mirror up to her and not only making her look at herself, but telling her what he saw in that mirror too. She let out a laugh. The first time she met him she thought he was no deeper than a puddle. She never thought she was one to jump to conclusions about people, but she sure did with Rich, and that fact embarrassed the hell out of her. He must have thought she was just like Kendal, Tristan, and the rest of the crowd they'd just walked out on.

She was wrong to tolerate her friends' behavior over the years, but she never acted like them. Today her friends crossed the line. It was one thing when they started with the pity comments about her losing the estate. She couldn't really care less about that or her diminished net worth—not that they or anyone but the IRS knew what it was. When they asked how it felt to go slumming and talked about Rich the way they'd always talked about her mother's men, that was when she'd lost her temper.

Rich opened the door, got in, and tossed a key in her lap. "Wanna tell me what that look is for? Please say you just got off the phone with your worst enemy because I don't think I could handle it if I did anything to piss you off."

"No, I'm not mad at you. I was just thinking."

He slid his hand up her back, wrapped it around her neck, and pulled her toward him for a long, deep kiss. "Bec, I want to hear all about what you were thinking later. But right now, I want to take all your clothes off using nothing but my teeth, starting with that cute little top you're wearing."

"Oh." She swallowed hard. Thank God they were only fifty feet from the carriage house.

Rich pulled up in front of the carriage house and killed the engine as Becca flew from the car and ran for the front porch, key in hand. He was right behind her. By the time she had the door unlocked, her pants were unbuttoned, unzipped, and his hand was already firmly entrenched in her panties. Incapable of moving, she braced herself against the door jamb as his other hand slid beneath her shirt and unhooked the front clasp of her bra to tease her breast. His teeth scraped her neck as he pressed the heel of his hand against her mound and slid two fingers deep inside her. Her breath froze in her lungs. His fingers, like heat-seeking missiles, came in contact with their target, and air mixed with a ragged moan ripped from her throat. Becca's short nails bit into the wood as she came apart in his arms.

Still shuddering in the wake of the most amazing orgasm she remembered, Rich licked the side of her neck, soothing the spot he'd raked his teeth over, and slid his hand from her pants, making sure she could stand on her own before nudging her inside. "It's a damn good thing it's cold out, and everyone has their windows closed. Still, we better get inside before someone calls 911."

When she turned her head to look at him, he had both fingers in his mouth, sucking on them like a five-year-old with a grape popsicle. "God you taste sweet. Now hurry up, we only have an hour before they bring dinner over, and I want you as my appetizer."

Becca was still in a post-orgasmic stupor, or at least she hoped that's what caused the fact she had to repeat what he'd said in her mind once or twice before she made sense of it. "You ordered dinner?"

He grinned as she stumbled over her own feet. It didn't help that her pants were sliding down her legs, and her ass was suddenly cold without having Rich pressed against her.

"For us and Tripod. I called Henry and Wayne and asked them to feed him. He can be scary when he's hungry. As for our dinner, I told the owners we were going to check out the Jacuzzi tub."

Becca hiked up her pants and tried not to fall on her face. "Dinner and breakfast?"

"I know, it boggles the mind. But right now, I'm more interested in sating other hungers. I'm not done with you, babe. Not by a long shot."

God she hoped not.

Rich flicked on the light switch, illuminating the small cottage. He took Becca by the hand and led her to the steps. "The bedroom is on the second floor."

She caught glimpses of warm, creamy walls and antique furniture before being nudged up the stairs. The bedroom was painted a soft celery, with gleaming cherry furniture and a king-sized canopy bed.

Rich stepped in behind and pulled her into his arms. "Thanks, Bec."

She tilted her head back against his shoulder to see his face. "What for?"

He slid her jacket off her shoulders and tossed it on the chair. "For nixing the trashy hotel idea. I don't know what I was thinking."

She laughed, pulled her sweater over her head, and tossed it in the direction of her jacket. Her bra, still undone, hung from her shoulders. She let it drop to the floor while she spun around and threw her arms around his neck. "There, does this spark your memory?"

"I want to make love to you. No one makes love in a trashy hotel room."

His eyes locked on hers, all signs of humor vanished. He stared as if he could read her mind. She wondered if he could. It would help if he'd clue her into what he saw, because right now, all she knew was what she felt. There was the ever-present lust, a fierce protectiveness of him, fear for herself, and the terrifying feeling that she'd completely lost control of her life. She couldn't choreograph this dance. He led, and she seemed to have no choice but to follow.

"You're thinking too much. Don't think, just feel. We'll deal with the rest in time. Right now, I just need you."

Need. Need was dangerous. Love didn't scare her because she could control it. Becca loved her brothers, her parents—yes, even her mother, and she loved Annabelle. But loving someone was very different from needing someone. Loving meant she cared for them and shared only that part of herself she felt safe to share.

She'd avoided needing people at all costs. Her shrink said it was due to revolving nannies and the lack of stability she and Chip suffered since birth. Maybe he was right, or maybe she just saw how weak Chip seemed when he begged for everything he needed, from love

and attention to money. Becca had vowed that once she
became an adult, she'd never put herself in the position
to need anything from anyone. She'd been extremely
successful until Rich.

The thought that she might actually need him para-
lyzed her. He had a way of taking a part of her without
her permission. It was as if he held a key she never knew
existed to the lock on the side of herself that kept safe all
she refused to share. But looking into Rich's eyes, she
knew that had changed, and she didn't know how to get
back to the safe place she'd been in just that morning.

His kiss was soft and undemanding. He didn't try to
take. He gave. He breathed life into her, and she put
herself in his hands, trusting him to cushion her fall. She
landed gently between soft sheets and hard man. Their
clothes disappeared along with her anxiety, and once she
accepted that there was no safe way to go back, she gave
into it and experienced freedom.

Rich had never felt such need to connect with another
human being. He always considered himself a good lover,
but now it seemed that everything he'd done before this
moment had just been going through the motions. Becca
was different, maybe because nothing came easy with
her. But the way she looked at him made it all worthwhile. Somehow he'd succeeded in breaking through the
wall she built to hold everyone at a safe distance.

He kissed his way down the column of her throat,
trying to keep a tight grip on the thin thread of control.
He'd been doing just fine until she wrapped her legs
around his waist. His cock met warmth and wetness,
and it was all he could do not to thrust deep inside her.
"Don't move, baby. If you do..."

She did, and Rich found out what heaven felt like. He'd never not worn a condom. His mind screamed stop. His body screamed go, and hers was already gone, drawing him deeper into the intense wet heat. Christ, it was a damn good thing he didn't know what he was missing all these years. Still, he clenched his jaw and pulled out.

He managed to speak. "Condom."

"Pill."

"Thank you, God." He kissed her as he gave into a need so strong, so essential, any finesse he may have had evaporated with his first thrust. He took her mouth with the same need. Rich swallowed her moans and breathed the air she expelled. With each moan, each sigh, each kiss and touch, she gave him more of herself. When their eyes met, hers were so clear and open the intensity shocked him almost as much as the sense of responsibility he felt to live up to the trust she bestowed.

Becca raised her hips, arched her back, and screamed his name. The intense wet heat shocked him as every muscle in her body strained, and he lost what little control he'd held as he thrust again and again and again before he let go, and together they exploded.

He wasn't sure how long he'd been lying prostrate on top of Becca, crushing her. Long enough for the both of them to have their breathing somewhat under control. He needed that to make sure he could speak. "Bec, if you haven't had a relationship in two years, why are you on the pill?"

Becca opened her eye a crack. "There are a lot of reasons a woman goes on the pill other than pregnancy prevention, you know. It keeps my periods regular and light. It also helps with cramps, and lucky for you, PMS."

"I wasn't accusing you of anything, I was just wondering." She didn't look like she believed him, but she didn't look mad either. He gathered enough energy to kiss her. Right at that exact moment, a stomach growled, but he couldn't say whose. "One of us is hungry."

She ran her hand down the length of his spine. "Probably both of us since the last food we ate were those biscotti."

"Told you that was the breakfast of champions, and you didn't believe me." He pushed himself up onto his elbows and took a deep breath. "Dinner is going to be here any minute. I'll bring it up just as soon as they deliver it."

She yawned and snuggled closer. "I don't want to let you go."

He hissed out a breath as he pulled away, and she tightened her hold. "Babe, if you don't eat, you'll never be able to keep up with me." He kissed her quick and rolled onto his side.

She rolled toward him and rested her head on her hand. "Maybe it's you who won't be able to keep up with me."

Rich grabbed his pants off the floor, pulled them on, and had a hard time tearing his eyes away from the picture she made. "God you're beautiful."

She looked well-loved, and where some women might look disheveled and worn, Becca glowed. He wanted to jump back in bed and see who came out on top. Then his stomach growled, and hunger overtook lust. Becca sat and threw her legs over the side of the bed to join him when he stopped her. "I'll be back with food. You keep the bed warm."

"You don't have to. I'm capable of going down to eat."

"God you're stubborn. Can't you give a guy a chance to impress you? I went to a lot of trouble."

She raised her chin and one eyebrow. Damn, she probably spent a year in front of a mirror practicing that look. If it didn't make him so damn hot, it would piss him off. "Okay, not a lot of trouble, but I oughta get points for trying." When he heard the knock on the door, he turned his back on her and went to get the food.

Becca heard Rich clanking around downstairs and realized that no matter what he'd said, she was going to see what he was up to. She pulled on a plush robe she found hanging in the bathroom and followed the noise and cursing.

When she found him searching the cabinets in the kitchen, she stayed in the shadows admiring the way his back muscles flexed as he moved. She still couldn't get over how beautiful he was. "What are you looking for?"

He looked over his shoulder, grinned, and then scowled. "I thought I told you I'd bring the food up?" He continued his haphazard search.

She closed the distance between them and wrapped her arms around his waist, resting her cheek against his back. "Rich, if you think I'm going to follow orders, we've got a real problem. Now, tell me what you're looking for, and maybe I can help."

"Candles. I was trying to be romantic." His tone of voice was more pissed than romantic.

Since she was still behind him, she rolled her eyes. He was such a guy. "I'll bet they're in the dining area. I'll go look."

The table was set for two, linen tablecloth, fine china, and of course, candles. The fireplace was stacked, ready for a match, and when Becca turned to take in the rest of the room, out the bay window she saw it had begun to snow—the first snow of the season. "Rich, come here. I found something."

She heard Rich grumbling, but it stopped as soon as he stepped into the room. "I told them to put the food in the kitchen. The other guy must have set the table while I tipped the one setting out the food." He looked at the romantic table. "I guess this is a better idea than dinner in bed."

He came up beside her, held her close, and joined her in watching the snow. Another perfect moment in time.

Becca kissed his neck and nodded. "How about you start the fire and light the candles, and I bring in the food?" For once he didn't argue. He was just macho enough to think that fire starting was man's work, and she was woman enough to let him.

They ate at the table since the fillets required cutting. Of course the meat was so perfectly cooked and tender, it could have been cut with the side of a fork. Rich slid the last bite of his meat through the béarnaise sauce before finishing his asparagus and potato. Becca looked down at her remaining food. "Can you eat some more? I'm getting full."

Rich reached over and stabbed an asparagus stalk. She just took his empty plate and exchanged it for hers and watched him dig in. He cut a bite of the meat and held it on the fork and looked as if he was about to say something then changed his mind.

"What?"

Rich chewed and shrugged. "I was just wondering if you were all right."

"How do you mean?"

"Well, you know, it can't be easy living as an artist. I mean, there's no steady paycheck or benefits, and without those it must be hard qualifying for loans. You probably had to put up a huge down payment for your part of the brownstone."

She didn't say anything. She let out a silent scream inside her head. NOOOOOO!

He wasn't stopping. Her lungs constricted; she was unable to expel air. She inhaled just fine, but she couldn't exhale. Panic began clawing at the edges of her consciousness.

"...I was just thinking with the market the way it is, it's not a good time for anyone. Bec, I know you won't ask your parents for help, so I just thought... I've got a pretty hefty nest egg, if you need anything." He looked up from his food. "Now don't go getting pissed because I offered. Just know it's there if you need it."

All the air that had been trapped inside rushed out with a sob. She never before felt such a sense of relief, and there was no stopping the tears. She was so embarrassed that she wanted to crawl under the table.

Rich looked terrified. Obviously, he wasn't comfortable with women who couldn't control their emotions. Not that she was one of them, but at first, she thought she'd been wrong about him, and then when she realized what he was saying, it was so wonderfully sweet, the floodgates opened. All the stress she'd been holding seemed to have taken over, and well, she was a mess.

He got out of his chair and crouched down next to hers. "I'm sorry."

She tried to speak, but it was pretty much impossible.

"Okay, I know. You want to do it yourself. Forget I said anything. It's okay." He drew her out of her chair and brought her to the couch in front of the fire before pulling her into his lap. He didn't say much. He just held her until she could stop blubbering long enough to breathe.

"Almost done?"

She nodded, her wet face moving against his bare chest.

"You want to talk about this?"

She dragged a hitched breath in and straightened. "I don't need your money, but thanks."

"Baby, I don't want to pry into your finances."

"Then don't."

He lifted her off his lap and sat her down on the couch before he went to clear the table. Shit, she was a bitch. Here he was being so sweet, and she shut him out. It was a habit.

She followed him into the kitchen as he set the dishes in the sink. He looked as if he wanted to punch something. When he turned he stabbed her with a look. "I get it. Okay. I think you said enough."

He turned and left her staring after him. He came right back carrying more dishes. "I love you, Bec, but you sure don't make it easy on a man."

He loved her? Of course he said it while he was arguing with her, but he said it.

"...I know you think you can do it all by yourself, and believe me, I admire the hell out of you. But I'm a guy, and we're wired different. We're built to fix things, to take care of the women we love, to provide."

There he goes saying it again. She wondered if he even realized.

"We can't help it. So don't go holding the fact that I have a 'Y' chromosome against me. I understand your quirks. You gotta give a little too."

"I know. I'm not used to this. I'm sorry. I said the wrong thing."

Well, that seemed to take the wind out of his sails. "Oh, ah, okay then."

A different kind of tension filled the space his anger occupied. She searched for something to change the subject. A chocolate dessert fondue sat on the counter all ready to go. "Why don't we set all this up in front of the fireplace and have a picnic?"

"Okay."

His feelings were hurt, and he'd had his ego bruised. He grabbed the fondue pot and set it on the hearth while she followed with the tray of fruits and snacks. She knew he'd be even angrier if she told him how adorable he was. Men hate it when women think they're cute. She could just imagine what he looked like when he was a little boy getting into mischief.

He pulled her onto his lap and loosened the tie on her robe. His eyes sparkled as if he just had an amazingly naughty idea.

"Rich?"

She sucked in a lungful of air as warm chocolate dribbled onto her chest. He slid the back of the chocolate-coated spoon over her left breast and tossed it back into the pot. Oh God. Her head rolled back against his arm as he sucked her breast into his mouth and slid her off his lap onto the rug, licking, sucking, and nipping, and once he had her all cleaned off, he devoured her mouth in a chocolate-flavored kiss.

Becca couldn't wait for her turn. She tugged on the button of his jeans, and Rich didn't seem to mind her taking over. He let go of her long enough to scoot his pants down his legs and kick them away. He rolled back and looked shocked when she grabbed his cock with a chocolate-covered hand. She let the dribbled chocolate drip over the head of his dick, and then wrapped her hand around it and stroked the length of it, covering it with warm slippery chocolate.

Rich watched as her tongue slipped out to lick the bead of liquid that oozed over the chocolate. Chocolate and salt—it reminded her of a chocolate covered pretzel, which happened to be her next favorite thing to dip in chocolate. She slid her tongue around the head of his dick as Rich tightened the hold he had on her hair and cursed as she went down on him and gently rolled his balls in her chocolate-covered hand. By the time she finished lapping up all the chocolate, he was begging, and she couldn't wait another second. She crawled above him, sucking in his tongue as she slid down the length of his cock. He let out a strangled cry, grabbed her hips, and all Becca could do was hold on while he went wild beneath her. She threw her head back and ground against him, sending herself over into orgasmic bliss, screaming his name.

Rich rolled them over and continued his onslaught, rolling one orgasm into another until she was hoarse from screaming. His body tensed, and with each thrust, he exploded within her, over and over, sending her into yet another orgasm as he filled her.

"Bec, baby, are you okay?"

Becca snuggled closer to his heat, and when she moved she groaned. Her eyes shot open when he moved too, and his dick jumped within her. "Okay, you win." Her voice was rough with sleepiness. "I can't keep up with you."

"It's not a competition, baby. Just relax, and let me love you." He kissed her softly, stealing her thoughts as he made slow, lazy love to her. She'd never done that, just loved someone because she wanted to be close, not striving for completion, just trying to make her lover feel good. It was nice: long, slow kisses, the warm fire crackling beside them. Before long she was sighing, and then she was wanting, and then demanding, and then, oh God, she was coming again and again.

She heard Rich's voice as if it was echoing from far away. "Come on, Bec. Don't fall asleep. There are two perfectly good beds upstairs, and I'll be damned if we aren't going to sleep in at least one of them."

"Hmm?" Becca pried her eyelids open. She had no idea how long she'd been sleeping. "Sorry."

He pulled her up beside him, wrapped her in the warm robe, and led her to bed.

Rich slid out from beneath Becca without waking her and tiptoed down the steps to call the main house and order breakfast.

First, Rich needed caffeine and searched the cabinets for instant coffee, though the only coffee in the pantry was the real stuff, and he had absolutely no idea what to do with that.

Rich called the main house and tucked the phone under his chin.

"Good morning. This is Melody. I hope you had a nice night Mr. Ronaldi. What can I do for you?"

"You wouldn't be able to talk me through making a pot of coffee, would you?"

"Certainly, but I'd be happy to run a pot over if you wish."

"No, thanks, I'd really like to know how to do it myself, if you don't mind. Then maybe, just to be safe, you could bring a pot over with breakfast."

Rich tucked the phone between his ear and his shoulder and followed the detailed instructions. In less than a minute the coffee machine was making coffee machine noises, which he took as a good sign. It didn't hurt that it looked like coffee and smelled like coffee. He gathered cups he found in the cupboard and took Melody's suggestion and filled them with the instant hot water from the dispenser at the sink. She said it would take the chill off the cups. Rich was impressed because who thinks of shit like that?

Melody was probably used to clueless men, so she told him where to find the breakfast tray and coffee carafe, and said that a bowl of fresh fruit salad was in the refrigerator.

He leaned into the refrigerator and found the bowl. "There's yogurt there and some fresh mint. Just put a dollop on top of each serving and top it with a sprig of fresh mint. That should hold you over until breakfast arrives."

"Thanks, it looks great."

"When would you like us to serve breakfast?"

"Can you give us about an hour?"

"Certainly, Mr. Ronaldi."

Rich thanked her and figured fruit salad was a real improvement over a bag of biscotti. He found some green stuff that looked like weeds in the refrigerator. He sniffed it, hoping to hell it was mint. It smelled like chewing gum. Definitely mint. He dished out two bowls of fruit, plopped a heaping spoonful of yogurt on top, and stuck a few leaves on it. It looked pretty. After draining the hot water from the coffee cups, he set them next to the carafe of coffee and the fruit salad, and headed out. Spoons, shit. He turned back to grab a few spoons and napkins before retracing his steps.

When Rich walked in, Becca hadn't moved. He couldn't wipe the smile off his face; he'd really worn her out. Setting the tray on the bedside table, he poured the coffee before sitting beside Becca and pressing his face into the crook of her neck. He took a deep breath. God, she always smelled so good. "Becca, wake up."

"Mmmm."

The sheet fell to her waist as she sat up, shot him a beautiful sleepy smile, raised her arms, and stretched. Rich held back a groan.

"I smell coffee."

He ignored his hard-on, threw his feet up on the bed, pulled her against his chest, handed her a coffee, and then picked up his own.

She took a sip and smiled. "God, Rich, if you made coffee like this, I'd be in serious danger of falling madly in love with you."

"Really?"

"Yeah, but believe me, you have nothing to worry about."

"Nope, I'm not worried in the least."

She cocked a brow. "What's that supposed to mean?"

He took another sip of the rather amazing coffee—if he did say so himself—as he watched her mind whirl. She raised her chin—a sign she was getting her panties in a twist, not that she wore any, but it was his experience that women were more than capable of getting their panties in a twist even when said panties were hanging off a lampshade as hers were.

He grinned. "I think it means that I love you, and you're in serious danger of falling head over heels in love with me."

She looked shocked and confused, which he had to admit was way better than pissed.

"I made the coffee."

Chapter 12

RICH SAID HE MADE THE COFFEE AND TOLD HER HE PUT together a beautiful fruit salad and even thought to garnish it with mint, no less. Either Becca was the world's best Domestic God coach, or Rich was playing fast and loose with the truth.

"You're awful quiet. You're not in shock, are you?"

Becca took a sip of coffee and shook her head. "No, not shock, precisely."

Her mind raced trying to make sense of all the changes. Rich thought she was close to broke and offered her money. He said he loved her. He was amazing in bed, and if he wasn't lying, he made a damn good cup of coffee. Could it be that she'd discovered the perfect man?

Rich sipped his coffee and stirred his fruit salad. "Is there anything you want to do today before heading home?"

Becca sat straight up. "Oh my God, it's Sunday. Don't you have to go to dinner at your parents'?"

Rich removed a newspaper from a plastic bag and scanned the front page. "I called Mama yesterday and said I was helping a friend move so there's no rush. I think checkout is at noon."

She tossed the covers off her legs. "Shit, I'm supposed to meet Mike and Annabelle at ten."

He folded the paper over, seemingly unconcerned. "Doesn't look as if you're going to make it."

"Yeah, thanks. Like I couldn't figure that out on my own."

"Happy to be of help."

Becca swatted him with her pillow and scooted away. "I better call and cancel." Becca crawled to the foot of the bed and reached for her phone in her jacket pocket. Walking on her knees back to Rich, she flipped the phone open, turned it on, and saw at least a dozen messages from her brother. "Oh, God."

"What?"

"Mike's been calling me all night." She didn't even bother listening to them. "Something's wrong."

"You don't know that."

"Why else would he call a dozen times?" She hit the connect button, and Mike answered on the first ring.

"Becca, where the hell have you been? I've been worried sick. You think you can just disappear off the face of the earth and not tell anyone where you've gone?"

Becca's heart raced from its new position in her throat as she had flashbacks of Chip's death, and Mike was yelling at her. "You called me a dozen times because you were looking for me? I thought something happened to Annabelle and the baby. You scared me."

"Well good. Now you know what I've been going through for the last eight hours. Dad said you'd left yesterday afternoon, and you were going to meet friends for dinner before coming home. You never answered your cell. Rich didn't answer his either. No one knew where you were."

Becca reminded herself that Mike had, until recently, been an only child. He wasn't used to having a sibling and obviously didn't understand the fact that older siblings are not parents. She took a deep breath and spoke to him slowly. "I didn't know I had a curfew. Nor did I know I had to answer to you. I'm an adult, and believe it or not, I've been on my own since the day I turned eighteen, almost nine years ago. I'm not used to answering to anyone, and I don't plan to start now. I suggest you calm down and stop treating me like a six-year-old." Becca heard some commotion on the line.

"Becca, it's Annabelle. I'm sorry. I told him he was overreacting, and you probably just went off with Rich. You did, right?"

"Yeah. He's here."

"See, I knew you two were perfect together."

"Annabelle, I just wanted to tell you I can't make it back by ten. I'll see you tomorrow, okay?"

"Sure, just promise me one thing."

Becca ran her hands through her hair, which she realized was sticking straight up. "What's that?"

"As soon as Rich is gone, call me, and fill me in. But I really don't want specifics because he's my brother, so there's that whole ick factor. You know?"

Becca laughed. "Yes, I can totally relate."

"Just promise you'll call. I'll take care of Mike."

"You don't have much choice. You married him."

"There is that."

Becca heard the smile in Annabelle's voice. Mike might drive Annabelle crazy, but she loved him. Becca leaned back against Rich. "Good luck with my pigheaded brother."

Annabelle chuckled. "Good luck with mine."

"Thanks, I'm going to need it. I love you. I'll call you later." Becca flipped the phone closed. "You might want to ignore any messages from Mike. He's been trying to track me down."

Rich tossed his paper down and wrapped his arms around her. "Yeah, I heard. Don't worry. He'll be okay and so will Annabelle and the baby."

It was nice to hear, but it didn't stop that niggling fear she seemed to carry.

"Breakfast should be here in forty-five minutes or so."

Rich got up and walked into the bathroom leaving the door open. It sounded as if he was brushing his teeth. "What do you want to do with the rest of the day?"

Becca followed him into the bathroom, and he rinsed off the brush and handed it to her. When she looked at him funny he laughed. "Babe, we've been swapping spit for the last two days. But if you want, I can check the other bathroom for a fresh toothbrush."

"No. I just never... it's fine." Scratch that. It was weird. She'd had a lot of sex and more than a few part-ners. She wasn't a slut, but she liked sex, so when she did have a partner, she had a very active sex life. In all that time, she'd never done anything as intimate as share a toothbrush or take a shower with any of her lovers. That suddenly struck her as sad.

She put toothpaste on the brush and caught Rich looking at her funny. "I want to go home. I need to figure out what to do with my work and maybe update my portfolio." She stuck the brush in her mouth as she recapped the toothpaste and began brushing.

"Sounds good."

Becca finished brushing as Rich watched. She put the brush back in the holder, turned, and kissed him. "Thanks."

"For what?"

"For everything. This is the first time I have a chance to have my work judged on its own merit. Not because of my name, or because my dad got somebody's kid into med school, or they belong to the same country club. Emily Stewart is going to look at my work without knowing any of that. For me, that's huge."

"She's going to love it. You've got incredible talent."

"You're biased."

"Of course, but I'm no idiot. I love your work. It's a part of you."

Becca didn't know what to say to that, so she kissed him.

One thing Rich found out pretty quickly was that if he and Becca were ever to truly live together, they'd need a much larger place. He looked around the already crowded apartment, and they hadn't even emptied out half of the work they brought home.

"Where do you want this one?"

Rich turned to find Wayne holding the metal sculpture. He shrugged. "Just put it anywhere it won't be in the way for now. We'll figure it out later."

Wayne walked past Annabelle who had come to help, too, and tsked, "Don't you dare lift anything heavier than your purse." He turned and took a long hard look at her red-and-purple purse. "Come to think of it, you might want to re-think your choice there too. It's supposed to be a purse, not an overnight bag."

"I bought it to use as a baby bag. I'm trying it out to see if it'll work."

Wayne put his hand on his hip and shook his head. "That will only work if you plan on borrowing a baby to go along with it. Now stop this nonsense and enjoy carrying a little purse while you still have the chance."

Annabelle poured herself a glass of orange juice and rolled her eyes as Mike walked back into the kitchen from the mud room where he'd been checking out the fire damage. He came up behind her and took her in his arms. "Listen to Wayne, he knows what he's talking about."

"No, he just doesn't like the bag. It's two very different things."

Wayne laughed. "Sorry, Doc. But she's right. Red and purple are so last year."

Rich caught Becca looking at him funny. When he shot back the universal "huh?" gesture, she mouthed words. When it became obvious that he had absolutely no clue what she said, she walked into his bedroom and motioned him to follow. Great—just what he wanted to do with Mike watching his every move. If the look on Mike's face was anything to go by, he was not thrilled with Becca's choice in roommates or lovers. She might as well have waved a red flag in front of a pissed off bull or just gone and painted a target on Rich's back.

"Close the door."

Rich did and leaned back against it. "Do you really think this is a good idea?"

Becca hugged her arms around her. "I can't find Annabelle's present. I went to get it out of the car, and it was gone."

Rich smiled. "I'm one step ahead of you, babe. I took care of it just as soon as I found out she was on her way over from my parents' place." Rich slid the door to the closet open and pulled an old milk crate from the back. He dug through the dirty T-shirts and workout shorts. "I stuffed it in here."

"What's that on top of it?"

"Camouflage."

There was a knock on the door, and then it swung open. Mike poked his head in. "If you guys are done showing each other your etchings or… sorting laundry. We finished unloading the car, and everyone is heading to DiNicola's for supper, like anyone is going to be able to eat after lunch or dinner, or whatever your mother calls it."

Becca tossed Rich's clothes back on top of the crate covering the sculpture.

Mike gave Rich a sideways glance. "I thought this was your room."

"It is. Becca was just teaching me to sort laundry." Rich slid the closet door closed and kicked Becca's shoe under the bed. The last thing he needed was for Mike to see Becca's clothes littering Rich's bedroom.

"Nice sheets."

Rich raised his chin in acknowledgement and walked past Mike. "Yeah, that's what happens when you don't sort your laundry."

Wayne stood with his hands on his hips in the middle of the apartment and looked around. "What is Becca going to do? Start her own art gallery?"

Annabelle sipped her juice. "I've offered to take it off her hands. Lord knows, I've been trying to set up a showing for Becca for the last two years. She accuses me of nepotism. The fact that we're related has nothing to do with it, but she doesn't believe me."

Becca blew her bangs out of her eyes. "She's right. I don't believe her. If I make it in the art world, I'm not going to do it because my sister-in-law gave me a showing at her gallery. Sorry. I'm going to do it under my own steam or not at all. Besides, I have a few irons in the fire."

Annabelle gave her a questioning look, and Rich had the urge to put his arm around Becca and stand with her. He understood. He just wasn't sure if she would welcome that, or the scrutiny their relationship would receive.

Rich and Becca begged out of dinner and ordered pizza instead. He was impatient to see everyone leave, but there was no way to shoo them without it looking as if he had ulterior motives.

By the time they'd found places for all of Becca's work, the apartment looked like a small art gallery, and Rich loved it. The only problem was that there was no longer any room for Becca in the den.

They stood crammed together in the small room. Rich was never one to beat around the bush so he just tossed it out there. "Since we're sleeping together anyway, there's no reason not to move your stuff into my room. What do you think?"

She didn't say anything. Rich had heard of pregnant pauses, but he never experienced one quite like this. When he finally faced her, the only way he could describe her expression was shocked.

Okay, he knew things were a little awkward. They were both feeling their way through this new chapter in their relationship, but shit, you'd think she could say something. Leave it to Becca to make this difficult.

It was like waiting for the next act to begin. The inter-mission lasted long enough for him to take a piss and grab a beer if he'd wanted to, but instead he just watched her mind working—an amazing thing. It seemed like she mentally made her list of possibilities and crossed them off after she examined each one.

She opened her mouth as if to speak and then shut it only to double-check her list and finally took a deep breath. "But that would mean we're living together, living together."

Well duh. "Did you think we were going to go back to being platonic roommates after last night?"

"I didn't think. You told me not to."

"Since when did you start listening to me?"

"I don't know."

"And if you did listen, you'd remember I said we'd deal with all that later. So babe, it's later. Deal."

Okay, so he lost his temper. But shit, he said he'd loved her. He'd never told anyone but family that he loved them. He shocked the shit out of himself when he'd blurted it out the way he had. Forgetting she was standing in front of him, he swore in Italian.

"Are you cursing me or yourself?"

Rich sat on the edge of her bed. "Me. Look, Bec. I've never been where we are before. Lord knows, I doubt I could have found a worse way to tell you that I love you than in a fight—"

"Well, it was original, but you missed the mark if you were trying to make me melt."

"I made you melt eventually, didn't I?"

Becca sat beside him and knocked shoulders. "Yeah, and you did sleep on the wet spot."

Rich grinned. They were going to be okay. "Becca, for as long as we're together, I promise that you will never have to sleep on the wet spot."

"Ah, and I thought you weren't romantic."

While they waited for their pizza to be delivered, Rich pulled out his laptop and went through his work email. Several students had already emailed him their assigned papers; one of them was Brad. Rich opened the document. "What the hell?"

Becca looked up from her computer where she was going through slides of her work. "What's wrong?"

Rich shook his head and ran his hand through his hair. "I have this student who has been struggling. We've met several times, talked about the tests. Hell, I spent an hour last week helping him outline a paper. He just turned in the paper, and it's not the same one we outlined."

"Do you think he cheated?"

"I don't know." Rich scrolled down through the paper. It was a good paper. "Why would he write a completely different paper after outlining one with me if it wasn't someone else's work?"

"What are you going to do?"

"God, Becca. I don't know. I hate this. The kid's been trying, I've been helping him, and he's getting by. If he needed more help, I could have suggested a tutor. I guess I need to talk to him."

"Maybe he did find a tutor."

"Yeah, and maybe he bought the paper. Christ, he's a young kid. He's having a hard time adjusting to college life. If he cheated, it could ruin his whole future."

Becca put her computer down and scooted over to him. "Maybe you could give him the chance to correct his mistake. When was the paper due?"

"Not until tomorrow."

"Okay, what if you emailed him and told him you lost the email he'd sent. Ask him to resend the assignment— the paper the two of you worked on together."

"But I didn't lose it."

"I know that." She scooted toward him and took his hand. "Rich, don't you think everyone deserves one chance to correct a mistake? Don't you wish you got one do-over?"

Damn straight he did, but if he'd had one, he wasn't sure if he'd have learned from it, the way he'd managed not to learn from military school.

Becca continued. "If he did cheat, he's probably sitting there wishing he could jump into your email box and take it back. If you give him the opportunity, he might correct his mistake. He still has time to rewrite the paper. If he didn't cheat, he'll send the paper back along with a reasonable explanation."

Rich reached over and kissed her. "One do-over, huh?"

"Just one."

"Okay." Rich deleted the paper and wrote Brad a note explaining his confusion. He also asked to see Brad after class tomorrow. He hit send, put his computer down, and went to get a beer.

Becca followed him. "You're upset."

Rich shrugged, pried off the bottle top, and took

a swig. "I am. I'm there to help kids learn. I haven't figured out how to help Brad yet, but I'm working on it. If he did what I think he did, he not only insulted my intelligence, but he's given up. I thought we were a team, and he just threw in the towel."

Becca was looking at him funny.

"What?"

She shrugged. "It's good you care so much. Give Brad a chance. He might just surprise you."

Rich pulled Becca toward him. "I hope so."

On Monday morning Rich awoke slowly, and it took him a moment to realize he wasn't dreaming. Becca had her leg wrapped around him, her head just beneath his shoulder, and her hand curled under her chin. He'd never thought himself a very sentimental man, but he had to admit he'd be one lucky bastard if he had the chance to wake up like this every morning.

Last night after they ate they made love in the shower. It was in the shower that Rich realized that their apartment was so crowded with art, there wasn't room enough to stand with your back against the wall anywhere except the shower. Rich wasn't a huge proponent of sex against the wall, but after experiencing it with Becca in the shower, it was certainly growing on him.

Her clothes took up more than half of his closet, her surviving bras and underwear lay neatly beside his boxer briefs, and the first sculpture Becca created sat proudly on his bedside table. Life was good. He was tempted to kiss her awake, but after seeing the time, he thought he'd better not start something he couldn't finish.

He slid out of bed trying not to wake her and took a quick shower before dressing in the dark. With his newfound knowledge, he put on a real pot of coffee because he needed a caffeine infusion almost as badly as he needed to prove to Becca that the coffee he'd made the day before was, in fact, his. He also needed to prove to himself that his success wasn't a fluke.

After feeding the world's loudest, most demanding, and undeniably coolest cat, Rich remembered to heat the coffee cups. Since they didn't have an automatic hot water dispenser, he stuck the mugs in the microwave for a minute while he checked out what he could make for breakfast. He'd used his last bag of biscotti, and after the lukewarm reception to both his biscotti and his coffee in the past, he made the only other breakfast food he knew he wouldn't screw up. Toast. He buttered it, found a few of those little gift basket jelly jars, put them on the tray along with the coffee, and brought it to bed with Tripod bopping along beside him.

"Becca?"

"Hmm?"

"Wake up, babe. I brought you breakfast in bed."

Her eyes opened, and a smile teased her lips as she pushed herself up to sit with her back against the headboard. "You made me breakfast?"

He did his best not to stare at her bare breasts and focused instead on her eyes. "Yeah, it's real coffee—and real toast."

He took a sip of the coffee just to make sure it didn't suck. He probably should have done that before he gave Becca hers. He sighed in relief when he found it to be almost as good as the coffee he made at the B&B.

She took a tentative sip and didn't spit it out. "Thanks." Opening the jar of boysenberry jelly, she slathered it on her toast. "This was so sweet of you."

Sweet wasn't exactly what he was going for, but what did he expect? It was coffee and toast. Rich took a big bite of toast and drained his coffee. "I wish I could stay, but I have office hours in"—he checked his watch— "forty-five minutes. So I'll see you back here for dinner?"

"Okay, I have to go to the brownstone and see about the electrical permits. I don't think I'll be late, but I'll call if something comes up. Oh, and let me know what happens with Brad."

"Will do." He sat his cup on the bedside table, and Tripod walked across Becca's lap heading right for it. Rich had forgotten to leave him some. "You might want to drink your coffee before Tripod does."

"Hmmm?"

"Tripod is a coffee-holic. Make sure he doesn't burn himself." He kissed away the confusion on her face. "Have a great day. I love you." Rich didn't wait for her response because as pushy as he was, he'd wait until she came to grips with the fact she loved him. He wasn't worried. Becca might be cautious, but she was one smart cookie. Once she made her lists and checked them twice, she would come to the only possible conclusion: she had fallen ass over coffee cups in love with him. He hoped.

Becca started to say, "You, too" about having a good day, not about loving him. But she stopped. She didn't want that because she wasn't sure she did. Okay, maybe that wasn't entirely true; she wasn't sure she wanted to love him. Let's face it. The man was difficult and pushy and too good-looking for his own good. The phone rang. Becca put her coffee down and picked up the receiver. "Hello?"

"Is he gone?"

Becca leaned back against her pillows and nudged Tripod off her lap. "Yes, Annabelle. Rich just left. Your timing is impeccable."

"Oh, good. Now, tell me all about it."

"I don't know what to say. I'm still trying to figure everything out."

Annabelle let out an obviously frustrated breath. "You're going to make a list, aren't you?"

"What do you have against lists? They help me see things."

"Sweetie, lists are for organization, not for feelings. If you need to figure out your feelings, you need to talk to your best friend—i.e., me."

Becca moved to grab her coffee only to find Tripod with his head inside her cup, his ears peeking out over the rim. "Tripod, stop that, baby. Coffee isn't good for cats, no matter what Rich says." She pushed him away from the coffee, and he began licking the toast crumbs off the plate. "Your brother has been feeding Tripod coffee."

Annabelle laughed. "Yeah, that sounds like something Rich would do. Remind me never to let him babysit."

"Well, not without supervision, at least."

"Are you planning to be the one supervising?"

That's exactly what she'd pictured, but she wasn't about to admit it. "How is Mike?"

"I'm not going to let you change the subject. How

many times did you force me to talk to you when Mike and I were seeing each other?"

"Okay. You got me. What do you want to know?"

"Where were you when Mike was freaking out looking for you?"

"Rich and I met Tristan, Kendal, and the others at The Big Easy."

"God you're brave."

"Stupid is more like it. I don't know what I was thinking. It was so awful."

"Don't tell me Rich did something—"

"No, he was wonderful. It was Tristan. He actually told your brother that he couldn't believe I had the guts to show my face after losing the estate and half my trust to—excuse the expression—some bastard."

"And Rich let him live?"

"He looked like he wanted to kill Tristan, but just calmly told him that that bastard was his brother-in-law and one of his best friends and that Tristan needed to get some manners. Well, that's before I took over…"

"I'm sure you had a thing or two to say."

"You know I did. But Annabelle, I'm so ashamed. I dragged Rich there only to have them ask me what it felt like to go slumming. I swear, if I hadn't been in a public place, I would have ripped that little bitch Kendal's face off."

"I would have paid to see that. I always hated Kendal."

"Now Rich thinks I'm broke. He actually offered me money."

"We're talking about my brother—Richard Antonio Ronaldi? It must be love. Either that or he's finally gone off the deep end."

"Yeah, well, he did say he loved me. Of course, he blurted it out while he was yelling at me."

"It's the Italian way. Still, he must have meant it if he said it while he was upset. Be careful with him, Bec. I don't think he's ever said that to anyone who doesn't swim in the same gene pool with him—murky water that it is. Rich has had a lot of girlfriends, but no one he ever really cared about, at least not that I know of. Do you love him?"

"He looks at me sometimes like he sees something everyone else doesn't. You know?"

"Uh huh. I saw him trying to figure you out yesterday. He's a smart guy, Bec. He's been in psychology for how long?"

"You think he's psychoanalyzing me?"

"No, I think he's tuned into you, and he understands you, or he's trying to. Why else would he fall in love with you? It's not as if you're the most open person. You always call me repressed, but let me tell you sister, you could give lessons on the subject yourself."

"I am not repressed."

"There's a difference between being sexually repressed and being emotionally repressed. I love you, but you have to admit that you hold so much of yourself back from people."

"But—"

"I know why you do it, sweetie. And it's okay, but you can't do that with the man you love. So go ahead and make your lists if they make you feel better, but I have a feeling the deed is done. You love Rich. He loves you. Now you just have to let him in and trust he's not going to hurt you. I told him I'd have his kneecaps broken if he did."

"I figured as much."

"Becca, just try to picture your life without him in it. If what you see is your everyday happy life, then the two of you have nothing in common but hot sex. You do have that, don't you? Hot sex, I mean."

"Yes."

"Good, hot sex is an important part of a relationship. Now, if you picture your life without Rich in it, and it sucks, then I suggest you open yourself up to him and see what happens. There's really no other choice."

"There's always a choice."

"Sure, okay, you can be miserable without him, or you can take a chance on becoming blissfully happy. It's a no-brainer, sister."

Becca laughed. "Yeah, that's easy for you to say, Mrs. Blissfully Happy."

"You got that right. Jump on in, the water's fine."

"Spoken like a true newlywed. I've got to go and find some coffee *sans* cat spit."

"Okay, I'll be at home all day if you need to talk."

"Thanks." Becca hit the end button and began her day. First thing, have a cup of coffee and then make a list.

Becca poured her coffee and went into the spare room to find her notebook. She had a real thing for notebooks. It was a sickness. Every time she walked into a store, she was in danger of finding a notebook she just couldn't live without. Sketchbooks, notebooks with lined paper she used for making lists, handmade, cheap—it really made no difference. She wanted them all. She grabbed her favorite, a robin's egg blue leather Levenger Circa notebook and the matching fountain pen she spent way too much for, and got down to the business of making a list. Probably the most important list she could make.

Pros

1. Rich was an amazing lover and had no problem keeping up with her sex drive.
2. He could take direction, both in bed and when it came to household chores. Not that he was the Domestic God he professed to be, but he was trying, and that meant a lot to her.
3. He liked and supported her work.
4. He wanted her even though he thought she was broke.
5. He liked her body just as God had made it. Long-limbed, skinny, and flat-chested.
6. He put up with her eccentricities and wasn't trying to change her.
7. He said he loved her.
8. He loved Tripod. And the cat was near impossible to love.
9. He stood up for her, but allowed her to fight her own battles.
10. When she saw the fire truck outside the apartment and thought something had happened to Rich, she completely lost it.

Cons

1. He gave her cat coffee.
2.

She couldn't come up with any more cons. That was almost as annoying as the fact the pros came so easily. She'd never gotten above two or three pros with any other man she'd ever dated, and the cons were always too many to list.

Shit, Annabelle was right. Becca loved Rich, and she couldn't come up with a good enough reason to dump him.

Not that she was looking for a reason.

She didn't think she was looking for a reason.

So what if she was? She still couldn't come up with one, so that's what counted, right?

She slammed her notebook shut and threw it across the table. Now what the hell was she supposed to do? She'd never fallen in love with a man before.

Becca did what she always did. She took her mood out on clay. She dumped a huge chunk and pounded it into submission. It took forever, but she loved the process, pressing all the air out of it, softening it, the feel of it when she'd worked it until it was perfect. Annabelle always said clay was like a drug to Becca. She'd go into a trancelike state, let the clay speak to her, a picture of what could be appeared in her mind, and then she'd work to create it. The picture that entered her mind was of a naked couple, the man holding the woman in front of him, his arms wrapped around her waist. She'd leave what they were doing to the imagination of the observer. She didn't need to make a sketch. She just pictured Rich holding her and went for it. Halfway through roughing out the piece, she'd decided to give it to Rich. Maybe then he'd replace that horrid first sculpture he'd grown so attached to.

Chapter 13

WHEN RICH GOT TO THE OFFICE, HE FOUND AN EMAIL from Brad. The kid sent the paper the two of them had worked on. After class, Brad followed Rich back to his office where they had a nice long talk. Rich went through the student handbook regarding rules of conduct; they talked about styles of learning and different strategies Brad might use to study. The relief on Brad's face was evident. Becca was right. Everyone deserved a do-over. Brad's new paper wasn't as good as the first, but it was definitely his.

Rich had a smile on his face as he packed his briefcase. He couldn't wait to go home to Becca and tell her about what happened with Brad. His hopes deflated when Craig Stewart stepped in and made himself comfortable in the chair opposite Rich's desk. His face took on that faraway, philosophical expression the dean wore when he was discussing the abstract. Rich never minded the philosophical discussions before, but then he never had anyone to go home to before either.

"Emily was very impressed with Becca. We're both looking forward to that dinner we talked about."

Rich leaned back in his chair. "Yes, Becca and I are too. We're still settling in, but I'll talk to her tonight about setting a date." Rich piled up the papers left on his desk trying to give the dean a subtle hint.

"You know, Rich. I spent a lot of time in this very office."

Rich dropped the pile, sat back, and tried to feign patience.

"I worked here for years doing the same thing you're doing, and doing it well. Nothing ever came easy for me. But let me tell you son, you've impressed me. I always knew you had the skill, but it seems as if since you've settled down with Becca, things are beginning to go your way. Now that I've met Becca, I can see why. With your hard work and her support, not to mention her background and family connections, I have no question that you'll go far."

Rich sat forward. "I appreciate your confidence." Now the only one who had any questions as to his ability to play the game was Rich. Just when had he sold out to the man? "But what do you know about Becca's family?" Rich had a bad feeling about this.

"Rich, I'm sure you realize how important Becca's family is. We're talking old money. Christopher Larsen, Becca's father, is a world-renowned cardiologist and a Columbia Medical School alumnus. With Rebecca by your side, you have a fabulous future ahead of you. As a matter of fact, I just got off the phone with the president of the university. He met Rebecca at the benefit Friday night and called to tell me how impressed he was with you both. You never mentioned that Rebecca's father and the president were in the same class."

"I didn't know myself."

"Well, congratulations, Rich. The president and I both agree you're the right person for the job. Your probationary status has been lifted, and you are on the road to tenure. And if you and Becca play your cards right, I see even bigger and better things in your future."

The dean stood, and Rich followed shaking his hand. "I never thought I'd see the day when you were speechless."

Not so much speechless as nauseated. He stood and watched the dean leave, closing the door behind him. He should feel happy. He got exactly what he wanted—a permanent position.

The phone at his desk rang, "Ronaldi."

"Hey, Richie, it's Nick. Are you up for a game and a beer before dinner?"

Rich looked on the shelf where he kept his gym bag. "I have to call Becca and tell her I'll be home late."

"Ah, so that's the way it is now?"

"No, I just said I'd be home for dinner—"

"Yeah, right. I heard a lot of shit from Mike. He's not thrilled, but that's his baby sister so you can't hold it against him."

"I don't."

"Good, because he's going to be there too. Him and Vinny. You better be on your toes."

"Great, thanks for the warning."

"My pleasure. I know you can dish it out. I want to see if you can take it."

"What are you talking about?"

"I remember answering the door and getting cold-cocked by you when you thought I was messin' with Lee."

"You were messin' with Rosalie."

Nick laughed. "At least I didn't knock her up, which is more than I can say for Mike and Annabelle, and I don't remember you cold-cocking him."

Rich scrubbed his hand over his face. "I so don't want to discuss my little sisters' sex lives."

"Yeah, I get you. Just remember that when Mike is around. He's still trying to wrap his head around the fact that he has a little sister, not to mention that she's sleeping with his brother-in-law. And how weird is that? We give the term family affection an all new meaning."

"Let's just not go there."

"Works for me. So, how long will you be?"

"An hour?"

"Good. You better call Becca and tell her you'll bring home dinner. You know Vinny'll be pissed unless he sends us home with the special of the day."

"Okay. Later." He hung up the phone and grabbed his cell and walked over to the shelf to get his gym gear. "Hey, Becca, it's Rich."

"Hi. Are you on your way home?"

Aw damn, she was waiting for him. "That's the thing. Nick called and asked if I'd meet him and the guys for a quick game of hoops and a beer. I was thinking I could bring home dinner. We usually get a beer at DiNicola's anyway, and Vinny gets pissed if we don't let him feed us. Are you up for Italian?"

"Sounds good. I'm at the brownstone, so I'll go see Annabelle for a little while. I guess I'll see you when you get home."

"Love you, Bec. I won't be too long." He disconnected the call and set his briefcase on the shelf. When he got home, the last thing on his mind would be grading papers, so what was the point in pretending otherwise? Rich tossed his gym bag over his shoulder and locked the office door behind him.

Becca hung up the phone and smiled to herself. She really did need some time with Annabelle. This gave her a perfect excuse. She took the elevator down and stepped out to find Ben, Annabelle's boss, waiting by the door. "What are you doing here?"

Ben turned and smiled. He had that windblown cowboy thing going on. He wore a leather duster that didn't look like one sold on Fifth Avenue—definitely not Kenneth Cole or Cole Haan—it looked worn and rugged, like it had spent days on horseback. Between that and the real—as opposed to Prada—cowboy boots, he either just got back from Idaho or was on his way.

"Hey, I didn't think I'd see you here. I need to go over a few things with Annabelle about the gallery. I didn't know she already mentioned it to you."

"Huh?"

Annabelle answered the door and squinted at Ben. "It's really hard to believe you're the same person I worked with on Saturday. Tell me, does it feel like you're dressing up to play cowboys and Indians?" She spotted Becca. "Bec, I wasn't expecting you, but I'm so glad you're here. It's serendipitous."

Becca laughed. "Have you been reading Mike's books again?"

Annabelle ushered them in. "No, but I saw this cute movie on TV the other night. It was called *Serendipity*. I had to look up the word in one of Mike's dictionaries. It's a great word, isn't it?"

Ben shrugged out of his coat. "And one perfect for the situation."

Annabelle took his coat and groaned from the weight of it. "I guess this means you're heading home tonight or in the morning."

Ben nodded. "Have you two discussed my offer?"

Annabelle shook her head. "Becca was away this weekend. I was going to talk to her when things calmed down. I didn't realize there was a clock ticking on the deal." She looked down and rubbed her belly. "Well, except for peanut here."

Becca held up her hands to stop them from talking over her. "Hold on. First of all, don't be calling my niece or nephew 'peanut.' If it's a boy, you'll give the poor kid a complex." She took Ben's coat from Annabelle and hung it and hers in the closet. "Secondly, does someone want to clue me into this discussion instead of just talking about what I haven't been privy too?"

"Ben's offered to sell me a controlling interest of the gallery, but with the baby coming, I was hoping to decrease my work hours, not the opposite, so he mentioned that you would be a perfect candidate for a partner, and I totally agree."

Ben sat down in Mike's favorite chair and put his feet on the leather ottoman facing Becca. "I'm right. I've known you almost as long as I've known Annabelle, granted, not as well, but that will come in time. And between the two of you, you can handle the day-to-day operation. I'd be more of a silent partner."

Annabelle shot him an incredulous look, and Ben smiled, holding up his right hand as if to pledge. "I swear. I have too many irons in the fire as it is, and with my grandfather's illness, I have to take over a majority of his duties. Unfortunately, I can't do it from here. I'm going to have to spend most of my time in Boise."

Annabelle bounced on the couch with excitement. "Just think, Bec. If we owned the gallery, we could do a showing of your work, and it won't be cheating."

"Cheating?" Ben looked from Annabelle to Becca.

Annabelle nodded. "She's got this thing about her family money. She doesn't want to show her work if her family name, influence, or money got her the gig."

Ben nodded. "Ah, sometimes being filthy rich is a real handicap, isn't it? I guess it's better than the alternative, but still, it does make one question one's self-worth. I've been there, done that, got the tuxedo."

Annabelle continued as if she never heard Ben. "But if we bought majority interest in the gallery, you could show your work, put it out there, and see what the critics say. I don't care what your name is and neither do the critics. Plus, we'd be working together! It would be great. What do you think?"

Becca liked the idea—she and Annabelle had always dreamed of doing something like this, but now that they were related, it was different. "I'm not sure. You know what they say about going into business with family."

Annabelle rolled her eyes. "Becca, it won't be like that for us."

Ben cut in. "Besides, I'll be around to referee any fights. It might even be fun. We can set up a mud-wrestling pit in the back."

Becca ignored Ben's comment this time and questioned him without even reacting. "Would it be the gallery as a business or the building, too?"

"We could handle it either way. I keep an apartment upstairs. I suppose I could rent it from the partnership and handle it that way. The building is paid for, so I can hold the note, too."

Becca nodded and checked her watch. "Why don't you email me a P&L, aged accounts receivable and payable statements, a current balance sheet, and I'd like to get the current market value of the building. Once I have time to look over all that, we can get together and discuss it further."

Ben raised an eyebrow. "I guess you'll be in charge of the books if this goes through."

Annabelle laughed. "That works for me. Lord knows, I'm no good with numbers."

It was obvious that Ben had something personal to talk to Annabelle about so Becca stood. "I've got to get going. Ben, I'll look for those numbers in the next week or so?"

Ben stood too. "I'll have my accountant get right on that along with a rough deal memo, which goes over the percentages and what-have-you. It's all up for discussion though."

Becca slid into her jacket. "Of course. Okay, have a safe trip or whatever. Annabelle, I'll talk to you later." She was out the door and rushing home. She wasn't sure why, though she did want to get back to the sculpture she'd started. She loved this part of the work—at least that's what she told herself. Missing Rich had nothing to do with it.

Rich threw himself on the bench, pulled his shirt up, and wiped off his dripping face. Mike had been riding him the whole game. Rich rubbed his side. He'd been elbowed so much, he was pretty sure he'd have a bruise. At least Mike would too; Rich knew how to play dirty, hell, he played basketball at the military academy, which was populated by rich kids, who because of their parents' money, served their time there instead of jail or juvenile hall where they belonged. Rich gave it as good as he got, but stopped before it turned into a hockey game.

Nick and Mike collapsed beside Rich. Vinny, who didn't make it that far, lay on the wood floor huffing like a freight train. "I'm gettin' too old for this shit."

Nick nudged Vinny with his foot. "You're not too old. You're too fat. It's all that good cookin'."

He pushed up on his elbows, his stomach sticking up more than before. "I gotta go on a diet or somethin'."

Mike looked over at Vinny. "When was the last time you had a physical? Come to the office, and I'll give you a full workup and put you on a healthy diet."

Vinny groaned, and he got off the floor. "Nothin' personal Mike, but there ain't no way I'm dropping my drawers and coughin' for you, bud. Uh uh. No freakin' way."

Mike rolled his eyes. "Fine, if you won't see me, I'll give you the name of someone else."

Rich pushed himself off the bench and offered Vinny a hand. Vin grabbed it, and Rich had to throw all his weight back in order to get Vinny off the floor. "You might want to take him up on it. At least the diet part."

Vinny took his towel from around his neck and snapped it at Rich.

"Christ, Vin. Cut that shit out."

They all lumbered into the locker room to shower and change and then tossed the ball back and forth between them on the way to DiNicola's. Rich spun the ball on the top of his finger only to have Mike knock it away. That was the last straw. Mike had been in his face since they hit the courts, playing dirty, trying to push him around, and Rich had pretty much ignored it, until now. Rich took both hands and shoved him, hard. "What the fuck is your problem?"

"You're my problem." Mike shoved Rich right back. "I don't like the way you're taking advantage of Becca. She's not just some convenient piece of ass."

Vinny and Nick stepped in and separated them, which was probably a good thing, since Annabelle would have killed Rich if he'd beaten the shit out of her husband like he wanted to.

Rich half-heartedly tried to shake Vinny off. "You better take that back or so help me, I'll make you eat your words. I love Becca, you asshole. And you better hope to hell she doesn't hear you talking shit like that about her."

The three guys were silent, just staring at Rich open-mouthed.

"What?" He pulled his arm out of Vinny's beefy grip.

Mike picked up the forgotten ball and tossed it to Rich. "Dude, why didn't you just say you loved her?"

Rich tossed it back to Mike, a bit harder. "I told her. I didn't think I had to tell you. Where do you get off? When you were dating Annabelle, I didn't give you shit after I delivered the hurt-her-and-answer-to-me message. Your Big Brother technique sucks."

Mike tossed the ball back and shrugged. "Yeah, I get that. Sorry. If it means anything, I'm pulling for you and

Becca to work out. I don't want to have to go through this ever again." Mike rubbed his chest like he had a bad case of *agita*. "Fuck, I really hope the baby is a boy. If it's this bad with my sister, what would it be like with my own daughter?"

Vinny groaned. "It's hell. The first time Mia looks crossways at a guy, it's off to the convent with her."

Rich dribbled the ball. He'd never thought about it with any of his other girlfriends, but the idea that Becca would be with someone else was enough to send bile up the back of his throat. He'd never thought he was the possessive type. He was wrong. Becca was his. He just wished like hell that she knew that. Shit, no wonder he'd always avoided serious relationships. All this bullshit had him questioning why he bothered, then he remembered the way he felt when he wasn't with her, how he couldn't stop thinking about her, the great sex, the way Becca looked at him that made him feel like freakin' superman, how she challenged him, made him laugh, and the way she touched him without realizing it. That's what made it all worthwhile. At least he hoped to hell it did because if it didn't work out, he wasn't sure he could let her go. He couldn't imagine his life without her, or maybe he was just afraid to. "Christ. Come on, I need a drink."

Vinny watched his boys toss the ball around just like old times while they made their way to the restaurant. Only back then, he was in much better shape and could take on any one of these bozos. Today, when he had to hold Rich back, he was thankful Rich wasn't too angry. He really was getting too old for this shit.

Mike seemed to have gotten his head out of his ass about Richie diddlin' his little sister. And poor Rich looked as if he just got hit upside the head with Cupid's sledgehammer. Vinny could almost see those cartoon birdies flying circles around his noggin. The poor guy had it bad, and as much as Vinny wished him well, he wasn't sure about that Becca chick. She wasn't like any woman he'd ever known. Though, really, how different could she be? Okay, she grew up rich, but she didn't live that way. Not if she was livin' with Richie Ronaldi she didn't.

Vinny opened the back door of the restaurant and took the ball away from Nick and set it on the shelf inside the door.

Nick walked into the kitchen. "Hey, Nino. We're gonna be in the back room. You want to put together dinner for two for all of us to take home? Make mine a big one. I skipped lunch."

Nino grimaced. "I suppose you want me to pack up some of my meatballs for that dog of yours too."

Nick grinned. "You know how much Dave loves his doggie bags."

Nino tuned on the whole crowd. "All of you, get out'a my kitchen." He turned his eye on Vinny. "Eh, when you're off, it'sa my kitchen, so don't give me no shit."

Vinny held up his hands. "Did I say anything?"

The four of them headed straight for the bar. Vinny poured beers and set a bottle of Jack Daniels and glasses on the bar tray. "Come on."

He led the way, sat at his personal table, poured two fingers of Jack into each glass, and passed them around. When he was finished, he raised his glass. "*Saluté.*"

All the guys raised their glasses. Everyone seemed to have recovered from their game, except maybe Rich, who looked stricken, but Vinny didn't think it had to do with the game or even with Mike giving him a hard time. He saw hints of a problem from the moment he'd joined them, but now that he wasn't playing b-ball, he had nothing to distract him from whatever the problem was. "So Richie. How did that big dinner thing go with your dean?"

Rich downed his Jack and chased it with beer before answering. "Great. Becca went with me, and she impressed the hell out of the dean and his wife."

Vinny sat back and rested his beer on his too-big belly. He should have poured himself a light beer. Too bad he couldn't stand any of them. "So you got what you were after then. You proved you're a stable kinda guy, in a serious relationship, and that you're not gonna end up doing something—what was it you did at Dartmouth? Oh right, you were screwing the dean's daughter. Yeah, that's enough to get your ass fired."

"Hey, I wasn't fired. I resigned. I wanted to come home."

Vinny watched Rich cave under the pressure of three sets of knowing eyes.

"It's true, but I'll admit that the dean did everything possible to make my life miserable. Still, you don't need to make it sound as if Darcy was fifteen. How was I supposed to know she was off limits? It's not like she wore a sign around her neck or anything. She never mentioned who her father was, she didn't have the same last name, and she certainly didn't look anything like him."

Vinny nodded. "I guess it's an easy mistake to make.

So you got it all now, eh? A nice girlfriend you're in tight with, a stable job. Everything you ever wanted."

Rich shrugged. "Yeah, yay me."

Nick rocked back on his chair, and Vinny shot him a look that had all four chair legs hitting the floor in a split second. Nick took a sip of his beer. "What's the problem?" He checked his watch. "Look, my wife is waiting, so I don't have all night to listen to you whining before getting down to the issue."

"I'm not whining. It just doesn't feel right."

Mike set his beer down on the table with a thunk. "You having second thoughts about Becca?"

Rich shook his head. "Hell no, I'm having second thoughts about my career. The dean came to me and said he was impressed with my work and with Becca. What should it matter who I'm sleeping with—not that Becca's not the best thing that ever happened to me. But I'm not a better professor because I've got her. I mean, maybe I am. But how would you feel if Annabelle was one of the reasons you got a job?"

Mike nodded. Nick tossed his Jack Daniels back. After exhaling and taking a slug off his beer he wiped his mouth with the back of his hand. "What do you want to do? Frankly, I've always been surprised that you're teaching at the college level. I thought you wanted to teach kids. Kids you can make a difference with. At least that's what you talked about when we were young."

"You mean when I wasn't stripping cars?" He and Nick both laughed even though neither looked as if he were having much fun. Rich shrugged. "I guess I got into psychology looking to do just that, but when I was working as a doctoral candidate, I started covering a few of my professors' classes and enjoyed teaching. I'm good at it. I don't actually remember ever thinking, 'I want to be a college professor.' I just fell into it."

Nick rocked back in his chair. "Do you like it?"

Rich shrugged. "I guess. I like teaching, I like the research, I hate the politics, and I wish I was making more of a difference in my students' lives. But I guess you can't have everything."

"Nothing says you have to stay a college professor. You could teach middle or high school, or, with your background in psychology, you could be a school counselor. Hell you could even open a private practice, couldn't you?"

Rich shrugged again, and Vinny had a feeling there was more to this story.

Nick continued, oblivious to the signs. "I guess it depends on what you're looking for. You can make a huge difference in kids' lives, but it doesn't pay as well or have the same caché as being a professor at an Ivy League university."

Rich looked into his glass as if he wondered who drank it. "I guess. I never considered that."

Nino came through the swinging double doors carrying four grocery bags filled with food. "Dinner to go. From soup to what they say—nuts? You explain to me who eats nuts? I guess you could put them on your gelato. But still, why not antipasto to dessert?" He set the bags in front of each of them and smacked Nick upside the head. "That's for feeding that dog of yours my good meatballs."

"Eh, I pay for them. And you gotta admit, Dave

has very discerning taste. He won't eat anyone else's meatballs. Only yours, Nino."

Vinny sat forward. "Nick, cut that shit out, or Nino's gonna make sure you wear the meatballs home."

Mike got up first. "I better go feed Annabelle—she's eating for two, and lately if her blood sugar falls, she gets cranky."

Nick grabbed his bag, too. "Hmm—Rosalie always gets cranky if her blood sugar goes down. It has nothing to do with the pregnancy. It's probably just a family trait."

Nick and Mike took off for home, and Vinny sat watching Rich finish off his beer. "Something else on your mind, Rich?"

"It's just that Becca met my dean and his wife, and it turns out that Emily Stewart is the head of some art foundation and wants to see Becca's work."

Vinny nodded. "Yeah, so that's good, right?"

"It's great. This is the first chance Becca's had to show her work to someone who isn't swayed by her highbrow family."

Vinny leaned back and rested the beer on his belly again. Shit, he really did need to lose some weight. "So, what's the problem?"

"Today the dean told me how much he liked Becca, and I was thinking that's good, because Becca's great. But then he said something like her old money and high social standing makes me look better, and with her by my side, I can go far. It shouldn't matter if Becca's got a mint full of money or not. It's not my money. And why should her money make me look better?"

Vinny shrugged. He wasn't sure what to say, not that Rich would let him get a word in edgewise. Maybe that's what they call one of those rhetorical questions teachers always ask. They don't expect anyone to answer unless they're called on. Obviously, Richie wasn't calling on him. And until he had something important to say, he wouldn't interrupt. The boy was on a roll.

"I don't think Emily gives a shit about Becca's family, but if Becca thinks there's even a chance Emily's interest in her art is because of her family, she's so freakin' stubborn, she'll pull out."

"Are you gonna tell her?"

"I don't know what the hell to do. See, when my dean told me to settle down, I'm not sure if it was my dean talkin' or if it was my friend and mentor, Craig. You know what I'm sayin'?"

Vinny rubbed his stubbled chin. "Yeah, it's like when we're having a meeting here at the restaurant. I gotta tell Mona what's what 'cause I run the place, and she handles the serving staff, but she's also my wife. It gets confusing."

Rich nodded. "Exactly. If I tell Becca what Craig said, she might cut off her own nose to spite her face. And if I don't tell her, and Emily likes her work, I have to smile and make nice with Craig and pretend that I don't resent the hell out of the fact that Becca's family connections pushed me over the edge and into a tenure track position instead of telling him he can take his job and stuff it up his ass."

"Yeah, that's probably not a good thing to do."

Rich ran his hand through his hair. "If I do, then Becca's the one who's going to lose."

"Plus, it's probably not a good idea to make waves at Columbia either. Don't forget you got out of Dartmouth without much damage to your rep—"

"There was no damage."

Vin raised an eyebrow. "Don't bullshit a bullshitter. Don't tell me you left with a glowing recommendation after dumpin' the dean's daughter the way you did."

Rich poured another Jack and sipped it.

"So now you gotta figure out what to tell Becca. Then you gotta decide if you gonna play the game and stay the big man on campus. If you do, you're goin' against your nature. You were born pushing the boundaries."

"Yeah, but if I leave, then I screw up Becca's chances. I can't do that."

Vinny filled their glasses. "You're walkin' a fine line here. If Becca finds out you kept somethin' from her, that ain't gonna look good. I guess you gotta decide if you'd rather give her all the information and let her decide what to do about it, or keep it to yourself and maybe screw up your whole relationship."

"I love her, Vin. I want her to have this chance."

"Are you sure that's all there is to it? If she goes for this, then you're part of the package, aren't you?"

"What the fuck are you trying to say, Vin?"

"I'm just wondering if you're afraid to tell Becca because you're her in with your boss's wife as much as she's your in with your boss."

Vin slid his seat back, because the look on Richie's face told him he may be pummeled soon. Still, he had to say it. "If she goes for this then she's tied to you, right? Once she finds out about the whole family thing, you know she's gonna take a pass, and she won't need you anymore. So I guess the real question is if she doesn't need you, will she stay with you?"

Chapter 14

THE WHOLE WAY HOME RICH THOUGHT ABOUT WHAT to tell Becca. Vinny was right. He wasn't sure she'd stay with him, and if that didn't dent the old ego, then all he had to do was think about what the dean had said to take a wrecking ball to it.

He gave himself a mental smack upside the head. Wasn't that exactly what he was going for when he practically begged Becca to pretend she was his girlfriend? Now that they weren't pretending, it suddenly felt dirty. He was annoyed that his plan had worked.

If the president thought they were going to benefit from his relationship with Becca, he obviously hadn't heard about the new heir to the Larsen throne and that Becca wasn't as loaded as she used to be. Not that Rich knew how much Becca was worth or even cared. Well, okay, he cared, but only because he'd hate to see her not able to do what she wanted to do with her life because she needed a paycheck. But Rich made pretty good money, enough to take care of her while she worked and made her mark in the art world. He was no art critic, but he knew what he liked, and he was floored by the work she did.

He wanted that for her, which kind of freaked him out. He never thought about taking on that kind of responsibility before. But the more he thought about it, the more sense it made. If they stayed together they'd need a larger place, and the apartment she was renovating was almost twice the size of their place. Besides, she and Annabelle were putting an art studio on the fourth floor, so she'd want to be close so she could work whenever she got the urge. He supposed he could take over the mortgage. They'd have to watch the cash flow, but he'd been saving ever since he started working and had never touched it.

He tossed the idea around in his mind, which was, unfortunately, slightly addled thanks to the Jack Daniels. He wasn't sure he wanted to share a brownstone with Mike and Annabelle. Not that they would be in each other's hair. He supposed it would be like living next door. As long as Mike didn't have a problem with it, Rich thought it would be okay. He liked Mike a lot and had always gotten along well with Annabelle.

The problem would be that if he and Becca moved in together, his family would never accept the fact they were just roommates, not that he thought for a minute they bought it now. But they'd stop turning a blind eye if he and Becca moved into the new place together and made it permanent. Which meant they'd have to get married, or he'd be disowned.

The thought of being married to Becca didn't scare him as much as the thought that she might not want to be married to him.

Rich let himself into the quiet apartment, put the food on the table, and tossed his gym bag in the laundry room. He heard pounding coming from Becca's old room and went in to find her up to her elbows in a hunk of clay. Tripod lay beside it, attacking what looked like a wooden knife. He had the blunt end in his mouth, his front paws holding it while kicking it with his one remaining back paw.

Tripod spotted him before Becca did and let out one of his catcalls. She turned her head and smiled the most beautiful smile he could ever remember seeing.

"You're home." She wiped off her hands on a muddy looking rag, not that it seemed to do any good, and wrapped her arms around his neck and kissed him.

Damn, he could get used to coming home to this every day.

"Emily called a little while ago and asked if we were busy Saturday night. She said she was really looking forward to seeing my portfolio and the few pieces I brought." She pulled away from him a little, which only served to force her pelvis against his. He held back a groan as she wrinkled her brow. "Do you think we could get your Aunt Rose's lasagna recipe, or better yet, talk her into making it?"

Rich grabbed her ass, keeping her pasted against him, while trying to follow the conversation without thinking about how right this all seemed. He figured he had to be at least a little drunk to be thinking of marriage without breaking into a cold sweat. "Whatever happened to you insisting I make the lasagna?"

She kissed his neck and sucked his earlobe into her mouth. Shit, that bed beside her was looking pretty good.

"Let's just say I've come to appreciate your other talents. Besides, I can't expect a gourmet meal from a guy who didn't know to take the plastic off the cheese before cooking it, and I don't want to take the chance of poisoning anyone. That won't help either of our chances."

Nothing like dousing the flames of passion. Christ, he needed to tell her something. He just didn't know what to tell her. After drinking a beer and he wasn't sure how many Jacks, it probably wasn't the time to make life-altering decisions. But if he didn't mention that he was made a full-fledged professor, she would wonder why. Wouldn't she? That wouldn't look good. At the moment, he couldn't see the downside to telling her, but that didn't mean there wasn't one. Fuck. He should never drink on an empty stomach.

Becca tasted the beer and something stronger when she kissed Rich, and he didn't seem quite himself, not drunk exactly, but not sober either. "How much have you had to drink?"

He rocked back on his heels. "I had one beer. That I know. It's just the Jack Daniels I'm not sure of. Vinny was pourin', and then Nick—maybe, even me, I don't know."

"Did you eat?"

"No, I brought home food though. You see, I'm a good provider."

"Yeah, a real prince. What did you bring me?"

"I don't know. Nino packs up whatever. He doesn't give us much choice. But it's all good."

Taking his hand, Becca led him out of the room toward the table. Before they hit the hallway he roped his arms around her waist and pulled her back to him. He was a little drunk and a lot horny.

"Becca, you feel so good."

She loved that he always seemed to want her. One of the men in her past went so far as to tell her she might want to find another boyfriend in addition to him because he couldn't keep up with her. Rich didn't seem to have a problem with keeping up, and he certainly would never recommend that she take on another lover. It was one of the positive things she'd put on her list. She smiled as his hands ran up her torso to her breasts. He seemed to love her breasts, what there was of them, and never once mentioned having them surgically enlarged, another plus on her list. She made it to the table just as his mouth met her neck, kissing, nibbling, tormenting her while she tried to concentrate on her list. Her hands hit the table as he unbuttoned her sweater and unhooked the front clasp of her bra. She still couldn't come up with any minuses.

"Since we have to reheat dinner anyway, why don't we wait a while longer? I'm really not hungry for food."

"Me either."

He slid her pants down her thighs and kissed his way up from her lower back. Every touch sent sparks up and down her spine as he pushed her sweater over her head, so it and her bra slid down her arms, leaving her wearing nothing but her panties. Standing straighter to rid herself of the garments, she pressed her ass against him and felt nothing but Rich. She wasn't the only one who lost her pants. When had he done that? "Rich?" She kicked her pants away as he pulled his sweater and T-shirt over his head.

"Yeah, baby?"

She pushed the bag of food further down the table. "Don't you dare rip my undies. I don't have many left."

"Then I guess we'd better take them off, hadn't we?"

He kissed his way down from her neck, hitting

erogenous zones she never knew existed. He tantalized slowly. The man didn't rush. The way he nibbled her back, side, and hip while his hands skimmed under her panties, brushing against her, but not lingering, brought her so close to the edge she was sure she'd come the second he entered her.

Becca bit her lip, waiting and wanting and wishing he'd hurry the hell up. Her breath was choppy, and by the time he slid her panties down, she was pretty sure he could wring them out. Kicking them off her feet, she widened her stance, and for the first time in her life, thanked God she had long legs. She looked over her shoulder, and he slid slowly inside her. Her muscles clenched, pulling him deeper as she lost patience and pressed back against him, wanting more. He wrapped his arms around her waist. She gripped the edge of the table with both hands out, anchoring herself.

"Relax, Bec." He pulled her up to him, her back to his front. "Perfect. God you're sexy. You feel so good." His hand slid down to massage her as he slowly pulled out and thrust back into her, driving her mad. "Open your eyes. Watch me love you, baby."

Her eyes fluttered open, and he was mesmerized by their reflection in the mirror on the wall over the sideboard. "Oh." It was exactly how she pictured them together. She was amazed by the accuracy of her work as much as by the feeling that both the image in the mirror and the sculpture produced in her.

He surrounded her, his dark hand on her white breast, the other between her legs. The way he watched her, read her, and moved her took her breath away. They looked as if they belonged together, as if they fit in reality and in her imagination. He had somehow completed the picture of love she'd only just imagined. It was eerie. Whatever this was could never be put on a list. It was indefinable. It was as simple or as complex as they wanted to make it. But the one thing that could no longer be denied was that this was love. She wasn't sure if the act spurred the emotion or the other way around, but it didn't seem to matter.

"Tell me what you see, Becca."

"Beauty. Love."

"I love you, Becca."

She watched him watch her. The emotion clogged her throat; she could only nod. She closed her eyes to hold in the sudden tears that stung her eyes.

"Stay with me, Becca. I want you to see how I love you."

She tried blinking them away, but one escaped, and then another. If there was any question in her mind that she loved him, her certainty increased with the intensity of his thrusts, his breath, his moans. She met his eyes, his thrusts, his breaths, and his love. Her head rolled back against his shoulder. It was too much—the intensity of the sex, the emotion—and she let go. "Rich... oh God." She didn't bother fighting it. She came with a ragged cry, and he joined her, drawing out her orgasm and shattering any semblance of equilibrium she had.

Rich lowered her to the table, his body covering hers. She rested her hot, tear-stained face on the cool table and was in no rush to move. She was probably incapable.

"You okay, Bec?"

"No. I'm in love with you. I may never be okay again."

"You're sure? Don't tell me that unless you're sure you mean it."

"I'm sure. I even made a list."

She heard and felt Rich laugh, which sent a bunch of mini-orgasms zinging through her. God, he was still hard. She sucked in a deep breath, and he slid in deeper as he reached for the notebook that lay just beyond her head. "In here?"

"Oh God. Don't…"

"Don't look, or don't stop."

"Both." But he already had it opened to the list and was reading it.

"Since you love me, and I love you. There's only one thing to do."

Becca struggled to come to terms with the fact that he could see what she thought of their relationship in black and white. "Yeah, what's that?"

"Marry me, Becca."

Rich couldn't believe he actually proposed in the middle of great sex and on the dining room table no less.

Actually, the question of whether this was the middle or the end of great sex was dependent upon the answer. It could be the middle if she said yes, or even maybe. If she said nothing or no, it would be the end. The longer the silence stretched out, the less likely it became that this was the middle of sex and not the end. Shit.

Rich quickly figured out that the only thing worse than proposing marriage in the middle of great sex was the silence that followed said proposal.

It was too late to pretend he was joking, which he

wasn't. It never occurred to him before how much he really wanted her to say yes. It also became apparent that there was no graceful exit to this debacle. What was a guy to do? Pull out and walk away leaving her spread out on the table like a buffet? He really should have planned this, but he wasn't a planner. That was Becca's job—she was the planner. She was the list maker.

Since he had to do something and after her lack of an acceptance the only thing he could assume was that Becca's answer was a resounding "no."

Becca lay there stunned on the table, unsure of what to do or say. He shrank away literally and left her unable to move, not knowing what to say to stop the downward spiral they were caught in. She heard a door shut and tried to wrap her mind around what just happened.

Marriage? Could he be serious?

She'd just told him she'd loved him, and he proposed marriage? Who does that?

Only Rich.

Shit, she should have expected this. It was just like him to jump into the deep end of things without looking where he was going or even thinking about the aftermath.

She took a deep breath, made sure her feet were under her, and stood. Oh man. He'd picked up her clothes, folded them, and set them on the chair beside the table. She had a feeling she'd just let something wonderful slip through her clay-covered fingers. Her lungs seized, and panic took a firm hold. Had she lost him? Was that the end?

"Rich?" She turned and went to their room. She thought about knocking and then refused to give him the opportunity to deny her access. By the time she got up the guts to open the door, he'd dressed in an old pair of sweats and a T-shirt. He looked at her with vacant eyes.

"I'm sorry." She noticed her nakedness and wished she had a robe to throw on, but of course, she didn't. She grabbed his lucky shirt, which was still hanging off the footboard of the bed, and threw it on before sitting beside him. "I wasn't expecting you to—"

"Don't rub it in. Let's just forget I said anything."

"Rich. Stop." She pushed him down on the bed and straddled him. "I'm not going to forget it, and neither will you."

He tried to push her off him, but she locked her feet under his legs. He let out a long breath, threw his arms up over his head, and lay there as motionless as a corpse. Great, now what?

She ran both her hands through her hair, the shirt she'd thrown on wasn't buttoned, and the movement left the shirt open. He didn't even notice. He wasn't looking at her. She buttoned it as quickly as she could. "Jesus, would you at least look at me?"

He grimaced first, but he opened his eyes. Once he did she reached for his hands, lying over him so they were nose-to-nose. She smiled when she felt his body react to hers. "I love you, Rich. I'm sorry I hurt you. I didn't mean to, but I just got to the 'I love you' stage. Obviously, you're way past that. You've got to give me some time to catch up at least."

He cleared his throat. "So, what? You couldn't have said that then?"

Fine, he was being belligerent. What a typical male response. She made a mental note to add number two to her list of cons. "Okay, I can see we're not going to be able to deal with this until after you've stopped sulking. So go right ahead. After you're finished with your I-am-man-hear-me-grunt theatrics, and you're ready to come out of your cave, let me know."

He flipped her over so fast, she hardly knew what happened, other than the fact that she was now staring up at the ceiling and had two hundred pounds of angry man pressing her down into their bed. Damn, he was good.

He held her hands beside her head and pressed them farther down into the mattress to make a point. "Real men don't sulk, and we're not into theatrics."

"Oh, pardon me. I didn't mean to offend your tender ego."

He rested his chest against hers; their mouths close enough to kiss. "Really? Because you're sure doing a hell of a job of it. I asked you to marry me, and what did you say? Let me think. Nothing. Absolutely nothing."

"I'm saying something now, but you're being too belligerent even to hear me." She wiggled beneath him, but he wasn't budging; it definitely wasn't having the effect she wanted. Rich only pressed his body to hers. "Babe, believe me, you haven't seen belligerent." He smiled as she held back a groan.

She arched her back trying to get out from under him and gave up. It was useless. "Are you finished exhibiting your physical prowess?"

"Do you want me to be? I was under the impression you like it when I get physical."

"This isn't about sex. This is about—what you said."

"You mean when I asked you to marry me? You can't even say it, can you?"

"As I said before, it would be nice if you would give

me some time to catch up. I'm not where you are. I've never thought about marriage. There, are you happy now? I said it. I never thought about marrying anyone. Ever. It's not you, it's me."

"Ah, that's the kiss of death, isn't it? You're going to start with the whole it's-not-you-it's-me breakup talk."

"No. It's just that I've never seen a happy marriage." She could see he was about to argue, so she cut him off before he even opened his mouth. "Don't use Mike and Annabelle as an example. They've only been married for a few months. That doesn't count."

"Plenty of people are happily married."

"Name three, and not your sisters. Who else do you know who are truly happily married for more than five years?"

"Dean Stewart and Emily."

"You don't know that. I know for a fact your parents are miserable. My parents were miserable, before the divorce, that is."

"Vinny and Mona are happy and have been as long as I can remember."

"That's one couple. Anyone else?"

Rich shook his head. "No, I don't know anyone else, but we could be if we wanted to."

"How do you know?"

He shrugged and rolled off her.

Becca rolled over to her side, missing the weight of him and the warmth he always infused. She rested her head on his shoulder, wrapped her arm around his chest, and tossed her leg over him. It took him a moment, but his arms came around her. She took a breath of relief.

"Okay, I can understand why you wigged out. I'm

not like you. I don't think things to death. I go with my feelings, and I want you Becca. I don't want to wake up some morning wondering where you are. I want you with me all the time, even when you're wearing those god-awful baggy rags you call clothes and making your lists. I want you even when you're pissed at me, and I don't want to live my life without you, even when you're being difficult."

"The way you're talking makes me wonder why you bother."

"I bother because I love you, babe. I bother because being without you would suck so bad, it hurts to think about it."

Becca slid on top of him and kissed him. He felt so good, tasted so familiar, so caring yet wild, and when his tongue fought hers for control of the kiss, which quickly went from tentative to frenzied, she pulled away and kissed his neck. "Rich? Do you think we could put the marriage discussion on hold, eat, and then skip right to the make-up sex part?"

His hands slid to her hips and pulled her tight against his erection. "Only if you really can't wait to eat."

Chapter 15

BECCA SAT CROSS-LEGGED ON THE BED AND ATE HER container of goat cheese and eggplant ravioli and almost all of the grilled vegetables in the other to-go container like a starving woman. She wasn't sure if the sex or the marriage proposal was to blame for her appetite, or the thought that she couldn't possibly say something terrible if her mouth was full.

Rich leaned back against the footboard of the bed facing the same meal, watching her, and eating quietly, which was very unlike him. The man did nothing quietly. He talked during sex, and if she wasn't imagining things last night, he even talked in his sleep. He must have been dreaming of work because he got this very professional quality to his voice.

Becca wasn't about to ask what was going through his mind, because even though the sex was, in a word, amazing, Rich probably wouldn't be thinking of sex, or love, or anything any normal person would think about when someone just dropped the L bomb. No, Rich was anything but normal. He couldn't be happy that she filleted herself to tell him that she loved him. No, that wasn't good enough. Rich had to top it and drop the M bomb. She still reeled from his proposal and had no idea what to do about it or how to put the two of them back on a level playing field.

Sure, they tabled the marriage discussion for the moment. They made love, and finally ate, but the problem lurked in the background like termites eating away at the foundation of their relationship. Becca had to deal with it soon, before much more damage was done. But what could she say? She didn't know if she wanted to marry Rich. She loved him. She was happy with him so far, but marriage? Why couldn't they just stay the way they were?

Rich tossed his to-go container on the bedside table with its contents only half eaten and nudged her with his foot. "How's the construction coming along on the studio and the apartment?"

She swallowed a piece of grilled zucchini before answering. "Good. The plumbing and electrical are almost complete. The inspector is coming in a few days, and then they'll start on the drywall."

Rich took on a Mr. Darcy-esque aura, all dark and brooding. "How much longer until you get an occupancy permit?"

"I don't know. A couple months maybe. It's hard to tell. There's a lot of finishing that needs to be done." She tilted her head trying to read his thoughts. Maybe he wanted an "I Do" or nothing. "Are you looking forward to getting rid of me?"

"If I were, would I have asked you to marry me?"

Becca looked down at her container and found it empty. The veggies were all gone too. She piled the container onto the table and scooted closer to him. "You can always move into the new place with me. There's plenty of room."

Rich shook his head. "I just want to know how long I have to work on you." He finally smiled. "I'm good at wearing you down."

Becca wasn't sure what he meant by that, but she wasn't brave enough to ask. It seemed a good time to change the subject. "Are you going to call your Aunt Rose and ask if she'll make the lasagna?"

"I guess I could, but maybe you should. She likes you."

Becca fluffed her pillow and thought about getting up to brush her teeth, but that would involve moving, and she was bone tired. She yawned as she lay down. "Your aunt did tell me she'd teach me how to make it when I wanted to learn."

Rich lay beside her and pulled her close to him. "See, I knew you could handle it."

"Of course I can. That doesn't mean I should. If I have to put up with a cooking lesson from your crazy Aunt Rose, you should too."

"Are you afraid of a little old Italian lady?"

Becca thought about the last time she had seen Aunt Rose and what she'd said. "Damn straight, I am. You're not making me deal with her on my own."

"Fine. You know my schedule. Just let me know when you set it up, and I'll be here to protect you."

"Oh good." She rested her head on his shoulder and curled her fist under her chin. "I feel so much better now."

Tuesday morning Becca awoke alone. When she rolled over, she found the dishes from last night had been removed, and in their place, a thermal cup of coffee waited for her. She took a tentative sip; it was still hot and surprisingly good. Either Rich mastered the art of making good coffee, or he was paying someone to sneak in every morning to make it. Tripod butted his head against the cup and yowled. "Did Rich forget to give you the dregs of his coffee this morning, big boy?" She scratched his neck and around his ears.

Tripod answered her in the affirmative as she unearthed her robe and slid it on. "Come on then, you caffeine-deprived kitty."

Tripod followed her to the kitchen and waited as patiently as he could for her to pour a little coffee with cream into a saucer. She wasn't sure if he liked sugar, but then thought about what she was doing and almost smacked her own head. She definitely needed psychological help. Who in their right mind wonders how a cat takes his coffee? Becca supposed it was a good thing that she lived with a psych professor, though she wondered if that's why she needed the help in the first place.

When Becca had awoken in the middle of the night wondering what to do about Rich, her first thought was to call Annabelle. This was something she needed to talk to her best friend about, but the fact that her best friend was also Rich's sister put the kibosh on that. She sipped her coffee and considered all of her other friends. Unfortunately, the only other friends she had were the ones who had asked her what it was like to go slumming with Rich. Not good candidates either.

Peering into the refrigerator, Becca looked for something to make for breakfast. She found nothing enticing to eat and was about to give up when she heard Henry and Wayne above her. She could talk to Henry and Wayne. They were perfect. They knew everyone involved but weren't related to anyone, and they would make wonderful sounding boards. Relieved, she grabbed the phone and called upstairs.

Wayne answered on the second ring. "Well, it's about time you called your lowly neighbors. How are you, Becca?"

"How did you know it wasn't Rich calling?"

"We saw him leave earlier."

"Do you and Henry want to come down for coffee?"

"Sure, we'd love to. I just made cinnamon rolls. Have you had breakfast?"

"No, not yet. Do you want to bring them down, or should I come up?"

"We'll be down in a couple minutes. I've been meaning to stop by. I have a toy for Tripod."

Becca smiled. "I hope it's not catnip because he's already jacked up on coffee."

"This I gotta see. We'll just be a minute."

"Great. See you soon."

Becca looked around the apartment. Artwork covered every available flat surface. If she and Rich were having the dean and Emily over on Saturday night, they'd have to figure out where to put everything. Not to mention that she'd have to make the dreaded call to Aunt Rose and beg for help. She grabbed her notebook and started a new list. She'd just gotten down to number three when the guys knocked. She nudged Tripod off her lap, much to his loud displeasure, and let the guys in.

Wayne held a tray covered with iced cinnamon rolls.

"Hi, come on in. I made some room at the table."

The guys came in while Becca corralled the cat to keep him from running out. Wayne sat the tray on the table and gave Becca a hug before going into the kitchen and putting the kettle on. "Henry likes tea. You don't mind, do you?"

"Not at all. Help yourself."

Henry examined her closely. "Don't you look all rosy? Things with Rich must be going well."

"That's why I called. I was hoping I could talk to you guys about something. I need to bounce some ideas off you."

Wayne smiled to Henry. "I told you so. Didn't I?"

Henry took plates out of the cabinet. "Maybe we should wait until Becca actually tells us what she wants to talk about before you start saying I told you so."

Becca knew when she wasn't needed. She sat at the bar and watched as Wayne and Henry moved around the kitchen. They danced around each other as if they'd choreographed it. They both knew where everything was kept and even had a stash of Henry's favorite tea in the cupboard. She wondered how long it took two people to be as comfortable around each other as they were. Then she thought back to the way she and Rich were, and she had to admit they were getting there.

Wayne stopped at the entrance of the kitchen. "Where's Tripod?"

He held something in his hand and wound it up. Tripod trotted into the dining room when he heard his name and let out one of his catcalls.

"There you are. Look what Uncle Wayne has for you." Wayne put the toy down on the tile kitchen floor. It looked like a mechanized ferret with a big, bushy tail. It began spinning around the kitchen, and Tripod went wild chasing it. "There, that should keep him busy." He grabbed the plates and butter before coming back to the table and sat as Henry poured the hot water into a teapot.

Wayne pulled out a chair for her to sit beside him and passed her a plate. "You have our full attention. I'm dying to hear the news, sweetie. So spill."

"Wow, there's nothing like being put on the spot, is there?"

Henry sat beside Becca and calmly poured his tea. "Sometimes these things are best delved into judiciously. Take your time, honey." He took a sip and seemed satisfied. "Why don't you begin by telling us why you've turned this place into a virtual art gallery? Oh, and let me know if the pieces are for sale. I especially love that metal piece. It's really gorgeous. Actually, I think all your stuff is beautiful, but that piece speaks to me."

"Thanks." Becca laughed when she saw the impatient look Wayne shot to Henry, who just sipped his tea and ignored Wayne. She ran her hands through her hair and jumped right in. Not even Henry was going to be able to keep Wayne down for long. "The day I moved in here, Gina broke up with Rich." She threw up her hands. "It had nothing to do with me. As far as I know, she didn't even know I'd moved in. But Rich came home and began trying to get her back—"

Wayne waved that statement away. "Those two are sooo not right for each other."

Becca couldn't agree more. However, the fact that she was thrilled they saw it too didn't bode well for her ability to think rationally about the situation. "Rich's dean has been pressuring him to grow up, settle down, and become a good little professor."

Henry set his cup down and reached for a cinnamon roll. "After the way Rich left Dartmouth, it's not surprising. Not that Rich did anything too terrible. Still, dating the Dean's adult daughter and dumping her is never a good idea."

Wayne took a bite and nodded his assent.

Becca took that as a hint to continue. "Rich had an invitation to attend a benefit as a guest of his dean and the dean's wife and was expected to bring his girlfriend. When Gina refused to take Rich back, he asked me to pretend to be his girlfriend…"

Wayne laughed, "Girl, don't believe a word out of that boy's mouth. He's had his eye on you from the first moment he saw you at Annabelle's engagement party. Anyone with eyes in his head could see that."

Becca wasn't sure she believed either Wayne or Rich, since he'd said the same thing. Still, part of her wanted to sigh. Another bad sign. "I was trying to be nice, so I agreed to go with him, but when we were there—"

Henry set his cup down. "Don't tell me. The lines between fiction and reality blurred."

"Exactly."

Wayne scrubbed his hands together. "So you and Rich are together?"

"Yeah, and I was okay with that."

Wayne smacked her hand. "Okay? Come on, girl. This is me you're talking to. Rich is yummy." He smiled at Henry. "Of course, he's not my type."

Henry laughed. "Which is a good thing since you are definitely not his type."

Wayne shook his head. "Of course not, but you have to admit he is one perfect specimen of he-manhood."

Becca relaxed a bit. "He does have certain attributes. And I seriously have a thing for him. He's sweet, and loving, and he tries so hard."

Wayne nodded, took a sip of his coffee, and held his coffee cup out to make a point. "Just don't let him anywhere near your fine washables."

Becca tried not to laugh. "The thing is, well, last night he proposed."

Wayne spit out the roll he was biting into, stood, pulled Becca out of her chair, and hugged her as he jumped up and down, forcing her to jump along with him. "Oh my God! That's so romantic. How'd he do it? Tell me all the details."

Henry stood and extracted Wayne from Becca. Becca wanted to kiss Henry—talk about a soothing presence. Henry held Becca's chair and motioned her to sit. "Wayne, some things are obviously private."

Wayne smiled as he took his seat and leaned closer. "Don't tell me he popped you and the question at the same time? He did, didn't he?" Wayne was exasperated. "What is it with men? I swear it has to be something in testosterone that causes the male brain to shut down while doing the deed. Will they never learn? What did you say?"

"That was the problem. I only just figured out that I love him. It's so new. I just told him, and then he dropped the M bomb. I didn't know what to say, so I didn't say anything."

Henry leaned forward, too. "Oh, that couldn't be good."

Becca shook her head. "No, it wasn't. He took off, and well, we had a fight."

Wayne nodded, "I heard some yelling coming from down here. Thin walls, shoddy construction. But I thought you two were just enjoying yourselves, if you know what I mean."

Becca refused to go there. "Once he stopped being belligerent, we were able to table the marriage discussion, but it's still there, lurking. I don't know how else to explain it."

Both guys nodded.

"I don't know what to do now. Dean Stewart and his wife Emily are coming for dinner Saturday night, which is why I brought a bunch of my work here. Emily is the head of a small arts council, and she knows everyone who's anyone in the New York art world. She can really help my career if she likes my work, and it sounds as if she's interested…"

Wayne nodded. "But now there's this big pink elephant in the room. You don't know how to deal with Rich, and you're understandably nervous about this big dinner. Wow, you've got a whole lot going on, don't you, girlfriend?"

Becca took a bite of her roll and nodded. "Yes, and it's not like I can talk to Annabelle about it. It's bad enough that she's Rich's sister, but she's living her happily ever after with my big brother." Becca set her food down and refilled her coffee. "Is there anything worse than an Italian woman in the honeymoon stage of a relationship? Annabelle sees hearts and flowers wherever she looks, and she wants everyone she loves as happy as she is."

Henry passed her the cream. "And you're not?"

Becca took the time to fix her coffee and was thankful that Tripod had finally caught his prey. He bopped over and laid the dead ferret at her feet. She stopped to rewind it and let the toy go on the carpet off to the side of the table. Tripod went wild—he was wild to begin with, but with all the caffeine buzzing through his bloodstream, he was even more insane than usual. The guys were fascinated and gave her time to think of an answer. When their attention returned to her she took a deep breath. "I'm happy where things are. I never thought about marriage, other than to avoid it, at all costs. I'm the product of a shotgun marriage that ended badly. Hell, it was bad from day one."

Henry leaned over and patted her hand. "Becca, honey, history doesn't always repeat itself. There's no reason you can't have a happy marriage."

"I know that in here." She tapped her forehead. "But I don't think I've ever seen a happy marriage. I've only seen the miserable ones, and that makes a real impression. I can't think of anything worse than being married to the wrong person. I've never been in love before. I'm not even sure how to do this."

Wayne crossed his arms and studied her. "Never?"

Becca rolled her eyes. "Okay, I thought I was once, then I found out my mother was sleeping with him, too. It tends to leave a bad taste in your mouth."

Henry's eyes went wide. "I can understand that. I'm so sorry."

Becca shrugged away his pity—she was so over that. "I just wish I could slow things down. Get used to being part of a couple. I don't know why he had to ruin what we have right now."

"Did he?" Henry sat back and cradled his teacup in his hands. "It seems to me that he just made his intentions clear. He's obviously crazy about you. Heck, that was evident to me that day we came down to welcome you to the neighborhood."

Wayne nodded. "Rich strikes me as an evolved alpha male. And if you ask me, they're the best kind. He's the kind of man who wants to take care of his woman, but he's evolved enough to know that caring for a smart, independent woman doesn't always involve all the macho pissing match crap that drives women nuts."

Becca nodded. "I agree, but that still doesn't help me figure out how to handle all this marriage talk without hurting him. I've already done a bad job of that. I need a plan."

Henry sat forward again. "Becca, there's no way to plan affairs of the heart. The best advice I can give you is to just talk to him about it. Tell him your concerns, and let him tell you how he feels. Make sure you really listen to him, and hear what he says, and realize that what a man says is not always what he means. I wonder if there's something else going on. It sounds as if he might be afraid of losing you for some reason."

"Why would he think that? I haven't given him a reason to think I'd leave him. Just the opposite, I asked him to move into the new place with me."

"I'm sure you did, but men need to be told how much you care. As sweet as you are, Becca, you seem the type to keep your cards close to the vest. I might be way off here, but in my experience, most men don't just jump into a marriage proposal unless someone's put their feet to the fire. Find out what's going on with him."

"Do you think he might have asked me to marry him because of pressure at work?"

"No, I didn't say that. But it could be that he's afraid of losing you for a reason that's purely internal. The point is you'll never know unless you ask."

The buzzer went off, and Becca set her cup down and went to see who it was. "Yes?"

"Becca, it's Aunt Rose Albertini."

"Come on up." She pressed the door release and turned to the guys. "I'm sorry. I wasn't expecting her."

Henry and Wayne stood and began clearing the table. Henry grinned. "From what Rosalie and Annabelle always said, the old bird's psychic. She must know you need to talk to her."

"Yeah, I just hope she doesn't know anything else."

Becca opened the door to Aunt Rose who stepped in, hugged Becca, and kissed both cheeks before patting one. "See, I told you, you no stay skinny for long. I see my Richie is feeding you."

Becca looked down. She didn't think she'd gained weight.

Aunt Rose turned and saw Henry and Wayne. "Sit, sit. I just come for a rest and a cup of coffee."

Wayne stood. "I'll make some."

Aunt Rose handed Becca her twenty-ton black purse and her coat. "Nonsense. I make'a myself." She bustled into the kitchen, opened a drawer, took out an apron Becca never knew existed, and tied it around her thick waist. "You boys so nice, visiting my Becca. She gets lonely when Richie's away."

"Aunt Rose—"

Aunt Rose waved Becca away. "She don't think she needs friends or a husband." She lowered her voice. "She'sa gonna learn though. Life is nothing without love, family, and friends." She turned to Becca who had crossed her arms and was tapping her toe while she bit her tongue. "You sit. *Mangia, mangia*. Tell me how my godson is."

Becca sat. She figured it was easier that way. "It's funny you should stop by. I was planning to call you today."

Aunt Rose put coffee in the filter. "Si, I don't like'a the phone, so I came for a nice visit." She turned to the guys. "Becca and Richie are having a big dinner. They need my lasagna."

Becca sat and shook her head. "So, Rich called you?"

"Richie doesn't call unless he wants someting."

It didn't escape Becca that Aunt Rose never really answered the question, but since the hair on her arms was already standing up, she decided not to pursue it.

"When you make'a one of those lists you so good at, make'a sure you put to borrow my big espresso pot. You can't have a nice dinner wit' no espresso. Eh? I give you my special coffee. You like. And tell Richie to buy good Zoom Zoom."

Becca opened her notebook and added "espresso pot" to it. "Zoom Zoom?"

"Sure, you know, Annisette, Sambuca—Zoom, Zoom. If'a you want, I can get Maria to make'a you her tiramisu. Just don't tell her you serving my lasagna." She shook her head. "Maria don't like that I'm a better cook. But eh? What can you do?" She took a plate out of the cabinet. "Wayne, you made cinnamon rolls?"

"Yes, why don't you have some? I'll get the coffee when it's finished. Sit and rest your feet."

Aunt Rose left the kitchen, and Wayne held her chair while Henry rose. She waved him down. "Such'a nice boys."

Becca looked over her list. "Why don't I write down all the ingredients we need so I can shop and have everything here when we start cooking?"

"No, we shop together. I'll bring'a my cart. We go to the butcher, the cheese man, the vegetable stand, the bread man."

"Oh, okay. When do you want to shop? The dinner is on Saturday."

Aunt Rose took a bite of her roll. "Mmm. Wayne, it'sa so good. *Grazi*." She patted his hand before continuing. "We shop on Thursday, cook and'a clean on Friday."

Becca shook her head. "Rich and I will take care of the cleaning."

"Richie? Clean?" She looked at Henry and Wayne. "If'a my Richie cleans, it'sa either love, or he'sa crazy." Aunt Rose shrugged. "It could be both, eh?"

Wayne unsuccessfully covered his laugh with a cough and went into the kitchen, returning with a cup of coffee for Rose.

"*Grazi*." She poured milk and stirred her coffee while looking around the crowded apartment. "You and my Annabelle. Such talent and so little—how you say? Confidence?" She nodded. "*Si*, confidence."

Henry cleared his throat. "Well, it's been lovely, ladies, but I've got to get back to work, and I know Wayne has a busy day ahead of him."

Wayne nodded. "Just keep the rolls. I have plenty more upstairs."

"Thanks, guys." When Henry and Wayne reached for the dishes, Becca waved away their help. "I'll take care of everything." She stood and hugged them as she walked them to the door. "I'll bring your tray up later."

After the guys left, Becca sat next to Aunt Rose and smiled. "Why don't you just cut to the chase? You came here for a reason. Say what you came to

say and don't pretend it has anything to do with the
dinner party."

Aunt Rose shook her finger at Becca, making Becca
wonder if she should duck. She was half expecting to see
a lightning bolt fly from Aunt Rose's fingertips. "You
too smart for your own good. You think'a too much.
Life is simple. You find a man, you want the man, you
marry the man, you learn to love him, and when he dies,
you wear black. Simple.

"Aunt Rose, you don't know—"

Rose held up her hand. "I know what I know. You
make'a your lists. Those lists make'a you look for the
wrong ting. You no look for the good. You look for the
bad. That might work in business, but not in love. Love
don't make sense. It don't fit into'a one of your pretty
pictures. It's confusing, it'sa messy, and if you fight it,
you can lose it. Be careful. Listen to your Aunt Rose."
She took a sip of her coffee and watched Becca with
intelligent eyes.

Becca had a feeling that Aunt Rose knew what she
was going to say before she even said it. "You know
everything?"

Rose wiped her mouth with a napkin. "I know Richie
wants to marry you. I know you're scared. I know you
trust no one, not even yourself."

"What do I do?"

"I just told you, but you don't hear it. It'sa shame.
You're a good'a girl. Richie, he's a good'a man with
you. He loves you, but you don't want to see that." She
patted Becca's hand. "You gotta trust in Richie, or you're
gonna lose him." She gathered the plates and took them
into the kitchen as Becca sat stunned. Lose Rich? She

wasn't sure what she was feeling, but she didn't like it. It was close to panic, but that was ridiculous. She just had too much caffeine. That's why she broke out into a sweat; maybe she was coming down with something.

In the time she sat there, thinking, trying to make sense of what Aunt Rose said, Aunt Rose had cleaned the kitchen. She came back to the table and shook Becca's shoulder. "I gotta go. I'll see you on Thursday. Meet me at the butcher at nine. Richie can tell you where it is. We'll shop."

Becca forced herself out of the chair. "Oh, okay." She helped Aunt Rose with her coat and accepted the hug and two kisses. "You and Richie, you'll be okay in the end, but only you can choose which path to take—the hard path, or the easy path. Knowing you, it'sa gonna be the hard one. You gotta lot to learn about love."

Chapter 16

WHEN RICH GOT HOME FROM WORK, BECCA HAD HER damn lists all over the place, and she'd rearranged everything so he couldn't even find a place to charge his cell phone. He picked up the sculpture of the horse and her foal, trying to figure out where to move it so he could plug in his phone. When he turned to put the sculpture on the dining room table, he found Becca with her hands on her hips, glaring at him.

"Your aunt just happened to stop over today for coffee and a rest. I don't suppose you called her?"

Becca was clearly agitated. He missed the warm homecoming he'd begun to get used to. "No, I thought you were going to call her. I guess you didn't have to after all."

She scrunched up her brow, and Rich got the definite feeling he was in trouble for something. He didn't think he'd done anything awful, well, not lately, anyway.

"Why did you ask me to marry you?"

Okay, that came out of left field. Rich set his phone on the table forgotten. "What kind of question is that?"

"A good one. Men don't just pop the question for no reason. What was yours?"

Rich approached her slowly and put his arms around her. She didn't change her stance or lean into him like she always had before. Something was definitely wrong. "I love you. You love me. It seemed like the next logical step."

"In what galaxy? People just don't fall in love and get married for no reason."

"Yes they do."

She pushed away from him. "So that's it? That's all the explanation I'm going to get?"

"What were you expecting? I've got three months to live, and I want to spend every second of the rest of my life with you? I'm sorry to disappoint you, babe, but all I can say is that I love you. I don't want to live my life without you even when you're acting like a lunatic. How's that for a reason? Does that pass whatever test it is you're giving me?"

She wrapped her arms around herself. He'd like it a whole lot more if she wrapped her arms around him, but at least she didn't look as angry. "I'm not giving you a test. I just want to know what the hell you were thinking."

"I thought you wanted to table the marriage discussion."

"I do, but it doesn't mean I don't think about it. Guys just don't go play basketball, have a couple of drinks with their buddies, and on the way home suddenly decide to propose."

"That's exactly the way it happened. I don't know what clown is giving you your information, babe, but I'll tell you a little secret: I'm easy. What you see is what you get. I love you. I want to be with you. I want to marry you. If you're looking for some deep-seated reason, or someone with a psyche that takes years to understand, you've got the wrong guy." He expected her to say no, she had the right guy, but she didn't. She just stood there with that weird look on her face and stared. "Have you been reading my psych textbooks? I know I botched the proposal big time, and I'm sorrier than you can imagine about that, but it's not like I can take it back." Lord knows, the way things were going he wished he could, so that next time he could do it right. "Why don't you tell me what's going on?"

"Nothing's going on."

He let it drop, but he didn't believe her, any more than she seemed to believe him, which gave a little nudge to his guilty conscience. He hadn't told her about what the dean said, but that didn't factor into his wanting to marry her. If anything, it would have been smarter for him to wait to propose, but far be it from him to do the smart thing.

As they fixed dinner together, he found her staring at him as if she was trying to read his thoughts. After the third time, he cornered her, trapping her between him and the counter. "Talk to me, Becca. I can't help you if I don't know what the hell is wrong."

"Nothing."

"Nothing is always something. We talked about this before."

"Oh right, your pop-psychology email. When I say it's nothing, I mean it's nothing."

"No, you mean you don't want to talk to me about it."

"Fine, believe what you want."

"Good, then I choose to believe that you're madly in love with me and that eventually you'll tell me that your life will never be complete without me in it, and you'll ask me to marry you. I'm sure you'll be much better at proposing. Just think, you can make a list, write out the pros and cons. You can plan the whole thing. Hell, knowing you, you'll practice getting down on one knee with Tripod. At least he'll give you an answer."

"Yeah, don't hold your breath." Becca fought a smile, but when he kissed her, she finally kissed him back.

"I'm not holding my breath, but I'm looking forward to it. You think proposing is easy now. Just wait."

Tripod obviously heard his name, strode into the kitchen, dropped the mechanized ferret at Rich's feet, and let out a weird "rrupt."

"What? You can't catch a real rat so you bring me a toy one?"

"Wayne bought it for Tripod. He wants to share his ferret with you, so go ahead, wind it up. Just be careful, he gets even crazier than usual."

"It seems to be the running theme in the house tonight."

Saturday dawned clear and cold. It was one of those beautiful, late-fall days that made you want to reach for a rake and build a mountain of leaves just to jump into them and splash around. Unfortunately, Becca was stuck in the apartment with Tripod. Her phone rang, and she ran into the bedroom to get it. She checked the caller ID. "Hi, Annabelle. Have you heard from Ben? What did he think of the offer?"

"He liked it. There were a few things he wanted reworded, but basically, it sounds good. His lawyers are going to contact our lawyers, and you know, handle all the legalese. When he comes back next month, we'll have a meeting and get down to figuring out our new roles in the partnership. I can't wait! Becca, remember all those nights at art school when we would dream of having our own gallery?"

"Yeah, I dreamed it, but you've made it happen. Thanks for letting me hang on your coattails."

"Don't be ridiculous."

"It's true, even back then, you were the one planning the space, remember?"

Becca could almost hear Annabelle's eyes rolling. "So, are you alone too?"

"Richie's not there?"

Becca moved Tripod to Rich's side of the bed and lay down. "No, since I spent the last week working to make everything perfect for tonight's dinner with his boss, he figured he could go out and play basketball with the guys. I thought Mike would be with him. They're part of the fantastic four."

"I guess he could be. I woke up from a nap, and Mike was gone. He left a note saying he'd be back by three. I assumed he was going to the hospital." She yawned loudly before continuing. "I haven't talked to you all week about anything but business. You sound really pissed at Rich. What did he do now?"

"Nothing. Which is exactly the problem. He bragged to his dean about how wonderful the family lasagna is, and I'm the one spending half the day Thursday shopping with your psycho-psychic aunt."

"You actually went shopping with her? You couldn't make something other than lasagna?"

"If I could, believe me, I would have. Spending an afternoon walking all over Brooklyn with an old Italian lady ordering me around and probably cursing me in Italian is not my idea of a good time. You should have heard her. She talked to the butcher, the cheese man, and the lady at the vegetable market in Italian. They all seemed to know who I was. What did she do? Take an ad out in the *Post*?"

"Ha, the *Post* ain't got nothin' on the Italian grapevine."

"Tell me about it. I am now known all over Brooklyn as Richie's Becca. Aunt Rose told everyone that Richie's Becca needed help cooking. Richie's Becca wasn't Italian—as if that wasn't obvious—but she said that was okay because I'm a nice girl, so the family was dealing with it. Annabelle, I bit my tongue so many times, it felt swollen."

"I'm sorry, Bec. I told you she was scary."

"Yeah, and Rich talked his way out of doing just about everything to get ready for the most important dinner of my life."

"I thought this was Rich's boss. Why is it so important to you?"

"Annabelle, Dean Stewart's wife is Emily Stewart. Ring any bells?"

"From the arts council? Wow! Okay, I understand why you're nervous, but Bec, if it makes you feel better, she's supposed to be really nice. She's also has impeccable taste."

"Thanks, but it would help if Rich had been here helping out instead of leaving everything to me. Granted, he was working, but it's not as if I have nothing else to do. I've been on the phone every few hours with Ben's accountants, his lawyers, my lawyers, and I spent all day yesterday cooking with Aunt Rose, cleaning the apartment, and trying to figure out how to display my work in a room with zero lighting." She slapped her hand onto her right eye to try to stop the twitching. "Annabelle, my eye is twitching."

"Oh, that's not good. But I told you that no one sees it but you."

Becca watched Tripod lie on the bedside table with his head hanging over the edge trying to bite the knob on the drawer. She shooed him away. "Tripod, you are not getting your toy back, so cut it out."

"Aw, give the poor cat his toy, you meanie."

Becca walked back into the living room and began fluffing the couch pillows. "I was fine with his toy until he began attacking it on every piece of furniture that held my work. I tell you Annabelle—this week has been, in a word, a nightmare."

"At least it's almost over. I'm sure dinner will be great, and Emily Stewart is going to absolutely love your work. I know it. I have impeccable taste too."

"Thanks." Becca sat on the couch, picked up the notebook she'd left on the coffee table, and looked over her list. "It will probably be fine, but that doesn't mean I still don't want to take a hoop and wrap it around Rich's neck."

"Yeah, I know the feeling. Still, you gotta admit they are good to have around to open jars and screw in light bulbs among other things."

Becca looked up when she heard the door being unlocked and tossed her notebook back onto the coffee table. "Speak of the devil. I gotta go. I'll call you later, okay?"

"Sure, good luck, sweetie. I know everything will be great. If it's not, then I'll hold Rich down while you beat him."

She laughed and turned her back to Rich. "I'll hold you to that. Love you."

She disconnected the call to find Rich towering over her with a raised eyebrow. "Who do you love other than me?"

"Your sister." Rich bent to give her a kiss, and Becca leaned back and waved a hand in front of her face. "You look and smell like something Tripod only dreams about dragging in. Besides, you're still on my shit list."

"Aw, come on, Bec. I brought you dessert and Zoom Zoom like you asked."

"Yeah, you probably picked all of it up from DiNicola's restaurant after the basketball game and a beer."

Rich didn't deny it though he looked a little disappointed to get caught.

"Here, take this." Rich handed Becca the dessert boxes and put the bottle of Zoom Zoom on the coffee table. "Be right back. I left one thing in the car."

"Thanks for the warning." Becca went to the kitchen with the stack of bakery boxes all tied up with string and was tempted to open them to see which of the DiNicola's amazing desserts Rich had bought. After the door slammed announcing his return, she asked, "Do these need to be refrigerated, because if they do, we may have to bring them upstairs and see if the guys have room. Our fridge is full..." She looked up from the boxes and found Rich holding the largest, and by far, prettiest, bouquet of flowers she'd ever received. "You brought me flowers?" She let out an exasperated breath and rolled her eyes. "Isn't that just like a man? Here I was ready to kill you, and then you go and do something sweet. You really know how to screw up a perfectly good mad."

Rich looked like he'd just survived one more round of *American Idol*. "It's a gift."

He bent down for a kiss. "So, you were talking to Annabelle and relaxing?"

Okay, so maybe he didn't ruin it after all. "You think I was relaxing? I've been working my ass off all week—shopping with your crazy aunt, cooking, cleaning, and running back and forth to the brownstone. I sit down for five minutes to have a conversation with your sister, and you think I'm relaxing?"

"Is this one of those trick questions?"

"No, it's rhetorical. I'm hoping to instill in you the realization of what an incredibly inane question you asked."

"Okay, why don't we just forget I asked and cut right to me telling you what an amazing job you've done and how much I appreciate how hard you've obviously worked."

"Okay."

Rich grabbed her before she could get away. "Come on, let's get a shower, and you can explain why your eye is twitching like a meter in a checkered cab."

"Annabelle said no one else could see it but me."

He took her hand and headed toward the bathroom. "She lied." Rich kissed the retort from her lips and took his time undressing her.

Becca did her best to ignore his hands, the little kisses he placed here and there, as they waited for the water to heat. Unfortunately the water didn't get as hot as she did. Becca only hoped that by the time they stepped into the shower, the water would cool her off. It didn't.

Rich didn't think he'd ever seen anything lovelier

than Becca wet and slightly pissed off, which made him question his sanity. He wasn't sure why he found that to be such a turn-on, but he figured it was a plus since she seemed to spend an inordinate amount of time being angry with him. He quickly soaped up and then started working on transferring all the soap on him to her.

"Rich, if you don't get your hands off me, I'm gonna have to hurt you."

"Fine." He pulled his soapy hands from around her and tried to ignore his erection—not an easy thing to do. "Anyone ever tell you that you get bitchy when you're nervous?"

She tilted her head under the water to rinse her hair. "Anyone ever tell you it's dangerous to call a nervous woman bitchy?"

He couldn't resist touching her, so he didn't. He slid his soapy body against hers and nearly groaned. "Babe, the house is clean, we have plenty of time, and sex is known to be a great tension releaser. I bet your eye will stop twitching."

He ran his hand over her breast, and the nipple pebbled almost instantly. He loved the way her body reacted to him, even when she wasn't happy about it. "Come on, Bec. You know you want to, and we're wasting time talking about it when we can be releasing all your tension."

He faced her and massaged her shoulders and back before moving to her breasts, only this time, he used his mouth, starting with her left, and then moving over to her right, since he was a fair guy. When he kissed his way back up, she looked so serious. With her lips all pursed and impatient, it was as if she was daring him to give her an attitude adjustment. He spent a minute nibbling her lips before deepening the kiss and tongue wrestling until she pulled her mouth from his, breathlessly.

"Okay," She wrapped her long leg around his hip and grabbed at his shoulders. "But make it a quickie—you know what those are, right?"

God he loved every bossy hair on her head, and well, everywhere else too. "I've heard a rumor. I'll see what I can do." He slid his hands down between her legs and found her slick and wet. She sucked in a breath and gave an impatient shake. She always amazed him—whenever they were together she seemed to want him as badly as he wanted her. Becca arched her back, and he slid right home.

"Oh, God." Every time he entered her he had to stop for fear he'd completely lose it. He waited for the sheer awesomeness to wane, but it didn't. Every time was like the first, and every time it was over, he just wanted her more.

That serious look returned to her face. "Rich, do I need to explain the central theme of the act of a quickie?"

He couldn't hide his smile. "Babe, there's a difference between a quickie and an embarrassment. I admit it's a fine line. All the work is done. We have plenty of time before the Stewarts get here, so let's just enjoy this." Kissing him, she wrapped her leg tighter around his, ground against him, and he nipped her earlobe. "You're pushing your luck, babe."

"This from a man who spent the last ten minutes driving me to distraction. Pushing my luck is the least I can do."

Becca groaned as he nipped her shoulder and lifted her, pressing her hard against the cold tile as she wrapped both legs around his waist.

She sucked in a breath as Rich slid slowly back in. He watched her face as he made love to her. He throbbed within her, and every time she moved sent him closer and closer to the brink. If she wanted a quickie, she wouldn't be disappointed. When Becca nipped his neck, Rich lost any finesse he might have possessed and just let go. Holding her waist, he pistoned his hips, and when he felt the intense heat and almost a splash of wetness surround him, tight within her, he ground into her and went so deep he could swear he hit her cervix. Her screams ricocheted through the small bathroom, urging him on, shattering his self-control. He came so hard his vision blurred, and he worried he'd drop her. He leaned into her and thanked God when she put one foot down before rocking against him, drawing out his orgasm and kissing him. She shivered in his arms; he wasn't sure if it was from the cold or the aftershocks zinging through the both of them.

"Okay," She rested her head on his shoulder and blew out a breath. "I guess you do understand what a quickie is after all."

Becca opened the hot oven. The stuffed mushroom hors d'oeuvres were browning nicely and ready to be served but would be fine for another few minutes. She pulled the foil off the lasagna, took the garlic bread out of the fridge, and stirred the sauce she left warming on the stove. The antipasto she and Aunt Rose put together was already dressed and on the table. Everything was ready. She took a deep breath, another sip of her wine, and went into the living room where her guests were chatting with Rich. She sat on the arm of his chair and felt his arm come around her, giving her waist a squeeze.

Dean Stewart smiled at them and lifted his glass. "Here's to your promotion, Rich."

"Promotion? Really? That's fabulous." Becca leaned into him, wrapping her arm around his shoulders.

Dean Stewart looked at Becca quizzically. "He didn't tell you on Monday?"

Rich straightened and put his wineglass down. "Craig gave me the news that I've been made a full-time professor and that I'm off probation. It's hardly a promotion."

Becca's head swam. "Monday? Why didn't you tell me?"

Rich cleared his throat. "I had other things on my mind I guess."

Becca forced a smile. "Sure. I remember."

Dean Stewart smiled back. "I told Rich that with his hard work, you supporting him, and your family back-ground and connections to Columbia, he could go far."

Becca found herself nodding. "Of course."

"We're hoping to see your father at our next alumni dinner."

She stood quickly and then regretted the speed. They probably thought Rich had pinched her, which was still better than what he had apparently done—namely fucked her over, lied to her, and used her. A regular trifecta. Becca was used to getting hit with one or two, but all three? "The hors d'oeuvres are ready. I'll be right back." She smiled and felt her jaw lock up. "Rich, do you want to give me a hand since you're so helpful in the kitchen?"

As soon as they were out of the Stewarts' line of vision, Becca turned on Rich. She willed herself to calm down and did her best to whisper. "You had other things on your mind? My, that's convenient. The only thing you had on your mind was finding a way to reel in a sucker like me. I'm surprised at you, Rich. I would think even you would come up with a better idea than proposing."

"Becca, it's not what you think."

She snatched the potholders off the counter and opened the oven. "It's exactly what I think." She pulled the mushrooms out and set them on the stove before grabbing the serving plate and spatula. "You proposed to me to ensure your promotion." She moved the mushrooms from the tray to the plate while she blinked away tears. "How could I be so stupid? This is even more mortifying than Nat sleeping with my mother. But then you're probably sorry you missed your chance to do that, too."

Rich turned around in a circle and then stuffed his hands in the pockets of his chinos that she'd spent ten minutes ironing. She was the biggest fool.

He picked up the empty mushroom tray and put it in the sink and then stepped close to her and held her shoulders as he whispered. "This is neither the time nor the place for this discussion. But did it ever occur to you that maybe you're so psycho about your family, I'd be afraid to mention it, because I didn't want you to cut your nose off to spite your face and miss this opportunity with Emily?"

"No. How long did it take you to think up that lame excuse? Next time you pull a fast one, you might try rehearsing your explanation in a mirror. Maybe then it'll be believable. God, I can't believe I fell for you." She hissed, sounding more like her mother than in her worst nightmares. God help her.

She handed him a stack of small plates and forks and left him standing in the kitchen with his mouth hanging open. She slammed the door on the flood of her emotions and put her heartache out of her mind. There would be plenty of time later to alternate between kicking herself and crying.

She could do this. She was great on autopilot. Lord knew, she'd spent most of her life practicing smiling when required, nodding, and making small talk. She placed the hors d'oeuvres on the center of the coffee table with a flourish, took the plates from the dumb-struck Rich, and served.

Becca offered Emily a plate. "I love your scarf. Where did you find it?"

"This cute little shop in SoHo. You should come with me sometime. I find the most unusual pieces there."

Becca handed Craig his plate. "I'd love to. SoHo is one of my favorite parts of the city, but with work and the remodel, I haven't had much time to get out."

Craig looked around. "I sure hope your new place is bigger than this one."

"Oh my, yes. It's over fifteen hundred square feet, not including the studio that Rich's sister, Annabelle, and I will share." Becca handed a plate to Rich, took hers, and sat on the arm of his chair again. "When Annabelle and I were roommates in art school, she regaled me with tales of her big brother. I felt as if I knew Rich before I ever met him." She smiled and bumped his shoulder with hers. She was just as capable as he was of pretending everything was freakin' hunky dory. Either that, or he didn't care, which was a distinct possibility.

Emily sat forward. "You're building a studio? I'd love to see it."

Becca cut the mushroom she'd been so looking forward to tasting until ten minutes ago when she'd lost her appetite for many things, especially a certain tall, Italian, lying user. "You'll have to come over once it's finished. I think there's another couple of months work to do. I was hoping it would be completed before Christmas, but I'm not optimistic. Everything seems to take twice as long as I think it should."

Craig laughed. "I hear remodeling is a real test to any relationship."

Becca forced herself to take a bite of her mushroom before setting the plate down. She nodded. "It would be if we were living there. Being away from it certainly lessens the pressure."

Emily nodded. "If your studio is under construction, where are you working now?"

"In the guest room. It's not the best, but it's temporary." Emily had no idea how temporary, and from the way Rich was shoveling in his mushrooms, neither did he.

"Really? I'd love to see what you're working on, or are you one of those artists who refuse to show anything until it's complete?"

"Not at all." Becca stood and picked up her wine. "I'd be happy to show you." She almost laughed when Emily all but popped off the couch. "You're not allergic to cats, are you? I have Tripod locked up in there."

"No, I love cats, so does Craig. Tripod—what an odd name."

Becca pushed open the door, and Tripod belted out a greeting. She looked at Emily over her shoulder. "Not really, when you consider he's only got three legs. It suits, and he seems to like it. He's answered to it since the day I rescued him."

Emily stepped into the room, stopped, and stared at the couple set in clay. She didn't even notice Tripod jumping out past her. "Oh, it's magnificent."

Becca shrugged. "It's coming along."

Emily shook her head. "The emotion just pours off it. It's breathtaking, really. You could stop now, and it would be perfect."

Becca laughed. It was a good thing, since she'd never touch it again. Christ, what a sucker she'd been, believing Rich. "It's a thought."

Emily circled the table it sat on. "It's rough, edgy, almost raw. It's positively sexual."

"Yes, that's what I was going for."

"What do you call it?"

"Star-crossed lovers."

"Becca, I love it just as it is."

"Thank you."

Emily threaded her arm through Becca's as they left the room. "Your work is so varied. So many times you find a fabulous artist who seems to do much the same thing over and over again. Your work is all so different, wonderful, but looking at your collection of work, you'd never think that they were all by the same artist. It's an extraordinary talent."

Becca laughed. "My art professors thought I had

attention deficit disorder. They may have had a point. I
get bored easily." She stopped by the dining room table
and turned toward Rich and Craig. "Why don't we all sit
down? The lasagna will be ready soon. Let's get started
on the antipasto."

Rich stood and carried their glasses to the table. "The
mushrooms were great, Bec." He kissed her cheek.

Becca smiled. "I can't take the credit. I used your
Aunt Rose's recipe. She said they were your favorite."

Rich filled everyone's wineglasses. "They are. She
used to always let me eat the left-over stuffing."

Becca laughed at that, trying really hard not to sound
like the Wicked Witch of the West. "She told me, so I
saved the leftovers for you."

Rich gave her a hug. "Just one of the many reasons
I love you."

Becca wanted to gag, but smiled instead, before
returning to the kitchen. She removed the lasagna from
the oven and set it out to cool for a few minutes. Aunt
Rose said if she didn't, the cheese would be too hot and
would make a mess when she tried to serve it. Since
the night was already a complete disaster, there was no
need to add to it. With the lasagna cooling in the serving
tray, she popped the garlic bread under the broiler and
set the timer. She didn't want to forget it—she'd eaten
enough of Annabelle's incinerated garlic bread to last
her a lifetime.

When Becca returned to the table, Rich stood and
held her chair for her. She nodded her thanks as he took
his seat. "This is a little difficult to serve. Why don't you
pass me your plates?"

Craig took a sip of his wine and watched her. "Becca,

I was under the impression that between the two of you, Rich was the cook."

Becca slid a lettuce leaf topped with prosciutto, Genoa salami, olives, roasted red pepper, artichoke hearts, and cheese onto a plate and passed it. "Rich and I share a few of the kitchen duties. In this case, he was responsible for the dessert and coffee. Rich's Aunt Rose wanted to teach me the secret to the family lasagna, and I didn't want to pass up the chance. Since my schedule is more flexible than his, I handled the rest."

"Ah." Craig shook his head. "The sharing of house-hold responsibilities is a sign of a strong relationship."

Becca almost choked on that one.

Emily placed her napkin on her lap. "Everything looks and smells wonderful."

Rich nodded. "Becca really did a great job throwing everything together."

"Thanks, I had a lot of help." She didn't bother mentioning that none of it was from him.

Rich dug in, while Becca picked at her food. She was thrilled when the timer went off for the bread. Rich followed her in, and she had him carry the lasagna, sauce, and meat to the table. They were in full view of the Stewarts, so when he kissed her, she didn't push him away even though she wanted to. Becca took her time cutting the bread and arranging it in the cloth-lined basket, just wishing she could disappear. Her head was killing her. She hadn't had a migraine in years, but she knew one was coming on. Fabulous. The only thing she could do was pop four ibuprofen, hoping to keep ahead of the pain, and get through the night.

Becca put on her cheery face and went back to the

table with the bread and served the lasagna. It was perfect. Looking at the bright side, at least she now knew the secret to Aunt Rose's lasagna. Not that she'd want to eat it for a good long time, but still, it was something she got out of this sham of a relationship.

Rich took a sip of his wine and took a bite of the lasagna and smiled when he realized it was fabulous. The schmuck.

Craig moaned in appreciation and nodded to Rich. "I know what I'm going to ask you to bring to the next faculty potluck."

Emily nodded. "It really is wonderful. I'm so impressed with both you and Becca. It's so inspiring to see the two of you so obviously perfect for each other. Two young people with such bright futures—Becca's in the art world, yours in the world of academia—is a very impressive thing. I wish you both all the luck in the world."

Rich leaned back in his seat and squeezed her thigh. "Thank you." All Becca could do was nod as she saw both her relationship and this opportunity die. Since the food was so good, not much more was said. She somehow got through coffee and dessert, and as soon as she said good-bye and Rich walked the Stewarts out, she went into the bedroom armed with her suitcase and began packing.

Chapter 17

RICH WATCHED AS THE STEWARTS WALKED ARM IN ARM toward the train. He offered them a lift to the station, but they claimed they needed to walk off all they ate. They did eat a lot, but then, no one could resist Aunt Rose's lasagna.

He was pretty pleased with himself. The dinner went well, and after Becca's initial reaction to the news of his "promotion" and that stupid remark Craig made about her family, she calmed down and did her queen-of-all-things perfect hostess shtick. Damn, the girl knew how to drive him crazy. He must have imagined peeling that dress off her a dozen times. It was soft and clingy and didn't have one button or zipper. His guess was that it was one of those dresses you can pull up, and it would stay up while you did whatever you wanted. He couldn't wait and hoped to God she wouldn't insist on doing the dishes tonight. He'd gladly do all the dishes in the morning if he could just get his hands on her tonight.

He made his way into the house. The table still needed to be cleared, and the dishes done, and Becca was nowhere to be seen. He checked the bedroom hoping she hadn't already changed out of that hot dress. Instead of finding her changing, he caught her packing. Rich stopped dead in his tracks, unable to believe his eyes. She had her suitcase thrown open on the bed and was tossing her clothes in without even folding them. Becca always folded everything, even her underwear.

"Why are you packing?"

She glanced at him without ever stopping. "Someone with three post-secondary degrees should be smart enough to figure that out for himself, don't you think?"

"Becca, hold on." He stepped between her and the closet. "Calm down and talk to me."

"Calm down? You want me to calm down after you used me, fucked me over, and sold me out. Not likely. How about I tell you calmly to get the hell out of my way?"

"No." Rich grabbed a handful of clothes sticking out of her bag, still on their hangers, and put them back in the closet. "I didn't sell you out. The only reason I agreed to the dinner was for you."

Becca looked about to clock him. He figured even if she hit him with that bat of hers, it would hurt a hell of a lot less than it would if she walked out on him.

"Ha! That's just so like you, isn't it? You think you can stand there looking all innocent, lie to my face, and get away with it. I know I was a fool to fall for you, but believe me, I won't make the same mistake twice. Now get the hell out of my way." She pushed past him. "You got what you wanted from the deal. You got your precious job."

Rich was beginning to sweat, which kind of freaked him out. He just wanted to grab her and make her listen to reason, but she was way past reasonable. "Babe, I don't care about the job. I just care about you, and I know how much you were counting on this thing with Emily."

"Oh yeah, and you took full advantage, didn't you? You pimped out my name. Did you tell them that I'd make sure Daddy sent a nice check to the alumni association if they gave my boyfriend a job?"

Okay, now Rich was getting angry. "Hey, I don't need your name or your daddy's money to get a job. If it wasn't for you, I would have canceled the dinner."

"But you didn't, did you? What, did you need to seal the deal?"

Rich couldn't believe his ears. This was a fuckin' nightmare, and there was nothing he could do to prove himself. But worse, how could she think he would hurt her so badly? His guts tightened up. Christ, what was he going to do?

She started throwing all her clothes from the drawers into another suitcase. "I was such a fool, falling for your act. You're good. Offering me money was ingenious. I gotta hand it to you—of all the guys who went after my money, you were by far the most original."

"What the hell are you talking about?"

"You thought you could get a two-fer. My trust fund and a great job. So what'd you do, Rich? When you were snooping through my artwork and my underwear, you checked out my portfolio, too?"

"Bec. Stop this. I love you. I love you and want to marry you. I don't give a shit how much money you do or don't have. Babe, I should have told you what Craig said, but I thought you'd refuse to let Emily see your work, and I wasn't sure if you could afford to miss this chance with Emily. After you lost all that money that went to Mike, can you afford to keep working on your art? Are you going to have to get a job? I don't want you to have to do that. I can, you know, support you."

"Rich, let me give you a hint. You can stop the act now. It's over."

"What's over?"

"This sham. You got most of what you wanted. Just be happy with that, and let me get the hell out of here."

Rich stood between her and the door. Not before she calmed down enough to talk sense into her. "Becca, it's late. You can't travel when you're so upset. Just stay here. I'll sleep on the couch if you want me to. We'll talk tomorrow after you calm down."

"No way. I'm outta here."

"Not until you calm down and talk to me."

"Oh right. Who's going to stop me?"

"I am. You're not going anywhere until after you've calmed down, and we've had a rational discussion."

"Are you delusional? Nothing that you say tomorrow is going to change my mind. You're a liar. A really good liar. I thought I could spot them all. Well, you got by me, you lied to me, and I fell hook, line, and sinker in love with you, and you would have had me if you hadn't gone off and proposed."

Damn, she looked just about ready to crumble. She stood board straight, all strong and pissed, but every now and then, he'd see that hurt little girl. Christ, she thought he was just like those bozo friends of hers, her mother, and sometimes even her father. Shit. He just wanted to grab her, hold her, and tell her it would be all right. But she'd already convicted him.

Rich went to his side of the bed and grabbed a pillow. "I'll be out on the couch when you decide you want to talk to me."

"Don't hold your breath, or on second thought, do."

"Bec, I didn't do any of those things. Once you look at this rationally, you'll see. I love you."

"Please just go. Please?" A big tear rolled down her cheek, followed by another, and another. Each one was like a punch in the gut and made him want to hit every person who'd ever hurt her. Himself included. He'd fucked up royally.

As soon as Rich left the room, Becca tried to pull herself together. She needed a plan. She grabbed her notebook and turned to a fresh page in her book and her life. She needed to find a place to live. She wouldn't survive living with Mike and Annabelle. Their incessant happiness would only highlight everything Becca didn't have in her life. She swallowed back a sob, cleared her throat, and looked for her phone. She could stay at a hotel, but as soon as Annabelle found out where Becca was, she'd be dragged back to the brownstone. Right now, Becca just wanted to be alone to lick her wounds and figure out how to get past this.

The other day when she'd met the appraiser at the gallery to get an appraisal on the value of the building, she'd done a walk-through of Ben's place, which was currently empty, since Ben was spending an extended period of time in Idaho. It would be perfect for her. She thanked God for the two-hour time difference and called Ben in Idaho.

"Hi gorgeous."

"Hi Ben."

"Why are you whispering?"

"Because I don't want Rich to hear me."

"Trouble in paradise?"

"More like a nuclear explosion. I need a place to stay, and I don't think I can take staying with Mike and Annabelle. Can I crash at your place until the construction is finished on mine?"

"Don't you mean *our* place?"

"Hey, nothing's been signed. Until then, it's *your* place. So what do you say?"

"Becca, it's fine. Are you going to be okay alone? Maybe you should go to Annabelle's."

"I'm a big girl. I've spent most of my life alone. I'll be fine." Maybe if she kept repeating that, she'd start to believe it. Right now she felt physical pain. She hurt everywhere.

"What about the keys?"

"I have a set. I needed them when I met with the appraiser the other night."

"Okay, good. Go ahead and make yourself at home. You can use the guest room for as long as you want. It looks like I'll be staying here for a while. Just take care of yourself, and let me know if you need anything."

"Um, Ben, how are you with cats?"

"Other than allergic?"

"Oh. Okay. I can probably leave Tripod with Rich until my place is finished. If not, maybe Mike and Annabelle can take him."

"I'm sorry, Becca."

"No, it's fine. Thanks so much, Ben. I'll be in touch about the deal. It's looking really good to me right about now."

"I'm ready to finalize things whenever you are. If you want to move up the date, it's not a problem."

"I'll think about it. Thanks again for everything. I owe you one."

When Becca disconnected the call, she looked around her at her packed luggage. She knew she was going to have to start building her new life all over again. She'd leave with less than she came with, because Rich had stolen her heart, and no matter how little sense it made, she still loved him. She wished love could be turned off, but no matter how hurt and angry she was, she still felt it. Even knowing what he'd done, she missed him. And even with all the pain he caused her, she wished she could go back to being blissfully unaware. She wrapped her arms around herself and lost the battle with tears.

Rich sat on the couch listening to Becca cry. Every sob was a knife to his heart. He forced himself to listen, wanting to break the door down, gather her in his arms, and make it better. But how? She wouldn't even look at him. He'd never felt so damn helpless. The situation had spiraled out of control, and he couldn't do a thing to stop it.

He'd lost her, and Christ, he had no idea what to do to get her back. Tripod crawled onto his lap and lay against Rich's chest. "I fucked up bad, buddy."

Tripod responded with something that sounded amazingly like "now what?"

"I don't know. I don't know what I can say to make her believe me." Rich shook his head wondering if he was going off the deep end. Maybe this was what insanity was like. If it was, it sucked, it hurt, and he had a feeling it was just going to get worse—not that it really mattered. Nothing mattered anymore, not without Becca. He took another sip of his Jack Daniels. Drinking was probably not a smart thing to do since drinking Jack Daniels was what got him in this position in the first place. He needed to find a way to make things right. Rich pulled his phone off the charger and called Vinny.

"Fuck, Richie. What the hell are you doing calling me at one in the morning?"

"I got a problem."

"Just one? What the hell do you want me to do about it?"

"Vin, she's leaving me."

"Whoa, okay. What the hell did you do?"

"I asked her to marry me on Monday—"

"And I'm just hearing about this now? What the fuck?"

"She didn't say yes."

"What the hell did she say?"

"When I asked? Nothing. Then later she was all suspicious. 'Why did you ask me to marry you?' like I had some kind of ulterior motive."

"You did. You were afraid you were going to lose her. I guess I should have warned you not to pull a stupid stunt like that, but I didn't think even you'd be that dumb."

"Thanks, Vin. You're making me feel so much better."

"Eh? What do you want from me? Do you want me to help you, or do you want me to be like one of your professor friends and blow sunshine up your ass?"

"Christ, what am I gonna do? She's packing her things and crying. I hurt her, Vin. Dean Stewart told her I got the promotion and that with her family connections and her rich father, I could go far. She thinks I used her to get my job, and that by marrying her, getting her trust fund is like a two-fer."

"Look, the bar is open. Why don't you come down here, and we'll, you know, think of something."

Rich took a sip of his drink and ran his hand over Tripod's stomach. "I can't. If I leave, so will Becca."

"What are you doing? Holding her hostage or something?"

"No, but I'll be damned if I let her leave me without at least talking about this. Vin, she thinks I used her. She thinks I lied to her—that I'm after her money or somethin'. I made her cry."

"Fuck, I hate it when they cry. I'd rather have a freakin' rectal exam than have to listen to Mona cry. But Richie, you can't make her stay, and you can't make her talk to you. All you can do is let her go and then do everything you can to get her back. Prove to her she's wrong about you. She is, isn't she?"

"Fuck you."

"Eh, I gotta ask. It's Mickey's little sister we're talkin' about here. If you hurt her on purpose, we're gonna have words."

"I hurt her, but I didn't mean to. Shit. You're not helping at all."

"You want help? Here's what you do. You get on your fuckin' knees and beg her to give you another chance. Grovel, and if that don't work, you're gonna have to prove her wrong and pray to God she comes back to you."

"How the fuck am I supposed to prove her wrong?"

"I don't know. One thing at a time. You gotta try groveling."

"I did. She won't listen."

"Fine, then I guess we gotta figure out a plan B, but you better make sure she's the one for you, because I gotta feeling you've got a hell of a lot of work to do.

She's a hard one, your Becca. She ain't like the girls you're used to dealing with."

"Don't I know it."

Becca didn't sleep; she tossed and turned and cried. Her migraine was so bad, it hurt to think, but she couldn't turn off her brain. After waiting hours, Rich finally fell into a hard sleep and started snoring. She tiptoed out of the bedroom, praying she could get past Tripod without him sounding the alarm. When she saw the two of them curled up on the couch together, she realized Tripod was more Rich's cat than hers. Just one more thing Rich stole from her.

Tears burned her already raw eyes as she slipped out the door and headed to Ben's place alone.

Becca let herself in and sat in the dark living room trying to figure out what to do next. Cold and exhausted, she curled up in an oversized chair and pulled a throw around her. She'd just fallen asleep when her phone rang. She looked at the caller ID. It was Rich. She waited for it to go into voice mail and called her brother. He picked up. "Hey Bec, what's got you up so early?"

"Mike? Could you do me a favor?"

"Are you okay?"

"Yeah, I'm fine. I just need some help. I'm at Ben's place. Rich and I split up—"

"I'll kill him."

"Mike, Rich is your brother-in-law, and this has nothing to do with you, so for the sake of your marriage, just stay the hell out of it. If you can't, you'll be no help to me."

"What do you need, Bec?"

"My luggage. I packed but left after Rich fell asleep, and I can't handle seeing him right now. It's over, and I don't feel the need to rehash the whole thing. I just need you to pick up my bags and make sure it's okay for Tripod to stay there until I can move into my own place."

"You just left without even talking to him? What are you running away from?"

"Nothing."

"Did he hurt you?"

Becca wiped a tear from her eye and heard Annabelle in the background. "Of course he didn't hurt her."

"Becca, it's me. What happened? Are you okay? Where are you?"

"I'm fine. I'm at Ben's, and God, Annabelle, I left Rich. It's over." Becca sobbed. "I'm sorry. I can't talk. Could you just get my stuff from the apartment and don't let the guys beat each other up?"

"Sure, I'll be there in a little while."

"No—" She was speaking to dead air. Shit, Becca just wanted to be alone to wallow in her misery. Now she was going to have to deal with Annabelle.

Vinny got up early as usual, and twenty minutes later, Nick was on the line calling for backup. He asked if Vinny could meet him and Mickey at Rich's apartment to haul out Becca's stuff. Which was just what Vinny wanted to do on a Sunday morning. Still, it was probably a smart move considering Mike and Richie almost came to blows when Rich and Becca were just dating. Once Mickey heard that Richie made Becca cry, he was going to want to rearrange Rich's face.

Vinny showed up early at Richie's place and thought that maybe he could have most of Becca's things packed out before Mickey showed up. He pressed the button on the intercom. "Eh, Richie. Open up. It's me, Vinny."

"Okay." Rich buzzed him through the security door and had the apartment door opened before Vinny got there. Rich looked like shit.

"How you doin', Vin?"

"Better than you. But then most people on life support would look better than you." Now this was what a man looked like when the woman he loves dumped him.

Vinny looked around the apartment. Everything was neat, clean, and normal except for the three-legged cat sitting on the coffee table drinking out of a big ass coffee cup. "You got a cat?"

"Tripod's Becca's cat."

"I guess you didn't do too good keeping Becca from leaving."

"I must have fallen asleep, and she snuck out. I've been trying to call her. She's not answering."

"I guess right now she don't want to talk to you. But it's a good sign that she wanted to make sure her big brother didn't beat the shit out of you. Your sisters and Becca sent Nick to babysit Mickey, and I'm assigned to you, so don't pull no shit, okay?"

Rich sat back down. "I don't want to fight with Mike. I want him to help me get through to Becca. She won't listen to me."

"And you think Mike's gonna want to listen to you?"

"You got any better ideas?"

"Actually, no. I don't."

The door buzzed, and the cat ran for it. Richie picked up the cat. "I'm going to lock Tripod in the mud room so he can't escape. You want to let Nick and Mike in?"

"Sure." Vinny buzzed them in and opened the door. Once Mickey got a glimpse at how pathetic Richie looked, he lost the murderous gleam in his eyes.

Richie stood his ground, not lookin' like a wimp, but he wasn't the same cocky bastard he usually was either. It takes a real woman to take a man like Richie and cut him off at the knees. It looked as if that was exactly what Becca had done.

Rich nodded. "Hey Mike. Nick."

The three of them stood with their hands in their pockets, staring at each other.

Vinny wanted to smack them all upside the head. He got both Richie and Mickey, but Nick was too quick and ducked. "Come on, yous guys. It's obvious Richie fucked up and wants Becca back. I know for a fact that everyone in this room has been in Richie's shoes, so the least we can do is listen to what he's gotta say."

Rich shrugged. "Yeah, what he said. I fucked up."

Mike rolled back on his heels. "Well, that's obvious. Why don't you tell me something I don't know, like why my little sister is crying her eyes out over you?"

Rich held up his hands. "Shit, okay, I'll tell you, but you gotta help me get her back."

Mike crossed his arms over his chest, and he and Richie just stared at each other.

"Mike, I love her. I didn't do anything wrong. Well, okay, I fucked up, but I didn't do what she thinks I did." He ran his hand through his hair. "I need some coffee. You guys want some?"

Nick followed Rich to the kitchen and leaned against the breakfast bar. "Are you makin' it?"

Rich turned and laughed. "Yeah, I learned how to make a damn good pot of coffee, brought Becca coffee and breakfast in bed every morning, and she still dumped me."

Vinny and Mike went to join Nick. The kitchen was immaculate. Vin smiled. He always liked a clean kitchen. Even the dishwasher was running. "You did the dishes from last night?"

"Yeah, I was hoping Becca would come back for her stuff so we could talk. She taught me how to clean, so I've been straightening up. I washed the tablecloth and napkins and vacuumed. It's hard to sit still."

Nick watched Rich count out scoops of coffee. "Yeah, I always clean when I get stressed."

Mike nodded. "It's really relaxing, and at least you feel as if you're accomplishing something instead of just pacing the floor."

Rich looked up from what he was doing. "It sounds like you've been there."

Vinny rolled his eyes. "Okay, it looks like I gotta play Doctor Phil or somethin'—just don't expect me to get teary-eyed or nothin', okay?" He ran his hand through what was left of his hair. "Rich, why don't you tell Nick and Mike what landed you in deep shit?"

"Okay. I told you what my boss said on Monday, right? Dean Stewart said because I got Becca by my side, I'd go far. Her dad's an alum, and well, she's got this queen-of-all-things act, which means she's great at the schmoozin' professors and deans have to do. Now, when he said that, I was pissed. After all, I'm a really good professor, and it shouldn't matter who I'm with."

Vinny cleared his throat. "Come on, Richie, we're aging here. We ain't got all day."

Rich took cups from the cabinet and piled them into the microwave and turned it on. "I was afraid that if I told Becca what Dean Stewart said, she'd freak out."

Vinny groaned. "You might want to tell them about your dumb-ass move now."

Rich took the cups out of the microwave and groaned. "I asked her to marry me."

Vinny shook his head. "Yeah, a dumb-ass move especially when she didn't say yes."

Rich cringed. "Thanks for reminding me. She didn't say anything. Then when she finally did talk, she asked to table the whole marriage discussion."

Vinny grabbed the coffeepot. Shit, if he was going to wait for Richie to pour, he'd be there all day. "That was until the dinner when the dean spilled the beans."

Rich passed around the cream and sugar. "Yeah, at first Becca was pissed, then she seemed to be fine."

Nick stirred his coffee. "Oh man, when a woman goes from pissed to fine in a blink of an eye, that's the time to start sleeping with one eye open."

Richie nodded. "Right. See there I was thinking everything was copacetic. I walked Dean Stewart and Emily out, and when I come back in, Becca's packin' her stuff. When I asked what the fuck was goin' on, she's calling me a liar and a user and said that I only proposed to her to get the job and her trust fund. She accused me of looking though her investment portfolio."

Nick shook his head. "Man, that's harsh."

"I know I fucked up. I should have told her about what the dean said. But it's not like she's been one hundred percent straight with me either. When we went to Philly we ran into some assholes who claim to be her friends, and they said that most of the money in her trust fund went to Mike. So I'm thinking she might be hurtin' for funds and might have to get a job instead of working on her art, so I offered to lend her money if she needed it."

Mike laughed. "Rich, she's hardly destitute."

"Well, how the hell was I supposed to know that? Have you ever seen how the girl dresses?"

Vinny, Mike, and Nick all nodded. Vinny took a sip of his coffee and was surprised by how good it was. "She's usually in clothes ten times too big."

Rich took a drink and rummaged through the refrigerator and pulled out a tray of biscotti left over from last night. "When she dresses up, let me tell you, she's gorgeous. Last week at that ball, I was wishin' she'd wear another one of her potato sacks. I felt more like a bodyguard than a date."

Mike sat on the stool and took a bite out of his biscotti. "So what are you going to do?"

Rich shook his head. "What can I do? I told her I love her, I want to marry her, and I didn't do all those things she accused me of, but it's not like I can prove it." He stared into his coffee cup as if it was a crystal ball.

Mike shook his head. "I don't know, man. That's rough. You should have seen Becca the day our dad said he'd gotten her work into an art gallery because he got the owner's son into med school. She flipped out. She's real sensitive about that."

Vinny finished his coffee and sat the cup down. "It looks to me like you two have some communicatin' to do."

Rich ran a frustrated hand through his hair that was already standing on end. "Yeah, how the hell am I supposed to communicate with her when she won't even talk to me?"

Nick, Vinny, and Mike all answered at the same time. "You have to wear her down."

Rich blew out a breath. "Yeah, thanks for the advice. It helps a lot."

Vinny walked around the bar into the kitchen and threw his arm around Richie. "We'll work on her too, and I'm sure Mickey and Nick will talk to Annabelle and Rosalie. Once they find out what happened, they'll take your side."

Richie didn't look like he believed them, but really, there wasn't much he could do. His face brightened when he looked at Mike. "I guess I can drop by your place and maybe bump into her."

Mike took the last sip of his coffee and walked to the sink to rinse his cup. "She's not with us, and I'm not allowed to tell you where she's staying. I've been sworn to secrecy. Give it some time, Rich. If she's in love with you, she'll have as hard a time being away from you as you will being away from her. If she doesn't, it's not meant to be."

Nick nodded. "Man, when Lee and I hit the skids, it was the worst month of my life. Christ, I'm so glad I'm not you."

Mike left the kitchen and walked toward the bedrooms. "Rich, you couldn't take pity on me and move her freakin' bags into the guest room?"

Rich shrugged. "What's the point? You practically caught us in the act the last time you stopped by. Do you pretend you're not sleeping with my sister?"

"I married your sister."

"Sure, and I'm doing my best to marry yours, so get over it already."

"Fine. Oh, I almost forgot. Becca can't take the cat until she moves into the brownstone. She asked if you'd take care of him. Either that, or I'll have to take him to my place, and it's not good for pregnant women to be around litter boxes, so I'd like to avoid that."

Rich nodded. "It's fine. I guess she'll have to get in touch with me eventually if she wants the little guy back. Not to mention all the artwork."

When they had all of Becca's things packed into the van Nick brought, Richie looked even worse than he did when they got there. Vin gave him a hug before he left, and he could swear he saw Richie's eyes watering. The poor guy. "We'll work on it from our end. You work on it from yours. And remember, when you see her, you grovel. It's worth the embarrassment every time."

Rich turned around, and Vinny let him. He didn't want to see a grown man cry any more than Rich wanted to be seen. "Thanks for coming by. I'll see ya. Oh, and let me know how Becca is, okay?"

Chapter 18

BECCA HEARD ANNABELLE COME IN AND WAS TRULY afraid for the first time in their friendship that she might lose her best friend and maybe even her new brother. She'd spent the last hour berating herself for doing something as stupid as falling in love with Rich Ronaldi. Not just because she ended up feeling as if she was dying inside, but because Rich was Annabelle's brother, and as he once reminded her, blood is thicker than water.

"Becca, where are you?"

She was in bed with a cool compress over her swollen, burning eyes. "In the guest room." She pulled the washcloth off her face and sat.

Annabelle waddled in, sat beside her, and pulled her into a hug. "I'm so sorry. Tell me what happened."

The entire time Becca talked, Annabelle was quiet. She nodded, but the longer Becca went on, the more scared she became. "Would you say something?"

"I understand where you're coming from, and I admit that from what you said that Rich looks like a real schmuck. But Bec, I know my brother, and I know he would never do that. He'd never use you to get a job."

Becca raised an eyebrow, which ended up twitching, and sent a stabbing pain through her head.

Annabelle continued. "Okay, I'll admit he tried to fake a relationship so he could look good, but Rich is way too conceited ever to take a promotion under false pretenses."

"Right, he had no problem begging me to pretend to have a relationship with him so he'd look like a good little professor."

"Oh, come on. Richie's always been good at whatever he's done. He wouldn't take a job he wasn't sure he more than deserved. And you know if he wasn't qualified, pretending to have a relationship wouldn't have made a difference. If Richie let the dean get away with saying that, he must have had a damn good reason."

Becca pulled her legs up to her chest and wrapped her arms around them before resting her chin on her knees. "Like a trust fund?"

"No, Rich is too proud to live off someone else's money. If anything, money would be a deterrent for him. All I can think was that Rich knew how sensitive you are to any sign of nepotism and was afraid you'd give up a perfect opportunity to showcase your work."

"I would have. But that's my decision."

Annabelle rolled her eyes "Of course it is, but he's an Italian man, which means he not only has the 'Y' chromosome, he's *über* protective, wants to give you the world, and he thinks he knows what's best for you."

"Then why did he ask me to marry him?"

"When did he do that?"

"Right after his boss dropped the big bombshell. Remember when the guys went to play basketball Monday?"

"Yeah, that's why you stopped by and talked to Ben and me."

"Right. After the game they went to DiNicola's, and he and the guys had a few drinks while waiting for takeout. Before dinner, and in the middle of sex, he asked me to marry him."

"Oh my God, what did you say?"

Becca cringed when she thought about it. "At first, nothing. Then, when I was able to breathe again and got my head together, he was pissed and belligerent. It wasn't pretty. We finally agreed to table the marriage discussion for the time being, but then I was talking to Wayne and Henry the next day, and they both agreed a guy doesn't just go out for a drink and on the way home decide to propose marriage. Not without something holding his feet to the fire."

Annabelle crossed her arms and rested them on her belly. "It's obvious. He was afraid of losing you. He must have been pretty upset when his dean said what he said. And instead of saying something and ruining your chances with Emily Stewart, he swallowed his pride. He did that for you, and by doing so, put your entire relationship in jeopardy."

"And you know this how?"

"Because I know my brother. He's not the devious type, and he's not money hungry. Why do you think he made such a shitty criminal? But why he did what he did really isn't the issue here. This issue is that you don't trust him."

Becca didn't know what to say to that. Annabelle was right. She didn't trust him; heck, she didn't trust anyone except Annabelle and Mike.

Annabelle kicked off her shoes and scooted up to rest against the headboard. "Do you want to know my theory on love?"

"Do I get a choice?"

"No, but this is a good one, so listen up. Trust and respect are more important than love in a relationship because no love will last without equal amounts of respect and trust." She rubbed Becca's hand. "Love, trust, and respect are decisions only you can make, sweetie. There's nothing Rich can do to prove to you he didn't check out your financial papers. He can't prove what he was thinking when he was given the position. He can only explain it and hope you love, trust, and respect him enough to believe what he says."

Becca had to admit it made sense. Still, she didn't know how to do that. It's not like there were some self-help books on how to trust—or were there? All the therapists she ever saw told her she needed to forgive the people who hurt her. She didn't know how to do that either. Of course, it might be easier to forgive people if they'd stopped hurting her or at least asked for forgiveness. As soon as she figured out that would never happen, she gave up.

Becca was lost in thought when Annabelle pulled the pillow under her head and lay beside her. "Mike called when he left the apartment. He said Rich looked worse than most corpses." Annabelle yawned. "Mike said Rich seemed relieved that you left Tripod with him. It didn't look like Richie wanted to be alone. Instead of wanting to beat the poor guy up, Mike ended up feeling sorry for him."

"What am I supposed to do now?"

Annabelle rolled onto her side. "I guess you need to think about it. Remember when I asked you if you saw your future without Rich as the same or sucky?"

Becca nodded.

"I guess you get to experience it firsthand and see if you were right. I know when Mike and I broke up, I was devastated. I never want to go through that again for as long as I live."

Becca lay there a while thinking about how sucky it was. So far, it really stunk. She rolled over to face Annabelle and tell her so, only to find her sound asleep. Becca got up, covered Annabelle with a throw, and waited for Mike to bring her things to her. At least then she'd have something to do, she could unpack. She wondered how long she could drag that out.

Rich sat in his office wishing he were dead. He'd stopped drinking by five o'clock in the afternoon thinking he could sleep through the hangover. Obviously, he was wrong. He woke up feeling like shit. Coffee, water, and aspirin didn't touch the pain in his head or his heart, and he wasn't even going to think about the damage he'd done to his stomach.

He kept his office blinds closed and the lights out, hoping that anyone who was dumb enough to show up for office hours on a Monday morning would at least have the intelligence to go away when they saw a dark office.

Rich leaned back in his wooden desk chair, his head resting on the wall behind him with his eyes closed, when some asshole opened the door and flipped on the light. Florescent bulbs blinked on beyond his eyelids. "You had better have an extraordinary excuse for inter-rupting a perfectly good imitation of death."

"I don't suppose the three students leaving messages regarding questions they would have asked if you'd been available during office hours would suffice? Especially since I witnessed your arrival and know you're here in body if not spirit."

Rich pried one of his eyelids open, and sure enough, Dean Stewart was standing there looking all collegiate with his tweed blazer and brown slacks. All he was missing was the bow tie and the damn pipe. "I'll talk to them. Thanks for letting me know."

"That's the only explanation I'm going to receive?"

Rich sat up and stared at Dean Stewart. "Do you think I'm a good professor?"

"With the exception of your behavior today, yes I do."

"Good, then I suppose it won't make any difference that Becca left me, and it doesn't look as if I have a prayer of getting her back. Hell, I don't even know where she is. She won't answer my calls or emails, and no one will even tell me where she's staying. I guess, if nothing else, I should be happy knowing that at least my job is secure."

Craig sat down and leaned forward. "Look, Rich. I know I'm your superior, but I'd also like to think that we're friends. You two looked so happy the other night. What happened?"

Rich shook his head and then regretted the movement. "Becca is very sensitive when it comes to her family name and their money. I screwed up on several counts, only one of which was failing to tell her about my promotion. She's been hurt before, and probably because of that, she questioned my intentions. Unfortunately, there's no way to prove my intentions."

"Why didn't you tell her about your promotion?"

"Because she was so looking forward to Emily seeing her work without knowing she was Rebecca Larsen of the Main Line Larsens. If she knew that wasn't the case, she'd have canceled the entire thing. She's so hell-bent on making it on her own that she's going overboard and destroying great opportunities."

"Ah." Craig leaned back in his chair and crossed his ankles out in front of him. "It's not easy falling in love with a woman with a pedigree and the money to back it up."

Rich raised his eyes to meet Craig's. "Emily?"

Craig nodded. "Emily Talbot-Stewart."

"Christ, that benefit? That was her family's foundation?"

"Of course, you don't think she is able to run a foundation like that on my salary, do you?"

Rich shrugged. "I'm so far out of my element here, Craig. I have no idea. I thought she worked for the foundation. I had no idea it was her family's."

"Emily was very impressed with Becca's work, and it had nothing to do with her pedigree, I assure you. As for you, I've known you since you were eighteen. I give you a couple of days to lick your wounds, and then you'll be busy figuring out how to get back in Becca's good graces. I'm sorry if what I said caused trouble between the two of you."

Rich rubbed his bloodshot eyes and groaned. "I guess it was bound to happen sooner or later. She doesn't trust me. I don't think it's personal. She doesn't trust anyone. Unfortunately, it's something I have no control over. She's got to decide whether to give me the benefit of the doubt or not."

"Well, my door is always open if you need anything. I wish you luck. I really like Becca. The two of you remind me of Emily and myself twenty years ago. It wasn't easy, but I have to admit, even with all the problems that come along with the marriage of two people from two very different social classes, it's well worth it."

"Thanks Craig. I'll keep it in mind."

Rich shook Craig's hand and watched him go. Rich felt trapped in his office so he checked his schedule for the day, called one of his doctoral candidates in to teach, left his lecture notes with the secretary, and headed to the one person who might be able to help him. A half hour later, he was on the stoop knocking. "Aunt Rose, it's Rich."

She opened the door but didn't let him in. "You tink I don't know that? *Maddòne*. You didn't come to dinner yesterday. You didn't go to church—too busy drinking the whiskey, eh? You better call your mother and go to confession."

"Yeah, okay."

Aunt Rose opened the door for him and smiled as she patted his cheek. He bent down to kiss each cheek and thanked God she didn't pinch him. "Aunt Rose, Becca left me, and no one will tell me where she is. They won't tell me if she's okay—nothing."

She motioned him to follow her to the kitchen, and he sat in the antique modern Naugahyde and chrome dinette set she'd had since before he was born. She tied an apron around her waist and started cooking lunch. "She's a'livin' in the city." She poured him a glass of wine and set it down in front of him. "Here, drink'a this. It will make you feel better."

The last thing he wanted was more alcohol, but Aunt Rose wouldn't answer until he did as she said. They didn't call her "The Colonel" for nothing. He took a tentative sip, which went down surprisingly easily.

"Where in the city?"

She gave him that look that said, what are you, *stunad*? Then she shook a disgusted head and pointed a huge meat fork at him. "What do you think I looka like? A street map? I don't give addresses. My Becca, she's in a nice man's apartment. He got some kinda money, that one."

"A man?"

"*Si*, but he no' there." She put a pot of water on the stove and pulled the butcher paper off a package. Rich's stomach rolled when he saw steak. "I make this special for you. You don't think so now, but it make you feel better." At least she wasn't forcing him to eat her mustard greens; he hated those. Aunt Rose dropped the steaks in a hot cast iron frying pan, the kind she used to threaten to hit him with. "She got a bad headache from cryin' over you. What'a you thinkin' askin' her to marry you like you did? No ring, no romance. What she supposed to tella' your children when they ask how poppa proposed?" She mumbled under her breath, and he could swear she said something in Italian about all men being assholes, but then he didn't really want to know if he was right.

"Do you know everything?"

"I know what I know." She pointed at him, which always gave him the creeps. "You don't deserve her." She made a slashing motion and turned back to her cooking. "*Stunad*."

She tossed some homemade pasta in the boiling water and stirred the sauce she had heating on the stove beside something else. Shit. He knew it. "Aunt Rose, I ain't eatin' those greens."

"Fine, you no eat the greens, then you drink the water I cook them in. You need the vitamins—it'sa good. Clean out the poison. What's it gonna be, Richie?"

"I'll eat the greens. There's no way I'm drinkin' that stuff. Just put some sauce on it. Maybe it'll cover up the taste."

She tsked as she fixed his plate, steak, pasta, greens. She set it in front of him and put the cheese on the table. "*Mangia, mangia.*" She waited for him to take a bite. Once she saw him eat, she turned back to fix her own plate, sat, said grace silently, and dug in. After one bite, she was pointing her fork at Rich again. "If you want your Becca back, you gonna have to work. It'sa not gonna be easy for either of you."

"Yeah, and just how am I supposed to do that?"

Rich took a bite of rare steak; he was starting to feel better, not that he'd tell Aunt Rose that, but then, knowing her, she knew already.

"You not. That'sa the hard part. You want to go find her, make her see your way." She shook her head and twirled her pasta. "No, that would make her angry. Better you leave her wondering, that one. You just do what you do. Let her see you're the boy she fell in love with. She's gonna miss you and that strange cat of hers. She might come to visit when she thinks you're away."

"She will? When?" Rich took a bite of the mustard greens. Even drowned in sauce they were bitter and rank.

"You ever hear that saying, absence makes'a the heart grow fonder?"

He swallowed the forkful of greens as quickly as possible and chased it with the rest of his wine. "Yeah." He held his glass out for a refill; he'd be drunk by the time he finished his vegetables.

"Listen to Aunt Rose. You leave her alone. Let her come to you. Just make sure you're ready for her when she does. And whatever you do, buy the girl a ring, and then when you do ask her to marry you, use your other head, eh?"

"No way, Aunt Rose. I'm not gonna ask her again. I told her if she ever wanted to marry me, she was gonna have to ask me."

Aunt Rose got up, and Rich wondered if she was gonna hurt him. Instead she took his face in her hands and kissed both cheeks before slapping one. "You think so, eh? You might just change'a your mind. You're stubborn, but not as stubborn as your Becca. You see reason eventually. That'sa why you're my favorite nephew."

"I'm your only nephew." He laughed, feeling much better as she shrugged and sat to finish her lunch.

After the deal went through, Becca and Annabelle became majority owners of the Benjamin Walsh Gallery. Before the ink was even dry on the contracts, Becca officially took over the studio down the hall from Ben's apartment, and Annabelle gladly moved back to her old office in the gallery.

Annabelle was chomping at the bit to give Becca a showing, but Becca didn't have the energy to even think about it. It was all she could do to get by day-to-day. She slept when she could and worked when she couldn't. Her days and nights seemed to meld to the point she'd have to look out the window to figure out if it was morning or night. She missed Rich, she missed Tripod, and as the days and weeks passed, and the pain and loss didn't diminish, she wondered if she was actually getting worse.

It was cold and wet, and looking out the window, she wondered if the weather mirrored her moods, or if her mood mirrored the weather. She paced Ben's apartment and tried not to think of how much she missed Rich's. Ben's place was very minimalist—all hard lines, bold shapes, cold and stark where Rich's was comfortable, warm, and laid back.

She checked the time. Rich would be at school for the next several hours. She pulled on a hoodie over her sweater, grabbed her coat, iPod, and purse. She was going to visit her cat; she just hoped she didn't get caught.

When Becca let herself into Rich's place, the first thing she noticed was that it was immaculate. Tripod yowled, and when she bent to pet him, he bit her. "Ow!"

The little bugger broke the skin. Becca sucked on her finger and dropped her purse and coat on the couch before going into the bathroom to wash her wound. The bathroom was cleaner than it had ever been when she and Rich shared it. She found herself taking inventory, and as much as it killed her to admit it, she was relieved to see that there was only one toothbrush in the holder, until she remembered that he didn't mind sharing.

God, the pain stabbed at her again so badly, she could hardly breathe. Maybe coming here was a bad idea. Tripod certainly didn't seem happy to see her. Just the opposite. She washed her hands and glanced at his bedroom. He kept it clean too. It was a far cry from the first day she stepped foot in Rich's place. She opened the first aid kit and squirted some Bactine, sucked in a breath when the sting began, and then blew on it. "It was easier when I didn't like him."

Tripod snaked around her leg and seemed to agree with her. "You're nice to me now? What was the bite about? Were you punishing me?"

Becca put a Band-Aid on the puncture wound, thankful that Tripod had all his shots. She tossed the wrapper, put the first aid kit away, and went back into the living room. All her work was where she left it. Everything looked exactly the same as it did when she walked out, only cleaner. Even her notebook lay on the coffee table right next to her favorite pen. She picked up the leather notebook and the pen and opened it to take out her Loving Rich list. She had thought of a few more cons, not that she was going to write them down. She just didn't want one of his bimbo girlfriends to find it. She paged through the notebook and couldn't believe her eyes. What the hell?

Someone else was writing in her notebook. She turned back to the beginning and then saw her name. It was dated just two days after their breakup.

Becca,

Aunt Rose said you might be stopping by to visit Tripod. I'm sure he'd love to see you. He seems to miss you almost as much as I do. So when I found your notebook, I thought since you won't return my calls, the only way I have to communicate with you is to write to you. Since I don't know where you call home these days, I'm hoping Aunt Rose is right about you visiting. I'm counting on that, and the hope that if you do come by, you might read this. In any case, I guess it's cathartic. Either that, or I'm just into self-torture, which is a distinct possibility. So here goes.

Hi Babe, God I miss you something awful. I don't think I've ever felt quite like this. It's as if someone stole a part of me, and I'm left with a gaping hole where my heart used to be. The only thing I can compare it to is the one time I lost my wallet. I know you're probably rolling your eyes, but work with me here. Okay? There was that initial adrenaline rush, when I frantically searched high and low for it, then after I knew it was gone, out of habit, I kept reaching for it.

I thought about all the things that couldn't be replaced, the social security card I signed when I was twelve, the pictures of my family, the Mass card from my grandmother's funeral, the fortune that was too good to throw out. And every time I'd reach for my wallet, I had the same reaction, over and over and over again.

That's the way it's been since you left. I wake up without you, and I gotta tell you, babe, I don't

know how to stop reaching for you, and every time
I do it hurts. I love you, Becca.

Rich

The tears just flowed, and she didn't even notice them dripping on the page. When she tried to brush them away, the ink ran. She didn't know what to do. If Rich looked, he would see it, but then if she took the notebook, he'd know she'd been there too, and he might stop writing her.

She cried through every note he wrote, one for every day they were apart, and by the time she got to the last entry, she was sobbing.

Becca closed the book, and then cried all over Tripod. God she was such a mess. She saw the clock and knew she had to get out of there pretty soon. Rich would be home, and the last thing she wanted to do was run into him now. It was hard enough leaving him when she was irate; now, all she knew was that she missed him so much, it scared her.

She put the cat down and wiped her face on her sleeve, left everything just where she found it, and took off out of the apartment, going the opposite direction from the one she knew Rich would be walking.

Rich turned the corner and saw a woman hurrying down the sidewalk ahead of him. She wore a hat, but the way she walked and dressed reminded him of Becca, but then he'd been having Becca-spottings everywhere he went. The other day at Starbucks, he'd even called out her name and grabbed a strange woman's elbow. That's when he decided he needed to get a little more of a life than the one he had. Spending every night writing notes to Becca, notes that she may never see, might not be the best use of his time.

Rich unlocked the door and pushed it open. He pulled off his jacket, took a deep breath, and swore he smelled Becca's shampoo. "Fuck, that was her." He hightailed it out of the apartment, down the front steps, and into the street, searching for her. He ran two blocks before he admitted he'd lost her.

He pulled off his cell phone and dialed her. "Becca, it's Rich. Babe, please come back." He turned a full circle looking up and down the cross street. "I'm waiting for you, Becca. Come home. If you won't come back, at least give me a call. I miss the sound of your voice. I miss everything."

Rich flipped his phone shut, walked back to the apartment, grabbed a beer out of the refrigerator, and microwaved the leftover salmon he'd made the other night and didn't eat. He hoped he'd have better luck tonight but decided that from now on, he probably shouldn't cook anything he made with Becca here—which was his entire culinary repertoire. The last time he'd stopped at Vinny's, he borrowed one of his cookbooks and brought it home with him. Maybe if he started cooking, he could get his mind off Becca and onto something useful.

He took his plate out of the microwave and cut off a piece of fish for Tripod, put it on a small plate, and brought them both over to the couch. He set Tripod's plate on the coffee table, and when Tripod went to sit on Becca's notebook, Rich pulled it out from under the little guy's butt. Rich cut a piece of his fish and opened Becca's notebook to find the ink had run. What the fuck? Shit, the pages were covered with tears. He'd made her cry again.

Chapter 19

RICH WENT INTO WORK THE NEXT MORNING DREADING the day. When he walked past Dean Stewart's office, he was called in by the dean's assistant. "Dean Stewart would like to see you, if you have a moment. Just go ahead in."

"Thanks." Rich knocked before sticking his head in. "You wanted to see me?"

Dean Stewart waved Rich in while he finished his telephone call. As soon as he hung up the phone, he smiled and rubbed his hands together. "I've got some interesting information I think might help you out."

Rich unbuttoned his trench coat and sat down. "Okay."

"Now, I hope I'm not making things worse, but I've found out that there's been a deal brewing between Becca, Annabelle Flynn, and Ben Walsh to sell them a majority interest in the Ben Walsh Gallery."

Rich's first thought was, *way to go, Becca*. It would give her a place to show her work, which would have nothing to do with her family. The second thought wasn't quite as positive. "You said this has been brewing for a while?"

"Yes, they've already finalized it. I would think it would take weeks, if not months, to put something like this together."

"Months, huh?" Rich picked up his briefcase and stood. "I have something personal to take care of. If it's okay with you, I'm going to take the day off. I'll call one of my doctoral candidates to cover my classes."

Dean Stewart smiled. "I was hoping that was what you'd say." Dean Stewart walked around his desk and slapped Rich on the shoulder. "Good luck, Rich. Take as much time as you need."

Rich set everything up before leaving his office and headed home. Everything made sense now. Like what Aunt Rose said about Becca staying in the city in a man's home. That man had to be Ben. She'd been living over the gallery the whole time they'd been apart, which meant that she had this deal brewing before they ever split up—not that she saw fit to mention it to him.

The entire time they'd been apart he'd been beating himself up, convinced that the breakup was all his fault. What a joke that was. Well, at least now he knew it was over. He was tired of living in limbo, hoping and praying she'd come to her senses.

As soon as he got home, he locked Tripod in the mud room and started packing Becca's artwork into the back of his SUV and felt more loss with every piece he removed. The apartment looked empty, like a blank canvas—all the spark, the life that made it his home, dwindled with every trip he made to the car. He lovingly wrapped the statue Becca had made of Annabelle and left it in the crate he'd used to hide it. The only thing left was the first piece Becca had ever done—the one piece that exhibited everything that he loved about her. He sat on the bed, staring at the slightly crooked piece, and knew he should pack it with the rest of her things, but he couldn't bear to part with it.

Rich let Tripod out and gave him back the toy he'd found hidden in Becca's bedside table along with several more notebooks. He took all the notebooks he'd found, along with the one he'd been using to write to her, and threw them in the crate. His place looked empty, kind of like the way he felt.

Becca was in the middle of shaping the nose on a face that looked suspiciously like Rich's. There was a knock on the door. She wiped her hands off. "Come on in."

She threw the towel down on the workbench, turned, and her breath caught. "Rich."

God he looked good. He was in jeans and a Henley shirt with a fleece-lined hoodie over it. She didn't notice the anger until she got to his face.

He put the crate down beside the wall. "I guess I was the last one to hear that you and Annabelle bought the place. I packed the rest of your things and brought them over. The piece you've kept under wraps is in there." He motioned to the crate filled with a half dozen notebooks, her favorite notebook, the one he wrote his letters to her in, was thrown on top. Her stomach took a dip. "Where do you want the rest of it?"

"Rich—"

He held up his hands. "Look, Becca. I know this has been over for you for a long time." He ran his hand through his hair. "Maybe I was just lying to myself thinking we were ever really together. I know you have to hit me over the head with a two-by-four sometimes to get through my thick skull, but you buying the gallery did it."

"I didn't—"

He shook his head. "Let me finish. You made a big

stink about me not telling you about my promotion when the whole time you were planning this without ever mentioning it to me? What did you do, talk my sister into keeping it quiet, too?"

She didn't know what to say; she hadn't thought about it at the time, but he was right. She didn't mention it to him, and after she left, because she was so concerned with him finding her, not sure she'd be able to resist him, she had asked Annabelle not to mention it. "I'm sorry."

He just nodded. "Yeah, me too." He shoved his hands into his pockets and looked at his boots. "Look, I'll just move your stuff into the downstairs storeroom, and I'll be outta your hair and your life. You can figure out what you want to do with it on your own."

She wanted to grab him and not let him go, but when she stepped forward he turned away from her. "Good luck, Becca. Be happy."

He turned and walked out, and instead of taking the elevator, he took the stairs. The echo of his footfalls rang out until the door finally clicked shut.

Becca reached for her notebook looking for the notes he'd written her. They were gone. Oh, God.

Becca sat on the couch, hugging herself, wanting to go stop Rich, but not knowing how. It had been so much easier to see him as the guilty party. She thought she'd cried all the tears she could possibly cry over the man, but when she remembered the look on his face, she realized how wrong she was.

Annabelle walked into the studio and slammed the door behind her. "What did you do to him?"

"I hurt him, and he finally gave up on me. I guess I got what I deserve. Oh, God, Annabelle. I lost him."

"What? You're just figuring this out now?"

"I don't know. I was so mad at him, thinking he'd used me to get the position at the university, and then when he asked me to marry him—I guess I kind of freaked out. I didn't realize that I'd been keeping things from him too. But if I had told him about buying the gallery—"

"He would have known you were rich, and you thought he was only in it for the money. Girlfriend, you really have to work on your self-esteem. Don't you think anyone could just love you for you?"

"No one ever has before."

"I have, you idiot. Even when you're acting like an ass. Like now, for instance."

Annabelle sat down beside her and gave her a sideways hug. "Okay, at least now you see you were both imbeciles. It happens. The question is what the hell are you going to do about it?"

"What can I do? He's so angry, and he looked so, I don't know, shut down."

"Kinda like he did after he asked you to marry him?"

Becca sniffled and brushed the tears from her eyes, probably leaving streaks of mud. God, she was a mess. "Yeah."

"Well, what did you do then?"

"I jumped on him and made him listen to me."

Annabelle rubbed her back. "It worked once. Chances are it will work again. But before you leave, you may want to wash your face and put on prettier clothes, not to mention nicer shoes." She looked down at the mud-splattered Crocs Becca wore. "I can't believe you wear those things on purpose."

Rich stopped on the way home and bought a bottle of Scotch. There was no way he was going to DiNicola's and getting drunk; he'd rather be alone. When he turned the corner, he found Aunt Rose pressing the intercom and talking to him.

"Aunt Rose, I'm here."

"You're late."

"No I'm not. What are you doing here?"

"I came to talk to you. You gonna invite me in?"

"Look, Aunt Rose, this really isn't a good time."

"You tink I don't know? You got someting better to do than talk to me?"

Rich shook his head. He might as well get it over with. There would be no drinking until Aunt Rose left. "Fine, come in."

"I brought you dinner and someting you need."

All Rich needed right now was the bottle of Johnny Walker Black he carried in the crook of his arm wrapped in a brown paper sack. Still, he carried her shopping cart up the front steps of the brownstone and showed her into the apartment.

"Where's all of Becca's art?"

"It's gone. I just dropped it off at the gallery. Becca, Annabelle, and Ben are partners now. The only thing she has left here is the cat, and she'll take him as soon as she moves into her new apartment."

"Ah, I see how it is." She put her pocketbook down on the breakfast bar in the kitchen and rooted through it.

"Really? Then why are you here? Whatever Becca and I had is over, Aunt Rose. Becca never loved me enough to trust me. She thinks I was after her money."

"Oh Richie, it's not you she don't trust, it's her. She don't tink she's worth loving for anyting but her money. But don't worry. That won't last long. Here." She handed him a small, worn black velvet jeweler's box. "This I give to you. You'll need it and a nice dinner."

"What is it?" Rich opened the box expecting a cross or a St. Christopher's medal; instead, he found a honking diamond engagement ring. "Wow. What are you giving me this for? I just told you. Becca and I are through."

Aunt Rose shrugged. "You never know. Me, I know what I know, and I know you need this. Remember what I told you. You want to marry the girl, you ask nice, and you give her a ring. *Capisce*?"

"*Capisce*." What was the point in arguing? Aunt Rose obviously got her wires crossed.

"This ring was always meant for you. I just thought I'd be dead before you needed it." She crossed herself. "For once I was wrong." She took the packages into the kitchen. "I'll put your dinner in the oven to heat. I set'a the timer so you don't forget."

"Okay."

"Take'a the flowers and put them on the table, eh? I brought you my good candlesticks too, so you can be romantic."

Rich did as he was told and was thrilled when she kissed him good-bye at the door. He was finally alone. He opened his bottle of Scotch, downed a full glass, and went to take a shower in the hope of drowning something, his sorrow, himself—anything would be an improvement over the way he felt right then.

Becca couldn't believe the getup Annabelle made her change into. You'd think she was going to a costume party dressed as a high-class call girl, not to beg for a second (or was it a third?) chance at love. She pulled down the short, short skirt that had every man on the subway eyeing her. It was almost as bad as the *über*-uncomfortable, thigh-high, fuck-me boots Annabelle foisted on her. By the time she arrived at Rich's apartment, she had blisters on top of her blisters and cursed herself for not getting her car out of the damn garage and driving. Shit. What if this didn't work out? What was she going to do? Get a ride back from Rich? Fuck. It had to work. She certainly wasn't going to be happy taking public transportation back to the city.

When she entered the apartment, she found an empty glass on the table, Rich's hoodie thrown on the couch, his humongous work boots kicked off under the coffee table, and the shower running. She peeked into the bedroom and found a trail of his clothes. His jeans, boxer briefs, his shirt littered the floor, and the door to the bathroom was ajar. One little push and the door drifted open. Tripod crouched next to the tub, jumped up, hitting the closed shower curtain, and bounced back down, only to repeat the action. Judging by the amount of steam rolling out of the bathroom and Tripod's obvious impatience, Rich had been in there awhile.

"Jesus Christ, Tripod. Keep your pants on. I'm getting

out. Don't you dare try to bite me because I'm in no mood to deal with you today, buddy."

The shower curtain zipped open, and one very hairy leg stepped out, followed by an equally hairy, and beautifully naked, Rich.

Becca stared. "Hi."

For a second, she wondered if he was going to slam the door in her face. Instead, he turned around and looked for his towel.

He walked past her. "What do you want, Becca?"

"Your towel is hanging on the bed."

"You came all this way to point that out to me?"

She shook her head. "No. Of course not."

Rich grabbed his towel, taking the time to dry off his hair and his chest and his back before wrapping it around his waist. "What? You might want to check your list so you don't forget any pertinent points. We wouldn't want you to have to come back and finish me off later."

"I didn't make a list. I didn't even think about it. I just came over."

"Dressed like that?"

"Annabelle made me change."

Rich nodded, crossed his arms over his chest, and stared.

"The thing is…"

Rich stood there, not moving a muscle. He was no help at all.

"What's the thing, Bec? I'm aging here."

"So, you're going to be belligerent? I don't know why I'm surprised."

Rich sat on the bed. "Hey, you're the one who just

strolled in here. Uninvited, I might add. Say what you came to say and leave. I'm done."

"Fine." She pushed him back down on the bed and straddled him. As Annabelle said, it worked before. She just wished he wasn't wearing the damn towel. "There, that's better." Rich moved his hands to her waist to pick her up and throw her off him, so she hooked her heels under his legs.

"Ouch, watch the spikes, babe."

"If you don't want me to have to hurt you, you'll let me finish."

"I don't see how you could possibly hurt me any more than you already have." Rich blew out a breath, grimaced, and stayed still.

He was really making her work for it, and she had to admit, she probably deserved it. "Would you stop looking at me like that?"

"Like what? Like a crazy woman who just broke my heart, stomped all over it in four-inch heels, and came back to make sure the job was done?"

She lay down on him so they were nose-to-nose. God she'd forgotten how wonderful he felt. "I came back to tell you I love you, and to say I'm sorry, and to ask you…"

"What?"

"Can we just go back to where we were?"

"Where we were an hour and a half ago, or a month ago, before you walked out of my life?"

"How about back to the night you came home from the basketball game?"

She pushed herself back up so she sat on him; it was better to be able to look him in the eye. Rich blew out another frustrated breath, but he didn't say no, so she figured she'd go for it. "You came home right after I figured out I was in love with you. I love you, you know. I've tried to not love you, but I can't."

"Thanks, that makes me feel so much better."

"I should have told you about Ben and Annabelle offering me a partnership, but then you asked me to marry you, and I'm sorry, it completely freaked me out. The thing with the gallery just slipped my mind."

"Right. Don't insult my intelligence, Becca. You didn't tell me about the offer because then I'd know you weren't broke. You treated me as if I was one of your asshole friends only interested in your dough."

"It wasn't like that."

He raised an eyebrow.

"I just couldn't figure out why you wanted to marry me. No one has ever wanted to marry me before—not because they loved me. The only reason anyone ever wanted to marry me was to get my trust fund, and when I heard the dean, well, I thought history was repeating itself. I jumped to conclusions, and I said some horrible things. I was wrong. I'm sorry."

"Damn straight you were wrong. I don't care about your money. I don't want your money. Hell, all I ever wanted was you. Why is that so hard for you to believe?"

"You're the psych professor. Ever hear of conditioned response? But then Annabelle says I have low self-esteem." She shrugged and wrapped her arms around herself. "Maybe she's right. I'm sorry I called you those names. I'm sorry I didn't trust you. I'm sorry I didn't tell you about the partnership offer. I miss you, and I want you back. I want us back. But there's something you need to know first."

"What is it now?"

"It's about my money. You see, I never spent a penny of my trust fund. I wanted to make it on my own."

"Wow, that's a surprise."

Becca barely kept from rolling her eyes. "I invested every cent of the money that came to me through my trust, and I'm good at it. I've done very well. So, in the interest of full disclosure, you should know that I'm extremely wealthy."

"Here's a news flash Bec—I never gave a shit about money, yours or anyone else's. My only concern was that you had enough to support your art. If you needed it, I would have helped."

"I'm sorry."

She moved forward to meet his eyes. Okay, now would be a good time for him to say something or do something. Frankly, she was pretty much all talked out, but he just lay there staring. She couldn't even read his expression. "Rich?"

"Hmm?"

"Aren't you going to say anything?"

"No, I'm kind of enjoying watching you squirm."

She nudged his leg with Annabelle's spiked heel. "You're such an asshole!"

Rich moved so quickly she screamed, landed flat on her back, and had the air knocked out of her when all two hundred pounds of him landed squarely on top of her. He pinned her down, his hand holding her wrists over her head.

He grinned, and for the first time in over a month, Becca felt whole. "God, I missed you."

Becca tried to free her hands to no avail. "That's it? I spill my guts, and all you have to say is you missed me?"

Rich pulled the towel from between them and slid between her legs, pushing the skirt she wore higher as he kissed the corner of her mouth. Becca's heart pounded, and her breath was so shallow and rapid, she wondered if she would hyperventilate. She tried to get her mind back on the topic at hand and away from the way he pressed against her panties.

"I love you."

Still not what she was going for. "Is there anything you want to ask me?"

"Just one thing. Could you leave the boots on?"

"What? Did you just ask me to leave my boots on?"

Rich raked his teeth over her neck. "Yeah, they're really hot boots."

"That's it? That's the only question you want to ask me?"

"No, but I can't very well ask you to marry me again until I put my pants back on, get down on one knee, and you know, try to do it right this time. Aunt Rose will come back and smack me upside the head, and frankly, that would be a bit embarrassing considering our relative position. So, what do you say?"

This time Becca wasn't making a mental list. Rich supposed that was a good thing. She shot him a beautiful watery smile before nodding, and then she said the one word he wanted most to hear. "Yes."

"Thank God." He released her hands. She wrapped her arms around his neck and kissed him. Nothing before had prepared him for the cataclysm of emotion that shot through him with one kiss. It was a mixture of hope, love, and energy mixed with excitement, passion, and a whole lot of need—the need to belong, the need to love, and be loved. He let all the feelings he'd held back for the past month flow out of him.

With one flick of the wrist, Becca's panties were history. He swallowed her groan as he joined his body with hers. He reeled from the heat, the intensity, and the emotion. When he opened his eyes and saw their reflection in hers, it sent them both spiraling out of control. It was a melding of souls but with the power of the big bang. She wrapped her legs around him, her boots digging into his back, urging him faster, harder, deeper. He pushed her top up and sucked her breast deep into his mouth as she came apart. The combination was all it took to send them both over the edge of sanity straight into heaven.

"Rich, the kitchen timer is going off."

He cracked one eye open, which was about all the movement he was capable of. Becca was stuck under him, and he wasn't sure if he'd ever be able to move again.

"Rich?"

He grunted. That used the rest of the energy he possessed.

She flexed her inner muscles and had him blowing his breath through his teeth. "What's the matter?"

"Just recovering from a near death experience—give me a minute, okay?'

"Sure." She patted his shoulder, planted a boot on the bed, arched her back, and slid out from beneath him. "I'll go take care of whatever it is you have in the oven."

He may have grunted again, and he could swear she kissed his neck before he floated back into a blissful sleep. When he awoke, he was alone. Panic ripped though him. "Becca?" He vaulted out of bed, grabbed his jeans, and was jumping up and down pulling them on when she came in.

"What's the matter?"

Rich ran his hands through his hair. "You were gone, and… Christ Bec, I thought you'd left."

Becca came to him and wrapped her arms around his neck. She was dressed in a pair of her old ratty sweats she'd forgotten in the laundry when she left. He never thought he'd see the day when he was happy to see her dressed like Becca again. She held him tight and nuzzled his neck. "I was just putting dinner on the table. It looks as if Aunt Rose spent all day cooking for us. We really shouldn't let it go to waste. Besides, I'm starving."

Rich ran his hands down her back and pulled her closer. "Okay, let's go eat." He stepped back, went to his closet, grabbed his lucky shirt, and slid it on. "We need to talk about a few things." He grabbed her hand and led her out of the bedroom, not wanting to let her go.

Becca sat and looked at him. There was a worry line between her eyes. "What kind of things?"

Rich poured the wine that Aunt Rose had left to breathe. "Don't look so worried. I just need to make sure we're going about this the right way. I don't think I can take another screw up. I swear I think I've aged ten years in the last month."

Becca took a gulp of her wine. "Okay, I agree. So shoot."

"I'm thinking of leaving Columbia."

"What? Why would you do that?"

"I don't want you to ever resent the fact that I'm there, and your family is well known at Columbia. I didn't get where I am because of you and your family. I know that. I hope you do too. But if we're together, we're going to be expected to play an active role in the university. If that's a problem for you, it would be better if I don't renew my contract."

"You'd do that?"

"Babe, I've been a professor without you. It's a job. It's not my life. You are. There are plenty of things I could do for a living that won't put a wedge between us."

"But what about your students, your research? You're a great teacher."

"I can teach anywhere. I can be a high school counselor. I can start a private practice. There are a lot of things I can do."

"But what about kids like Brad?"

Rich shrugged and cut into his chicken. "There's no shortage of professors."

"No, there's just a shortage of good, caring professors." She got out of her chair and went to kneel beside his. She took his hands in hers and swallowed hard. "Rich, I've learned a few things over the month we've been apart too. I've spent so much of my life running away from who I am, I almost lost myself in the process. No matter what, I'm always going to be Dr. Christopher Larsen and Bitsy Larsen's daughter, but that doesn't define me. My life and what I do with it does. If you want to change your career, do it. If you're happy at Columbia, stay. I'm going to be fine with it either way."

"You're sure?"

"Positive. So, is that it?"

"What do you mean?"

"Is that what you wanted to be sure of so we don't screw this up?"

He knew he was looking at her strangely, but heck, what did she expect? "Yeah, that about covers it."

"Okay. Good." She put both hands behind her neck and unlatched a necklace she wore, dropping it into the palm of her hand. "Rich." She took a deep breath and blew it out.

"Becca, what are you doing?"

"I love you, and the last month we've been apart has been awful. I saw my life without you in it, and it's not the life I want to lead."

"Bec—"

"Please don't interrupt. I've been practicing, not with the cat, of course, because he's been here with you. But I did practice what I would say in my head on the subway on the way here. It's not like I could kneel down in the getup your sister made me wear so just let me finish."

Rich slid off his chair and pushed it away so he was kneeling in front of her. "Okay."

"I want to be with you forever. I want to share my life, my love, everything I am, and everything I'll ever be, with you and only you. You told me once that you'd never ask me to marry you again. You said if I wanted to marry you, I'd have to do the asking. So I'm asking you. Rich, will you marry me? I made this puzzle ring years ago at school. I thought that someday I'd give it to the other part of me. I want you to be a part of me. It's two pieces that fit perfectly together—just like us." She slid the two pieces of the ring together for him. "And then it makes the eternity symbol, because I want to be with you forever and a day."

"Becca, I was going to ask you to marry me. Only this time, I was going to try to do it right. Look." He dug his hand in his pocket and pulled out the ring Aunt Rose had given him. He shrugged. "I didn't make you the ring. Hell, I didn't even pick it out. Aunt Rose gave it to me because she wanted you to have it."

"You were going to propose to me? But you said—"

"Since when do you listen to what I say?"

Becca smiled and sniffled at the same time. "I always listen. I just rarely do what you tell me to do."

"Becca, will you marry me?"

She laughed. "Oh, no you don't. I asked first."

"Technically, I asked first. You asked second."

Becca rolled her eyes. "Are you going to answer my question, or are we going to fight about this?"

"If we fight, then we get to make up again."

"Rich, I have a feeling we're going to be making up for the rest of our lives."

He kissed her as he slid his ring on her finger. "God I hope so."

The End

Acknowledgments

Even though writing is a solitary endeavor, publishing isn't. I'd like to thank the people who have helped me.

First and foremost my husband, Stephen, who is the most loving, supportive man I've ever known and is a true Domestic God.

My children, Tony, Anna, and Isabelle, who don't complain when Mom is on deadline and they're eating sandwiches for dinner.

April Line, who read countless scenes and answered the all-important question: Does this suck?

All my friends at the Carlisle Crossing Starbucks who kept me in coffee and laughter.

My agent, Kevan Lyon.

The whole Sourcebooks team, especially my friend and editor Deb Werksman, publicist Danielle Jackson, and my publisher Dominique Raccah.

About the Author

Robin Kaye was born in Brooklyn, New York, and grew up in the shadow of the Brooklyn Bridge next door to her Sicilian grandparents. Living with an extended family that's a cross between *Gilligan's Island* and *The Sopranos*, minus the desert isle and illegal activities, explains both her comedic timing and the cast of quirky characters in her books.

She's lived in half a dozen states, from Idaho to Florida, but the romance of Brooklyn has never left her heart. She currently resides in Maryland with her husband, three children, two dogs, and a three-legged cat with attitude.

Robin loves to hear from readers. Please visit her website at www.RobinKayeWrites.com.

Romeo, Romeo

BY ROBIN KAYE

Rosalie Ronaldi doesn't have a domestic bone in her body...

All she cares about is her career, so she survives on take-out and dirty martinis, keeps her shoes under the dining room table, her bras on the shower curtain rod, and her clothes on the couch.

Nick Romeo is every woman's fantasy— tall, dark, handsome, rich, really good in bed, AND he loves to cook and clean...

He says he wants an independent woman, but when he meets Rosalie, all he wants to do is take care of her. Before long, he's cleaned up her apartment, stocked her refrigerator, and adopted her dog.

So what's the problem? Just a little matter of mistaken identity, corporate theft, a hidden past in juvenile detention, and one big nosy Italian family too close for comfort...

"Kaye's debut is a delightfully fun, witty romance, making her a writer to watch." —*Booklist*

978-1-4022-1339-7 • $6.99 U.S. / $8.99 CAN

Too Hot to Handle

BY ROBIN KAYE

He sure would love to have a woman to take care of...

To Dr. Mike Flynn, there's nothing like housework to help a guy relax, while artist Annabelle Ronaldi doesn't have a domestic bone in her body.

When they meet at her sister's wedding, Mike is sure this is the woman he wants to take care of forever. While Mike sets to work wooing Annabelle, she becomes determined to sniff out the truth of the convoluted family secret that's threatening to turn both their lives upside down.

978-1-4022-1766-1 • $6.99 U.S. / $7.99 CAN

SEALed

with a *Kiss*

BY MARY MARGRET DAUGHTRIDGE

THERE'S ONLY ONE THING HE CAN'T HANDLE, AND ONE WOMAN WHO CAN HELP HIM...

Jax Graham is a rough, tough Navy SEAL, but when it comes to taking care of his four-year-old son after his ex-wife dies, he's completely clueless. Family therapist Pickett Sessoms can help, but only if he'll let her.

When Jax and his little boy get trapped by a hurricane, Picket takes them in against her better judgment. When the situation turns deadly, Pickett discovers what it means to be a SEAL, and Jax discovers that even a hero needs help sometimes.

"A heart-touching story that will keep you smiling and cheering for the characters clear through to the happy ending." —Romantic Times

"A well-written romance...simultaneously tender and sensuous." —Booklist

978-1-4022-1118-8 • $6.99 U.S. / $8.99 CAN

SEALED
with a
Promise

BY MARY MARGRET DAUGHTRIDGE

NAVY SEAL CALEB DELAUDE IS AS DEADLY AS HE IS CHARMING.

Professor Emmie Caddington's quiet intelligence and quirky personality intrigue him. When he discovers that her personal connections can get him close to the man he's vowed to kill, will their budding relationship be nothing more than a means to revenge…or is she the key to his salvation?

Praise for *SEALed with a Kiss*:

"This story delivers in a huge way." —Romantic Times

"A wonderful story that will have readers experiencing a whirlwind of emotions and culminating with an awesome scene that will have your pulse pounding." —Romance Junkies

"What an incredibly powerful book! I laughed and sniffled, was turned on and turned inside out." —Queue My Review

978-1-4022-1763-0 • $6.99 U.S. / $7.99 CAN

Lucky IN LOVE

By Carolyn Brown

Beau hasn't got a lick of sense when it comes to women

Everything hunky rancher "Lucky" Beau Luckadeau touches turns to gold—except relationships. Spitfire Milli Torres can mend a fence, pull a calf, or shoot a rattlesnake between the eyes. When Milli shows up to help out at the Lazy Z ranch, she's horrified to find that Beau's her nearest neighbor—the very man she'd hoped never to lay eyes on again. If Beau ever figures out what really happened on that steamy Louisiana night when they first met, there'll be the devil to pay…

Praise for Carolyn Brown:

"Engaging characters, humorous situations, and a bumpy romance… Carolyn Brown will keep you reading until the very last page." —Romantic Times

"Carolyn Brown's rollicking sense of humor asserts itself on every page." —Scribes World

978-1-4022-2435-5 • $6.99 U.S. / $8.99 CAN

HEALING
LUKE

BY BETH CORNELISON

She can't escape her past...

Occupational therapist Abby Stanford is on vacation alone, her self-confidence shattered by her fiancé's betrayal. Romance is the last thing on Abby's mind—until she meets the brooding and enigmatic Luke...

He won't face his future...

Scarred by a horrific accident, former heartthrob Luke Morgan is certain his best days are behind him. Abby knows how to help him recover, but for Luke his powerful attraction to her only serves as a harsh reminder of the man he used to be. Abby is Luke's first glimmer of hope since the accident, but can she heal his heart before Luke breaks hers?

"Beth Cornelison writes intriguing, emotionally charged stories that will keep you turning the pages straight through to the end. Fabulous entertainment!" —Susan Wiggs

"Healing Luke is a breath of fresh air for romance fans... a stirring novel and a five star read!"
—Crave More Romance

978-1-4022-2434-8 •$6.99 U.S. / $8.99 CAN

Love at
FIRST FLIGHT
BY MARIE FORCE

*What if the guy
in the airplane seat next to you turned out
to be the love of your life?*

JULIANA, HAPPY IN HER CAREER AS A HAIR STYLIST, IS ON HER WAY TO Florida to visit her boyfriend. When he tells her he's wondering what it might be like to make love to other women she is devastated. Even though he tries to take it back, she doesn't want him to be wondering all his life. So they agree to take a break, and heartbroken, she goes back to Baltimore.

Michael is going to his fiancee's parents' home for an engagement party he doesn't want. A state's prosecutor, he's about to try the biggest case of his career, and he's having doubts about the relationship. When Paige pulls a manipulative stunt at the party, he becomes so enraged that he breaks off the engagement.

Juliana and Michael sat together on the plane ride from Baltimore to Florida, and discover they're on the same flight coming back. With the weekend a disaster for each of them, they bond in a "two-person pity party" on the plane ride home. Their friendship begins to blossom and love, too, but life is full of complications, and when Michael's trial turns dangerous, the two must confront what they value most in life...

978-1-4022-2006-7 • $6.99 U.S. / $7.99 CAN